W9-ACW-915

continued . . .

The Accidental Human

"I highly enjoyed every moment of Dakota Cassidy's *The Accidental Human* . . . A paranormal romance with a strong dose of humor."

—*Errant Dreams*

"A delightful, at times droll, contemporary tale starring a decidedly human heroine . . . Dakota Cassidy provides a fitting, twisted ending to this amusingly warm urban romantic fantasy."

—*Genre Go Round Reviews*

"The final member of Cassidy's trio of decidedly offbeat friends faces her toughest challenge, but that doesn't mean there isn't humor to spare! With emotion, laughter, and some pathos, Cassidy serves up another winner!"

—*Romantic Times*

Accidentally Dead

"A laugh-out-loud follow-up to *The Accidental Werewolf*, and it's a winner . . . Ms. Cassidy is an up-and-comer in the world of paranormal romance."

—*Fresh Fiction*

"An enjoyable, humorous satire that takes a bite out of the vampire romance subgenre . . . Fans will appreciate the nonstop hilarity."

—*Genre Go Round Reviews*

The Accidental Werewolf

"Cassidy, a prolific author of erotica, has ventured into MaryJanice Davidson territory with a humorous, sexy tale."

—*Booklist*

"If Bridget Jones became a lycanthrope, she might be Marty. Fun and flirty humor is cleverly interspersed with dramatic mystery and action. It's hard to know which character to love best, though: Keegan or Muffin, the toy poodle that steals more than one scene."

—*The Eternal Night*

"A riot! Marty's internal dialogue will have you howling, and her antics will keep the laughs coming. If you love paranormal with a comedic twist, you'll love this book."

—*Romance Junkies*

"A lighthearted romp . . . [An] entertaining tale with an alpha twist."

—*Midwest Book Review*

More praise for the novels of Dakota Cassidy

"The fictional equivalent of the little black dress—every reader should have one!"

—Michele Bardsley

"Serious, laugh-out-loud humor with heart, the kind of love story that leaves you rooting for the heroine, sighing for the hero, and looking for your own significant other at the same time."

—Kate Douglas

"Expect great things from Cassidy."

—*Romantic Times*

"Very fun, sexy. Five stars!"

—*Affaire de Coeur*

"Dakota Cassidy is going on my must-read list!"

—*Joyfully Reviewed*

"If you're looking for some steamy romance with something that will have you smiling, you have to read [Dakota Cassidy]."

—*The Best Reviews*

Burning Down the Spouse

DAKOTA CASSIDY

B
BERKLEY SENSATION, NEW YORK

THE BERKLEY PUBLISHING GROUP
Published by the Penguin Group
Penguin Group (USA) Inc.
375 Hudson Street, New York, New York 10014, USA
Penguin Group (Canada), 90 Eglinton Avenue East, Suite 700, Toronto, Ontario M4P 2Y3, Canada
(a division of Pearson Penguin Canada Inc.)
Penguin Books Ltd., 80 Strand, London WC2R 0RL, England
Penguin Group Ireland, 25 St. Stephen's Green, Dublin 2, Ireland (a division of Penguin Books Ltd.)
Penguin Group (Australia), 250 Camberwell Road, Camberwell, Victoria 3124, Australia
(a division of Pearson Australia Group Pty. Ltd.)
Penguin Books India Pvt. Ltd., 11 Community Centre, Panchsheel Park, New Delhi—110 017, India
Penguin Group (NZ), 67 Apollo Drive, Rosedale, Auckland 0632, New Zealand
(a division of Pearson New Zealand Ltd.)
Penguin Books (South Africa) (Pty.) Ltd., 24 Sturdee Avenue, Rosebank, Johannesburg 2196,
South Africa

Penguin Books Ltd., Registered Offices: 80 Strand, London WC2R 0RL, England

This book is an original publication of The Berkley Publishing Group.

PRINTING HISTORY
Berkley Sensation trade paperback edition / July 2011

Library of Congress Cataloging-in-Publication Data

Cassidy, Dakota.
    Burning down the spouse / Dakota Cassidy.—Berkley Sensation trade pbk. ed.
      p. cm.
    ISBN 978-0-425-24108-0
  1. Separated women—Fiction.   2. Women cooks—Fiction.   3. Greet Americans—Fiction.   I. Title.
    PS3603.A8685B87 2011
    813'.6—dc22

                                                                            2011007735

PRINTED IN THE UNITED STATES OF AMERICA

10   9   8   7   6   5   4   3   2   1

ACKNOWLEDGMENTS

For the Rainbow Diner back in Pleasantville, New Jersey. You have no idea what a haven your diner became for me when nothing else was open and I needed to escape the fears of my pending single parenthood. I couldn't afford more than one cup of coffee, but no one ever balked because I didn't order food, and you kept my cup filled. Thank you for allowing me to keep my dignity when I was nose to nose with the bottom of the barrel.

And to Guy Fieri of *Diners, Drive-ins and Dives* fame. Dude, your show was invaluable in my research. With diners pretty few and far between in Texas, and never having been in the kitchen of one back at my old stomping grounds in New Jersey, I needed some insider info, and your show was a ginormous help to me. Plus, you're kinda funny, but seriously, walk away from the spice jokes. The Ginger/Mary Ann reference is pushing some comedic boundaries. No. I kid. Because I love. Really. Also, Tyler Florence, who tweets the most amazing cooking information almost like he knows, by some weird osmosis, just when I need it. You're the "ultimate" personable, fan-friendly celebrity chef.

And to Barry Manilow for the song "I Made It Through the Rain." Those who know the song will understand what it means.

Most of all, to my father, Robert Cartwright, who watched every single Food Network show known to man with me and adored, among many, Rachael Ray. Each time I cook a meal these days, I remember

Rachael Ray's infamous word—one Dad repeated to me daily at dinner—"yummo." So yummo, Daddy. A big yummo from down here. I miss you.

Dakota Cassidy ☺

CHAPTER ONE

See, the problem is that God gives men a brain and a penis, and only enough blood to run one at a time.

—ROBIN WILLIAMS

So maybe things had gotten a little out of hand, Frankie Bennett reflected. Through the lingering clouds of black smoke, she perused the carnage now littering her husband Mitch's made-for-TV kitchen with a rather detached view.

But really, live tapings were all about the unexpected, right?

No doubt, the ratings for *Mitch in the Kitchen*'s first-ever live show on the Bon Appetit Channel would be ginormous.

And all because of her.

God, she really was a giver.

"Jesus Christ, Frankie! What the hell are you doing?" a male voice whisper-yelled from the floor below, drawing her attention to the assorted utensils scattered at her sneakered feet.

Jesus Christ, indeed.

Frankie looked down where one of the stage crew was slinking across the tile on his belly, his hands over his head like they were in a war zone.

Her eyes shifted, catching the debris littering her brand-new Nikes.

Hoo shit. She'd totally mangled Mitch's favorite wire whisk, the one he demanded always be to his left when the recipe he was cooking called for one.

The stank would surely fly for that offense.

It was part of his new collection of kitchen gadgets and overpriced casserole dishes no one but a Hilton could afford to buy.

It was also shiny, she noted. Very shiny.

Frankie waved her hand in the air and wrinkled her nose. Wow. Who knew one little flick of a Bic could create so much kitchen towel wreckage? Oh, and look. Mitch's stupid thousand-dollar-a-pound black French truffles lie smashed to smithereens against the wood flooring, so flattened by Frankie's foot they looked like those Parisian pancakes Mitch loved to brag he'd created the recipe for. Well, with one little exception. The truffles were black, and Mitch's pancakes weren't.

But there was always the five-second rule, right? Maybe he could have his assistant-slash-ass-kisser Juliana scoop them up off the floor and salvage what she hadn't done the watusi on. No doubt, she could definitely use some help scraping them off the bottom of her shoe.

That insight made her giggle, a little high-pitched, and if she was honest, it did sound a little crazy-assed, which drew more slack-jawed astonishment from everyone around her.

Mitch would dock her pay for those thousand-dollar truffles.

Black French truffles do not either cost a thousand dollars a pound, Frankie.

That was true, but you'd think they did the way Mitch had reacted when she'd taken them down with one fell swoop of her arm. There'd been a lot of yelling, hands flying, and red-faced, vein-popping fury on his behalf.

It was to be expected. They were, after all, million-dollar-a-pound black French truffles.

"Cuuuuuttttttttt!" a male voice yelled.

Well, screamed—on a hacking cough, no less.

Pretty loud, too, considering the amount of smoke inhalation he'd probably incurred.

Probably Epson. He was a control freak of a director. If they were thirty seconds to live and everyone wasn't in their exact spot marked with the masking tape he'd so lovingly placed on the floor himself, he was dramatically putting his hand over his chest as though he could will himself to leave this plane just by thinking the words "heart attack." "Damn it! I mean—*go—to—commercial*!" he corrected, his anxious screech but a vague penetration through Frankie's eerie wall of calm.

Yep. That was her. Always rockin' the unruffled. Always keeping things on track. Always asking how high when someone said jump.

Frankie's shoulders slumped when the red light on camera three blinked off. She jammed one hand into the pocket of her tailored jeans, stepping over the glass remains of the mixing bowls Mitch preferred. He liked the visual effect mixing ingredients in them created for his television audience.

Her other hand clutched a wooden spoon. She made her way past the row of copper pots and pans hanging over Mitch's six-burner cooktop with the boil-in-eight-seconds feature. How peculiar, Frankie thought, pausing to see that the crew had all begun ducking and diving for cover with mouths open wide in horror.

Like they were all waiting for something bad to happen.

The crash of the spoon she wielded against the bottom and sides of all that copper did sort of sound like a xylophone, Frankie decided. Huh. She'd always wondered if it would . . . But it would probably sound much more pleasant to the ear if she had a stainless steel spoon. That'd make some righteous noise.

That decided, Frankie made her way to exit stage left and go home. Today had been brutal, her arm was strangely sore, her throat was scratchy and a little raw, and she had a killa headache.

However, by the look on hubby Mitch's face, one Frankie knew well, it didn't appear he agreed she was due some "me" time. She sighed with a forlorn whistle to it. There went the bubble bath and glass of Chardonnay.

Fucker.

Frankie's eyes searched for Kiki, her longhaired Chihuahua mix. Kiki was Mitch's on-air mascot. She'd attended every taping since Mitch's viewers had seen Frankie in the audience with her. After an abundance of emails from fans of the show who wanted to see more of Kiki, Mitch had dubbed her an asset—a mangy, smelly one who might get hair in his precious food, but an asset that couldn't be denied. Kiki turned into an overnight sensation when Mitch's fans found out she was a stray he'd rescued after finding her foraging outside the Bon Appetit studios.

What he forgot to mention was *he* didn't rescue anything. Mitch couldn't rescue something or someone if he had the paramedics with him. He didn't even like Kiki. Frankie had found Kiki at the Dumpster outside the studios, scrounging through a garbage bag carelessly thrown to the ground. To her husband's utter mortification, she'd fallen in love and promptly brought her home.

Scooping her up on her way out, Frankie chucked Kiki under the chin and whispered, "Tonight when you curl up in that crazy three-thousand-dollar bed of yours, thank the doggie gods you're deaf, Kik. I think we're in for a shit storm of verbal assault."

Mitch's hand wrapped around her arm, yanking at the sleeve of her carefully-picked-by-her-personal-shopper cashmere sweater. "What the fuck is the matter with you, Frankie? Do you have any idea what you've just done?" he roared so loud, her hair lifted off her shoulders.

Done? She'd done what she'd always done. Prepped Mitch's food to within an inch of perfection for the live show and put it in sequential order in the set's refrigerator. Checked not twice but thrice to be certain his spice bowls were filled with kosher salt and freshly ground black pepper, arranged each mixing bowl and utensil in the correct order of usage. Then she'd gone off to his dressing room to make absolutely certain he had ice-cold bottled Perrier for commercial break. That was her job at the Bon Appetit Channel—Mitch's whipping, er, food prep girl.

Once she'd completed those menial tasks, she'd smelled the lovely flowers someone had sent to Mitch while reading the attached card.

Dear Mitch,

Let's celebrate your stratospheric rise in the cooking world at my place after the show. I'll have your favorite massage oil and chai tea waiting.

Oh, wait. The flowers . . .

Was that what this was about? Was Mitch upset that she'd crushed them to oblivion like his stupid black French truffles? Jesus. He was so picky. It was just some water on the floor and rose petals. Big shit.

Kiki curled up over her neck, shivering. She might not be able to hear Mitch, but she certainly sensed his fury. "You're angry about the flowers," Frankie stated rather than asked, bouncing Kiki to soothe her. "They're just roses, Mitch. Go buy yourself twelve dozen. God knows you make enough money. I'm going home to take a bath. This last week with you before this live taping hasn't exactly been a game of Chutes and Ladders."

Mitch's grip only became more forceful, matching his rising anger. His fingers dug into her upper arm, refusing to let her leave. Eyes, lined with crinkly webs of an age he was finding harder and harder to hide, grew wide. "Are you fucking serious?"

"Just like one of those heart attacks Epson's always prepping for," Frankie responded, bland and disinterested. Once more, she made an effort to leave, ignoring the crowd gathering behind Mitch's back.

Mitch jerked her back, forcing her to face him and making Kiki cringe. A fury so crystal clear in his gray-blue eyes it scorched her with its venom. "You're a jealous bitch! You never could handle my success, could you, Frankie?"

"Handle it?" What was there to handle? It was all about Mitch or it wasn't. Easy-peasy. Successful or unsuccessful, Mitch was da man of the hour—every hour of every single day. All Mitch, all the time.

His mouth became a thin line, the veins in his neck, angry, blue, and pulsing. "Do you have any idea what the tabloids will do with that stunt you just pulled on *live TV*? They'll rip me to shreds!"

Frankie let her head fall back on her shoulders so she could properly display the huge amount of disinterest she was feeling about poor widdle Mitch and his poor widdle reputation. "So?"

"So? *So?*" His face became a mask of furious disbelief. "You just accused me of being unfaithful to you on *national TV*, Frankie—with another Bon Appetit Channel chef all while you set my kitchen towels on fire! But not before you trashed everything in your wake on a live set. Half the world saw you behaving like you had roid rage!"

Well, assuming half the world had actually tuned in . . . that might be a tad generous. Mitch's ratings were pretty damned good, but he wasn't exactly Emeril. Though, that was the intended goal for tonight. And it wasn't like she'd accused him of being a bottom-feeding infidel without cause. Why was he always so hard to please?

"Can you even hear me, Frankie? You've ruined my reputation. The tabloids will have a field day with this!"

Yeah. It would probably be pretty ugly and obviously, Mitch needed some form of validation from her to prove his point. Her job as ego-stroker extraordinaire was never done, was it?

Her shoulders lifted, despite the painful grasp he had on her upper arm. "Yeah. You're probably right. So they'll call you a disgusting, lying, cheating pig who's boning a chick half his age named Bamby? With a 'Y' on the end of it, in case you missed that memo. She's sent like twenty of them in the past month since she slept with the CEO and nailed *Bamby's Bakin'* to remind us. I don't know about you, but for me, Bamby With A 'Y's' repetitive nature is a little old."

Frankie paused, almost forgetting the original question. Oh, wait. She remembered. The tabloids. "Where were we? The tabloids, right? Is there some error in the statements I made while I trashed your live show and all of your ridiculously expensive *Mitch in the Kitchen* cookware? Did I miss a detail? If you want, send me an email memo so I'm sure I have it all ironed out and I don't get a single, filthy stat wrong, because we all know how meticulous you are about the smallest details. Do that and mark it 'IMPORTANT.' You know, all in caps like you do so I won't miss one out of the nine hundred you send me a day. For now"—she attempted to shrug off his iron fist, hiking Kiki up higher on her shoulder—"I'm going home."

Yet Mitch hung on to her. He might be fifty-eight, but he had some grip from all that hand mixing he did. "The hell you'll step foot in *my* home! Never again, Frankie Bennett! You got that? It's my brownstone. *Mine*. In fact, all of it's mine! I want a divorce. Do you hear me? And so is Kiki!"

Frankie sighed, cocking her head to the left, eerily detached. "Yep. I heard you. And Kiki's *mine*. I'd bet my left foot *and* my right hand your fans would love to hear who really found Kiki. She doesn't even like you. So forget it. And I guess I'm fired, too, huh? Bummer that. Good thing I'm blessed with the ability to color-coordinate food so it has camera appeal. Bet it's a skill that'll come in handy when I look for work. Oh, and geez, I hope my new boss is a total tyrant. I can't work unless someone's screaming at me. Know what else?

I really, really hope he's an anal, egotistical, self-serving, whiny, aging half-man who has manicures once a week like some soccer mom. I can't see why anyone would ever want to work for someone who doesn't have at least two of those traits." She yawned. "Okay. Gotta go. You and *Bamby* enjoy your *stratospheric success.*"

With a hard shove, she pushed her husband Mitch away from her for the last time, stepping over the smashed carton of organic eggs so she wouldn't slip and break an ankle, and made her way out of the studio.

She gave nary a glance to the crew and their wide-eyed stares when she sauntered down the long hallway leading to the exit.

When passing Bamby With A "Y," she held up Kiki, sticking the dog under Bamby's nose. Kiki hung there, her little legs dangling, wide-eyed with nary a blink. "Grrrrrrrrrrrr!" Frankie mimicked a much bigger dog than Kiki, giggling when Bamby squealed in terror.

Bamby hated dogs, probably as much as she hated the letters "I" and "E." Her leggy, tight body; her shiny, chocolate brown hair; her quivering with fear at Kiki didn't even make Frankie pause.

Frankie realized she should probably want to beat the bitch to within an inch of her life with a rolling pin—maybe a meat tenderizer, that'd definitely leave marks—but there was simply no fight left in her.

Stumbling into the warm night air, she dug around in her jeans to find the keys for her car.

Mitch might own everything. The brownstone was in his name. True dat. Every investment, vacation home, stitch of clothing in their walk-in closet, checking and savings account might be his, too. That's what prenups were for. Mitch had made sure she'd signed one when they'd married eighteen years ago. She'd done so willingly to prove her undying devotion to the head chef at Reynard's. Back then Mitch was just financially sound, but he'd clenched every penny as though it were his last.

Eighteen years later, he was now insanely rich and still clenching every penny between his tight ass cheeks.

Smart. He must've had some kind of crystal ball that told him he was going to be worth millions someday.

Yes, Mitch owned it all, Frankie mused ruefully.

But by God, her little Nissan Versa was hers.

Six months later

"She's asleep? It's almost three in the afternoon!"

"Tell me something I don't know, Maxine. I think it's depression," Frankie's Aunt Gail said. In fact, if she were willing to open her eyes and get out of bed, Frankie'd bet Gail was nodding her head full of shortly cropped white hair, while her finger rested under her bottom lip.

"Has she been diagnosed with depression?" whoever Maxine was asked.

"Are you kidding? She hasn't been anywhere in months to be diagnosed with anything. All she does is sleep."

"Gail Lumley, why didn't you call me sooner?"

"Because you're so busy with the new business and school. Not to mention your new husband. You have so little time alone with Campbell. I didn't want to intrude."

Maxine chuckled all warm and squishy, making Frankie clench her eyes tighter. "My new business is exactly the cure for this kind of depression."

"But she's so cranky when you wake her. Like a hibernating bear."

"Really? Well, that's too damned bad."

"I wouldn't," Gail warned.

"Yeah? Well, I would," Maxine said. "Now give me the cookie."

The door to her Aunt Gail's small second bedroom cracked open, shedding a slant of light across the floor, forcing Frankie to burrow farther under the knitted afghan and tuck Kiki closer to her. A slight shift, and the bed sagged with someone's weight, and her faithful little Chi was suddenly up and away. The faint sound of pig noises drifted to Frankie's ears.

"Frankie Bennett?"

No.

The someone in question made a rash move by dragging the covers off her in a whoosh of cold air. "I said, Frankie Bennett?"

"Who are you?" she moaned in response to losing her knitted cocoon.

A hand, slender and finely boned with neatly trimmed nails, was under her nose in a flash. "Maxine Barker. Get up."

Dragging a pillow over her face, Frankie ignored the hand and muttered, "What for?"

"So we can stop this farting around and get to the business of living. Bills don't get paid if you sleep until three in the afternoon. Now get up."

No, no, and no. She was never getting up. "Aunt Gail?"

"Yep, sassafras?"

"*Who* is this?"

"Maxine Barker, but she already said that. She's my best friend Mona's girl. Now get up, Frankie, and stop steepin' in your stink like some human tea bag."

Her nose slid surreptitiously to her armpit. She did not stink. She'd showered like . . . four days ago or something. "Please, Aunt Gail, I just want to be left alone." She really, really did. Forever and ever.

Maxine clucked her tongue with what sounded like disgust.

"Frankie? I'm here to help you help yourself. It's time to get out of this bed and join the land of the living. I'll take drastic measures if I have to."

Drastic this. "Go away." Frankie tacked on a "please" on the off chance this Maxine meant something to her aunt. Aunt Gail was good to her. She didn't want to offend her—probably as much as she didn't want to get out of bed.

"Gail?" Maxine said. "Out in the hall, please? And bring her little dog, too."

Soft footsteps shuffled back out of the bedroom, her traitorous dog in tow, giving Frankie enough time to locate the afghan and burrow herself back into it. Jesus. Broad daylight hurt your eyes. Why would anyone choose to get up and endure it?

But then the footsteps returned.

Damn.

"Frankie—I'll count to three, but if you don't get up, you'll be sorry," Maxine warned.

How much sorrier could she get than she already was? This woman Maxine was a novice if she thought there was any sorry left in Francis Bennett.

"Last chance . . ."

Hah. Let the counting begin.

"One, two, threee!"

Icy rivulets of water sloshed between the holes in the afghan and over the top of her head, plastering her hair to her scalp while dripping down to glue her torn T-shirt to her breasts. Frankie tore at the blanket, hurling it at Maxine, who caught it like a Yankees shortstop nabbing a line drive. Her berry-glossed lips curved into a smile of victory when Frankie jolted upward out of the bed.

"What the hell?" Frankie sputtered, water dripping into her mouth.

"I did warn you," Maxine countered, smoothing her hands over her crisp, white, fitted shirt with the smartly upturned collar. "The longer you lie around in bed, the easier it is for your limbs to atrophy. Now come with me."

The. Hell.

Frankie cocked her head questioningly in her aunt's direction as she used her forearm to wipe the droplets of water from her forehead.

Gail tightened her sweater with the small white buttons around her chest, curling a wide-eyed, typically silent Kiki against her. "Something had to be done, honey. You can't stay in bed for the rest of your life."

Said who? Was there a law written somewhere, declaring you had to participate? In anything? Ever?

Gail came to her side, using a tender hand to smooth the moisture from her niece's face. "Honey, I love you, just like my own, but this has to stop. By giving up, you're letting that dirty bird, Mitch, with the wayward wanker, have all the control. I won't have it. I can't stand to see you like this." She held up Kiki, her little dog's legs swinging in the air. "Little Kiki can't stand it either. Now Maxine here, well, she's had some tough times a lot like yours, but she came out of it in a blaze of glory. You can, too. Please, Frankie. *Please* do this for me."

Frankie's glazed eyes cleared momentarily, giving her a glimpse of her aunt, so worried, so intent, she crumbled. There wasn't much she wouldn't do for Gail, and if it would make this woman go away, she'd do it. "I'm not sure what you want me to do," she muttered, ashamed she was the reason Gail was so clearly upset.

Maxine put a hand on Gail's shoulder and squeezed. "Follow me, Frankie," she ordered, yet her tone was soft, her green eyes warm. She made her way around the edge of the bed and down along the short corridor to her aunt's guest bathroom.

Aha, Frankie thought when Maxine flipped on the light. The bathroom *was* pink and blue and sported a matching hand-crocheted doily doll with a flowing skirt to decoratively cover the box of tissues. She'd mostly only stumbled around here in the dark late at night after her aunt was long in bed.

The twin lights above the long mirror glared, making her eyes water painfully. Maxine came to stand behind her, placing her hands on Frankie's shoulders. "Do you see yourself?"

Yep. Frankie nodded, realizing that was what would make Aunt Gail happy.

And now she really didn't want to see any more.

Okay. Acknowledged. Were they done now?

Maxine's lips took on a thin line. "Do you remember what you looked like before you were divorced, Frankie?"

A snort almost escaped her lips. Yes. She remembered. She hated that she remembered, but she did.

"Do you see what you look like now?" Maxine lifted a long lock of her thick, pin-straight auburn hair and held it up to the light. "You're a greasy, pale, washed-out, shaky, undernourished mess, Frankie. Don't you agree?"

And she needed a dye job, too. Point made.

Maxine, shorter, even in heels, peered around her slumped shoulder. "So I have a couple of questions. Okay, maybe more than two, but they're compelling," she joked with an easy smile. "Why would you allow a man like your ex-husband, who's a mean, cheap, lying, philandering sonofabitch, have all this power? Did he define who Frankie was? Did you get up every morning just for him? Did you shower, put on makeup, and dress up only because he existed? Is it because he's no longer in your life that you've sunk so low you don't even want to get out of bed?"

Yes. Yes. Yessss. "Is this like some weird kind of intervention? Do they have those here in little old Riverbend, New Jersey?" she asked with dry tones, fighting to keep the crack of watery tears out of her voice.

Maxine smiled again, pretty, gentle, understanding. "You didn't answer the question, Frankie."

Her head sunk to her chest. For all her bravado the night she'd walked out on Mitch and Bamby With A "Y," for all her venomous, arrogant words, *yes.* The end of her marriage to a man she hadn't, if ever, seen clearly, hurt like hell, but adultery was the one and only thing short of murder she knew deep down she'd never be able to live with.

Realization, in all its ugly blatancy, was what had made her snap the night she'd found out about Mitch's affair.

Eighteen solid years and she'd finally seen the real Mitch. Self-centered, egotistical, bossy, and a cheat. He'd always been there. He'd simply done a bang-up job of lurking just below the line of decent, but she'd brushed those warning niggles aside, granting them excuses because she'd loved Mitch with all her heart.

Hearing about his infidelity in such a callous way had been a crass wake-up call—like being clunked over the head with a two-by-four.

It was as though all of a sudden she'd hit this brick wall she'd once always found a reason, even if it was flimsy, to climb over. But on that night, there was just no more rope for her to grab on to to help her scale that seemingly towering hurdle.

Not being able to live with Mitch's infidelity didn't mean it hurt less. Having divorce papers served to you two weeks after you made your big marital exit on national television didn't sting less because the man you'd devoted your life to was a prick.

"Frankie?" Maxine prodded.

Her breath was a long shudder. "Yes. Everything I did revolved around Mitch. I didn't realize the gaping hole not having to chase after him would . . . would leave." Her heart, quiet and unresponsive for six months, shifted with a painful jolt in her chest.

Maxine's ash brown head nodded in understanding. She gave Frankie's shoulders a squeeze. "It's like a big, black void of nothingness. Even if the tasks you performed as Mitch's wife were tedious, they gave you what you thought was purpose. Your lot in life, so to speak. You don't have to explain, Frankie. No one, and I really mean *no one*, gets that better than I do."

A tear seeped out of one eye. God damn it. She'd had the market cornered on numb. When and if she was awake long enough to think, she'd amused herself with inconsequential musings like how many drips it took before a ketchup bottle was empty. Anything much deeper and she shut it down, closing her eyes to seek solace in dreamless sleep.

Maxine turned Frankie to face her. "Listen to me, Frankie. I was a stay-at-home mom. A trophy wife just like you. I married my ex-husband Finley when I was twenty and he was forty. He was the first man in my life, and for twenty years, he was the only man in my life. Unfortunately, the same thing couldn't be said for Finley. He married me because I was a hot number back then, and he liked 'em young and hot. I married him because he swept me off my feet. We didn't see a movie and grab a burger like you'd do on a typical first date with someone your own age. We flew to Paris and had escargot."

Maxine's shoulders lifted in a wry shrug. "I got caught up, and when he was unfaithful, I blamed it on myself. When he was unfaithful for the third time, I'd just had enough. I hit the same wall I'm sure you hit when you confronted Mitch."

"On live TV," Frankie murmured. In front of an entire nation. Woo to the hoo.

Maxine chuckled, but it was laced with sympathy. "Yes. On live

TV, and it was ugly, and I don't doubt you'll have some living that incident down to do. But here's the thing, you hit that wall for a reason. I'm guessing because you were oppressed and tired of being Mitch's pretty toy. Sometimes it happens out of the blue, and there's no stopping it. You just explode."

Hindsight and utter humiliation made her wonder if she might have chosen a more private venue in which to do all that exploding, leading her back to the conclusion that she'd been plenty happy avoiding the memory.

"I'll give you this," Maxine noted. "You didn't stick around after you found out about his affair. Good for you. Me? Not so much. You did what your heart told you to do. But you didn't fail your marriage, Frankie. Mitch just stopped being a team player."

Looking back, Frankie had to wonder if she'd ever even been on the team. She mostly just remembered sitting on the bench. The idea made her want to retreat back to her bed. Now. "Look, I appreciate you and your story, but I'll figure this out alone. So thanks for stopping by." Frankie made a move to get around Maxine, but her aunt stopped her.

Gail's finger waved in a no-nonsense manner, blocking the bathroom door. "Oh, no, missy. This is the longest I've seen you upright in months. No way are you going back to bed. Not on my watch."

Maxine held up her left hand, a shiny diamond and wedding band catching the bathroom's light. "Look, Frankie. I can help you. I was broke and I had nowhere to go once, too. I lived here in the retirement village with my mother for almost a year, trying to get on my feet. Worse, I didn't have a single job skill to my credit but the ability to put together a fabulous dinner party—oh, and shop. So get in the shower. I'll go make some coffee with your aunt, and once you get dressed, we'll talk."

Frustration welled in the form of a tight ball in Frankie's chest.

The part of her that just wanted to keep right on drifting rebelled. Who the hell did this woman think she was? The Dalai Lama of divorce? All serene and all-knowing? So they had some commonalities. Married young to older men who liked the just-over-jailbait chickies.

Whatever. It was clear this Maxine wasn't down on her luck anymore. She was remarried, judging by the size of that rock—a rock that didn't come from the cubic zirconia store on QVC.

Maxine's life wasn't any different than it'd been when she was married to her last husband. She'd just taken a year off from her trophy-wife duties and laid in wait to nab another rich guy. Mission accomplished. Frankie didn't need lessons on how to snare rich potential husband number two. No more men. "I really just want to be left alone."

Maxine's tongue clucked again in admonishment. "I bet you do. But here's something to ponder while you wash your greasy hair and maybe attack a vat of deodorant, armpit first. How long do you suppose Gail can support you until you become a big, fat burden on her Social Security and retirement fund? What little money you have personally is running out."

Instantly, Frankie was indignant. She'd given Gail money every month for the food she'd barely touched and the water, according to her splendiferous odor, she'd hardly used. She would never stiff her aunt. "How do you know what my financial status is?"

Gail snorted, pursing her lips. "Someone had to open your mail, kiddo. You sure as hell don't. You don't have but two hundred smackers in that account of yours. Now you know I don't want your money, but I ain't gonna live forever. You have car payments long overdue, too. They're going to send in the repo man. If you want to keep that nice-lookin' car and some untarnished credit when all's said and done, you need to get it together. Plus, think of my Squeaky Kiki. She

has to eat. She needs shots and veterinary care. You have to get on
with the living, honey."

To what purpose? Frankie wanted to scream. What was there to
live for? Instead, she let her indignant chest shrink in defeat.

Maxine handed her a bar of soap and a fresh towel before reaching out to take Kiki from Gail. Kiki snuggled against Maxine's ear,
sighing with contentment. "Get in the shower, Frankie, and hurry up.
The day awaits."

Bone weary, her muscles just didn't want to cooperate. Her get-
up-and-go had gotten up and went and it was never coming back. She
couldn't summon the will or the energy to care about anything. Her
eyes, pleading and teary, sought her Aunt Gail's, searching for a crack
in her hard veneer. "Can't we just do this tomorrow? I promise I'll get
up tomorrow. Promise."

Maxine shook her head in Gail's stead, and it wasn't in the yes
mode Frankie'd hoped for. "Nope. *Today's* the day you start back on
the road to recovery. It's long. It really, really blows, but there's a
world out there that you have to be a part of unless you like card-
board-box living and soup kitchens. By the looks of that bed Kiki
sleeps in, I'd say she won't love living under a bridge. Get it together,
Frankie. It's time for you to suck it up, princess."

Maxine marched out of the bathroom with Kiki, followed by her
aunt, who'd refused to meet her eyes.

A long, deep breath later, thankful for the silence and the chance
to sit on the edge of the bathtub, Frankie almost collapsed in a boneless heap.

The effort it'd taken to get from one room to the other, coupled
with the sensory overload of Maxine's chatter after four months of
very few wordy exchanges with her Aunt Gail, and she was wrecked.

Frankie dropped the bar of soap and towel to the floor with jelly-
like arms, letting her head rest against the salmon pink tiled wall,

and attempted to make her mind go blank. She'd gotten incredibly good at it since she'd come to Gail's. There shouldn't be any problem summoning up some more numb.

Yet, she couldn't stop wondering.

Suck it up, princess?

What kind of new age crap was that?

"I don't hear water running, Frankie," Maxine warned from behind the door. "I'll put you in that shower myself. You've got ten minutes. Make that twenty—you'll need to wash that greasy hair twice—and then I'm coming in."

Frankie rose on unsteady legs, gripping the towel rack. She didn't doubt Maxine would do exactly as she stated. She also didn't doubt she had neither the strength nor the kind of oomph it would take to stop her.

Coffee wouldn't kill her. A shower wouldn't either.

It was the sucking-princess thing that worried her.

CHAPTER TWO

There are two sides to every divorce: yours and shithead's.

—AUTHOR UNKNOWN

"Well, look at you. Bright as a shiny new penny," her aunt crowed from a corner of her tiny kitchen. "Sit, honey, and I'll pour you some coffee."

The very idea made her stomach turn. Yet Frankie found herself dragging a dinette chair out and dropping into it, scooping a bewildered, silent Kiki up to sit in her lap. Her jeans gaped at her waist, pushing at the bottom of her thin T-shirt, and she wasn't even self-conscious enough to care. It was all she had in her to drag a brush through her wet hair and locate a pair of underwear.

Maxine sat to her left, texting on her iPhone with the neon green cover. When she looked up, it was with a smile of encouragement. "Admit it. You feel better."

"I feel cleaner. That's all I'm willing to cop to."

Gail snorted. "You sure smell better," she teased, plunking down a yellowish brown ceramic mug filled with steaming coffee. The cup brought a familiar ache to Frankie's chest, making her heart constrict. Her mother once had cups just like those.

Cupping the mug with her icy hands, she sniffed the liquid out of habit. A bad one. One Mitch had instilled in her. He used to say if she could smell the chicory, then she'd made an acceptable enough brew.

Gail nudged her arm with a grunt before dropping a plate of Danish in the center of the table and sitting to Frankie's right. "Not like the highfalutin stuff you're used to. I'd bet my pressure socks on that. It's just plain old Chock Full o'Nuts."

Frankie shook her head. "I'm sorry, Aunt Gail. That wasn't why I smelled it. It's an old . . . Just a habit." She bit her lip before swallowing a gulp of the steaming liquid that burned her tongue and made her stomach roil.

"A Mitch habit," Maxine, all-knowing, all-seeing, said.

Her eyes rolled upward. Yes. Mitch, Mitch, Mitch.

Maxine sipped her coffee before saying, "It's time to break all those old habits, Frankie. If you'll just let me help, I promise you'll be asking yourself, 'Who the hell is Mitch Bennett?' before long."

Frankie looked down into her coffee, unable to meet Maxine's eyes. Just hearing his name spoken out loud was like a small stab wound to her gut. This forgetting who the hell Mitch was could be done much more effectively under some covers. Asleep. "What is it exactly that you do, uh, Maxine? Are you a divorce coach or something?"

Maxine laughed, her bright face crinkling with a smile. "Uh, no. Though, that is a service we offer. We have a support group run by a retired therapist who once specialized in family counseling. I'm not a therapist. I have no official degree—"

"Yet," Gail interrupted with a grin, reaching over to stroke Kiki's back. "Maxie here's come a long way since she got the big D. She's going to college to get her business degree."

The pride in her aunt's eyes for Maxine made Frankie slink farther down in the chair. There'd once been the possibility of a degree in her future. Until she'd met Mitch, and he'd given her the perfect excuse to bail.

"Right. What your aunt says is true. Though, that didn't happen overnight. It took me a long time to get my act together enough to take courses. So it's like I said, I've been where you are."

Divorced. Right. So what? "I don't want to be rude, Maxine, Aunt Gail, but if you're just here to talk me off the ledge with your ex-trophy wife divorce story, I'm good. I like the ledge. In fact, I'm considering pitching a tent here."

Maxine's laughter, light and airy, once again filled the small dining area. "Bitter. Now that you're awake, and we've forced you out of your cave, you're pissed. That's a good sign. It means you still have life in you."

"Let's cut to the chase and stop beating around the proverbial bush. Just tell me why you're here, and then I can go back to bed."

Maxine and Gail gave each other sidelong glances.

"What?" Frankie fought a yelp in her frustration. "Hold on. Is Maxine some kind of hit woman? I know you hated Mitch, Aunt Gail, but we can't afford bail," she halfheartedly joked.

Gail barked a laugh. "I'd figure it out. I bet everyone in the village'd chip in. That Mitch deserves a good slap in the kisser and some ceee-ment shoes."

Because all the seniors had been witness to Gail Lumley's pathetic niece freak out on television while they ate their tuna casserole from TV trays. Oh. God.

"I'm not a hit woman, Frankie. I own an employment agency, one specifically geared to help women just like you."

"You mean ones who've aired their dirty laundry on a live cooking show?"

Maxine's expression turned pained. She blew out a breath of air, making her cheeks puff outward. "That was a lot."

A lot? A. Lot? She let her head sink into her hands. To say what she'd done was "a lot" was like calling the *Titanic*'s sinking a little mishap in the water.

"Look, Frankie, you're going to be recognized. That's a fact."

No siree. Not if she didn't ever leave her aunt's retirement village ranch, she wouldn't.

"Deal with it. Head-on. You have nothing to be ashamed of. Who wouldn't threaten to, and I'll paraphrase, 'mash her husband's testicles if—'"

"Cubes," Gail said with a firm nod. "Frankie said 'cubes.'"

Maxine nodded back. "Right—her husband's *cubes* with a potato masher after finding out he was unfaithful? I can think of ten women offhand who'd give their eyeteeth to do it on national television. I'd bet there are a million women all over the nation still smiling over that particular broadcast of *Mitch in the Kitchen*. But it's over. You can't hide from it. And before you say it, you have to leave the village sometime."

Wasn't it funny all the things she *had* to do? Where was this universal rule book that had all these requirements located anyway?

"Not only do you have to leave the village, but your checking account says you have to work," Maxine reminded her.

Frankie's cheeks stained red, a hazard of her fair skin. "Doing what? I have no skills other than being someone's bitch." She was quick to cast an apologetic glance in her aunt's direction for her language, but it was the truth. She prepped food for a television show, and the only reason she'd been given the job in the first place was due to her nagging Mitch. She'd wanted to be more involved—to be more productive.

Whoever the hell said idle hands were the devil's playground was full of horse puckey.

"My employment agency helps train women just like you. Trophy and even some non-trophy wives who've been sedentary in the workplace for long periods of time, and you do have a skill or two, Frankie. You just don't know it yet."

Yeah. She could work the shit out of a Magic Bullet. Definitely employers all over the globe would trip over themselves to hire her because of that priceless skill.

Yet Maxine's smile was infuriatingly serene. "Tell me what you did when you worked for the Bon Appetit Channel."

"I did the food prep for Mitch's show. I chopped and organized, made sure everything was at his disposal. I'm good with color, size, and texture for a camera, and that's it. Seeing as I pitched a nation-wide fit, I don't think there's a television station from here to the remotest regions of Siberia that would hire me. I guess my camera-worthy food prep days are over. Now McDonald's might find me appealing, but I don't suppose I can earn a living there as head Big Mac maker." And she didn't want a job anyway. She just wanted to go back to bed because that whole slew of sentences had taken way more energy and focus than she had to give.

"But you probably learned a lot about cooking because you were exposed to so much of it, right?"

Oh, she'd learned. In fact, she was responsible for many of the recipes Mitch featured on his show. But she'd also learned early on—shortly before Mitch proposed to her—she hated to cook. Like really hated it. Her shoulders lifted in a small shrug. "I know enough."

"Those are valuable skills, Frankie. How could you not see that?"

Gail waved a cheese Danish at her. "Tell her where you went to school, Frankie," her aunt prompted, a hint of the pride she'd earlier shown for Maxine in her words.

Her voice lowered in more ugly shame. If this kept up, she'd have to hyphenate her name with the word. "I dropped out of the Culi-nary Institute of America."

"Because of Mitch?" Maxine asked, folding her hands on the table, staring directly at her.

Her eyes began to feel heavy, every word an effort. "Not just

because of him, no. He made for a good excuse, though. The truth is
I really hated cooking school. It wasn't nearly the fun my mother
made it while I was growing up."

"Frannie was a good cook. The best of the best, my sister was,"
Gail chirped, her eyes glassy from unshed tears.

Yes. Her mother, the woman she'd been named after, had been
the best of the best. Frankie would give up a major organ just to be
able to talk to her right now.

Her throat tightened, but she pressed onward, hoping to speed up
Maxine's departure. "There's a lot of pressure in a professional kitchen
versus the one you grew up in where no one flipped if you did something wrong. I just didn't love the process the way I thought I would.
I kept thinking, 'It's just food, not the cure for erectile dysfunction.' I
could never buy into the big deal a chef would make if someone
screwed up an order, but to them, it's like an offense of the highest
order. Anyway, I was waiting tables and going to school when I met
Mitch. At the time, he was the sous chef at the restaurant I waited
tables for. He loved food enough for the both of us. I used to really
love to watch . . . to watch him . . . cook." Frankie gulped.

Maxine pressed a hand to hers in comfort. It felt strange and reassuring all in one touch. "And then he changed, I take it?"

Had he—or was he always the self-absorbed, callous prick she'd
born witness to the night she'd caught Mitch and Bamby? She
couldn't remember if he was always so domineering or if at that time
in her life, his dictatorial behavior was the kind of guidance she'd
needed rather than resented. "I don't know. Maybe I changed . . ."

Maxine nibbled on a Danish with pretty white teeth. "It's neither
here nor there. All of those things can be worked out later in our
group sessions. For right now, you have a job interview. So go get your
pretty on, and we'll go." She turned her attention back to her coffee,

nonchalantly stirring it with the spoon, as though she hadn't just set off a grenade.

Frankie's mouth fell open. A job interview? With whom? Who would hire her to do anything but maybe babysit their cave? "I'm not ready—to—I"—she sucked in an anxious breath—"I can't . . ."

"No, you can, and you will." Maxine gave her the mom look, brushing crumbs from her hands onto the yellow paper napkins Gail provided. "You have to. You've been in bed for six months. Do you have any idea how much time you have to make up for? So no more lollygagging. Go put on something that says 'hire me,' and hurry. We have to meet Nikos at five at the diner."

The diner. The. Diner. Unmoving, Frankie said, "The diner."

"That's right. The diner," Maxine confirmed, her eyes sharp with amusement. "Are you going to give me grief because it's not a five-star restaurant and insult all the hard work it took to nab you this interview?"

Gail grinned, holding out her hands to Kiki. "Good then, it's a date. I'll babysit. Come see your Auntie Gail," she cooed to a stoic Kiki.

White-knuckled, Frankie's legs shook, and she wasn't even standing yet. There was absolutely no way in friggin' hell she could go on an interview, let alone work in a diner. Or anywhere.

Well, so much for protests. There was something to be said for the brand of vitamins Maxine was taking. She'd pried Frankie's fingers from the molding around the door with the strength of a sumo wrestler.

Leaning against Maxine's passenger door, Frankie huddled deeper into her sweater, reluctant and petulant. It was the heaviest piece of outerwear she still owned, but it wasn't cutting it against the sharp November air. Her teeth chattered and her body shook.

"You're cold because you haven't been eating, Frankie." Maxine's observation came as she yielded into traffic.

"Thank you, FDA," she muttered.

Maxine's tongue clucked in disapproval, but her grip on the steering wheel was relaxed. "If you could put as much effort into preparing for this interview as you did into clinging to the doorway at your aunt's, you'd be golden."

"How am I supposed to prepare for something I wasn't aware of until fifteen minutes ago?" Oh, she sounded so peevish.

"Someone had to throw you into the deep end. It wasn't going to be Gail. She's too soft, and she loves you too much to upset you. I, on the other hand, have no compunctions about dragging you from your cave, and I don't care if it upsets your precarious balance or your beloved pity party."

She might not have felt a whole lot in the past six months, but today, right this second, she hated Maxine Whatserface for forcing her to do something she didn't want to do. "So who are you? The patron saint of divorced, depressed ex-trophy wives? And how did I get the label ex-trophy wife anyway?"

Maxine pulled into the parking lot of a place called Greek Meets Eat Diner, touting a huge banner that read, "Home of the World's Best Meatloaf," and laughed. "You're snarky. I like that, and no, but I already told you, I know where you are. I know how hard it is to even consider surviving, let alone summon up the will to want to when you've been dumped in such a public way. I know what it's like to have nothing. Absolutely nothing. So I started an employment agency for women just like you and me. Which leads me to the definition of an ex-trophy wife. Typically we're pretty young things who marry a much older, rich man who likes to display his eye candy in the way of nubile. When we're not so young and nubile anymore, we're down-graded, and many times we lose everything because we were stupid enough to sign prenups. Hence, we're not so trophy anymore."

Frankie grunted. Thank God she knew who she was. The wife formerly known as trophy. Labels were good. She didn't get it. If Maxine was back in the black, why did she give even a small hoot about women in a predicament she was no longer in? "And so you bought an employment agency to help ex-rich girls out? With what? Your new rich husband's money?"

Maxine's smile was glib when she put her car in park, but she didn't rise to Frankie's bait. "You know what, someday, when you get past behaving like a spiteful three-year-old who's been forced to potty-train and give up her sippy cup all in one day, I might tell you exactly how I came upon the money to open my own employment agency and why I did it. Until then, let me just be really clear. I'm not the enemy. You're your own worst enemy. I want to help. But you have to help me help you. Financially, you're in dire straits right now. You might not care because you're all caught up in the 'bury your head in the sand' stage of divorce recovery, but the time will come when you will care, and it'll be too late, Frankie Bennett. Your aunt asked me to help because she was at her wits' end with worry over you, and she didn't know where to turn. I've never seen her as upset as she was yesterday at my mother's. She was good to me at a time when good was hard to come by. I never forget that kind of good."

Remorseful tears stung her eyes again. One minute she was rail-ing in defensive rebellion for being dragged from her hibernation, the next, she was weepy and repentant. No matter how depressed, she'd never intentionally hurt Gail. "I'm sorry. I know my aunt is try-ing to help. I don't want to hurt her."

Maxine cocked her head, turning in her seat to capture Frankie's gaze. She reached out a hand and rested it on her shoulder. It brought curious warmth to the pervading chill her body couldn't shake. "I know what you're doing isn't intentional, Frankie. You just want to be left alone. Sometimes, during something so life altering, so painful, you withdraw because hiding's easier than getting back in the game. You're lethargic and disinterested in everything. It's depression."

"Wow, I sound like one of those commercials where everything's gray and dreary until you take a Xanax or, in this case, a Maxine, whatever it is, and poof, it magically makes your world go all bright with shiny colors again. Well, except for those nagging side effects like the anal weeping and eyeball leakage."

Maxine chuckled, then sobered. "The thing is you *are* like one of those people, Frankie. The only difference is you haven't been clinically diagnosed. But we could change that, if you'd like. I'd be happy to take you to the doctor," she offered with her irritatingly pleasant tone.

Frankie sobered, too. She didn't need a pill. She needed a bed with a blanket.

"Look, while you mope, the people around you, who love you, suffer, too. That's why you have to get up off your ass and do something about it—even though you know it'll suck. So here's the skinny—get over yourself long enough to at least give this a try."

Frankie lowered her eyes to her ice-cold hand in her lap. "And suck it up, princess, right?" Such a dumb expression.

Maxine chuckled again, her eyes crinkling at the corners. "That's exactly right. It's my life mantra. Now c'mon. You'll like Nikos and his family. They all have a hand in the diner in one way or another. They're a big, loud Greek family who'll fatten you up in no time flat. Not to mention, they'll provide you with a distraction while you heal."

Heal. Like she had the flu.

Her stomach began to revolt by rumbling while waves of anxious panic swept over her. She couldn't possibly convince anyone to give her a job in this state. She hadn't been out of her aunt's house but maybe ten times in six months. She'd forgotten what kind of common courtesies and communication were involved in meeting new people.

How in all of fuck could she possibly meet and impress a possible employer? Frankie's fingers went to the handle on the door, gripping it for all she was worth. "I don't think I can do this, Maxine. I—"

"You're panicking. Understandable. But you *will* do this, Frankie. Even if you don't get the job, it's a beginning. A starting point. So just pretend this is a practice run." With those words, Maxine hopped out of the car and went to the passenger door as if she were skipping through a vibrantly scented field of wildflowers.

Frankie locked it with fumbling hands.

Maxine's eyebrows rose, but her smile was wicked when she held up the key fob with two fingers. The beep signaling the door unlocking made Frankie jump.

Maxine popped it open, holding out her gloved hand. "I win. So c'mon. If nothing else, I'll buy you a bowl of soup and a sandwich. Now gird your loins and get crackin'."

Frankie's breath shuddered in and out, the cold air blowing steam from her panicked gasps. Maxine took hold of her arm, pulling her toward the diner's doors, doors that were see-through with etchings in gold, giving Frankie a glimpse of the diner's interior.

Red and silver booths with jukeboxes at every table were the first thing she was able to focus on before being swept into the warm rush of air. The next was the smell—redolent with so many different varieties of rich spices and garlic, she couldn't place one from the other.

Christmas lights were strung in winking bright white where the wall met the ceiling. Frankie winced. Christ. The last holiday she could clearly remember, and that was only due to the disrupting noise of it, was the Fourth of July. Was it already December? No, it was just two days after Thanksgiving. The distant recollection of her Aunt Gail and her friend Mona planning a Black Friday shop-a-palooza tickled her memory.

A small tree decorated with tinsel and multicolored blinking lights stood by the cash register. A young woman, her hair the color of black satin, in black hip-hugging pants and a white shirt with black vest smiled in Maxine's direction. "Hey, Max! How are you?"

"Adara, it's so good to see you! Home for Christmas break?"

Her sleek head bobbed up and down. "Yep. I'm working Papa over for some extra cash," she said with a teasing grin.

Maxine pulled off her gloves, dropping them into the pockets of her jacket. "Connor's coming home in three days. I'm so excited to see him, I could scream. Campbell even went out and bought an Xbox 360 so they could play video games together."

Adara's head cocked, her eyes, as black as her hair, lit up. "So he likes school then?"

Maxine's light brown head nodded. "Loves it." She glanced at her watch and pursed her lips. "I hate to rush, but I have dinner with Campbell in an hour. Adara, this is Frankie Bennett. She's interviewing with Nikos today."

Adara stuck out her hand and grinned again, her smile a thing of utter beauty. "Awesome to meet you. Welcome to the home of the World's Best Meatloaf."

Meatloaf.

At Greek Meets Eat Diner in Riverbend, New Jersey.

Hookay.

Frankie hesitated until Maxine nudged her with an arm. *Right*, she mentally reminded herself. *Be polite, cave dweller*. She took Adara's hand and gave her a faint smile. "Nice to meet you, too."

Coming around to the front of the cash register, Adara hitched her jaw in the direction of the doors Frankie assumed led to the kitchen. "You want me to go tell him you're here? I think he's in the back with Mama and Cosmos."

"Please, Adara," Maxine said with a smile. As Adara went off to find Frankie's would-be employer, Maxine leaned into her and whispered, "Adara is Nikos's sister, Cosmos is his brother. And in case you're wondering, every last one of them is as good-looking as the next. I don't know what they feed those kids, but they're all like Rodin sculptures."

No pressure, but seriously, no shit.

Frankie gave a self-conscious glance at her baggy jeans and faded T-shirt, tightening her sweater around her and pushing at the loose strands of her ponytail, windblown and askew. Then she gave up. What difference did it make what she looked like? There wasn't a hooker's chance at the debutantes' ball she'd maneuver a job looking the way she did—especially with her dormant social skills at an all-time low. Retreating back to the recesses of her mind, Frankie decided to pretend this wasn't happening. A sigh escaped her lips, drawn out and disinterested.

When the kitchen doors popped open, Frankie gave only a cursory glance upward before returning her eyes to her sneakers. Thankfully, she'd purchased them with her Bon Appetit salary just before she and Mitch had broken up or they'd have gone the way of the prenup, too.

"Max!" a throaty timbre greeted.

"Nikos, it's great to see you!" Maxine responded, disgustingly cheerful. Hugs were apparently exchanged due to the rustle of material. Suddenly, Maxine's arm was around her shoulder and her hip was nudging Frankie's.

Another one of those signals to behave accordingly in a social setting.

"Nikos, this is Frankie Bennett. Frankie, Nikos Antonakas."

Antonakas. She found she had trouble even considering rolling a name like that over her thick, underused tongue.

Frankie took her time looking up, letting her eyes scan the leather-worn work boots Nikos wore, following his length by way of his thighs. His hard, muscled thighs in black jeans.

Whether it was genuine curiosity to see if his bulky thighs matched the rest of him, or some of her social graces were thawing, Frankie glanced upward, letting the fringe of her unadorned lashes keep her eyes undercover.

Oh.

Shazam.

Rodin had nothing, *noth-ing* on this man.

Holy spanakopita.

Stunned by Nikos's breathtakingly chiseled good looks, Frankie's head swirled, and her legs trembled. He really was that beautiful. Even in her stupor of postdivorce lunacy, she could not deny the appeal of his hard, classic features. His hair was thick, the color of midnight in the height of a winter chill, falling just past his chin. A widow's peak in the center of his forehead drew her attention to his eyebrows, raven and arched. His ruddily toned skin held two patches of color along the angular slant of his cheekbones. Eyes the color of black olives assessed her with a smile full of straight white teeth.

Oh, that smile. Disarming with a hint of playful.

He had a dimple in his chin, too, and catching sight of it made Frankie's breath hitch.

Shit. Had they been introduced? Maxine gave her arm a discreet pinch. Frankie coughed to hide her embarrassment. "I'm Francis— Fran . . . kie. Uh, Bennett."

The dark Adonis put out a hand for her to shake. "Nice to meet you, Frankie. Welcome to Greek Meets Eat. Home of the World's Best—"

"Meatloaf," she muttered to avoid his hand. Oh, no. If she shook that hand, long fingered and wide, she'd pass out.

Maxine coughed in Frankie's ear, "Shake his hand, *princess.*"

Immediately, Frankie did as she was told, their fingers connecting for a moment before she tugged her hand away, shoving it into the pocket of her jeans. His skin was warm with just the right amount of callusedness, burning an imprint against her icy flesh.

Nikos's expression said he wondered if she was deranged, but he hid it well when he called over his broad shoulder, "Let's go back to the office and sit and talk. You want coffee, Max, Frankie?"

"No!" Frankie faltered behind the shelter of Maxine. "I mean, no, thank you."

Maxine smiled over her shoulder with encouragement, following Nikos to the end of the wide diner. His fingers turned the brass doorknob on a broad, red enamel door, holding it open for them to enter with a sweep of his long muscled forearm.

Maxine found a chair, patting the one beside her as Nikos took his place behind the desk cluttered with papers and a computer. "I appreciate you coming to Trophy Jobs, Nikos."

He grinned, alarmingly warm and charming, making Frankie's already slow breathing hitch again. "Don't thank me. You're pretty impressive, lady. I know you didn't expect a lot from Lacey, but she was one of the best damned short-order's we've ever had."

Maxine's chuckle and the glance she exchanged with Nikos bordered on mysterious. Frankie fidgeted in her seat, uncomfortable with the fluorescent lights of Nikos's office. "Who knew Lacey, of all people, would want to go off and study at Le Cordon Bleu?"

His laughter was hearty, his eyes warm with fondness. "We miss her, but she sends us postcards all the time. Anyway, with the kind of luck we had the first time around, you were the person who came to mind."

Who was Lacey, and oh, my God. She was in a diner. *A diner.* A diner boasting the world's best meatloaf. *Meatloaf.* Food for heathens who had no taste buds, if you listened to Mitch.

But she wasn't listening to Mitch anymore. Bamby With A "Y" was.

Strangely, that made Frankie want to bust a grin.

But it hurt to consider moving her facial muscles. So she didn't.

"So you have all the information on Frankie's work history, right? I had Bettina fax it over this morning."

Nikos slapped the papers on his desk with a loud hand. "I don't need paperwork, Max, but yep, I got everything."

Good. That was good, Frankie mused. She wondered if he had the DVD of famous chefs' wives gone wild, too. Sliding down into her appointed chair, she pulled her sweater closer around her chin.

"Okay, good then," Maxine said, rising.

Whoa, whoa, whoa. Where was the divorce guru going? Surely Maxine wouldn't leave her here all by herself with the reinvention of gorgeously glorious. Not when she was as fragile as eggshells and liable to crack at any given moment.

Oh, but she would. Maxine gave Frankie's shoulder a reassuring pat. "I'll just wait outside and let you two talk. I think I'll have some of that coffee while I do." And then she was gone.

And they were left staring at each other.

His glance was openly curious, but cheerful.

Hers was petrified, and well, petrified.

Nikos cleared his throat, rustling the papers Bettina had sent. "So, Frankie. Do you have any experience working in a diner—maybe a restaurant?"

I was a crappy waitress. But I can work a Slap Chop like a breast implant salesman works an A-cup convention. She shifted in her chair, pulling the sleeves of her sweater over the palms of her hands. "No."

"Any food experience in general?"

"I've been known to eat it." Oh. Jesus.

His chuckle was thick and sexy. Just like him. "Right." He patted his hard abdomen. "Me, too. What I mean is, Max says you have experience as a chef."

Right. Max would say that. "Define 'chef.'"

Nikos rolled his tongue around the inside of his cheek. "Well, aren't they usually people who cook? You know, like that food thing we talked about."

"Yes, they are, and no, I'm not a chef. I hate to cook." That said, she waited while he processed her response and shipped her back off to Maxine. Screw her car. The repo man could come and take it. She didn't need to drive if she never planned to leave the house again.

He nodded his sleek black head, all agreeable. "Well, that's a good thing. We don't need a chef."

Damn. Foiled again.

This was ridiculous, and she was doing nothing but wasting his time. So if she frigged up the interview, she could go back home to her aunt's dark guest bedroom and get back into her nice warm bed. Let the frigging begin. "Can we be frank with one another?"

He sat back in his chair, running a hand over the dark stubble on his chin. "I want you to be whoever you want to be."

Frankie ignored the joke in favor of her purpose, a warm bed and nothingness. "You can't possibly expect me to believe you don't know who I am."

"Should I know who you are, Frankie?" When he said her name, slow and easy, a chill of unadulterated pleasure swept along her arms.

Her laughter was filled with bitter irony. "Maxine told you to pretend you didn't know, right? So I wouldn't be humiliated on my first official public outing."

His face remained placid, his smoldering black eyes perfectly blank. "Have you been in jail?"

"Jail?" If she had any gumption, she'd be affronted. But she didn't. So no affronting from her side of the desk.

"You said this was your first 'official public outing.'"

"It is. And, no. No jail." Though, she'd come precariously close after the judge viewed the tapes of her outburst. Destruction of property, blah, blah, blah.

"Hospitalized?"

Frankie's return gaze was filled with cynicism. "What you really mean is institutionalized, don't you?"

Nikos waggled a finger in admonishment and gave her a playful grin as a chaser. "Uh-uh-uh. *You* went there. I didn't."

"No. I haven't been institutionalized. Though, after my display, I'm pretty sure some would say I should be." In fact, Mitch had. On *Hollywood Scoop*. With his best sad-sympathetic face. Oscar statues had wept from near and far at his performance.

"Display? I have no idea what you mean."

Who on the planet, and probably twelve other alternate dimensions, didn't know who she was? She'd been on every rag mag and television gossip show for months, speculation about her mental well-being the primary focus as they'd replayed in every speed imaginable her infamous symphonic wooden spoon debut.

Quite frankly, on that night, she admittedly had looked like someone who'd escaped a full-body butterfly net and gone off her prescription pharmaceuticals. Hair wild, eyes wide and glazed, spittle forming at the corner of her mouth—all in perfect focus thanks to close-up genius, cameraman number two, Andy Jeffers. Add in the spoon she'd wielded like a sledgehammer, and she made one scary-looking lunatic.

Mitch and his PR crew had put some spin on her outburst, too, making him look like the poor, suffering husband of a woman whose mental state was challenged by the voices in her head.

"You really don't know who I am?"

Nikos shook his dark head back and forth, the light catching the deep gleam of his thick hair. "Nope. Not a clue. You wanna tell me who you're supposed to be so I can behave accordingly? If you're royalty or something, I want to be sure I bow appropriately," he said with a teasing tone.

"I'm Mitch in the Kitchen's wi . . . um, ex-wife." There. The elephant could leave the room.

"Mitch in the where?"

Wow. Not only super-fantastical looking, but gracious and kind. "Kitchen."

Yet, his eyes read thoroughly perplexed. "And why would I pretend I didn't know you were Mitch in the Kitchen's ex-wife when I don't even know Mitch? In fact, I don't know anyone named Mitch. Unless we're talking Miller, and he defines the word 'dead.' God rest his soul."

Frankie sighed. His denials made her head swim. "Because Maxine told you to be nice to the pathetic, broke ex-trophy wife who, by the way, wants a job like she needs another useless ovary."

His thick eyebrow arched. "You were a trophy wife?"

Frankie flapped her hands in concession, not at all offended by his surprise. "I know. Hard to believe, looking the way I do, right? But as Valentino is my witness, I was a trophy wife with all the bells and whistles. Maxine said so. Clothes, hair, makeup, personal massage therapist. The only boat I missed was the plastic surgeon's, and

I just know Mitch would have talked me into double Ds before long. So yes, I was a trophy wife. For eighteen years. Now I'm not. I've been replaced. Hardcore replaced. But you knew that because Maxine told you." She fought not to make it sound like an accusation, but he wasn't making this easy.

Nikos frowned, delicious lines marring his smooth forehead. "Maxine didn't tell me anything other than she had an applicant for an opening I have here at the diner for a prep chef. There was never any talk of a Mitch or a kitchen or for that matter, a display."

She rolled her eyes, brushing an impatient hand over her bangs. "Oh, she did, too. *Please.* You don't really think you're fooling me, do you? I mean, it's very nice that you're going out of your way to be so kind, but your performance isn't exactly red carpet worthy."

"What exactly is a Mitch in the Kitchen anyway? Is that like the ShamWow guy?"

Okay. She'd play along. "It's a television show on the Bon Appetit Channel."

"The one with all those fancy chefs? Nuh-uh . . ."

"Uh-huh. The one with all those fancy chefs." And fancy women with names like Bamby.

"Your husband had a show? Like a real television show?" His disbelief was growing more convincing by the second.

Frankie's head cocked to the right. "Yes. You really don't know who Mitch Bennett is?"

Nikos leaned forward on his desk and propped his hands on either side of his jaw, his mouth slack for a moment before he recovered and answered, "Nuh-uh. But I'm still in awe that you were married to a guy who had a television show. In fact, color me a little starstruck."

She was used to this kind of reaction when people realized she was married to a celebrity. *You're not married to a celebrity anymore, Frankie.* She fidgeted with the tie at the waist of her sweater.

"Do you have any idea the kind of customers the diner'd get if they knew a celebrity's wife from the whatever channel worked here?"

This wasn't going according to plan. He wasn't supposed to be excited. He was supposed to tell her she lacked experience, not to mention enthusiasm, and then politely respond by telling her he'd get back to her. "Are you kidding me?"

Nikos slapped a large hand on his desk, sending papers scattering. "Not even a little. You're rockin' my socks off right now. That kind of experience alone is all golden and shiny as far as I'm concerned." His words were followed by a hearty laugh, straight from his not as hearty hard-planed belly.

Hello. What about her pain and suffering was rocking-your-socks worthy? Sudden anger tweaked her already raw nerves. "Did you hear me the first time, or did you miss the part about me being an *ex*-trophy wife? I'm no longer married to Mitch. So no celebrity."

Flapping his tanned hands, Nikos waved at her dismissively. His grin was wide and effusive. "That's neither here nor there. You have infamy on your side, and you worked at the Bon Appetit Channel. Bet you have a bunch of secret recipes running around in your head. That's all I need to know." He shook his head and shot her a wry grin. "Damn, this is some awesome turn of events," he stated with obvious glee, hopping up from behind his desk to head to the door in two strong strides.

So cute and dense went hand in hand with Nikos Anta . . . Anta . . . Chakalakaboomboom. Whatever.

"Max, c'mon back in here!" Nikos shouted out into the diner, his voice a cheerful bellow.

Frankie shrunk farther down in her chair as she listened to the muffled words exchanged between Maxine and her employer-who-almost-was.

"Frankie Bennett?" he crowed back into the room.

She rose to turn and take him in, pushing down the baggy folds her jeans created when she stood. Her face held a question she was too tired to ask.

Nikos stuck out his hand to her while Maxine gave her the big thumbs-up sign behind his broad shoulder. "I don't care if you can't boil water. You're hired."

Shut. Up.

CHAPTER THREE

From the reluctant (very, very reluctant) journal of ex-trophy wife Frankie Bennett: The first rule of the Princess Club? Suck it up. Please. This is by far the most ridiculous thing I've ever done. I don't want nor do I care to document my postdivorce road to recovery so I can look back one day and smile at how far I've come. Seeing my pain in black and white isn't therapeutic at all. And PS, Maxine Barker's a flake. I'm only doing this to appease my Aunt Gail because she's looking over my shoulder right now and making me feel like I purposely didn't go to confession. So in the interest of keeping her happy, here's my first entry. And Maxine Barker's still a flake.

"You do so know who she is, Nikos. That was a crappy thing to do," his brother Cosmos chided with a slap to his back as they watched Maxine and Frankie cross the parking lot. Nikos mentally noted the drag in Frankie's step, the slump of her shoulders that were too damned skinny, and the sag of her jeans on what he'd bet his left lung had once been a sweet ass.

He fought a grin. "Giving her a job was crappy how, Cos?"

"You know what I mean, you shithead. I heard everything while you pretended not to know who she was, then went about making like she was the second coming."

Nikos winced. Yeah, he was a shitty improviser. "That just sort of happened. My bad. But she was working pretty hard to avoid getting herself hired. Max told me she would because she's post something or other traumatized."

"Postdivorce."

"Yeah. That was it. She said she'd be sullen and disinterested. So I just went with it. Steamrolled her, so to speak."

"How do you suppose it made her feel, knowing you plan to use her infamous freak on television as a promotional tool?"

"I would never do that. You know it and I know it. I just didn't want her to run away, so I did a little off the cuff. Max'll tell her I was just kidding. Besides, I owe Maxine. She was really good to Kelly. I wanted to return the favor," Nikos said, reminding his brother of the help Maxine had given their cousin after her ugly divorce.

Cosmos nodded his sleek, dark head. Only an inch shorter than his older brother, he gazed up at him with narrowed eyes. "Yes, Max was great to Kelly. If she hadn't stepped in when she did, I'd bet Aunt Dora'd be in the crazy house after that jackass and Kelly broke up. But if Frankie didn't already feel uncomfortable—and judging by the way she won't look anyone in the eye, she's a wreck—you only made things worse by telling her she'd bring the diner business with her supposed celebrity."

"Okay, so it wasn't the best plan."

"So what *is* the plan?"

"The plan," their mother, Voula, said, poking her head out from the kitchen doorway, "is to fatten her up! Ack! Did you see, Nikos? She is so skeeny. I will make lamb. You think she like lamb?"

Nikos smiled at his mother, short, big-haired, and boisterous. "Who wouldn't like your lamb, Mama? I agree, Frankie needs to eat."

Voula nodded, tightening the knot of her apron around her thick waist. "Good. I make baklava, too. Maybe even spanakopita." She headed back into the kitchen, determined to fatten up the poor, unsuspecting Frankie.

Cosmos took in Nikos once more. "So the plan? She says she hates to cook. I heard it right through those paper-thin walls. How does that help you and me in the kitchen with the prep work?"

"The plan is to give her a paycheck she probably wouldn't get anywhere else due to her limited skills. Besides, what's Kelly always telling us Maxine taught her? To suck it?"

"Suck it up, princess," he corrected.

"Right. Max said Frankie needs to stop indulging in self-pity and get back on the horse. She told me she has to take it like a man, and she needs a paycheck to do it. Frankie's Aunt Gail was so worried about that woman, she cried. You know how much I love the ladies from Leisure Village. They bring us a ton of business for the early bird special, and I really like Gail and Mona. One hand washes the other, bro. Plus, if I remember reading correctly, Frankie got custody of that little deaf dog, Kiki. Kiki's cute. She needs to eat."

Cosmos pursed his lips. "Does she have *any* idea what she's in for? She looks like you could scare the skin right off her bones just by bumping into her. We're not exactly known for the use of our indoor voices, Nik."

Nikos sighed, running a hand through his hair. "I agree we're probably not like spending a day chanting with Tibetan monks, but if what Max says is true, she's had all the quiet time she can handle without spiraling into therapy and meds. Maybe chaos will keep her so busy she'll forget she was dumped by a limp dick like Mitch Bennett. Either way, take it easy on her, would you?"

"Easy-shmeasy. I need someone to *help* me, not hinder."

"It'll be fine."

"Did you really say 'rockin' my socks off'?"

"I did."

"That was ridiculously lame."

Nikos chuckled. "Maybe so, but she's had a hard time of it, and she does know how to prep food. Max told me she did it for that asshole of an ex-husband of hers. On *TV*, pal. She's very organized, something you and Mama could definitely use back there, and she knows her way around a knife."

Cosmos barked a laugh. "Oh, don't I know it. I saw the way she was wielding that Mitch's spoon like it was a samurai sword. I plan to tread very lightly around her."

"Look, if worse comes to worst, I'll put her on cashier duty. Adara'd love to have some time off to see her friends and shop, okay? Now, don't you have a slew of chickens to marinate?"

Cosmos threw a white kitchen towel over his shoulder. "Yeah, yeah. I'm out, but just remember this. I have my reservations about this woman, and if she takes a kitchen knife to *my* cubes, I'm comin' for you, brother."

Nikos slapped him on the back with a grin. "I take full responsibility for any and all cube dicing."

Cosmos visibly shuddered, sweeping past the long row of stools at the counter before disappearing into the kitchen.

A glance out the window revealed Maxine and Frankie still in the car, heads bobbing, hands waving. Nikos smiled. Frankie was probably giving her shit about the new boss who wanted to exploit her, and Maxine wasn't taking any. It was clear Frankie didn't want a job. Not just this job, but any job.

Couldn't say as he blamed her. She was right. Her television debut had been some "display" as she'd called it, and he definitely didn't need some food snob criticizing his diner's food. Yet, there was something about her he couldn't pinpoint that made him want to help her, whether she wanted it or not.

Nikos knew exactly who Frankie Bennett was. He, like a million and two other people, had seen the constant replay of her infamous fit all over the place. He'd also cheered the kind of gutsy fortitude she'd shown when she'd threatened to whip Mitch's dick to a stiff meringue-y peak with his souped-up mixer.

Unlike most of America who'd fallen for the bullshit about his wife's mental instability, Nikos saw Mitch Bennett for what he was—an overblown ego with a penchant for beautiful young women less than half his age.

Unfortunately, he'd seen that firsthand.

Right here in his own diner.

With his best friend's wife.

Prick.

~ ℓ ~

Frankie flipped through the pamphlet Maxine left her just before she'd skipped out the door of Gail's and off to the loving arms of her rich hubby.

"Messages of hope," was what the pamphlet proclaimed. Inspirational speeches of the "giving up your Ferrari for a used Yugo didn't have to suck" variety littered the pages. Phrases like "big girl panties" and "Walmart can be your friend" left her more desolate that she'd been to begin with.

The words began to spin and blur. Her eyes were grainy from so much awake-and-not-allowed-to-wallow time, and her stomach was a sea of roiling acid. "Oh, look, Kiki." She held up the pamphlet, which Kiki assessed with calm eyes along with her owner. "Maxine says cash is cash, and there's no shame in starting at the bottom of the job chain."

Nikos's offer had been generous, considering a prep chef was an entry-level position. When Maxine heard the salary he'd offered her, she'd whooped—loudly, making Frankie wince. But she couldn't summon up the kind of excitement Maxine apparently felt over the idea that she'd be able to afford her own cell phone and tampons in no time.

"Where would we be without Maxine, Kik?"

"I see you got Maxine's Survival Guide for Ex-Trophy Wives."

Frankie grunted at her aunt. "Whether I wanted it or not," she said on a wide yawn.

Gail glanced at the clock on the wall with the Amish couple in the center. "You've been up a whole three hours. Takes a lot out of a girl, eh?"

She was too tired to care that she was being poked with a stick. Her fingers tugged at the elastic band holding her ponytail, yanking it out and running a hand through her hair. "Just breathing takes a lot out of me."

Gail sat on the arm of her plaid couch, placing an arm around her niece's shoulder to give her a squeeze. "Did you even read the pamphlet? I spent a week typing that up on a computer, sunshine. Used to do almost a hundred words a minute back in the day."

Frankie pressed it tight to her chest. "I'll treasure it always," she teased.

Gail pinched her cheeks and smiled. "Don't be a smarty pants, young lady. So tell me all about how you nabbed this job and on your very first interview while I make us some dinner. Pretty impressive for someone who's been in the crapper for six months."

Her shoulders lifted as she followed Gail into the kitchen, watching her pull out two TV dinners from the freezer. The thought of food made her want to retch. She dropped Kiki at her food dish, giving her little black-and-white bottom a nudge toward the bowl. "No, Aunt Gail. None for me thanks."

Gail's eyebrows rose. "What? Not fancy enough for your overdeveloped palette?"

Frankie let out a sigh. "No, it's not that at all, Aunt Gail. I'm not as much of a food snob as you'd like to think. There were plenty of nights when Mitch was off globe-hopping that I ate TV dinners." Though, if Mitch had known, he'd have had an apoplexy. "I'm just not very hungry."

Gail's forehead wrinkled. "Nonsense. You need energy for your new job tomorrow. I just bet you'll need energy to keep up with that hunk Nikos Antonakas. Phew, he makes my insides all squishy." She giggled. Like she was still in high school. "He's good-lookin', don't you think?" She peered at Frankie with covert eyes while poking holes in the plastic TV dinner.

Good-looking? If ever there'd been an understatement. Calling Nikos good-looking was like saying the Andes were just little mounds of dirt. He was gorgeous, and if her libido wasn't in a state of deep freeze, she'd acknowledge that very fact, but her hormones were officially ice cubes. "He's fine, Aunt Gail."

Gail plunked down some forks and folded paper napkins on the table. "Fine, you say? *Fine?* Did your eyeballs fall out of your head when you got that divorce? He's what the kids these days call brick shithouse."

A gurgle of laughter bubbled up from her throat at her aunt's use of modern-day slang. "Okay, he's brick shithouse, but it doesn't make a difference. I'm not in the man market. Though, apparently, I'm now in the job market." Albeit under duress and brute Maxine force.

The microwave dinged the completion of their meal. "Maxine said you were none too happy about it either. Why's that? It's a perfectly good job with a perfectly good-lookin' boss."

A tear stung her eye.

Yes. Everything was perfectly good. She just couldn't summon the will to care. Grateful was what she should be. What she wanted to be for her aunt's sake at the very least. Yet she was numb and unresponsive. As limp as the wet noodle Mitch once called his love machine. Each reaction to a kind gesture was merely by rote, and that was some kind of pathetic. "I think I'm just overwhelmed. I did more today than I have—"

"In months, and it's about time, too." Gail placed the Salisbury steak–mashed potato combo dinner in front of her. "I know, Frankie. Believe me, I know. You were sinking, kiddo. I had no choice but to call in reinforcements. Someone had to convince you to get out of bed and do something for yourself. You're young. A beautiful young woman who should be out celebrating her freedom from that wanker, not holed up in her bedroom, sleeping all day, drowning in depression. He's not worth that kind of vigil, my girl."

She knew that. She. Knew. Yet, it remained. This dark, dank hole of nothingness. Nothing to plan for, nothing to look forward to, nothing to get out of her own way for. Just nothing. "You're right," she agreed, flat and disinterested.

Gail tapped her fork on the edge of the plastic covering the TV dinner. "I'll wait until you say it like you mean it. And you will, cookie. I promise you, you will. Maxine was just like you. If you'd been interested enough to ask her, she'd have told you herself. She pulled up her bootstraps, and it wasn't easy, but she did it. Though she had more at stake with a young boy. What you need to do is find your purpose."

Why?

Frankie pushed the spongy Salisbury steak against her fork, forcing herself to take a bite, knowing it would please her aunt. "I'm not sure what that means anymore."

"It means you let your whole world revolve around a man who isn't worth the crud on the bottom of my shoe. You had nothing that was just Frankie's—it's why you're so lost. You were supportive long before he hit the big time, too. You arranged all his appearances and cookbook signings. You answered all his emails from fans and took care of that stupid FaceSpace or whatever ya call it. And he cheated on you, and left you with nothing."

Frankie fought to swallow the gritty mashed potatoes. "It's MySpace and Facebook, and I have nothing because I signed a pre-nup that said I'd get nothing. There's no one to blame for that but me." And it had never occurred to her to change that. Not once had she considered Mitch's empire hers, though she'd helped him build it from scratch.

She didn't even have a hobby. Jesus.

Gail threw her fork down in disgust. "He's a dirty bird, Frankie. I told you that from the get-go. He took advantage of your youth and those starry eyes of yours, all romantic and gooey. That he left you with nothing after everything you've done for him, whether you signed something or not, makes me want to sauté his man parts." She shook her head in revulsion. "Doesn't matter anymore. We're moving forward. Just like Max says. Now it's time for your world to revolve around you."

Maybe it could just stop spinning altogether and Mitch and Bamby would fall off the edge of it. "Forward," she mumbled on her last bite of spongy Salisbury steak, washing it down with the glass of water her aunt gave her.

Gail perked up, the hope in her eyes bright and bubbly. "That's the spirit. Now, if you finish all your dinner, you can have dessert. I made a nice peanut butter cup pie while you were gone with Maxine, hoping we'd have something to celebrate when you got back."

Yay.

She had a job at a diner.

Celebrate good times.

C'mon.

~❧~

"Frankie? Wake up." Gail's soft hand, covered in a light application of lily of the valley hand cream, caressed her cheek.

She struggled to force her eyes open, muttering, "Are you okay, Aunt Gail?"

"I'm fine, honey. Phone's for you." Gail opened her hand and put the phone in it.

She put it to her ear with a groan. No one called her anymore. "Hello?"

"Frankie?"

"*Who* is this?"

"It's Maxine."

Woot. The divorce fairy. A glance at the clock told her she was a divorce fairy of the early bird variety. Jesus. It was five in the morning. "Yes?"

"I'm calling to check and be sure you're up."

"For?"

"Work, Frankie. You have to be at work in an hour. You're working breakfast and lunch today, remember?"

Yesterday came back in a crash of mental visuals, featuring hunky Greek men and red vinyl stools that swiveled. She sat up with a speed that left her dizzy, swinging her legs over the edge of the bed to prevent a wobble. Kiki was instantly at attention beside her mistress, quiet as a mouse, eyes unblinking. "Right. Work."

"Right. Work," Maxine mimicked her. "You know, the place where you go every day to earn money to pay for crazy things like food and shelter."

Both of which she could care less about. All she really needed was a sleeping bag and a sturdy bridge. No fuss. No muss. Then she caught sight of the picture of her aunt and her deceased Uncle Gus, smiling at her high school graduation, and guilt crept up to bite her on the ass. "I'm up."

"Don't forget to shower. As a courtesy to those around you."

Funny. "I'll shower."

"Use soap. Lots of soap."

Frankie frowned. "I'm not ten." Heh.

"Then you won't forget to wash behind your ears, will you?"

Her jaw clenched. "Anything else?"

"One more thing."

"Just one?"

Maxine's laughter tickled her eardrum. "Smile today. Just try it once. I swear your lips won't fall off. But try to make this a positive experience instead of looking at it like you're walking the plank."

A male voice, low and muffled, said something in the background, something she assumed was intimate, and then Frankie heard Maxine giggle girlishly. "Gotta run, but I'll pop in later today to see how things are going, and maybe tonight I can bring you over to Trophy and introduce you to everyone. You go have a good first day. Bye, Frankie."

She didn't say good-bye. Instead, she hung up the phone with a trembling hand. A pang of envy shot through her, hearing that male voice so low and early morning grumbly. For an agonizing moment, she found herself longing for sleepy morning intimacies. Those first moments when you woke up and discovered an arm flung around your waist, and rather than get out of bed, you snuggled deeper beside your . . .

Frankie's heart began an uncomfortable thump. That had to stop. Mitch didn't deserve warm memories and gushy reflections from her.

Pushing back the covers, she rose to take Kiki out, then trudge to the shower and make good on her promise last night to Gail. She'd try and find two sticks to rub together and start a fire in her cave. Live, live, live for the moment and all that jazz. Booyah life.

But only for Gail.

The house was chilly as she made her way to the bathroom, flipping on the light to get her first peek at her mussed appearance.

A shower would never fix the jacked-up mess she was. It was like putting a Band-Aid on a gushing jugular. Her skin was pale, her eyes dull, her lips chapped, her hip bones jutting painfully from beneath her flannel drawstring pajama bottoms.

But whatever.

This wasn't Miss Universe. It was Miss Needs A Job.

Flipping on the water, Frankie let it heat up while she undressed, catching a glimpse of her breasts in the long mirror above the vanity. She cupped them, wincing at how small they were, noting they were also beginning to sag.

How fun.

Bamby had fluffy D-cups.

Maybe she'd been the inspiration for Mitch's comment when he'd said Frankie might consider a boob job.

Frankie shook off the memory with a shiver. Mitch was all up in her head today, and she had Maxine to thank for that. If she'd just left her alone, her numb state of denial could have gone on in a blissful haze of her own stench.

Kiki sat beside her on the bath mat, her paws primly in front of her, dark eyes observing Frankie in typical stoic fashion. "Just remember, I'm doing this for you—because kibble costs money. But I don't like it. Got that? If you didn't need to eat, I'd just stay in bed."

That train of thought became a theme for her first day at Greek Meets Eat Diner. Upon her arrival, loud crashes of pots and pans came from the kitchen followed by words, harsh and foreign, mingled with laughter and a lot of yelling.

Frankie winced, pulling the sleeves of her sweatshirt over her hands, unsure where to go, but desperately hoping to avoid the overwhelming chaos by finding a dark corner. It wasn't so much the yelling. God knew Mitch had yelled at her, more often than not, without her even realizing it, as their relationship disintegrated. It was the overstimulation she found abrasive and jarring. Like small needles puncturing her cocoon of quiet.

The diner held only one customer, most likely due to the fact that not even vampires were putting on their eye masks and night cream yet.

A man, just an inch shy of Nikos's tremendous build, and almost as handsome, skidded out of the kitchen, his face a mask of anger. Frankie backed up against one of the red vinyl stools lining the long counter. "You're here!" he all but shouted.

She was. Frankie nodded, wincing. "I am, and you're an awesome welcome wagon." She jammed a finger in her ear to stop the ringing.

The man grabbed her by the hand, dragging her back to the kitchen. With a harried look, he dropped her hand and spat, "I can't find my spatula."

Frankie's eyes went blank. "Your spatula."

He nodded like she should know exactly what he meant. "My spatula. Can't find it anywhere. How the hell am I supposed to make omelets for the morning rush if I can't find the damned thing?"

"I don't want to sound judgmental, but you only have *one* spatula?" What kind of cook had one spatula?

"It's my favorite," he reasoned.

No one understood that better than Frankie. Mitch had a favorite everything, too. If Mitch lost or misplaced his favorite anything, she was in charge of making it appear out of thin air. "Am I in charge of spatula recon?"

"I don't know your exact job title, but you're in charge of whatever needs taking charge of. You're Frankie, right?"

He didn't recognize her either? Please. Had televisions gone the way of Tears For Fears and ripped sweatshirts while she'd hibernated? "I'm Frankie. Yes. Frankie Bennett." She remembered to hold out her hand in introduction. If nothing else, she'd earn courtesy points on her work eval with Nikos.

The tall, dark man grabbed it and gave it a brisk shake. "Cosmos Antonakas. This here's Hector Louis, our other short-order cook, and he can't find my damn spatula either."

Jamming her hands into her jean pockets, Frankie rocked back on her heels. "You said as much, and nice to meet you, Hector."

Hector gave her a brief smile, one that didn't quite meet his eyes, holding up his hands to indicate they were covered in grease as a way to apologize for not shaking her hand. "Hey," he muttered before turning back to what he was doing.

Cosmos flapped his hands to indicate she should get moving. "So let's go. Nik said you were going to help organize the kitchen and do the prep work for the breakfast and lunch crowd."

"Oh, she is here!" A woman with big hair, fashioned in some sort of bouffant, and eyes resembling Nikos's, crowed from the corner of the kitchen. She rushed forward, her white apron fluttering about the tops of her knees, to envelop Frankie in her doughy-soft embrace.

She plucked at Frankie's arm and made a face. Her Greek accent had shades of light and dark when she said, "First things first. You are too skeeny. I make you spanakopita and you eat it. No make with the mouth about it either. It is a miracle you can hold up your head, never mind a whole body all skin and bones like you are. We must fix the skeeny."

Taking hold of Frankie's hand, she led her to the back of the kitchen, lined with ovens and an enormous grill, to a small space adjacent to the long stretch of steel countertop used for prepping. She patted a lone red vinyl stool. "Sit."

As though she instinctively knew Frankie was going to refuse her invitation, Voula raised one raven eyebrow flecked with gray, daring her to decline. Frankie's lips clamped shut. "I said no mouth about it.

Everyone eats to start the day right with Voula. It gives the brain energy and the body gas."

"Fuel, Mama. It gives her body fuel," Cosmos interjected with an indulgent chuckle, planting a kiss on his mother's cheek.

Voula waved her pudgy hands at him. "Fuel, gas, make no difference. Still the same. You fill up the body with both." She pulled a plate from beneath the warming lights used to keep customer orders hot prior to being served, and plunked it in front of Frankie. "I make this just for you, because Nikos said you are too skeeny. We have much to chop today. You need your strength."

Frankie's face flushed at the notion Nikos thought anything of her. Yet, she still planned an uprising. As Voula went off in search of what Frankie figured was silverware, Cosmos leaned into her with a crafty smile. "I wouldn't even consider telling her no. If you're totally opposed, make nice and I'll cover for you while you dump it, but telling her no is like poking her in the heart with a hot pitchfork. You would not believe the drama that woman can generate over the word 'no.' It's not in the Greek vocabulary when it comes to food."

Voula brought her silverware, placing the fork in Frankie's hand. "You eat. *Now*. I'll get coffee to put some color in your cheeks."

Frankie instantly sat. She might be reluctant, but she wasn't brain dead, and the last thing she wanted to do was embarrass her Aunt Gail, who'd cooed with delight about Nikos and his diner. Lifting the flaky crust, she almost smiled. The pastry was cooked to perfection, filled with gooey feta cheese, eggs, and spinach. Finding herself appreciative of the visual effect of the dish, she placed a piece in her mouth.

Wow. Had she ever underestimated a good meal all these months. The melt-in-her-mouth goodness, the combination of salty cheese and mellow eggs hit her stomach with a euphoric sigh of bliss.

Voula put a hand on her shoulder, giving it a gentle squeeze. She smelled of pastry and spices mixed with floral perfume. Her scent made Frankie's eyes sting with more unwanted tears. "It's good, right?"

"It's delicious. Thank you," Frankie said around another mouthful, hoping to avoid any more "skeeny" conversations.

"Hah! I bet all those pretty television food people you know don't know my spanakopita."

Frankie's stomach sank.

Further sinkage occurred when a now familiar voice boomed, "Mama! What did I tell you?"

Voula yanked the striped towel from her shoulder and swiped playfully at the dark Adonis, er, Nikos. "I think about this last night before I go to bed, Nikos. Frankie isn't a stupid girl. We don't come from the old country where there is no electricity. We have a TV. We saw what happened. If I was her and your papa was Mitch, that dirty, old man would lose more than his pride on the television. He would have lost his olives."

Frankie snorted before a cough erupted from her throat. Cosmos passed her a cold glass of water she downed in two gulps. Though, it didn't help the flame of her cheeks or the tingle of her scalp as Nikos leaned over her to pinch his mother's plump cheek. "Mama, that's not the point. Sometimes, even when you mean well, you dump salt in an open wound with your kindness."

Voula brushed a stray piece of hair back into its nest and made a face. "Bah! You don't put salt in a wound. You put peroxide. It makes everything okay. And I'm not gonna tippy-toe around here in my own diner. My memory is bad. I forget to keep the secrets. So we just let the rabbit out of the hat and get it over with—"

"The cat out of the bag, Mama," Nikos corrected, his grin fond and warm enough for Frankie to feel it.

"Yes, cats, rabbits, groundhogs. That's not the point. The point is we cannot have Frankie here afraid she is not with people who understand."

Voula turned to Frankie, cupping her chin, her dark chocolate eyes warm. "You were married to a bad man, Frankie. Now you are not. We will take good care of you, but we do it without all the pretending and nicey-nice like we don't know you did something people say is crazy. Okay?" Voula directed her question to Frankie, who'd semi-recovered.

She set her fork down, wiping her mouth with the napkin Cosmos provided. "Okay?" She wasn't sure if it was okay, but looking up at Voula, everything felt almost okay. Or if it wasn't, Voula would beat it with a rolling pin until it was.

Voula chucked her under the chin and smiled. "Yes. It's okay now. Would have been better if you married a Greek boy to begin with, but for now, it's okay. So finish and we begin." With that, she strode off to a door at the other end of the kitchen, letting it close with a thunk behind her ample backside.

Nikos eyeballed her, leaving her without much air in her lungs. His sharply planed face and luscious lips made her fingers wrap more tightly around the fork. "So Mama made you spanakopita? She doesn't do that for just anyone, you know."

Frankie's resentment at being so easily fooled seeped over the edges of her manners. "Just for loony-bin worthy women like me who make fools of themselves on television?"

He popped his lips. "And sometimes for loony-bin worthy women who make fools of themselves on a much smaller scale. But only the *really* loony ones," he teased with a grin.

More with the funny. "You said you had no idea who I was. Imagine my surprise."

Nikos crossed his arms over his wide, hard chest, the dark hairs on his arms making her stomach weak. "Yeah, and I was so convincing, Spielberg called. He wants me to star in his next movie about chefs' wives gone wild."

What little air she had in her lungs fled. "So you lied."

He sighed, making his gorgeous chest expand and deflate, drawing her eyes to it. "Yep, but I just wanted to make you more comfortable. You weren't exactly helping yourself in that interview. I got the impression you would have peeled your own skin off to get out of my office. But I promised Max I wouldn't let you get away with it. No need to get excited or defensive. Oh, and I've held off on the flyers featuring your name as the newest addition to the Antonakas diner family. In case you were worried we'd abuse your celebrity." Nikos winked, his thick, long lashes sweeping across his cheekbone in rakish fashion.

Frankie made a mock roll of her eyes in gratitude. "Well, thank God for that. I wasn't sure how we'd manage to find a cage big enough for me to fit comfortably in. Plus, there's always the hassle of the mess all those peanut shells make when it's feeding time at the zoo."

Hector snickered in the background, but Cosmos laughed directly over Nikos's shoulder. "She's funny."

Nikos nodded his dark head, the sleek shine of it deserving of every woman's envy. "That's good. She'll need her sense of ha-ha for Papa. He's cranky and difficult, and he refuses to retire."

"And I still have no spatula," Cosmos complained.

"Maybe you should have more than one. You know, as a backup," Frankie suggested, pushing the surprisingly half-empty plate away from her and rising to search for Cosmos's spatula. It didn't hurt to move away from the close proximity of Nikos to do it either. He smelled too good. Looked too good. Too. Good.

"She's not your keeper, Cos," Nikos chided, his black eyes gleaming. "Frankie, you don't have to look after Cosmos's cooking utensils.

If he'd put stuff back, he'd be able to find it. But he's a slob—a complete pig, and he thinks because he does most of the cooking that he has the right to behave like the Galloping Gourmet and pitch a fit every time he can't find a utensil only *he* uses."

"I do not," Cosmos denied, his handsome face distorted with mock hurt.

"You do so," Hector agreed before turning his back on them.

Nikos barked a laugh. "Yeah, little brother, you do. He can be difficult at best, Frankie. I'm warning you now. He yells when things get hectic back here because he can never find what he needs, and it's always someone else's fault. He rants about how everything's disorganized, but it's usually him who's responsible for the disorganization."

Her eye caught several glimmers of stainless steel shelves stored under the grill. She knelt to pull out a silver tray and rummaged through it until she located a spatula. "Is this it?" Frankie held it up for Cosmos to see.

A smile lightened his face when he scooped her up and kissed her full on the mouth, making her eyes go wide. "Yes! You're a lifesaver, and I do not yell." His staunch denial made Nikos laugh.

"You do, too. You're a diva, little man. Own it."

Frankie shrugged and looked down at her feet. "It's okay. I'm used to yelling. Mitch . . . Mitch was a demanding . . . well, he was demanding."

Nikos nudged her shoulder. "Don't you worry, Frankie. I won't let Cosmos push you around. You're not his slave. You're *mine*."

Frankie's chin lifted, her eyes unable to hide her alarm. She was skittish and sensitive, and she knew it. She just wasn't catching her reactions in enough time to keep people from crunching the eggshell-lined path to her doorway.

Nikos placed a warm hand on her shoulder, bringing ease and unwanted excitement to her tense muscles. "It was a joke. We do a lot of that here. We also eat a lot, and there's always chaos. We're loud, sometimes obnoxious, opinionated, but we love each other. Which means we hug a lot, but I promise in your servitude, I'll keep your chains slack so you can participate."

Frankie giggled, closing her eyes and running a hand over her tired, grainy eyes. "So what is my job description anyway?"

Nikos took her hand in his to pull her to a long stainless steel island, backing her up against it until her hips were pressed to it and he stood almost between her thighs. Almost. Or was she wishful distance thinking?

His cologne, fresh and clean, whatever its label, wafted to her nose, making her nostrils appreciate the strong scent of man. The tight black T-shirt he wore clung to what looked like a million flexing, sculpted muscles in his chest and stomach. He was almost painful to look at he was so beautiful.

It made her cast her glance away to the far corner of the kitchen where Cosmos cracked eggs on the flat grill.

But Nikos moved into her line of vision. He gave her a sly gaze, his eyes, like a river of chocolate she wanted to jump into and do the backstroke in, smoldered.

She shook her head, repeating the question. "So what's my job again?"

He raised an eyebrow with a lascivious arch to it. "I told you, Frankie. You're mine. *All mine.*"

Super-duper.

CHAPTER FOUR

From the still reluctant journal of ex-trophy wife Frankie Bennett: I don't care what Mitch says. Meatloaf and brown gravy with fries might well be fit only for cavemen, but the way Nikos Antonakas prepares it makes a girl want to grab her pelt and start a fire with two sticks and the sunshiny rays of high noon. Cavemen rule. *Greek* cavemen really rule. And oh, damn, look. I wrote this entry in pen. Note to self: Next time use a pencil with a big eraser in case of open-mouth, insert-foot emergency, genius.

Nikos's statement sent a shiver of awareness along her arms and up the back of her neck.

Cosmos laughed maniacally like some old horror movie villain.

Clearly catching her anxious dismay, Nikos chuckled. "Another joke, Frankie. I crack wise. You humor me and laugh," he teased, the fresh scent of his breath fanning her heated cheeks.

She gulped. Where had her sense of humor gone? *Down the shitter when you found out the joke was on you.* "Right. Joking. So being yours, all yours, what am I doing?"

Nikos pulled two aprons off a hook on the wall, tying one around his lean waist, leaving Frankie mesmerized by his long fingers. "You're my assistant."

"What am I assisting?"

He handed her an apron, then smiled. "Making my day a whole lot easier on my eyes."

She tilted her head to the right in question just as an older man pushed his way through the exit door directly in the back of the kitchen. His gray and black eyebrows knit together in a frown. The thick fall of his hair trailed over his forehead in deep ebony and silver waves as he dumped a bag on the island with a grunt. He brushed his button-down beige sweater with strong, thick hands. "You." He pointed a finger that might have been Nikos's if not for the liver spots at Frankie. "You chop."

"Papa," Nikos chided with obvious affection in his tone. "Say hello to Frankie. She's our new prep chef."

Nikos's father scanned her from head to toe with a cynical gaze, the wrinkles at the corners of his eyes deep with hesitation. He lifted his round chin and clucked his tongue. "Hello."

Brrrrr. It wasn't just cold outside.

Her hand flew out, hoping to turn this awkwardly strange moment around. "Frankie. Frankie Bennett. Nice to meet you, Mr. Antonakas." She tacked on a smile she hoped came across as genuine without being forced.

His lips pursed in clear skepticism. "Uh-huh. Yes. I know all about the skeeny Frankie Bennett who blew her gasket on the television. I like your dog, Kooky."

There was something to be said for honesty—it so sucked. "Um, *Kiki*," she offered in bright tones.

Nikos got behind him and pushed his father's arm outward, making his hand take Frankie's to move up and down in a handshake. He mimicked his father's tone of voice and accent perfectly when he said, "Nice to meet you, Frankie Bennett. I am Barnabas Antonakas, the cranky old man who's upset with his oldest son for making him rest instead of standing on his feet for fourteen hours a day. He's a bad, inconsiderate son, my Nikos."

Frankie fought a smile. Now she understood. She was taking over

Barnabas's duties as a prep chef of sorts, and he was resentful for the intrusion. Nobody got downsizing and trading up better than Frankie. "So I'm aiding and abetting, eh?" she teased.

Barnabas yanked his hand from Nikos's and tweaked his cheek. "You are a fresh boy. Nobody chops like Barnabas. You need me here, Nikos. You will regret the day you kicked me to the grass," he warned, but his eyes were loving when they gazed upon his eldest son.

"It's curb, Papa, and I won't regret not seeing you in the hospital with a bunch of tubes sticking out of that big schnoz of yours. Now go do something productive like watch *Family Feud*, and let me handle everything else."

Barnabas snorted in disgust over his shoulder when he muttered, "You will see. The skeeny Frankie won't chop like me. She'll be here all day long just trying to catch up to old Barnabas . . ." His voice trailed off as he pushed his way through the kitchen doors.

Nikos grinned. "Sorry. He's cantankerous, but he isn't intentionally rude. Just depressed as one era ends in his life and another begins."

Frankie eyed the bag Barnabas brought and realized it was filled with onions. Many onions. "I can definitely see how depression would set in if he couldn't chop onions. I'd be sad, too. Thankfully, it looks like my depression is in for a much needed breather." What had she gotten herself into?

Nikos grabbed a shiny knife and winked with another chuckle. "You do have a sense of humor. For now just peel, and I'll chop. But if you show me your Jedi skills, I promise you, too, can chop."

"You're afraid to give me a knife, aren't you?"

His eyes met hers. "Say again?"

"I said, you're afraid to give me a knife because they're sharp and pointy, and I'm unstable and unpredictable," she joked. Well, it was only sort of a joke. She had been unpredictable.

Nikos cocked his head back with a wink. "I love unpredictable, but I love unstable even more. So you'll be like the cement that holds my crazy together."

Now Frankie laughed, popping open the bag of onions, relaxing just a little. "I've got plenty of crazy."

"Good to know. You'll need it here. Now start peeling. By the looks of the orders piling up, we have hash browns and omelets to make."

Frankie looked down at the bag, pulling out the first onion, avoiding his dark gaze. "So how many do you need? Three? Four?" She handed him the first peeled onion, her eyes just barely beginning that familiar sting.

"The whole bag."

All ten pounds? No way.

He nodded his sleek head without looking up from the chopping board as though he'd read her mind. "Yes way."

"Why wouldn't you buy them prechopped?"

His hand rocked the knife back and forth over the onions with the skill of any trained chef she'd ever seen. "First, they're not fresh, and everything we do here at the diner is fresh and made to order except some of the pastries and pies, and they don't hang around more than a day. Second, they're expensive. Third, if I did that, you'd have no job security." The corners of his lips lifted when he wiped his eyes on the shoulder of his black T-shirt.

Frankie wiped the tears in her own eyes with her sleeve while she peeled. "Point."

"I have them. Not often, but when it happens, it's usually categorized as historic."

Frankie muffled a snicker, keeping her eyes on her work. Yet they kept straying to Nikos's hands, so fluid and graceful as he chopped. It was probably better he had the knife. She'd be here all day without the Slap Chop.

The back door in the kitchen creaked, capturing Frankie's attention.

"Morning, Nikos," cooed a lean young woman with a long, dark brown braid down her back and the best legs Frankie had ever seen. She pulled off a cute, knee-length jacket and hung it on a hook by the aprons.

Nikos barely looked up but muttered a polite, "Morning, Chloe."

She stopped short at the island where Nikos and Frankie worked and gave Frankie a thorough once-over with her round silver gray eyes, making no bones about the fact that she was sizing her up. "And who's this?"

Manners, manners, manners. She must display them in social settings. If that wasn't in Maxine's handy-dandy notebook, then it should be. Frankie wiped her watering eyes across the sleeve of her shirt, then swiped her hand on her apron. She jammed it in Chloe's direction, forgetting the constant source of embarrassment her name brought her as of late. "Frankie Bennett."

Chloe wrinkled her nose without extending her hand in return. "I know you. Your husband was on that show *Mitch in the Kitchen*."

Okay. So embarrassment was back.

Nikos's head snapped up, his eyes following Chloe's gaze with something hidden in them Frankie couldn't place. "Chloe Gianopoulos, meet Frankie Bennett, my new assistant. Frankie—Chloe, one of our waitresses."

"Nice to meet you," Frankie said, though, from the eyeball glare Chloe was giving her, Frankie suspected the feeling was not mutual.

Chole gave her a quick smile and muttered, "You, too," before turning to Nikos. "So I'll see you later on my break? Save me some

68   Dakota Cassidy

meatloaf and gravy." She brushed a hand over Nikos's arm in very obvious possession, shooting a pointed glance in Frankie's direction before skirting out of the kitchen.

Though Frankie noted Nikos didn't outwardly shun Chloe's affection, he didn't acknowledge it either.

Yet clearly, Chloe meant for Frankie to know Nikos was hers.

And okay. Message received. She didn't need or want a man. Especially this man. This beautifully hard, fantastical man. He had to be major maintenance in the mirror department. Not to mention the women who must line up in scads to take a shot at grabbing his attention. His body obviously didn't lack a good, hard workout either. Nikos Antonakas was work.

No more high-maintenance men.

Or maybe just no more men, high or low or anything in between maintenance.

She cast a furtive glance at Nikos through oniony eyes.

If he belonged to Chloe, and she was so totally okay with it, why did the idea make her more depressed than she already was? That was ridiculous. They'd just met.

Huh. Things to ponder.

Nikos stared at Frankie's slender back while she did half spins on the stool at the front counter, flipping through a magazine, headphones in her ears. She looked exhausted and grateful for her break. He busied himself counting her ribs, cursing Mitch in the Fucking Kitchen in a moment of protective anger. The surge took him by surprise when it crawled along the back of his neck and settled in his clenched fist.

There was no love lost between him and a cheat. What it had so visibly done to Frankie made him want to wrap his fingers around

Mitch Bennett's throat and shake the hell out of him until he shit gallstones.

"You're staring," his brother commented from over his shoulder.

"Was not."

"Were, too."

"Yep, you were," Hector parroted, joining Cosmos.

Nikos gave them both pointed looks. "So?"

"So, you probably don't want to tap that, bro. She comes with baggage, lots and lots of baggage. You've been down that road— remember—"

Nikos swung around and flicked his brother's hair with two fingers. "No one said anything about tapping anyone. Shut the hell up."

Cosmos grinned, displaying a set of perfect white teeth. "Could've fooled me by the way your eyes go all moony when she's in the room."

Nikos clenched his jaw. Usually, Cosmos couldn't get to him, but with no warning, Frankie'd become a sensitive subject. "She's not my type." And she wasn't. He liked them hippier, fuller, rounder, darker haired with an occasional blonde. Yet . . .

Yet what, Antonakas?

Yet shit. No more damsels in distress.

Cosmos crossed his arms over his chest covered in his dirty lunch-hour apron. "That's because she looks like she hasn't eaten in a year. Wait until she puts on twenty pounds. I saw all those pictures of her during that feeding frenzy the tabloids had with her after her divorce. She's pretty hot. Seriously hot, Nik. She has crazy long legs and an ass—"

"Shut it," Nikos warned with a growl of words he found he could barely contain. *The hell?*

Cosmos held up his hands like two white flags, but his playful grin remained. "Chill, Mr. She's Not My Type."

"She's not, but would it kill you to give her a little respect?"

"Anyway, Mama's right. She looks like she'll keel over at any minute if she doesn't eat."

Nikos rolled his tongue along the inside of his cheek in thought, forgetting Cosmos's rude comments. "Hook me up with some meatloaf and gravy, would ya?"

Cosmos grunted. "You got it." He gave Nikos a shove to his shoulder. "Quit staring. She'll have holes in the back of her sweater. She can't afford less insulation on her scrawny body, or she'll freeze to death."

Nikos ignored Cosmos and headed toward the stool next to Frankie, brushing against her when he sat with an unceremonious flop. His shoulder brushed hers, making her jolt a little. He motioned to her to take her earphones out. "So do you hate me yet?" Her red-gold hair, pulled back in a mussed ponytail, reeked of onions and garlic.

Frankie's red-rimmed, amber eyes gave him a thoughtful glance before returning to the magazine she was reading. "Well, I wasn't in love with you after onion ten or so, but the garlic really was uncalled for. So while 'hate' is a strong word, I wouldn't one hundred percent rule it out." She wrinkled her pert nose to show her distaste for the dozens of garlic cloves she'd peeled and mashed for him to use in a marinade.

Nikos folded his hands on top of the flecked countertop and smiled. "So I guess I should wait on my marriage proposal?"

He managed to elicit a small smile from her when she turned up one corner of her full, strawberry-colored lips, unadorned by gloss. Admittedly, it pleased him to garner that kind of reaction from someone so deadpan most of the time. "Uh, yeah. At least until I get the smell of onions out of my hair."

"Damn. And I was already booking the doves and fireworks."

"Birds are messy, and fireworks are sort of pretentious."

"Hah! You don't know my family. Doves and fireworks aren't even the half of it."

"Speaking of family . . . your dad . . ."

"He's crotchety and feeling displaced."

Her head bobbed in agreement as she set the magazine down. "By me. Thanks for that. Between bouts with Ellen DeGeneres, he's poked his head into the kitchen at last count eight times to scoff at my chopping skills—openly and with vigor."

"Don't let him get to you. My father isn't one to keep his feelings on the inside. He's not angry with you. He's angry with me for finally putting my foot down and making him let go of his duty to the diner when he had a bout with colon cancer."

"I noticed he's not afraid to express an opinion."

Nikos grinned at her "That particular gene runs in the family."

Frankie sighed. "Are there more of you who're unafraid to express their opinions? Because if so, I think we should just have one Frankie Bennett viewing and get all the 'she's too skeeny—Mitch is a letch' comments over at once. It works toward good time-management skills."

His glance in her direction revealed she was teasing, and Nikos found he'd been holding his breath while she spoke. "Speaking of skeeny," he said as Cos placed a plate in front of her, "eat. No one goes without a meal here."

"For the lady," Cosmos said, pushing a fork and knife in her direction before winking lasciviously at his brother.

"Oh, I'm not hungry," she protested, letting her head fall to her chest in her now familiar gesture of withdrawal. "But thank you." She flipped back through the magazine with distracted turns of the page.

Nikos pushed the side of the fork through the slab of meatloaf on the plate and used his other hand to tilt her chin up, holding the utensil to her mouth. Her skin was so soft he had to fight to keep from tracing his thumb over it. "Thank me after you taste this, and don't make me get Mama or you'll find out just how much drama one little Greek woman can create." He pressed the fork to her lips in encouragement.

Frankie's pretty eyes rolled when she opened her mouth, leaving Nikos fighting to ignore the kind of sensual visual she created. They widened when the flavors of Greek Meets Eat's famous meatloaf tantalized her taste buds.

"This is the famous meatloaf my Aunt Gail was talking about, isn't it?"

"Beats reading a crocheting magazine, don't you think?"

Frankie smirked, a dimple appearing on the left side of her mouth. "I'm trying to find a hobby. Because it seems I've never had one. Being married to Mitch . . ." She stopped short, her cheeks flushing a pretty shade of red. "Yes. That meatloaf is amazing. It totally beats crotcheting."

His nod was smug when she cooed her approval, taking the fork from his fingers. "I know. It's like ground beef and gravy nirvana, right? Mama's the only one who ever lays hands on the meatloaf. It's almost the only dish she won't let anyone else prepare."

Frankie wiped her mouth with the napkin and nodded with a grin. "It's delicious. I've never had meatloaf this spectacular."

"There've been three food critics and one franchise who've wanted to pay Mama for the recipe for that meatloaf, and she's turned every one of them down. I'd put it to the test against any professional chef's fig-and-goat-cheese-encrusted whatever."

Her head dropped again in a quick change of mood. "I'm not a food snob."

Fuck. She was offended. "I didn't say you were."

Pushing away from the counter, Frankie scooped up the plate with one hand and pursed her lips at him in obvious disapproval.

"You didn't have to. Everyone thinks because I was married to a famous chef, I can't eat anything that isn't impossible to pronounce, never mind spell, and prepared by the hand of someone trained at Le Cordon Bleu. Yet not one of you have any idea just how many hot dogs and ramen noodles I've consumed in this lifetime."

Nikos made a face at her to try and lighten her darkening mood. "You eat ramen noodles? How bohemian," he joked.

But Frankie clearly wasn't having it. Not if her stiff posture and narrowed eyes were any indication. "By the buttloads. So if you'll excuse me, I'm going to leave you and your preconceived notions here while I go in the back and finish my break, then get back to mashing a thousand more garlic cloves before my shift's over and I can go home."

She sashayed off in the direction of the kitchen while Nikos stared after her.

Okay. So she was a little sensitive.

Reason number nine hundred and ninety-two to stay far away from Frankie Bennett.

Far.

"I know it's wrong, but . . ." the petite brunette named Brandy said from the far corner of the circle the support group had formed.

"Whatever you're feeling is never wrong—maybe misguided and sometimes even unwarranted, but your feelings are never wrong, Brandy. As long as you don't let them eat you up and define you forever, it'll be okay. So share them with us," the pro bono therapist—some niece of a Leisure Village resident—prompted, her face kind, her words softly encouraging.

Frankie struggled to focus on what Brandy could possibly add to the already somber discussion about the struggle to pay your bills with your minimum wage job after years of being accustomed to spending your days shopping and having your highlights retouched. This supposed support group at Trophy Job's offices was about as uplifting as a day in the pokey.

Brandy's lower lip trembled. "You know when you enter a room? Like when you go to a restaurant or maybe a PTA meeting? I miss . . . I miss having his hand at the small of my back to guide me. I miss the security of it. The feeling that I wasn't so alone," she said, scraping an angry tear from her cheek. "I miss couple things. But at the same time, I hate that I miss it. He left me for my nanny. My Swedish nanny who was just nineteen! How could I miss *anything* about him?"

Words were exchanged, supportive and understanding, in sympathy for Brandy, but Frankie lost her focus because she understood Brandy's sentiments.

They gnawed at her with an ache awakened by Maxine's forceful entry into her cocoon of denial. Maybe it wasn't as much Mitch's hand as it was the idea of it she missed. What it represented.

Couple things. All those small, day-to-day occurrences and routines now lost to her.

She was single.

Woefully single.

Something she hadn't been in a very long time—if ever.

Tonight, she felt more alone than she had in six months.

Uncomfortable with this new rush of emotions dredged up by hearing these women spill their intestines, Frankie remained in her seat within the circle as everyone broke off into smaller groups.

The gorgeous, near flawless blonde to her left leaned into her. "Tissue?" She held out a pink Kleenex.

Frankie blinked, dragging a finger over her eyes to find them wet. Her breath shuddered in and out, taking the tissue from probably the most beautiful blonde Amazon on the face of the planet. "Thank you."

Her smile, perfect and warm, acknowledged Frankie. "I'm Jasmine Archway."

Of the famous Archway Tires?

Her smile, red and glossed, was knowing, too. "Yep, that's the one. Performance tires, truck tires, radials. Tires, tires, tires. Isn't it funny when the last name Archway is mentioned, Archway Tires is the first place people's minds go? Especially here at Trophy Jobs where everyone's jacked up. I bet the name wouldn't raise an eyebrow at the Stop & Shop. Anyway, I'm Ashton Archway's ex-plaything. Ex and now broke plaything, that is."

An ex-plaything named Jasmine . . . poles, showers of dollar bills, and thong-tha-thong-thong-thongs came to mind.

She chuckled, reading Frankie's thoughts again. "And no. I wasn't a stripper. My mother was a botanist. Jasmine was her favorite flower."

Frankie dropped her head to her chest, swiping at errant tears while hiding her shame for judging Jasmine.

She gave Frankie a nudge with her equally perfect round shoulder. "Don't feel bad. Looking the way I do, the stripper-slash-escort thing comes with the territory. I own it. All the labels a blonde like me conjures up—I own every one of 'em. I know I'm hot. I worked hard to maintain the gifts God gave me. Look where that got me, huh?" She looked down at the front of her tight ruby red sweater, catching Frankie staring with a question in her eyes. "And yes, this is my rack. Not the job of some fancy plastic surgeon. Though," she said on a wistful sigh, "I wish I'd reconsidered when Ashton said I could have a lift if I wanted it. These days, they're finding it harder and harder to breathe through all this underwire and steel."

Frankie burst out laughing, putting a hand over her mouth. "It's obvious I don't have the same problem. But on the upside—no boob sweat."

"Ah, but we have many other things in common. You're Mitch in the Kitchen's ex-wife, Francis."

There was just no hiding—even looking like a mere shadow of her former self didn't help. Frankie averted her eyes, fighting the rising swell of panic in her chest. She fought an uncomfortable fidget, forcing herself to stay seated instead of running out of the room as though it were on fire.

Jasmine placed a hand on her arm, her frosted white nails flicking at Frankie's wrist. "It's not like everyone doesn't know, Francis."

"Frankie." She cleared her throat. "It's Frankie."

"Okay, it's not like everyone doesn't know, *Frankie*. You did lose your mind on national TV."

There really was something to be said for phrases like "not in polite company" and "if you don't have anything nice to say, don't say anything at all." Her words were bitter in response. "Yep. That was me."

Jasmine shrugged her slender shoulders. "So own it. Your husband's off screwing a chick named after a deer in a Disney movie. He did something shitty, and you let him have it for most of the world to see. Is there any shame in calling someone on their craptacular behavior?"

"I think it's frowned upon in national television settings."

She let her blonde head fall back on her shoulders with a chuckle, throaty and rich and so open, Frankie envied her freedom. "Tough shit for Mitch. Maybe he should have been smarter and banged the maid instead. It certainly would've been less global and far more discreet."

Somehow, Jasmine, with her outspoken acceptance and brash observations, made Frankie feel a little less like a social pariah. "And maybe not quite as painful."

"Maybe. But here's how I look at it. You got out in the nick of time. Mitch isn't getting any younger. In fact, he's getting wrinklier by the day. Not that you're getting any younger either, but you're still a ways behind old Mitch. On the bright side, you're still young and pretty, though you've let yourself go these days because you figure why get your gorgeous on when you won't ever have Mitch's seal of approval again. You'll learn that was all bullshit when you find yourself again."

All wise words, except for one little problem. "Where exactly do I go to find myself anyway? I keep hearing that phrase bandied about like a tennis ball. Is there a place of business for it? Like the Find Yourself store?"

"If only it were that easy. We'd all be lined up. It takes time to figure out who you are when you're a scorned trained seal."

Frankie's smile was ironic. What a spot-on way to describe their former lives. She spread her arms wide. "Has any of this helped you? I mean Maxine's guides and pep talks and support meetings?"

Jasmine's head bobbed with enthusiasm. "I know it sounds hokey-guru-ish, all the crazy euphemisms she's got and pamphlets on how to adjust to being poor—which in and of itself is just pathetic, isn't it? Nobody forced me to become candy for some rich man's sweet tooth. I let that happen and, in the process, I became complacent. I didn't have to end up poor. That's on me. So yes, I've learned a lot since I found Maxine and Trophy Jobs. If it weren't for her, I'd be in the nearest homeless shelter. Instead, I have my own little studio apartment and a cat named Gary."

Nothing said enticing like a cat and a studio apartment.

Jasmine gazed at her, her hazel eyes, deep and alluringly seductive, capturing Frankie's. "I know it doesn't sound like much, but to me it's everything. I have more pride than I ever did as Ashton's wife, and I'm content. I can't say I was ever really content when I was married to him. My life is a whole lot simpler now, but I don't miss the privileges much. Okay, maybe I miss the weekly manicures and my masseuse, but there's something to be said for knowing you can take care of yourself, learning how to budget, making a living that's all yours."

Who knew Maxine Barker was such a goddess? "And Maxine did all of that for you?"

"Nope. She was just my port in the storm. She taught me to suck it up, but I did all the sucking," Jasmine said on a throaty giggle.

Suddenly, this was all too much information for her. It was a bit like attending an Amway convention with tips and advice for pitiful divorcees.

Jasmine patted her arm in consolation. "You're not there yet. You're still too resentful Maxine interfered, and sometimes these meetings can be overwhelming. All those sad stories of one-time rich women dumped on their saggy asses for younger, hotter babes. I wonder sometimes what someone on the outside would say about all this vapidness in just one room."

Frankie's eyebrow rose. "You mean the dreaded middle class?"

Jasmine barked a husky laugh. "Yeah. Looking back now, hearing some of the new girls and their stories, I have to remind myself I was once like them."

"You make this adventure sound like you're Cinderella, only in reverse."

"Trust me when I tell you that once Cindy was done running off with the prince, I'd bet my still perky ass she was bored to tears living in that castle with nothing to do but wait for Prince Whatever to come home on his white steed."

Frankie laughed again. Huh. For the second time tonight. Like real, honest to God laughter.

Jasmine rose, leaving Frankie strangely regretful she was planning to make her exit. "Some of us are going to Greek Meets Eat for coffee. You wanna come with?"

Oh, hell to the no. She'd had enough of the diner and hot-pants Nikos and his assumptions for one day. Frankie glanced at her watch. "I can't. I have an early day tomorrow. Maybe another time?" She found she meant that, too. Jasmine's approach to her very public divorce was to live out loud, and it piqued Frankie's curiosity.

Jasmine wrapped her equally red scarf around her neck and buttoned her jacket. "I'll hold you to that. It's good to get out, and coffee's cheap. Plus, the refills are free. Now give me your phone. I'll put my number in it. Call me if you ever need to talk, okay? Otherwise, I'll see you next week."

Frankie obliged by handing Jasmine her aunt's cell phone. "It's my Aunt Gail's phone. I don't . . . well, I can't . . ."

"Afford one of your own yet." Jasmine clucked her tongue between pearly white teeth. "You will. Soon enough. When you can, I'll show you how to bargain hunt for the cheapest, yet most efficient cell plan." She punched in her number and smiled when she handed it back. "Oh, and while you're hunting for a hobby," Jasmine said, looking down at the woodworking magazine she'd grabbed after deciding crocheting just wasn't for her, "try decoupage. It's cheap and you can use fun, inexpensive things like holiday napkins on sale for half off to do it. You should see the fabulous President's Day mirror I have in my bathroom. Anyway, see you next week, Frankie."

Decoupage. "Next week," she mumbled, watching the sassy sway of Jasmine's confident ass leave the conference room.

"I see you met Jasmine?" Maxine asked her from behind.

"In all her outspokenness."

Maxine's laughter filled her ear. "She's really something, and just an FYI, she's come a long way since I first met her."

"Because of you."

Maxine shook her head, the soft curls of her hair brushing her shoulders. "Nope. I had nothing to do with it. Okay, I had a little to do with it, but very little. I only helped her maximize skills she didn't know she had and use them in the workplace. She did the rest."

Curious, Frankie asked, "What does she do?"

"She's a bookkeeper."

"Where?"

"Fluffy's House of Ill Repute."

Frankie's snort escaped before she could stop it. "You mean the strip joint in the next town over?"

Maxine's grin was wide when she thrust her hands into the pockets of her black linen trousers. "Even strippers need to be paid. Jasmine's a whiz with numbers—we put that to good use while she takes accounting courses at night. For now, it's an honest living, if unconventional."

Again, Frankie smiled, her facial muscles sore from overuse.

"That looks good on you."

"What?"

"A smile. It really is okay to smile. Nothing bad will happen when you do."

"Nothing bad was happening to me when I was in bed. In fact, it was a whole lot less tiresome."

Maxine laughed again, tucking her hair behind her ear to reveal modest diamond studs. "How was your first day, anyway?"

"In a word?"

"One would be fine. An entire sentence wouldn't go ignored or unappreciated." She followed her wish with a grin.

"Overwhelming."

"The Antonakases will do that to you. They're a noisy bunch, but they have hearts the size of Texas."

Yeah. One in particular had something the size of Texas. Something that had littered her thoughts all day long since she'd taken sensitive to astronomic proportions. "They were very nice."

"You have no idea how nice. You met Hector?"

Frankie nodded. He was so quiet in his corner of the kitchen he'd almost freaked even her out. "I met him today."

"Then here's a little something you should know about your boss Nikos. He's a really great guy, a decent one. It's no secret Hector was a gambler and an alcoholic, but because he was some friend of a friend of the Antonakases, Nikos hauled him into a state-run rehab and then hired him at the diner. He's been clean ever since."

Frankie had little time to chew on the fact that Nikos was all things beyond supreme hotness before they were interrupted.

"Max, honey? We really have to get going if we're going to make the airport in time for Connor," said a tall, rugged-looking man in jeans and a down jacket who'd just entered the room.

Maxine's eyes lit up the moment she caught sight of him. She gave him a quick peck on his lips and smiled with so much affection, Frankie winced. "Frankie, this is my husband Campbell."

He held out a lean hand, tan and large, toward Frankie. "Pleasure," he said with a genuine smile, one that radiated warmth. Maxine leaned into him when he tucked her close to his side. Their obvious love for one another left Frankie with another pang of yearning, so sharp and biting, it stole her breath.

"Nice to meet you," she murmured.

"I've got to go, Frankie. My son's coming in for the holidays from college. But I'll check in with you later in the week, okay?" Maxine took her hand and gave it a quick squeeze. Pulling Frankie's ear to her lips, she whispered, "Oh, and look. No rich, old man in sight either."

Frankie let her eyes fall to the floor in shame. Okay. She'd judged. So sue her.

"It's okay, Frankie," Maxine reassured. "There's a lesson to be learned from your assumptions about me."

"That I'm judgmental and bitter?"

Her deliberate smile was a sly tease. "No. That all men who are rich have to be *old*."

For the third time that night, Frankie laughed.

Out loud.

With gusto.

CHAPTER FIVE

From the "still, but maybe a little less, reluctant" journal of ex-trophy wife Frankie Bennett: Okay, so Maxine was right. Sort of. Earning a paycheck *is* good for the soul. I do feel productive and useful. She was right when she said idle hands are the devil's tools and all that encompasses as an idiom, yadda, yadda, yadda. Score one for Maxine. But I've come to believe Nikos's hands are the devil's instruments, and I wouldn't mind them being idle on me. Sweet. Jesus.

"You're beautiful."

"You're blind."

"Sight impaired, thank you."

"So it makes perfect sense you'd be in a strip joint where there's nothing but a *visual* Utopia of thong-covered asses and naked breasts."

The man at the bar chuckled. "I see with my other senses."

Jasmine raised a skeptical eyebrow at this handsome man's cane and leaned her forearms on the shiny mahogany of the bar top, nodding a thank-you to Bert the bartender when he set a club soda and lime in front of her. "I'll bet you do."

His sandy blond head nodded in appreciation of her tone. "For instance, my sharply honed other senses tell me you're skeptical."

"Me and cynical are old friends," she only half teased, brushing her hair from her eyes. She wasn't in the mood to cavort with customers today, paying or not. Most especially with a blind man . . . correction, sight-impaired man in a strip bar. No matter how attractive. And indeed, he was attractive. Lean, with a healthy glow to his cheeks and a body bunched with hard muscle.

His smile was ultrawhite in the dimly lit corner of the bar where they sat. "I'll prove it to you."

Jasmine sighed, making her irritation at his intrusion clear. Men—young, old, and in between—had been hitting on her since she was thirteen, and since her divorce from Ashton, she'd decided she was fed up. If and when she wanted another man's attention, she'd make the moves—all of them—in her own damned time. For now, she was enjoying life in all its simplicity from her studio apartment with Gary. A man would only complicate her new path with silly romantic debris.

"I'm hurt you don't want to play with me," he chided good-naturedly, his deep green eyes looking at her as though they actually saw her. "I *am* blind."

Sipping her club soda, Jasmine gave a half smile. "So because you have a disability I'm supposed to indulge you and your come-on? I thought people with disabilities wanted to be treated equally? I'm perfectly happy to give you the same fair treatment I'd give any sighted man. So in the interest of equality—go away."

His linebacker shoulders shrugged in his blue football jersey. "Equality is overrated. I'm all about the pity card if it gets me what I want."

She began to hide a smile at his joke, then realized there was no need to. Jasmine ran her finger around the rim of her glass. "And what do you want?"

Mystery Man dragged his stool closer to Jasmine and leaned into her, their thighs touching. He smelled of department store cologne and chicken wings. Yet that didn't stop him from sending a chill of unadulterated pleasure along her arms when he said, "I want you."

Him and the rest of the free male world. "I remain unimpressed."

He reached with a deft hand to find the bowl of peanuts and pop one in his mouth. "How disappointing."

Jasmine chuckled before she could stop it. "Life's full of them."

"You're telling me?" he tapped the bar with his lean, well-manicured finger. "Blind guy here."

She waved a dismissive hand at him, forgetting he couldn't see it. "Right. Nice crutch."

He surprised her by laughing, deep and inviting. "Is it helping my cause?"

Another grin spread across her lips. "Not even a little."

"So sucks to be me today."

"Sir?" A tall man wearing a dark suit and dark glasses placed a hand on her would-be suitor's shoulder. "We really must go."

Mystery Man cocked his head back at the sound of the stranger's voice and smiled. "Aw, c'mon, Jeeves. Just two more minutes with the pretty lady, and I promise we're out."

Jeeves sighed from pursed lips. "Sir, it's Winchester," he scolded, nodding his head with acknowledgment in Jasmine's direction. "I'm Winchester Barclay—not Jeeves. Simonides loves a good joke." Putting his hand under Simonides's elbow, he encouraged him to rise from the bar stool. "Now, while the lovely lady would be a wonderful way to pass a cold and gloomy afternoon, I've caught what you yourself would call her vibe—and it distinctly screams disinterest. Even I, utter novice in the ways of a woman, could sense that from all the way across the room whilst I ate greasy peanuts. I say we call the game and head for your interview before we're late. You know how Oprah feels about tardiness."

Jasmine couldn't help but wonder at Mystery Man's name—and Oprah . . . "Simonides?"

Winchester gave her a curt nod. "Yes. Simonides Rhadamanthus Jones."

She sat farther back on her bar stool, stunned. *"The football player?"* Ashton had been a huge fan.

Simonides rose, allowing Winchester to place his cane back in his hand. He leaned into her. "Actually, it's just Simon. Or Blind Guy. Whichever makes you feel sorrier for me so you'll let me buy you dinner."

Jasmine looked to Winchester through the smoky haze of the bar.

Winchester smiled in return, broad and with a fond look to Simon. "Yes, miss. The football player."

Simon made a mock sad face at Jasmine. "Who's blind. Did I say *blind*?"

Winchester chuckled. "As a bat, sir. I think the nice lady is clear. Now shall we?"

Simon turned to obey Winchester but not without a parting shot sprinkled with amusement. "I'll be back, Jasmine Archway. Count on it."

Long after Simon and his friend had left, Jasmine sat on the bar stool, perplexed. Not just by the legend attached to a man with a name longer than a country mile, or the tragic accident that had left him blind, but simply that he knew her name.

Plucking a peanut out of the bowl, she found she wasn't in the least bothered by it either.

Just curious.

Very curious.

"Is she as hot as I remember, Win, or have things gone south for her? Not that I care as much as most think I would, but my curiosity has no shame."

Winchester settled in the backseat of the limo Oprah had sent, scoffing in Simon's direction. "What a shallow question, Simon. Answering it makes me feel cheap and degraded."

Simon gave a hearty laugh. "Answer the question."

"Don't you think a heterosexual male would be a much better candidate to provide you an answer?"

Simon visualized the face Win was making at him right now, sour and disapproving. "You know what a good-looking female is. You definitely know the kind of woman I find attractive. You also know I've waited a long time for this moment. This isn't some whim. This isn't some casual pickup."

"No, sir, not at all. This is what you as a child called backsies. In fact, what you're doing is as childish as the word 'backsies.'"

Simon placed his hands on Win's face, tracing his mouth and grinning. "I knew it. You're scowling at me again. No matter how blind I am, I can call up your 'Simon, I disapprove' face. It's a classic."

Win cleared his throat, turning his head away from Simon, judging by the sound of his voice. "Good. Then my message is clear. I wholly disapprove of what you plan to do to Jasmine Archway."

What he'd planned to do began to fade as what he'd like to do took precedence. "Maybe my plans have changed," he offered, vague and distracted while his mind busied itself changing courses.

His conversation with Jasmine, though brief and filled with roadblocks, had changed the landscape he'd so carefully honed in his mind's eye. "In fact, they've definitely changed, Win."

Definitely.

"Well, look what the cat dragged in," Gail crowed from her recliner, clicking off the Bon Appetit Channel as though she'd been caught surfing Internet porn.

Frankie leaned in to kiss her weathered cheek before plopping on the couch, lifting Kiki up to sit with her. "You don't have to stop watching because of me, Aunt Gail."

"Bah! I'd sooner have my tongue cut out than watch anything even remotely involving that dirty bird Mitch." She jammed a needle into the needlepoint she was working on.

"Oh, c'mon, Aunt Gail. You know you think Jean-Luc from *Viva La Vegetarian!* is cute. It's okay to admit it. Everyone thinks so—even I do, and he's nice, too. I'm not so bitter I'll never watch anything Bon Appetit televises. You shouldn't be either, though I appreciate the loyalty."

"Never mind the TV. Was today any better than the last four days?"

Frankie closed her eyes, grateful for the reprieve from her aunt's prying eyes. "It was fine." Everything was fine. Fine as fine could be.

"You say that every day when you come home, sassafras. I still don't know how every day is just plum *fine* with that hunk o' burnin' love Nikos for a boss. He's anything but fine, young lady. I'd reconsider my retirement for him and his cute butt."

Her face reddened. That was part of the problem. The more time she spent at Nikos's side as his assistant, which she'd discovered was really just a made-up position because Nikos owed Maxine something Frankie was still unsure of, the harder it was to ignore the fact that everything he did made her insides melt like cheese on the grill.

Pity employment, humiliating as it was, was dandy for now. Lusting for a man she was nowhere near ready to lust for wasn't dandy or even fine—it was nerve-wracking. When Nikos had fed her that meatloaf, he'd cinched the deal. He was dangerous with a capital H-O-T. Since that first day, she'd stayed as far away from him as she could on her breaks. Yet her eyes found him no matter where he was.

"I don't give what he looks like much thought. I'm just putting in my time so Maxine won't hunt me down and shoot me like an animal of prey." Kiki rose up on her hind legs, putting her paws on Frankie's mouth, silently accusing her of being a total bullshitter.

"Your nose is growing," was Gail's dry response.

She caught her fingers before they sought her nose and clenched them into fists. "Don't be silly. Yes, Nikos is lovely to look at. Denying that would be like denying the pope wears a pointy hat. But I'm not interested. He's my boss. Period." Period, period, period. Now if only someone would tell that to the Sandman so her dreams weren't littered with him in his tight jeans and T-shirt, she'd be golden.

"You wouldn't be the first girl to fall in love with her boss. But I think if we're going to make him fall in love back, we have to do something about . . . well, something, that's all. Your clothes are falling off you, and if I didn't know you, I'd think you were some crazy homeless bag lady. All you need is a shopping cart and another stray dog to complete your bag lady ensemble."

Frankie's face reddened again. How far the fabulous had fallen. Being Mitch's wife had been filled with the kind of pressure to be beautiful at all times, pressure only beauty queens and movie stars should endure. She *wanted* to feel the shame that her appearance had a homeless hint to it. Instead, her embarrassment came and went like a double coupon sale.

She shrugged off Gail's insult, though she knew her aunt had only said it out of love. Gail had never seen her as anything less than picture-perfect. To see the comparison now had to be a shock. Yet Frankie was making no apologies for this small freedom she'd found since walking out on Mitch. "First, let me set the record straight. No one's falling in love with anyone. Most especially not me and Nikos. No matter how Greek god–like he is. Second, there's a certain kind of freedom to not wearing makeup, and there's definitely no pressure involved in just rolling up out of bed, brushing your teeth, and going to work."

Gail snorted, rapping the needlepoint she held against the arm of the recliner she'd had since Frankie's childhood. "I'll say."

Frankie gritted her teeth. "I'm not working at the diner to impress anyone with my impeccable taste in clothes, Aunt Gail. I'm working because you and Maxine forced me to. I was happy where I was. It was the two of you who decided I needed to shower and find all this purpose and meaning in my life. So here I am. Clean and searching for the meaning of my life in a burger deluxe with a double side of fries."

Gail yawned. "You'll thank us both when they don't come take your cute car from you and put my Squeaky Kiki up for adoption at the pound. You need a cute car to romance a cute man. From what I hear, having your own set of wheels is important when you're dating so you always have an escape vehicle."

"Aunt Gail, I really think it's much too soon to talk about dating or Nikos or of all things, falling in love. I was married for eighteen years, and I'm just now realizing how unhappy I was for probably the last twelve of those years. I don't want to consider a relationship with a hamster, let alone a real, live man for a very long time." No matter how many nights she spent pondering one with Nikos. Were you supposed to do that so soon after you were divorced? This had to be chalked up to a rebound crush.

Gail trailed her fingers over her niece's, giving her a warm, albeit appeasing smile. "You'll change your mind. If you fall off the horse, you just gotta get right back on, kiddo," she said, blowing Frankie a kiss and planting one on Kiki's head before leaving the room.

Frankie let her head fall to the cushioned arm of the sofa in defeat.

Screw the horse.

No more riding lessons.

Kiki cocked her head at Frankie as if she knew her mistress was a big, fat liar. Her wide, liquid-brown eyes pierced Frankie's.

She'd better hurry up and find a hobby soon. Distraction was the key to her waking libido. "How do you feel about ceramics, Kik? I could make you a new bowl with your name on it."

With a sigh, Kiki dropped her paws from Frankie's chest, flopping to sprawl across her lap. Frankie gave her a loving nudge. "Fine. But if you're jealous when I bring home a 'handmade by Frankie Bennett' garden gnome to Auntie Gail, you'll have no one to blame but yourself."

—ℓ—

"Frankie?"

"Nikos?"

"Where are you right now?"

Cuddling the phone to her ear, Frankie decided every woman who'd been scorned and needed a pathetic, never-gonna-happen fantasy should have a wake-up call from Nikos Antonakas. It was decidedly sinful. After two weeks of working with him, she'd become a never-gonna-happen fantasy aficionado.

She burrowed deeper into the blankets, relishing the warmth of her favorite afghan and Nikos's silken voice in her ear. "Isn't that a rather personal question from my boss?"

"Well, I guess it would depend on why I'm asking."

Frankie frowned with a wide yawn, setting a sleepy Kiki on her chest. "Okay, why are you asking?"

"Can I ask you one more thing first?" he whispered, delicious and husky into the mouthpiece.

The visual she had of him, sitting at his office desk, in that tight-fitting black T-shirt, his chest hard, and screaming her name came to mind. He was probably gnawing on a pencil, his reading glasses propped on top of his thick head of hair while he did two things at once. So. Sexy. So, yes. Ohhhh, yes. He could ask her anything he wanted. Any—thing. "Uh-huh."

"Wasn't it me who hired you even though you were clearly unwilling to do anything other than feel sorry for yourself?"

Wow. What a harsh to her warm, fuzzy vibe. The haze of sleep she'd been in began to lift—and not pleasantly. "Wait a minute. I wasn't feeling sorry for myself. I was—"

"You were moping, and you did whatever you could to get out of getting off your backside and working. That's what you did. But I hired you anyway, and this is the kind of thanks I get for taking such a leap of faith with someone who has little or no skills?"

Leap of what? In an instant, she was wide awake. "Where are we going with this?"

"We're going to the unemployment line if you don't get your butt in here *now!*" he roared.

Holy hissy fit. Nikos almost never yelled. He was loud—boisterous even when the pressure was on during rush hour—but he never yelled in anger.

Frankie's eyes flew to the alarm clock on the nightstand in panic. Ten. It was ten in the morning. She wasn't scheduled to work until one thirty. She'd seen it with her own two eyes—right there on the board in the back room where she'd gone every day for two weeks to see the schedule.

It was also the only reason she'd stayed up so late last night, surfing the Internet on Gail's laptop in search of a hobby. Shit. She should have known better than to let herself get sucked into that ladies' blog about making furniture out of beer cans.

Frankie glanced at the clock again. It was only *ten*. She sighed with relief. "But I'm not scheduled to work until one thirty. So I'm clearly missing your point. Today's my late day." It was.

"Huh," Nikos rasped against her ear with a sarcastic drip to his words. "Funny. I'm looking at the schedule right now, and it says you should have been here an *hour* ago. So unless you want to find yourself out of a perfectly good job you need, I'd skip your morning massage followed by eggs Benedict and fluffy, freshly baked croissants and get the hell in here fast, *princess!*" he bellowed.

The phone went dead with a crackle while she sat stunned, but only for a moment.

Frankie threw the blankets off and shot into the bathroom, ignoring her pasty pallor and puffy eyes. Jamming the toothbrush into her mouth, she scrubbed her teeth, seething while she did. She'd seen that schedule and it had said one thirty, and when she got into that diner today, she was going to show Mr. Hot Pants he needed a new pair of glasses. She stuffed her unwashed hair into a ponytail, hurled an unfazed Kiki at her aunt with a plea to take her potties, and flew out the door, still unclear why she was rushing off to a job she hadn't wanted in the first place. Were people dying because she wasn't there to slice onions for onion rings?

And when had a job, especially *this* job, become so important?

Oh, I dunno, Frankie. Maybe it was when you decided there was still life and oh, hormones left in your waiflike body and they were all screaming Nikos's name?

Twenty minutes later she screeched into the parking lot, slamming on the brakes and throwing her car into park. She fought the harsh blasts of cold air, pressing her hands to her ears it was so sharp. A gust of wind later and she was inside the diner doors—the very quiet diner with only one patron.

She'd missed the breakfast hour rush—hoo boy.

Chloe greeted her from behind the front counter with a smile that never reached her beautiful sloe eyes. "Must have been some night for you to oversleep like that, huh, Frankie?"

Hector shook his head at her before gliding out from behind the counter and off to the back with a slight wave of his hand over his shoulder.

Frankie's eyes narrowed in Chloe's direction, catching her slender hands on her curvy hips and the glimmer of something in her gaze Frankie wasn't quite sure she understood.

One of the customers at the counter spun around on his stool. "Is *that* her?"

Chloe's dark head nodded in his direction. "That's her, Ralph. Mitch in the Kitchen's wife. Oh, sorry, ex-wife. Right here in our very own little diner. A real live celebrity, right, Frankie?"

Frankie froze, tightening her clutch on her purse. Her cheeks flushed while her feet refused to make a move for the nearest escape.

"You sure that's her?" Ralph asked, his slender, wrinkled face clearly unsure.

Chloe nodded, waving her hand in Frankie's direction. "Come say hello to Ralph, Frankie. He's a big *Mitch in the Kitchen* fan."

Ralph squinted his eyes. "You sure don't look like her. She was darned pretty and had some meat on her bones. I remember because the wife and I met her at one of them there book signings Mitch had. Drove all the way to Manhattan just to see him, too. What a pain in the keister, all that traffic in the city."

"Well, they do say the camera adds ten pounds, and you know, after her nationally televised *incident*, I imagine the stress shaved off an inch or three," Chloe offered helpfully while Frankie stood rooted in place like a teenager caught by a cop with a flashlight, macking it up with her high school boyfriend in the backseat of a car.

Okay, so now would be a really good time to run for cover. Hide beneath her shame like the sissy-Mary she'd become these past six and a half months.

Yet neither her legs nor her desire to avoid public punishment would cooperate.

Sad—so sad, Frankie. Who are you, sister, and when the hell did you trade in your spine for hush money?

"You know what else they say, Chloe?" a voice called from behind her on a chilly burst of air. "They say waitresses are nosy bitches with no lives. Until you, I might have begged to differ."

A hand with red fingernails attached to it planted itself on Frankie's shaking shoulder. A sultry voice whispered in her ear, "You can stand up for yourself any time now, Frankie. I know you're not afraid to. I've seen you in action with a wire whisk, among other kitchen accoutrements."

Jasmine.

Despite Jasmine's encouragement, Frankie's tongue stuck to the roof of her mouth like it'd been tarred in place. Whatever was up Chloe's ass wouldn't be pulled out by her razor-sharp wit at the rate she was going. "But Chloe didn't cheat on me like Mitch did. Anger has its degrees and all," Frankie whispered back, grateful for the musky scent of Jasmine's perfume and her warming presence at her side.

Chloe's face went from sly to sour in seconds. "Oh, look. It's Jasmine. Here to pick up another free round of coffee for your strippers so they won't fall asleep on their poles?"

Jasmine chuckled, as though she relished swooping in for Chloe's kill. Crossing her arms over her buxom chest, she purred, "No, kitten. I'm here for lunch. Now go be a good food service engineer and bring Jasmine some water—with a slice of lemon in it while I decide what I want you to *serve* me, please. Don't blow it now. I just shot a wad of big words at you, and I know you confuse easily, but your tip depends on you getting it right."

Me-ow.

Chloe's face turned several shades of an unattractive red before she scurried off to the kitchen, and Ralph made a stunned beeline for the door without a backward glance.

Frankie's mouth fell open.

Jasmine chucked her under the chin with a hearty chuckle. "Now that's how you put a little viper like Chloe in her place. Next time, speak up, Frankie. What she did was cruel and unfair."

Frankie's breath shuddered out on an exhale. "Thank you. I—I—"

Jasmine shrugged her shoulders before removing her coat and laying it on the stool at the counter. "You need to find your tongue is what you need to do, and don't be silly. No thanks necessary. Any chance I get to shoot down that conniving bitch makes it a beautiful day in the neighborhood."

"Obviously," Frankie commented, unsure if she should pry into the reasons Jasmine so disliked Chloe.

Sliding onto a stool, Jasmine patted the one next to her. "It's a long story, but there's no love lost between Chloe and me. That's all that you need to know. Oh, and that she's a jealous busybody. That's always good to keep in mind. Now sit with me. Do you have time for a break?"

Frankie frowned, pushing up the sleeves of her bulky sweater. "I might have time for a forever break if Nikos is still around. Do they hire older women at Fluffy's? I bet if I put on a couple of pounds what I lack in boobage I can make up for in sparkling personality."

Jasmine's giggle lightened Frankie's mood. "What happened?"

"I can't get into it now. Suffice it to say, I might be practicing my pole-dancing skills on the nearest lamppost if I don't get back to the kitchen, but I promise to spill another time."

"You free for dinner?"

Frankie snorted. "That was a joke, right?"

"A joke?"

"I live in a senior citizens's retirement village with my Aunt Gail, Jasmine. You don't have pressing engagements when you're in bed by eight. Well, unless there's a *Match Game* marathon. Then it's on. So yes, I'm about as free as unwanted advice and bird watching from a park bench where the homeless gather."

Jasmine smiled, tucking her blonde hair behind her ear. "Good. Then let's have dinner. Anywhere in particular?"

"Anywhere but here," Frankie said on a laugh.

"Welllllll, look who decided to work today," Nikos said from the kitchen doorway, his muscled forearm holding the door open. "Did you get your mani-pedi all taken care of? I hope you didn't forget that facial. I wouldn't want you to have clogged pores or anything on account of me and my grueling requirements for eight solid hours of your precious time."

"God, even when he's an asshole, he's beautiful," Jasmine whispered with a grin.

"If only that weren't the truth," Frankie said back in hushed tones. "Gotta go, but I'll call you later and we'll make arrangements to meet." She ducked under Nikos's arm, sticking her tongue out at him just before she did.

Exactly when her balls had decided to make an appearance, she was unsure. Though, they would've been much more helpful if they'd shown up when Chloe was in attack mode.

Nikos was right behind her, stalking her like so much prey. "So, princess, what held you up this morning? Shoe shopping?"

Whirling on him, Frankie poked a finger in his chest. The title "boss" flew right out the window hot on the heels of her common sense. "I told you what happened, Nikos. I read the schedule just yesterday and it said *one thirty*. Not ten. So while I realize you probably think my fifth-grade reading skills can be attributed to some sort of confusion in my pretty, pampered head, I know what I saw."

Nikos yanked the schedule from his back pocket, holding it up so she could indeed see it said ten.

Which was a bitch of a conundrum, but still it wasn't the same schedule she saw yesterday.

Stomping to the far end of the kitchen, she tore her apron off its hook. "I don't care what that says. I know what I saw yesterday." Frankie pulled a gleaming knife from the block and held it up, cornering him and his damned schedule. "And you'd better lay off the snide remarks about pedicures and facials. I couldn't afford a facial right now if I sold my soul to the devil, and you know it—which is why I'm working here with a beast like you for a boss. To remind me of those luxuries, and my lack thereof, is petty and preschool-ish. Now bring me a ten-pound bag of onions to chop. Nay, bring me two so I can make up for my spur-of-the-moment morning shopping spree!"

Nikos caught her by surprise when he laughed with total abandon, the cords of sinew along his neck strained. "Wow. That was nice."

The anger she'd spewed evaporated at his smile. Damn him and his smile. And his brawny body. Oh, and his stupidly sick rippling thighs. "Did it make you feel bad?"

"Not until you hit 'preschool-ish.'" He gave his chest a light-fisted punch. "That cut deep."

Now Frankie grinned up at him. "Good. You deserved it. You could have given me the benefit of the doubt, you know. I've been on time every day for two weeks, and I do all your dirty work for eight, sometimes ten solid hours six days a week. I really did read the schedule and it really did say one thirty—*yesterday*."

His eyes caught hers, pinning her. "You're right. I should have asked before I jumped down your throat. Sometimes we Antonakases forget the word 'communication' exists for a reason. We get excited first and ask questions later. Apology accepted?"

Her breathing slowed as he hovered over her. She caught her breath when Nikos lifted a thumb to swipe at the corner of her mouth. "Toothpaste," he muttered, but his finger didn't move when he was done wiping. Instead, it lingered in all its deliciousness.

"I didn't have time to rinse, you tyrant," she muttered back, hoping to hold on to her grudge, yet caught up in a strange trance they both couldn't look away from. Her heart began an erratic pattern of starting and stopping in jolts to her chest.

Nikos's chest rose and fell, too, in choppy breaths. "I did apologize," he said without a trace of antagonism. Though his reminder was slow, measured, and said with distinct distraction as his eyes followed her darting tongue gliding over her lips in nervousness.

Frankie swallowed on a hard gulp, using all her will to suppress the urge to capture Nikos's finger between her lips. "You did."

"Now you accept and we move forward. It's nice workplace etiquette," he muttered, the spot where his thumb rested burning beneath his finger.

Frankie found she didn't want him to remove his thumb—*ever*. "But you were pretty mean. I don't know if I can forgive and forget. I am known for my awesome ability to lose control. If I were you, I'd tread lightly," she teased with a flirtatious edge to her tone.

Whoa.

Frankie Bennett was flirting. Better still, it felt good.

Heh.

Nikos let his other arm rest on the wall above her head when he leaned toward her, amusement streaking his olive black eyes. "I'm not afraid of you and your wooden spoon of doom."

Frankie giggled. "I hear it was pretty psych-ward worthy."

Nikos wiggled his eyebrows. "You mean you haven't seen it?"

"Not the whole thing—no. Just the stills the tabloids splashed all over the front pages, and a snippet or two on TV. I don't remember much of it either. It was like I was possessed."

"All you needed was a good pea-soup spew. It was probably the best beat down I've ever seen, bar none."

His approval made her want to bask in the glory of his sun, even if she was basking for all the wrong, totally inappropriate reasons. "No one would have ever expected that kind of reaction to anything by quiet-as-a-church-mouse Frankie Bennett. I surprised even me. I don't know where that came from."

"From a place I imagine was a little sick and tired. Cheating's a crappy thing to do. It makes people do things they didn't think they were capable of."

Was that understanding from one cheated upon to the other? At the mention of Mitch's infidelity, the spell Nikos held her under was broken. Frankie sobered. The painful reminder that she wasn't enough for Mitch, despite the fact that in hindsight, he hadn't been enough for her for a long time, was still raw. "Yes. It was a crappy thing to do. Something I decidedly plan to avoid for, like, ever."

Yet Nikos didn't seem to be suffering the same effects of the moment's end she was. "Do you still love Mitch, Frankie?"

When he said her name like that, all interested and with a tender hint to it, she wanted to give in to her foolish impulses and melt against him. But his question was one she was still sorting through. What had she loved about Mitch to begin with? His physical presence never made her heart skip a beat the way Nikos's did. Looking back, there wasn't a particular time she could remember feeling cherished by him or needed for anything other than her ability to manage him to within an inch of his disorganized life. "I haven't given it much thought . . . But if forced to answer, no—I . . ."

"You're still sorting it all out. I get it."

How could he possibly understand her relationship with Mitch and the kind of heartbreak he'd created? Who'd ever dump Nikos so heinously that he'd know the sort of pain Mitch's infidelity wrought from deep within her? "Do you?"

He smiled, a smile that reached his warm eyes. "I do."

"Hey!" Cosmos stuck his head between the two of them. "Uh, I hate to interrupt, but Frankie? You got a phone call while you were catching up on your beauty sleep."

Frankie narrowed her eyes at Cosmos, ducking out from under Nikos's arm. "I was not, I repeat, I was not sleeping in like some diva!" she yelped, pointing the knife she still held in Cosmos's direction.

Nikos cleared his throat. "Lay off her, Cos. It was just a mistake." He winked when Frankie shot him a grateful smile, leaving her insides slushy.

Cosmos raised an eyebrow with a cynical lift to it. "Right. Whatever. Anyway, like I said. You got a phone call."

Who'd call her at the diner? Who even cared she was alive besides Aunt Gail? The tabloids had turned into a bunch of slackers the moment a new ass to chew had appeared. She hadn't had a call from anyone in, at last count, two months. "Who called?"

Cosmos didn't look her directly in the eye. Instead, his gaze strayed to Nikos.

"Well?" she almost demanded, her stomach finding that old familiar discomfort it'd grown so content with. It was something bad. It was always something bad as of late.

Cosmos's sigh was reluctant, his words short. "Mitch called, Frankie. It was Mitch."

Superfly.

CHAPTER SIX

From the "maybe even a little less reluctant than I was last entry" journal of ex-trophy wife Frankie Bennett: Maxine says it's crucial to create your own new life from the inside out. After your divorce, you're supposed to make it a point to experience new things, create new routines, get out and see the world, and let the world see you and your brand-new attitude. I went. I saw—the world, that is. I think my world is far better viewed from the confines of my cave. But no one, especially that hippy-skippy Maxine, can say I didn't try.

"If I was you, brother, I'd walk away now," Cosmos advised with a slap of his hand to Nikos's back.

"What am I walking away from?" he asked, keeping his head buried in the possible menu changes to avoid a glimpse of Cosmos.

"Don't bullshit me, Nik. I saw the way you were looking at Frankie today when you had her cornered—but what you didn't see, because you're as blind as the proverbial bat, was the way she looked when I told her her ex-husband called. You know why you didn't see it? Because you're not paying attention to the signs. Instead, you're making a checklist of things to do to save her. Do I really need to remind you of Anita?"

Nikos's shoulders bunched. No one needed to remind him he was the biggest ass where Anita was concerned. "I don't need to be reminded." He wasn't in the mood for the speech from Cosmos tonight. He'd rather be pissed off about Frankie's reaction to Mitch's phone call. A reaction he never expected after she'd just told him she didn't love the prick anymore. A reaction he shouldn't give a world of crap about, but found himself angry over nonetheless.

"Let it go, Cos."

"Fine. Just remember, I was the one who reminded you about your love of a chick who's hard up."

"Who is hard?" Voula asked, wiping her hands on her apron.

Nikos shot Cos a glare. "No one, Mama."

Voula pinched Cosmos's cheeks. "I hear that bad Mitch call today for our Frankie. You didn't tell her, did you?"

Cosmos let his head hang to his chest. "I did, Mama."

Voula scowled. "Next time you give Mama the phone. She will take care of the Mitch and his kitchen. Frankie looks better since she is here. She eats my meatloaf almost every day for lunch, and she smiles sometimes. I like this. That bad Mitch will only make her sad again. We don't want her to landslide, do we?"

"Backslide, Mama. And no, we don't want her to backslide," Nikos reassured her.

"Then if he calls again, Cosmos, you tell him we don't have no Frankies here, okay?"

Cosmos nodded with a sidelong glance at Nikos. "Done."

"Nikos? Did you tell Frankie about Marco and his bad wife?"

Nikos winced. No. He hadn't told Frankie about Marco. "Doesn't she have enough on her plate, Mama?"

"Her plate will break if she is caught with the surprise, Nikos."

"You don't really think Carrie will show up here ever again, do you? I don't think we should worry about it, and we definitely shouldn't add anything else to Frankie's troubles."

Voula wagged a finger at him. "I don't like the secrets, Nikos. And what about Marco? When he comes back from his trip, he will meet our Frankie. I don't want to see him sad again, Nikos."

A stab of guilt for his best friend and the heartbreak he'd suffered when his marriage went to shit made Nikos's gut twist. "How about we talk about this another time, Mama. You go home and have dinner with Papa."

Cosmos intercepted Voula, saving his brother. "C'mon, Mama, I'll take you home. You've been on your feet too long today."

Voula frowned when she removed her apron. "I like tired feet better than I like your cranky Papa."

Both brothers laughed. "It'll pass, Mama. He just needs to find other interests," Nikos said, planting a kiss on her forehead.

Cosmos threw his jacket on, giving Nikos one last pointed look. "Mark my words, brother," he warned.

Nikos waved him off, turning back to the menu changes. He wasn't interested in Frankie Bennett.

Not interested in her luscious, bare lips. Not in her flushed cheeks when she was tweaked. Not in her warm amber eyes when she smiled. Not in the comfortable groove they'd found working together. Not in the ridiculous smile he experienced when she consumed something he'd cooked for her. Not in the weird rush of something he couldn't explain that shot to his chest when he saw her flipping through endless magazines, searching for this hobby she hoped would motivate her to want to get out of bed every day.

Not.

~ℓ~

"Why in Sam Hill are you fancying up?"

Frankie smiled into the bathroom mirror at Gail's image behind her before blotting her lips with a tissue to soften the lipstick she'd found in the vanity drawer. "I have a date."

Gail's lips split into a grin. She gave Kiki, who sat on the vanity top, a scruff to the head. "I knew it was just a matter of time before all my prayers were answered." She mouthed a "thank you" to the ceiling.

"And what did you pray for, Aunt Gail? What do you suppose Auntie Gail prayed for, Kik?"

As though she waited for an answer, Kiki shot them both a somber glance before leaning back on her haunches, her large ears erect.

"I prayed my favorite Greek god Nikos would ask you out. God's been slacking a little where you're concerned, but I think when they say *he's* always listening, they mean it."

"I think *he's* still giving you a deaf ear."

"You're not going on a date with Nikos?"

"Nope."

Gail raised her eyes upward, palms to the ceiling. "What? What is it you want? I just stuffed my face full of Voula's lemon meringue pie. It ain't cheap, but I donated to the cause. Not to mention, I put twenty bucks in the coffer last Sunday! It's not like I asked you for a swarm of locusts. I was just looking for a little romance, and it wasn't even for me."

Frankie's giggle filled the pink and blue bathroom. "I don't think God takes bribes, Aunt Gail."

Gail's expression grew sheepish, then she bristled. "I wasn't bribing anyone, young lady, just offering to scratch a back. Father Tobias said the Sunday school kids need new Bibles. I help buy new Bibles, he prays Nikos asks you out. It wasn't like I was looking for a marriage proposal."

"Well, my date isn't with Nikos. You've been had," she teased, running a brush through her now almost waist-length hair. Scrutinizing her reflection, Frankie decided next paycheck she'd get a major trim. Instead of dragging it back away from her face, she let it fall where it may.

Gail lifted a strand and smiled. "You look pretty, honey. It's nice to see some color in your cheeks and your hair so shiny. So who's your hot date?"

"Jasmine."

Her aunt's sharp eyes widened. "A woman?"

"Uh-huh."

Gail reached for the top of the toilet seat, letting it flop down so she could sit on top of it. Kiki responded by scratching at the vanity top, her warm eyes concerned. "A woman . . . Are you having one of those midlife crises? I watched a Lifetime movie once where this woman got an ugly divorce then . . . well, then she became a lesbian. Can't say as I blame her. Her ex-husband could have turned any red-blooded, man-loving female into a lesbian. He was worse than even Mitch. But he was a serial killer. And before you get all persnickety with me, I just want you to know I support whatever makes you happy, but it'd be nice if you told me something like that so I can pray for the right thing—gender—whatever."

Frankie's laughter was uninhibited. She leaned down and kissed Gail's wrinkly soft cheek. "I'm not a lesbian, Aunt Gail. Jasmine's someone I met at Maxine's support group. Another ex-trophy wife or whatever we call rejects like us. She was married to Ashton Archway. We're just having dinner. No big deal."

"Okay then. I'll keep praying."

"Aunt Gail?"

"What, sassafras?"

"Lay off the praying for a while. At least praying for me to find a man. Maybe you should reach for something more attainable, like a studio apartment so I'm not in your hair anymore."

Gail rose, giving Frankie a hard hug. "I like having you here, sugarplum."

"But I bet Garner Barker doesn't like it so much. You two've been sneaking off to his place for the last month."

Gail gave her a guilty look, her sharp eyes hooded. "I didn't know you knew about me and Garner."

Frankie squeezed her aunt's arm with affection. "I think it's awesome you've found someone you want to spend your time with. I just hope he's good to you."

Gail winked. "Don't you worry about me. I'm plenty old enough to know what I'm doing. It's you we need to take care of right now. Speaking of taking care . . ."

Frankie paused while grabbing her purse, catching the look of concern in her aunt's eyes. "Ohhh, I know that look. Spill."

"That dirty bird called here. I told him we didn't want whatever he was sellin' when he got snippy with me, thinkin' I was keeping him from you."

Frankie's heart sank. What could Mitch want from her? Didn't he have everything she'd once had? Wasn't every stitch of clothing, two summerhouses (one on the beach in Malibu), a classic Camaro, and a partridge in a pear tree enough already?

Damn him for intruding on this new space she'd found. This precarious balance between survival and a cot with three squares a day. Her eyes sank to the pink and blue tiled floor. "Did he say what he wanted?"

Gail lifted her chin, her eyes determined black chips. "Don't you go crawlin' back into your cave, Frankie. You look me in the eye when I tell you that Mitch with the traveling penis called. You have nothing to be ashamed of. Stop acting like you do. Get mad, Francis!"

A tear stung her eye. Go figure she still couldn't shake her disgrace over Mitch. Her shoulders slumped when she scooped up Kiki, hugging her close. "I'm not mad. I know I'm supposed to be, but I'm not. I just want him to go away like he never existed in the first place."

Gail's jaw hardened, leaving a tic on her left cheek. "Maybe that's the problem. Maybe if you were mad, you wouldn't be so depressed. That you let that man steal one iota of your life makes me want to clunk you in the head. That you let him steal six months from you makes me want to wrap my hands around his neck and squeeze until a crime scene investigator shows up to make chalk lines around his dead body!"

Now Frankie sunk to the toilet seat, letting her hands rest between her knees. "You know what bothers me the most about Mitch's cheating, Aunt Gail?"

Gail smoothed a hand over the top of her head. "What's that?"

Without thought, she voiced one of her deepest fears. Inadequacy. "Why wasn't I enough for him? I did whatever he wanted all the time. I made sure the show ran smoothly for him. I took care of all of his fan mail. I was his buffer with the Bon Appetit Channel execs. I helped him research recipes. In fact, half of the recipes he used on the show were mine. I dressed up—I worked out. I took care of myself, not to mention catered to his every whim, and still it wasn't enough. I was always missing something, always lacking in one department or another. It was work. All day, every day. I'm never letting a good-looking man charm my stupid socks off again. Mitch charmed his way out of and into everything, and I fell for it. I'm never investing that much time in a man again. If I'd invested half the time in finding a career of my own as I did in Mitch and his greedy rise to celebrity chef stardom, I might not be living in my aunt's retirement village."

"You know why you weren't enough, Frankie? Because Mitch was too little. You can only overcompensate so much before someone collapses under that kind of pressure. Real men don't need someone to do everything for them short of hold their Mr. Peabodys when they piss."

The meaning of life in four sentences by Gail Lumley. Frankie swiped at her eyes, handing Kiki to her with a kiss on her furry head. "If Mitch calls again, tell him we have nothing left to say to each other. He has nothing left to take from me. I don't want to talk to him. I'm sorry if he gave you a hard time."

Gail's cackle bounced off the acoustic walls of the bathroom. "Like he could ever best your old Aunt Gail. I told him if he wanted to talk to you, he'd have to get past me and"—she lowered her voice to a mere whisper—a whisper that held guilt—"and your new boyfriend, Nikos . . ."

Her eyes closed at the horror. "You did not."

"Oh, yes I did, too," Gail shot back with fiery eyes. "And I'd do it again just to hear that wheeze in his gasp when he tried to hide his surprise. No use in him thinkin' you were pinin' for him like some puppy abandoned at the pound. Let him think you've moved on with your life even if you've only really just begun."

Yeah. Take that, Mitch. "Don't engage him anymore, Aunt Gail. If he calls again, just hang up."

Gail began a protest by screwing up her face, but Frankie held up a hand to quiet her. "Please. I really want him to leave me alone, and he won't if you encourage a good battle by antagonizing him. Better yet, look at the caller ID and if it's him, just don't answer the phone."

"Oh, fine. We'll let the weasel keep thinking it's okay to schtupp someone with the name Bamby."

"With a 'Y,'" Frankie reminded her on a chuckle, discovering it didn't hurt as much to mention the other woman's name as it once had.

Gal pinched her cheek. "You go have a good time with your new friend and forget all about the dirty bird. Kiki and I have a date with that hot geek *Chuck*."

With a wave, Frankie left, forcing herself to push Mitch out of her thoughts. He didn't deserve a nanosecond of brainpower.

Though, she had to admit, she was curious about why he'd call now after over six months of silence. There was nothing left to settle up—nothing to divide—nothing left he could take pleasure in reminding her was no longer hers.

So what the hell?

The only thing about his phone call Frankie could be certain of was that she didn't want to talk to him—and not just because he'd left her feeling stupid and intimidated. Instead, she found she simply didn't care what he was doing or whom he was doing it with.

Even if he was still doing it with Bamby and her "Y."

Woo to the hoo for growth.

$\sim\!\ell\!\sim$

Jasmine waved to her with her perfect smile from a far corner of Little Anthony's Italian Ristorante. Gorgeous in the low lighting with her smooth skin, fashionable kiwi-colored sweater, and matching scarf looped around her neck, Jasmine had probably threatened many a female in her time with her almost surreal brand of beauty.

But Frankie didn't have a shred of jealousy, even knowing she was mediocre at best compared to Jasmine. She was suddenly just glad to be out and doing something for herself that left her feeling like she was at least trying to pick up the pieces and learn the language in this new place called Divorcelandia.

Frankie took a peek around as she followed the hostess to their table, finding herself mentally comparing her surroundings to the diner. She frowned. Why was everything about Nikos and the diner? This was a perfectly nice little Italian restaurant with plenty of atmosphere and gorgeous murals on the walls. Christmas music played in the background, emphasizing how remiss she'd been about the coming holiday.

Jasmine jumped up and gave her a quick hug before Frankie sat down and settled in. "I'm glad you decided to leave your cave. It's bright out here in the land of the living, huh?" she teased.

Frankie mock-squinted. "And it burns."

Jasmine chuckled, flipping open the menu to peruse the selections. Her hair, loose and flowing past her shoulders, gleamed in the lone candle on the table. "I'm starving. So tell me what happened with Nikos. What was he so hinky over today?"

"I was late for work. A lot late. But I'm telling you just like I told that prehistoric excuse for a man, I saw the schedule, and I wasn't scheduled to come in until one thirty."

Jasmine's pink-glossed lips thinned into a line of distaste. "Chloe."

"What?"

"I'd bet my left nipple it was Chloe who changed the schedule."

Frankie let the menu fall to the table. "Your left nipple's definitely a serious commitment. So care to explain?"

Jasmine's shoulders shifted in her sweater, pulling back squarely. "Here's the deal with Chloe. I already told you she's a bitch. She's also a jealous, mean bitch."

"To be fair, I bet you can't count on one hand women who aren't jealous of someone like you, Jasmine."

Jasmine's eyebrow rose, but her expression was neither haughty nor condescending. "True that. I've had my fair share of women snubbing me since I turned thirteen and woke up one day with the rack the good Lord gave me. I'm not telling you she's jealous because of me, Frankie. I had my run-in with her and her Nikos fixation, and now she knows better than to come to the playground unarmed. I'm telling you she's jealous because of you."

"Me? What do you suppose she's most jealous of? My barely B

cups or my hot, twenty-pounds-underweight bodacious bod? Don't be ridiculous, because that's just what that is. Ridiculous." Silly, silly, silly. That the lovely dark, olive-skinned Chloe would be jealous of the pale, skeeny Frankie was absurd.

Jasmine peered over her menu, her eyes serious. "Have you seen the way Nikos looks at you?"

Only in my deepest, darkest, wildest fantasies. "Me?" Her question showed her genuine surprise.

"You, sister. He's definitely interested, no matter how angry he was today. That's bound to make Chloe want to gouge your eyes out with her cheap stilettos."

Taking a sip of her water, Frankie swished it in her mouth before speaking. "So you think Chloe messed with the schedule because she's jealous of me?"

"Yep. So you'd come in late and Nikos would fire you. Thus, eliminating the competition in the race for the smokin' hot Greek guy."

Frankie whispered her response. "Have you taken a good look at me lately, Jasmine? I couldn't compete even with double Ds and a Brazilian butt implant. I look like shit. Chloe has nothing to be jealous of, and I'm not in a race for anything but the will to want to survive."

Jasmine handed their waiter the menu after giving him her order. "Next time say it like you mean it. You are, too, interested in Nikos. There's nothing wrong with that. It's a good thing, a sign, as Maxine would say, that you're moving forward. It's healthy."

Frankie spouted off her order to the waiter and waited until he left to address the very unhealthy crush she couldn't deny she had on Nikos. "First, Nikos is way too charming for this girl. That kind of charming, his kind of brick shithouse, always turns into a lying, cheating slug. I know, I was married to one. Second, he's my boss. That can't be smart. Third, I'm pretty sure when Maxine sat down and wrote all that gibberish, she meant for us to play on a team within our leagues. You own a league all unto yourself. The rest of us are just dust in your wind. So I concur—it is not healthy to be interested in a man who can have any woman he wants. It's like hoping Clive Owen will show up and take you to prom."

Jasmine flicked her glass of wine, a gleam in her eyes. "So you admit you're interested?"

"No." Oh, wait. She kind of had. Shit.

"Your lips say no, but your scrawny, underfed body and its unique language says yes. Own it," she demanded, nabbing a piece of bread from the basket in the middle of the table. "And stop putting yourself down. You were no slacker in the looks department, Francis. You're just on a bit of a beauty sabbatical because you feel like crap. Once we get some food into you and some color in your cheeks, you're going to show that sneaky, cutthroat bitch Chloe what hot really looks like. And Nikos is a good guy. He's nothing like Mitch. Plus, Nikos is attracted to you at a level all women can only wish a man as treacherously beautiful as him would find them attractive."

Frankie's unplucked eyebrow rose. "Which level is that, Jasmine? The homeless bag lady level?"

"Oh, that's a load of crap. He's attracted to the hot mess you are—in spite of the hot mess you are. That's something to take note of when jumping back into the dating pool." Jasmine slathered a thick layer of creamy butter on the fragrant sourdough bread and handed it to Frankie. "Now eat. Your ass needs something to form middle-aged lumps on."

Frankie took a bite of the bread, savoring the tang of the sourdough, carefully planning her next words. No matter the outward comparisons she saw between Mitch and Nikos, despite the idea they both had more charisma than a television evangelist looking for charitable donations, there was no stopping her next question. "So what's the deal with Chloe and Nikos, and you, for that matter?"

Jasmine brushed the crumbs from her hands with a glib smile. "Is that a question from the uninterested?"

Frankie's eyes guiltily strayed to the checkered tablecloth. "No, it's a question from someone who ironically wants to keep her job and not end up on the playground alone without her bazooka for backup."

The waiter planted their plates of spaghetti in front of them, making Frankie squirm in anticipation of Jasmine's answer. She nodded her thanks before picking up her fork to twirl the noodles, pretending nonchalance.

"Nikos and I chatted when I first came into the diner a year ago. No big deal, clearly no attraction between us."

"I think you did the world a favor by not hooking up with him. There's only so much Brangelina perfect the world can take," Frankie teased.

Jasmine waved Frankie off with a dismissive chuckle. "Either way, I never thought twice about Nikos and the same went for him. Yes, he's divine on a million levels, but we just have no chemistry, and at the time, chemistry was the last thing I was thinking about anyway. But Chloe saw him talking to me as one usually does with a frequent customer and later made a snide remark. I set her straight in the most polite way a woman who's basically been called a whore can. She didn't like that, so she accused me of leaving without paying my bill. Thankfully, the customer who sat at the table next to mine said Chloe had picked up the money I'd left. Naturally, Chloe played like she'd forgotten due to the stress of lunch hour—which is a total load of shit, but it did get me free coffee for life. So when I say watch out for Chloe, I mean watch out for her. She's sneaky and conniving."

Things to ponder. "She definitely doesn't like me."

"That's because she's threatened by you and the attention Nikos pays you. Now, do you really want to know what's up with Chloe and Nikos?"

No. Yes. No. Oh, fine. Yeeeesssssss. She wanted to know if her obsession for Nikos really was like waiting for Clive Owen to show up and take her to prom. "Sure," she said, feigning indifference.

"Chloe's the girl Nikos is supposed to marry."

Well, damn. It would appear her Clive Owen forecast was looking cloudy with a chance of thunderstorms.

~ℓ~

Nikos pulled out a chair for his friend, waving off Winchester. "I got it from here, Win," he said with a smile. "I'll bring him home, too, if you have something else you want to do."

Win slapped Nikos on the back with a grateful smile. "Thank you, sir. I can't tell you the grumpiness I've had to contend with since the lovely Jasmine turned our fair Simon out like so much stale bread. He's been incorrigible."

"Women," Simon muttered, placing his cane between his legs under the table.

"Yeah," Nikos agreed, sitting in the chair opposite Simon with a wave good-bye to Win. "They suck. So what happened to make the great Simonides strike out? Not that I'm not glad you shot it all to hell, because I am. I like Jasmine, and I'd have totally blown your cover in the interest of keeping her from getting hurt. But I'd love to hear how it happened anyway. I mean, are you slacking these days or what? Didn't you give her your bank statement with your opening line?" he joked.

Simon sighed. "I would have if she'd given me the frickin' chance. She blew me off too fast. I even played the blind card, and still, she shut me down."

Nikos laughed, smiling at the waitress who'd brought a bottle of red wine and popped it open, pouring it into their glasses. "You really need to knock off the 'I'm disabled' line, pal, especially with smart women like Jasmine. So explain to me why Jasmine blowing you off is such a big deal."

"Have you seen her, Nik?"

"Uh, question is, have *you*?" he snickered, knowing Simon wouldn't take offence.

"Yeah. Yeah, I have. Before the accident. You know I have."

"But that was five years ago," Nikos reminded him. It worried him that his friend still held a grudge over a betrayal he hadn't known existed until much later in his life.

Simon grunted. "I bet she hasn't changed much."

Nikos had to agree. "Nope. She's still as hot as she ever was. She's also still a woman who doesn't deserve your scorn—even if it's only by proxy."

Simon ran his fingers over the table with a light touch until he located his silverware. "It's not about that anymore. I don't want payback."

Nikos searched his friend's blank eyes. "Then what do you want?"

"Her."

"Don't you say that about all the women you manage to woo into your den of iniquity?" Since his accident, and his subsequent divorce, Simon was all about the prey. Women were his favored sport.

"It's different this time," he offered, his tone quiet.

"How's that?"

"Can't explain it. It just sort of clicked for me."

Nikos shook out his napkin, placing it on his lap. "That I get."

"Ahhhh. What's this I'm hearing?"

Even blind, Simon could still read his best friend of over ten years like a book. "Nothing."

"Bullshit," Simon accused.

"Okay, maybe it's bullshit."

"So spill it. What's her name?"

"Frankie."

"The new girl at the diner Mama Voula was talking about? The one who was married to the famous chef? The new *not so Greek* girl?"

Nikos rolled his tongue in his cheek, fighting the twist of his gut when Frankie's name was mentioned. "Yeah. That's her."

"Shit, man. Your mother's going to have a heart attack when she finds out."

There was that. "There's nothing to find out, Simon."

"Hah! Don't bullshit the bullshitter. I can hear it in your voice. You like her, and you know damned well your parents aren't going to approve because she's not Greek. Because she's not *Chloe*. You know, the woman they handpicked for you to find marital bliss with?"

"That's sort of the point. Frankie isn't Chloe. It isn't like I haven't told the family and Chloe my feelings on that particular subject."

Simon slapped his hand on the table with a bark of cynical laughter. "Like that's stopped Voula from hoping Chloe will grow on you? Be real, Nik."

"What Mama wants doesn't change how I feel about Chloe. She's a good waitress, and that's about all the admiration I can summon up for her. Period. Though, she could make things sticky for Frankie at the diner, no doubt. Not to mention Pop's all in an uproar because she's doing what he's always considered his job, while he's forced to watch TV and mope himself into retirement."

"So what are you gonna do?"

What was he going to do about his growing attraction to Francis Bennett? "If I'm realistic, there's really nothing to do. Not now anyway. Frankie's pretty shot down after her divorce and touchy as hell."

Simon wrapped a hand around his wineglass and saluted Nikos.

"Right up your alley, buddy. Opa!" he muttered the Greek sentiment for happiness, though the real intonation behind it was "good job on finding yet another wounded soul, knucklehead."

Nikos frowned, tamping down his irritation at Simon's cynicism, grabbing a slice of bread to stuff in his mouth. "You sound a lot like Cosmos."

"That's because Cosmos was right there with me after Anita. Or don't you remember how much puke we cleaned up as a tag team after one of your all-nighters?"

Nikos flinched. "I say we can all discussion of women and focus on grub. I'm starving."

Simon didn't respond. Instead, he cocked his blond head to the left, putting a finger to his mouth to quiet his friend.

Nikos gave a glance around the restaurant. "What?"

A smile spread over Simon's face—wide and genuine. A rarity, indeed. "Did'ja hear that?"

"More fan girls who want to help you on your journey to self-fulfillment?" he cracked with a laugh. It was uncanny the ability Simon had to hear a gushing fan long before Nikos was even aware they were in the same room. Though by now, he was used to the kind of attention Simon drew whenever they were in public together.

"Naw, man. It's Jasmine."

"You're delusional. Wishful thinking because you crapped out with her. Now you're hearing her everywhere. It's your ego's imagination."

"Nuh-uh. She's sitting to the right and toward the back of the restaurant." Rising, Simon grabbed his cane and his wine.

Nikos was up, wineglass in hand, too, and hot on his heels, hissing, "Where are you going?"

"To eat with Jasmine, dipshit." He grinned, clearly pleased with his choice.

"If she wanted to eat with you, she would have said yes when you asked her out the first time, Simon," Nikos growled in his friend's ear.

But Simon wasn't listening; he was barreling ahead much like the quarterback he'd once been, rounding the big white columns at a speed Nikos marveled at.

Simon stopped short in the corner of Little Anthony's, throwing his arm with unbelievable accuracy and placement around his friend's shoulder just as Jasmine laughed. "Did I tell you, or did I tell you Jasmine was here? I didn't just hear her either. I smelled her perfume. Very distinct. Magically delicious."

Hoping to thwart Simon's intent to crash dinner, due to the pair of big, amber eyes looking at him with accusation like he'd just interrupted a discussion about feminine products, Nikos nodded with a cluck of his tongue. "You did. What you failed to hear with those big ears of yours was Jasmine's *date*. She's not alone." There. Mission aborted due to unfriendly fire.

"Oh, Nik. You have crappy game. You couldn't lie if someone gave you cold hard cash to do it. Jasmine's date is a woman. I can smell her perfume. So either join me, or turn tail and roll. I'm goin' in."

Nikos sighed; there was no stopping Simon when he got it in his head he wanted something.

Yes, Simon's balls were a thing of beauty due some primitive, cavemanlike admiration. Big and clanging, they fueled him toward the Jasmine goalpost, dragging a reluctant Nikos in with him.

And given that Frankie was scowling at him as though he were Hannibal Lecter rudely interrupting her dinner and demanding she hand over her thigh for him to snack on, this would be the time to display his very own set of balls.

In resignation, he acknowledged there was nothing to do but play along. So mission reevaluated. Proceed with caution due to unfriendly female.

Nikos smiled from behind Simon and cooed, injecting as much charm as he could into his greeting, "Heeeeey, ladies. Lonely?"

"Dude," Simon whispered over his shoulder. "Very lounge-lizard leisure-pants-ish, maybe even a little stalker creepy. Cool it."

"This from a man who *smells* his woman out?"

Using his cane to find his way to the edge of the ladies' table, Simon murmured, "Follow my lead, brother. We're goin' in."

Gun loaded, locked, and ready.

CHAPTER SEVEN

From the "no longer so much reluctant as just plain old, had it up to her eyeballs" journal of ex-trophy wife Frankie Bennett: I'm never going out of my aunt's house again. I don't care if the apocalypse is slated to hit only Jersey and safety awaits me in like, Fiji. I'd rather skip the sunburn and end it all in a fiery ball of Garden State Parkway and tsunami-like waves from the Jersey Shore. I want to go back to my cave. Call me melodramatic, but I personally believe I excelled at cave dwelling and was best left alone to do just that. Dwell. Oh, and I thought I was warming to Maxine Barker and her hokey-schmokey, helpful, ex-trophy-wife tips. My asshattery. Let me show you.

Jasmine gazed in total silence at Nikos and his friend, her haughty glare a sight different than the warmth of the laughter in her eyes just moments ago.

The blond, very large man with Nikos leaned down, with great precision for someone who was blind, directly in front of Jasmine. "Miss me, pretty lady?"

"Like I'd miss a public flogging."

He chuckled, low and with delighted relish. "Kinky." His vacant but warm eyes strayed in Frankie's general direction, a hand potentially capable of wrapping itself around her neck extended toward her. "I'm Simon. Nice to meet you, and you smell great."

Frankie took his hand and almost giggled until Jasmine gave her the girlfriend frown. The one that meant she was to find this man neither amusing, good-looking, nor, God forbid, charming. Like it or not. Frankie cleared her throat and put on her most stern frown in defense of the woman she liked more and more and hoped to appease in order to cultivate their budding friendship.

"Frankie Bennett, and thank—" Jasmine gave her another girl-friend glare of fire and brimstone, thwarting further planned courtesies. She clamped her mouth shut with a wince of apology in Jasmine's direction.

His jovial smile widened. "Really? *The* Frankie Bennett? I'm so jazzed to meet you."

Frankie's face fell in an instant. She shot a frost-filled dagger of a glance at Nikos, who feigned ignorance, before responding with intentional ice in her tone, "Yes. I'm *the* Frankie Bennett. The crazy, ex-media-proclaimed-trophy wife of celebrity chef Mitch in the Kitchen. And double yes to your next question. I'm also the woman that fully intended assault with a deadly wooden spoon upon Mitch Bennett's lying, cheating person, during a live broadcast of his show." She gave Nikos another narrow-eyed gaze, slamming her fork down on her plate of half-eaten spaghetti so he'd be really clear about her displeasure at turning her into a sideshow freak.

Simon guffawed, clearly thoroughly amused by her blunt statement. "You sound like my kind of girl, but that's not what I meant. In case you missed my clumsy approach, I'm blind. I didn't see the show, but it damned well makes me wish I could still use the old eyeballs. Must have been awesome retribution. I'm sure whatever happened, the punk deserved it."

"Always with the blind card," Jasmine huffed, slinking downward in her chair when Frankie gave her a look of admonishment. No matter the reason Jasmine didn't like Simon—and she'd held nothing back in showing her displeasure—he'd taken Frankie's side.

You had to like that in a guy.

Simon chose to ignore Jasmine's jab; the dazzling smile he wore never left his face. "I meant you're the Frankie Bennett Nikos is always talking about. Talk, talk, talk, talk, talk. That's all he does. Frankie this and Frankie that."

Oh. Well. That was a whole different ball of Frankie wax, now wasn't it? The warmth Jasmine was so determined to stomp out in Frankie returned—tenfold. So Jasmine and her wadded knickers be damned. And Nikos with the murderous glance at his friend Simon be damned, too. Damn everything but the music of Simon's words to Frankie's crush-starved ears.

"What Simon means is," Nikos interrupted, all smooth and unruffled, "I told him about how lucky we are to have found someone as good at peeling onions as you are."

Frankie rolled her eyes at Nikos, then addressed Simon. "My apologies. I'm a little touchy about the subject. I tend to overreact, and please, forgive my insensitivity to you." She made sure her tone of voice was extra shamefaced.

Simon gave her hand a quick squeeze before letting it go. "Totally understandable, Frankie. So why are you two pretty ladies having dinner alone when there are two perfectly willing men to eat it with you?"

"So I won't choke on my meatballs?" was Jasmine's catty response. Her harsh words were doing the same thing she'd accused Frankie of earlier—saying no, but her eyes on Simon, well, that was a different story. They virtually gleamed with the opportunity for a shot at some verbal sparring, and there was no hiding that.

"Well," Simon purred. "We couldn't have that, could we? But all's well. I know the Heimlich. So move over and we'll join you, just in case there's a medical incident." Simon somehow managed to locate the empty chair at the table next to them in the close quarters of the restaurant. He dragged it next to Jasmine's, sitting in it with the scarred wooden back facing the table.

Frankie began to giggle, but it turned into a muffled snort when Jasmine flicked her forearm hard, and Nikos's sigh of exasperation filled her ears.

Simon's hand trailed with deft fingertips over the table until his hand found Jasmine's. "So how's Foofy's?" he cooed.

"It's Fluffy's and it's still running rampant with naked women in thongs you can't see." She shot a catty smile at Frankie and Nikos while batting at Simon's hand.

Hoo boy.

Frankie's eyes slid back to the table, avoiding Nikos's altogether while she picked at her now cold noodles. "Your friend?" she muttered under her breath while Simon engaged Jasmine in rapid-fire conversation.

Nikos's shoulder brushed against hers, making her fight a shiver. "If I said no, he's just some guy I found outside who looked like he needed a meal, would you believe me?"

She chuckled. "I might, seeing as you feed the homeless guy who sleeps under the bench near the diner's parking lot almost every day. However, Simon's dressed too well. He's also pretty intent on getting Jasmine's attention, but then, who wouldn't be?"

He caught her eyes with his, captivating her without even trying. "You have beautiful hair. I like it down."

Preen, preen, preen. She tugged self-consciously at a strand to avoid a messy coo of pleasure. "It needs a dye job and a trim. My ends are split." *Very flirtatious, Frankie. It's a good thing you want to shrivel up and turn into a recycled virgin.*

When she'd been married to Mitch, she'd hit the salon religiously every six weeks. She was almost ashamed that she hadn't given her hair more scrutiny tonight before she'd left. Yet, that was all part of living life for herself and no one else. She didn't have to have her roots done. Such a rebel.

"I didn't know you and Jasmine were friends," he said, low and husky.

"We met at Maxine's support group meeting a couple of weeks ago. This is our first date."

"Ah, the ex-trophy wife club, right?" Nikos sipped his wine, his luscious lips wrapping around the rim of the glass, making her stomach jolt with a rush of heart-shattering desire.

The feeling was new and something totally foreign to her. So foreign, she had to grip her hands together in a clenched fist to keep her breathing even.

"Yep. It's where we go to bemoan the loss of our limitless platinum cards and learn how to clip coupons and survive on minimum wage. Fun, fun, fun." She tried to keep the sarcasm out of her tone, but it wasn't easy when she looked back on her old lifestyle and how pathetic and shallow it must seem to someone as hardworking as Nikos. Tonight, she'd been busy appreciating a delicious meal she could pay for herself, not crying about the fact that she wasn't eating the meal in authentic Italy. Which was a really nice place to visit, but somehow, not as nice as it had once seemed.

"Do you miss those luxuries, Frankie?"

Her head instantly moved in the negative, words spilling from her mouth she didn't realize she meant until the question was posed. "No. Not the way I guess most who've lived the lifestyle I have would. To be honest, I spent the better part of six months in bed since my divorce. So I was comatose during the socially acceptable mourning period over the loss of my Ferragamos," she joked. "Now those, I really do kinda miss, but not much else. I was never much into clothes or any of that until Mitch decided I had to be." Or demanded she had to be so she'd always be perfect when they made happy-couple public appearances.

His next question was one asked in solemn tones, and Frankie couldn't decide why he was asking it, or whether she should even wonder if there was a point to it at all—maybe he was just making conversation to pass the time until Simon ran out of Jasmine fuel. "Do you miss Mitch?"

Her breath hitched at such an intimate inquiry. It made her fight the ridiculous notion that Jasmine was right, and Nikos really was interested in her. "N . . . wait, I want to say this the right way. No. I don't miss Mitch. I miss the idea he represented. I miss the hours in my day his needs filled to keep me occupied. I miss what's familiar, and I'm scared witless of the unknown. I miss the feeling that I was part of something important—even if I was just a background player. But by the end of our marriage, anything intimate or warm and fuzzy was long gone. We had more of a working relationship than anything else. Now I know why." Those words were like shedding a skin, one that had become too tight and so constrictive, she could barely breathe.

Yet, Nikos didn't appear daunted by her admission. He leaned in, his cologne, tangy and woodsy, filled her nostrils, his stunningly handsome face showed apparent interest. "You mean because of Bamby?"

Her cheeks flushed, but in some bizarre way, saying it out loud, letting her personal introspection become not so private, somehow felt right. "Our marriage was over long before Bamby, I think. I don't know why I didn't see it then as clearly as I do now. I guess we got into one of those ruts everyone talks about. Everything became about Mitch and his career, doing whatever it took to keep him on the celebrity chef winning streak he was on. I was just his cheerleader-slash-gofer. Looking back, Bamby shouldn't have been the sucker punch she was. I should have seen the signs."

Nikos's beautifully chiseled face flashed an expression she didn't understand regarding her words, but would definitely pinpoint as relief. "It was a shitty thing to do. Shittier still that he left you with nothing. It isn't like he couldn't spare a dime."

Frankie heard his scorn, and she wanted to buy into it. So wanted. Instead, she nodded with a vague smile. "Established. But the nothing portion of this mess is entirely my fault. Mitch asked me to sign a prenup in the beginning of our marriage, and I did so willingly to prove my love wasn't about his wealth. I guess I just never thought our marriage would be reduced to numbers. But who does, right? In fact, I didn't think about the prenup at all until it was too late, making me not so bright and shiny."

"No, Frankie. It just makes you trusting. You were young when you married, right?"

"Too young. I was twenty."

"Jesus," he commented with a wry grin. "I was still having keg parties and hazing freshman."

"You went to college?"

He smiled that incredible smile. "I know. A guy who works in a diner with a college degree. Crazy that."

Frankie's face flamed again. "I didn't mean it like that . . ."

He put his hand on hers, warm and so large it completely covered Frankie's. "Joking. I was joking. Yes. I went to college. I have a degree in accounting, which I put to good use at the diner in ways I never imagined."

Frankie cupped her chin on her knuckles, refusing to move the hand Nikos covered with his even if her Nissan Versa depended on it. It brought with it more than just a scintillating tingle. It sparked something new, fanning an ember of need in her she couldn't remember having felt before. "Did you start working at the diner right out of college?"

"Nope. I had a high-powered job and a ridiculously expensive apartment in Manhattan. In fact, my job was how I met Simon—who'd be living in a one-bedroom walk-up in Hoboken if not for me and my genius with numbers. Instead, he has ten thousand square feet in Manalapan with an indoor pool and a bowling alley."

"You mean he doesn't just sniff out hot women with his uber-powerful nose. He bowls, too? I'm impressed."

Nikos laughed. "He does. It's a little out of control, but if you give him enough direction, he's a solid sixty-five. Blind hasn't stopped Simon, as you can see."

Frankie glanced at Simon and a Jasmine who didn't appear nearly as uptight as she'd been when Simon first approached her. In fact, Frankie heard a soft, albeit maybe a little reluctant giggle from their corner of the table.

But she forgot about Simon and Jasmine when she considered the reasons a man like Nikos would leave his career to come run the family business. He intrigued her. Okay. He did a lot of things to her, but right now, her hormones were in behavior modification mode, and she wanted to learn more about this man she had a ludicrous crush on. "So tell me more about this job you had in Manhattan. Why'd you leave?"

It was as though she'd asked him how many inches his man bits were. Nikos's face changed, and he didn't bother to hide the displeasure inching around the tightening of his lips. "Personal reasons."

Oh, Frankie. Booyah, for finding the touchiest issue you possibly could and asking about it. Leave it to her to take the one stab in the dark that actually hit the jugular. Silence settled between them, thick and uncomfortable.

As dark almost always turns into light, so did Nikos's face. "Sorry. I guess I have my touchy issues, too. I worked long, crazy hours at the firm. I didn't have much of a life. I hardly ever got home to see Mama and Papa. If you know just a little about them by now, you know they're all about family."

Frankie let out a relieved breath of air followed by a smile. Voula and Barnabas were indeed all about family. It was one of many reasons she was growing so fond of them "I know when your father mutters what a meddling brat you are as he hovers behind me while I wield seven inches of razor-sharp steel, he means it with big love."

He grinned with fondness. "Yeah. That's Papa for you." Then Nikos frowned. "He's not taking it out on you, is he? I told him he'd better behave when he's around you, or I'd take away his *Judge Judy* privileges."

Frankie shook her head with a chuckle. "Only in the way of long, dramatic sighs and the occasional snort of displeasure when he sees me chopping something in a way he wouldn't do it. Though last week, he only snorted like twice in a day between commercial breaks for *Regis and Kelly*. I think I'm growing on him," she joked, leaning into Nikos before she could catch herself, fighting the utter luxury having such a solid, delicious man in such close proximity brought.

The candle glowed between them, giving Nikos's eyes a seductive glint that sent a shiver along her spine. "You've grown on a lot of people, Frankie." He tilted his wineglass in her direction.

Swooning wouldn't be out of the question if it weren't for Jasmine tugging on her arm, totally harshing her Nikos vibe. "You look like a girl who needs to use the ladies' room, Frankie," she said with a suggestive tone, sending another girlfriend signal that screamed she was using the facilities whether she wanted to or not.

Frankie pointed to the left of Nikos with an apologetic smile. "I think I have to go to the bathroom. Excuse me." Slipping past him, she held her breath when he rose, allowing her room to shimmy out of her chair.

Once free of the confines of the table, Jasmine dragged her in the direction of the bathroom. "That man is infuriating," Jasmine muttered under her breath.

"Infuriatingly hot for you," Frankie teased. "I don't see the problem."

Jasmine stopped dead in her tracks, pulling Frankie to an alcove by the restaurant's bar. Her face a mask of hard anger, she hissed her words. "You know what the problem is, Francis? The problem is Simon's just like Ashton."

Frankie frowned at her friend, unsure where her sudden anger stemmed from. "Simon does tires, too?"

Jasmine shook her head with a sharp bob, placing the heel of her hand against her forehead. "No. Simon's an ex-NFL football player."

"Ohhhh, I don't know anything about football players. Just food. So Ashton played pro football, too? Before or after tires?"

Jasmine's beautiful eyes rolled upward. "No, Frankie."

"Then I'm lost. Take my hand—guide me to wherever this crisis you're having is. I'll follow."

"Simon's rich."

Frankie held up her knuckles, facing Jasmine. "Niiiice coup, my friend. You and Gary'll be moving out of that studio apartment in no time flat."

"No! Don't you get it? That's the problem, Frankie. He's rich. I don't want to ever become involved with another man who has boatloads of money to burn. When you can have whatever you want, when nothing's unobtainable, you lose perspective. The people around you become disposable. Not to mention, Simon's ten years younger than I am."

"He is not," Frankie scoffed. "You two could be the fabulous twins for all the blonde hair and good looks between you. If the two of you had children, no one would be able to bear looking at them for the shiny."

"He's thirty-six, for Christ's sake." Jasmine's lush lips thinned in disapproval.

"So?"

"So I'm not!"

Frankie rocked back on her heels. "Still don't see the problem. He's rich, attractive, has a great sense of humor, and he very obviously wants to date you. If only we all had those problems. Boo to the hoo for poor, gorgeous Jasmine."

"I'm forty-six years old, Frankie. That's too old to date some kid I could have almost given birth to."

Frankie's mouth fell open in surprise, but she managed to snap it shut. "You are not forty-six," she said with a shake of her head. "Jesus, I can't believe how unfair this is. You didn't just hit the gene pool lottery for the dazzling; the guy upstairs decided you should bathe in the Fountain of Youth, too? Do I need to remind you just how lucky you are? And another thing—if you could've given birth to Simon, I call we hunt your mother down and have her locked up for neglect. You're ten years older than he is, Jasmine. Not a hundred."

"It doesn't matter. Obscenely rich men are all the same. They just want eye candy—trinkets to wear on their arms. Ashton told everyone I was his most prized possession. Well, until I wasn't."

"So now wouldn't be the time to remind you Simon's eyes can't see your candy? That might sound incredibly insensitive, but that's Simon's reality. I'd say it's obvious he thinks there's more to you than big hooters and an ass you could crack a walnut on," Frankie joked.

But Jasmine wasn't laughing. "I'm never going to be someone's toy again."

Frankie cocked her head, her smile sympathetic. "Wow, and

people have the nerve to call me sensitive. I get it, Jasmine. I do. I was someone's toy, too. Okay, granted, I wasn't as shiny a toy as you are. I'm still not, and I'm almost ten years younger than you, too, okay, eight, whatever, but you just met Simon. How do you know he's just like Ashton? Even I, pathetic, jacked-up, beaten-down divorcee, know you shouldn't judge the poor guy before he's given you a reason to." Oh, dear God. Maxine's crazy-assed philosophies and cutesy euphemisms were in her head now, claws deep.

Jasmine's finger waved under her nose. "I know rich men, Frankie. They all just want young playthings, and when the young plaything gets old, they don't want her anymore."

"Yeah. I think you've said that four times now. Your argument's less effective when you use the same one repeatedly. Lest ye forget, I know rich men, too, and I don't want to be the one to smack you with the actuality of the situation here, Jasmine, but you're not a young plaything anymore."

"Score."

Frankie curtsied. "Okay then. Not that you aren't fabulous, and a whole helluva lot more so since I found out you're freakin' forty-six, but if we're playing by the numbers, only eighty-year-old men would consider you a plaything."

Jasmine threw up her hands with a wry smile. "Okay. Touché. I get it. The horse is beaten."

Frankie gave her a thoughtful glance. "So I guess we wouldn't be having this conversation if you didn't like him and might be considering dating him, right?"

Jasmine slumped against the textured wall, tucking her purse under her arms in front of her like a petulant child. "I don't want to like him."

"I don't want to have a zero balance in my bank account either while I sponge off my Aunt Gail. There are a buttload of things I don't want. Sometimes life hands you what you don't want. I can think of far worse things than liking Simon to not want. So knock it off and be grateful for the endless gifts the Big Kahuna seems to keep sending you while he neglects the rest of us to stew in our mediocrity."

Jasmine giggled, nudging Frankie with her shoulder. "You just told me to suck it up."

Frankie grinned, rather proud her mentality was slowly changing. "Yeah, I guess I did. So, ahem—in the esteemed words of our fearless, ex-trophy wife leader, Maxine Barker—suck it up, princess."

Jasmine laughed once more, squaring her shoulders with a groan. "I can't believe I'm being so whiny. Let's go to the bathroom so I can stare my lily-livered reflection down."

Frankie followed beside her with a snicker. "And do me a favor. Don't do that again, okay? I was the one in control of your freak. That should *never, ever* happen for as long as we're friends. Got that? I don't like you insecure. If you're insecure, then I'm surely suicidal. So while we're in there, make sure you hike up your spine. I might need to borrow it."

Jasmine's cackle rang through the restaurant, making Frankie laugh, too, distracting her for a moment from the hand that snaked out of another small alcove, grabbing her with an iron grip. "Are you Frankie Bennett?" a male voice slurred.

Jasmine was instantly between Frankie and the tall, lean man who had her arm, placing her hand on his wide shoulder to give it a light shove. "Hey! Back off, pal."

He gave Jasmine a wobbly nudge, pushing her out of the way and redirecting his glare at Frankie. A glare filled with distinct malice. "I said, are you Frankie Bennett?" His words washed over her in an alcohol-soaked breath so sharp, Frankie had to fight to keep from gagging.

Her head shot back as she took in the face looming before her. A nice enough face attached to a man whose red and black striped tie was askew and whose rumpled brown suit looked like it had forgotten dry cleaners weren't extinct.

Paparazzi maybe? Damn them. Her first night out of the cave, and already someone had found her. How was it possible in nowhere Riverbend? Frankie stared up into the stranger's bleary, aquamarine eyes lined with red rims, and fought to keep her calm.

She held up a warning hand in Jasmine's direction when her feet shuffled toward them. "Look, if you're hoping to dig up some gossip on me so you can write a story that's almost ninety percent bullshit, blow, buddy. There's nothing here to see, and if you don't let go of me, I'll pull a Mitch in the Kitchen repeat performance, the likes of which you've never seen!" Frankie tried to re-create that out-of-control lunacy she'd experienced when she'd trashed Mitch's set. The one that made her eyes wide and buggy.

But to no avail. Clearly her threats meant nothing to him. Instead, he gathered her up by her shoulders, his long fingers digging into her flesh and asked again, *"Are you Frankie Bennett?"*

"That's it!" Jasmine yelled, winding up her arm to clock him in his curly head of dark brown hair. She hit the perp's head with such force, the snap of Jasmine's plether bag made a thwacking noise.

The man's head snapped back, but he didn't let Frankie go. Rather, he dragged her backward with him, toppling chairs to the tune of yelping, astonished customers and the shattering of glass.

Just as Frankie saw the floor rushing toward her face, another hand reached from behind her, grabbing her around the waist to haul her upward and push her out of the way while the man fell to the floor as though a lumberjack had taken him out at the knees, his back hitting the tile with a crack of bones and the raucous skitter of chairs.

"Marco! What the hell are you doing?" Nikos roared, pushing his way through the toppled bar stools to hover over him.

A small, round man with a black dinner jacket scurried toward the group, but Nikos held up his hand. "I got it, Anthony. Just give me a minute, and send me the bill, okay?"

The man bowed out in quiet submission, his moon-shaped face full of concern, as though this kind of thing happened with Nikos and whoever Marco was all the time.

Frankie pushed her tousled hair out of her eyes, gasping for breath as Jasmine rushed up behind her, pulling her back away from the debris.

Simon was right behind Jasmine, finding her elbow with his hand. "Marco? What the hell are you doing? Has he been drinking, Nikos?" His nostrils flared. "Never mind. I can smell the Jack on him from here. Marco, my friend, you know what this means, don't you? Intervention, pal."

Nikos hauled Marco up off the floor with a rough jerk, setting him hard against the bar. The two standing but an inch apart in height, Nikos grabbed his jaw, giving his cheek a light cuff with the back of his hand. "Marco? What are you doing here? I thought you were in Botswana where they don't have phones or running water?"

"Who the hell is he?" Jasmine whispered to Simon.

"Thass her, Nik. Thass her, God damn it!" Marco shouted, his words blending together when he pointed an accusatory finger in Frankie's direction, slamming his forearm into Nikos's shoulder to break free of his grip.

Frankie cringed. Indeed. It was her. She was never sorrier it was her than she was right now. She turned to Simon when she caught her breath. "You know him?"

Simon clucked his tongue in Marco's direction while Nikos fought to keep him in check. "Yeahhhh. We know him. That's our other best friend, Dr. Marco Sabatini, DDS."

Jasmine snorted with a dry comment. "What a trio you men make. The obnoxious, the drunk, and the Greek. Nice manners, too. Kudos."

Marco began to barrel toward Frankie again, his eyes filled with not only the glassy effects of the booze he'd so undoubtedly consumed, but also something else she couldn't get a feel for. If she had to guess, she'd call it sorrow, deep and cutting. "Okay, so if he's not the paparazzi fishing for a story, how does he know me? I mean, I've had a rude comment or two from the male persuasion in Mitch's defense, calling me a ball buster for threatening his . . . well, his—"

"Junk," Jasmine offered with a snicker.

Frankie nodded her agreement. "Right. Junk. But no one's ever reacted like this. He's really a little over-the-top outraged on behalf of men caught cheating, don't you think?"

Simon blew out a breath of air. "Oh, if you only knew. Excuse me while I go put myself in the line of fire, ladies. Marco would never hit a blind man. I hope," he muttered, using his cane to find his way to the bar, narrowly avoiding a shattered brandy glass.

"Marco, my man! S'up, buddy?"

Marco reached upward to cup Simon's face. "Thass her, Simon. I seed—saaaw her in the paper. I haf to talk to her," he shouted on a wobble of very large feet.

Simon poked him in the stomach with his cane. "You'll do no such thing, pal. You leave Frankie alone and come home with me. Gimme your keys, and don't make me fish in your pants for 'em. People'll talk."

Marco shook his head with vigor, the curls on his head violently shuddering. "No. No. No. I haf to know if she's seen Carrie. I'm no— *not* leafin' 'til she tellss me."

"Marco—if you don't take your ass outta here, I'll haul you out myself," Nikos grated with a harsh growl. "Carrie's back where she belongs. In Idaho with her family. Frankie doesn't even know Carrie. Now knock this shit off now and go home with Simon."

Nikos pulled his cell phone from his pocket with a snap, using his thumb to scroll through it until he located the number he needed. "Win? It's Nik. Sorry to interrupt, but we need reinforcements." He frowned while he listened and nodded his head. "No, no. It's okay. We'll figure it out. Stay where you are. I'll call you."

By now Marco had slumped against Simon's shoulder, his mouth open and slack against the burgundy sweater Simon wore. Simon hoisted him up, letting his friend lean his back into the bar for support.

Frankie finally found her words. Who was Carrie and why did this Marco think she knew her? Her eyes narrowed when she approached Nikos and tapped him on the shoulder. "Who's Carrie?"

"Marco's ex-wife," he muttered, avoiding meeting her gaze by focusing on Simon's back.

Aha. "And why would I know her?"

"He's drunk, Frankie," was the impatient answer. "When he's drunk, he thinks everyone knows where Carrie is."

"Well, then maybe you might consider AA so he doesn't accost the wrong person on his hunt for the elusive Carrie?"

Marco's head reared up at the sound of her voice. "Your husband . . . He stoled my wife!"

Frankie heard Jasmine's sharp intake of breath and felt her own leave her lungs in simultaneous surprise.

"Ask Nik. Go ahead and asssk him!" Marco yelped with a weak struggle against Simon.

Nikos's sigh was ragged when he ran his hand through his thick head of hair.

"Shit," Simon spewed, clapping Marco on the back. "Just shut up,

Marco. Shut up and put your head down so you don't hurl all over my sweater. The last time you did that, I had to throw the frickin' thing out."

Jasmine was instantly at Frankie's side, throwing a hand around her shoulder to lead her out of the restaurant, but Frankie shrugged her off. "Hold up! Did I just hear him right?"

Nikos finally turned to her, his beautiful face full of concern, his response slow. "Unfortunately, yeah. You did."

"Care to explain?"

Jasmine shook her head, giving Nikos a warning look Frankie didn't miss, one very similar to the girlfriend glare but not. "Forget it, honey. Let's just go and forget this ever happened, okay? Who cares what Mitch did? He's an asshole."

Frankie's blood boiled. "No, Jasmine. I care what Mitch did. You know why I care? Because apparently Nikos knew Mitch did something and didn't bother to tell me—which would have been the courteous thing to do, seeing as his friend clearly wants my blood for it. Not to mention the fact that Nikos is friends with someone who could've shown up at the diner at any time to read me the riot act, and I wouldn't know why. Now wouldn't that have been awkward?" she ranted, glaring at Nikos. "So pony up, Antonakas!" she demanded, jabbing a finger into his chest, forgetting all about the fact that he signed her paychecks.

He grabbed at it, pulling her hand into his. "You're right, I should have told you, but you were so—so . . ."

Frankie's eyebrow rose when he stalled. "Pathetic. You can say it. Go ahead. Pathetic and fragile, and you were afraid to tell me whatever this is about for fear I might take a swing at your man parts, too, right?"

Simon barked a laugh from the bar.

Nikos frowned. "No. Yes. No . . . Okay, yes. You were in a bad space when I hired you, Frankie. Marco was off in Botswana, licking his wounds and fixing underprivileged kids' smiles. Obviously, he didn't lick long enough to make him stop this ridiculous bullshit over a woman who doesn't deserve to be the shit on his shoe. He wasn't supposed to be back until the spring. Either way, I figured you deserved a little time to adjust to being out in the real world again, get your feet under you, so to speak. But I really was going to tell you . . . given some time."

"Just not until you, Dr. Nikos, thought poor, unstable Frankie was capable of dealing with it without going into an uncontrollable fit of woman rage, right?"

Nikos sighed, yet he still held her hand. "Sort of. No. Look, Marco's had a shitty time of it. I'm sorry for his behavior. Tomorrow, when he's sober, he'll feel like an asshole. I promise he'll be begging for your forgiveness."

Frankie shook her head, tugging her hand out of Nikos's, refusing to mourn the loss of the steadfast warmth it brought. "I don't want him to apologize. I want to know what the shit he means when he says Mitch stole his wife. Mitch was boinking Bamby With A 'Y' last I heard. How exactly does a Carrie fit into all of this?"

Nikos's eyes hardened for a moment, before softening, going dark with sympathy. "I guess before Bamby, well, there was Carrie— Marco's wife."

She shouldn't be stunned that Mitch had been unfaithful on more than one occasion. But here she was. Stunned. "So Mitch slept with Marco's wife?" As if saying it out loud would give it more clarity.

Nikos nodded his head with a wince. "Twice, I think. No, wait. Three times—"

"*Shut uuuup*, you dipshit!" Simon yelled at Nikos in disgust. "Christ, you're a Neanderthal, Nik!"

Huh, of all the coinky-dinks.

Nikos was best friends with a man who'd also been, in an indirect way, hurt by Mitch's ever-randy, heat-seeking missile of love.

Frankie couldn't move for the one song that kept running through her brain.

It really was "A Small World After All."

CHAPTER EIGHT

From the journal of Frankie Bennett: I'm not at all reluctant when I write, Nikos Antonakas is infuriating on more levels than Donkey Kong has! He'd better color himself lucky I've retired my crazy, and that he's so damned gorgeous. Oh, God. Must. Resist. The. Cute. It threatens my pissed-off and, more importantly, my last tenuous hope of keeping myself from begging him to take me heaving-bosomed-slash-rakish-Lord style. That's right. I wrote it.

Frankie didn't bother to look back at the three men, nor did she bat an eye when she made her way to their table, throwing enough cash on it to cover her and Jasmine's bill.

Tears didn't sting her eyes until she hit the sidewalk outside the restaurant, for which she wanted to beat her chest in pride. Jasmine crashed into her, grabbing at her arm to steady herself on heels that scraped against the patches of icy pavement. "Frankie, honey, I'm sorry."

She let her chin fall to her chest, leaning against the lamppost festively wrapped with silver garland. "Is there a vagina on the planet that hasn't slept with Mitch?" she mused with dismal humiliation.

Jasmine tightened her scarf around her neck, then squeezed Frankie's hand in her now gloved one. "What upsets you more? The fact that Mitch did this more than once, or the fact that he had you so completely fooled you thought he only did it once?"

Yes. By hell, yes. The latter, not the former, was undoubtedly what made her want to yark. "Jesus! If Bamby wasn't the first, how many others do you suppose there were, Jasmine? How could I have been so completely blind?"

Her shoulders lifted when she brushed Frankie's hair from her face, wincing at the brutal wind. "Who knows, Frankie? But ask yourself this—who cares? Do you really care anymore? What Mitch did is done. There's no changing it."

Frankie shook her head, her chest so tight she feared it would explode from the weight of her naïveté. "I care, Jasmine. I care because it goes to what a total idiot I am. Nikos and what he knew all along aside, I care that everyone must have thought I was such a blind fool. How many people in Mitch's entourage knew what was going on? People who said they were my friends. People who never once called to see if I was okay after I was tossed out on my ass. What really kills me is while I was slaving away, working my ass off night and day to create new recipes for him, keep his entire world on track for that roving penis of his, Mitch was off banging who knows how many women! What does that say about my womanly intuition?"

"You're not gonna like this, but I'm going to say it anyway. I think it says that maybe you weren't all that interested in what Mitch did with his free time, honey. I don't mean he should have spent it rediscovering his youth in a barely legal vagina. That you'd obviously drifted apart is absolutely no excuse for him to stick his junk where it didn't belong, but I bet you didn't really want to know, or you'd have made it your mission to rekindle your relationship. I think you fell out of love, Francis, and you didn't know it until long after it happened. So you buried yourself in things that kept your mind busy and out of Mitch's line of fire."

A revelation clapped her in the head as sure as thunder had struck. She was dizzy from the knowledge.

Frankie spun around in a circle, pointing her finger to punctuate her realization. "You know what, you're right! I found Mitch less and less appealing in the last years of our marriage. As a matter of fact, I did whatever I could to be anywhere but where he was. If he was coming, I made it a point to be going. My marriage should have ended a long time ago. When I outgrew him. When I no longer needed a father figure. I just didn't know marriage wasn't supposed to be the way ours was. So I let it ride."

"Oh, I get complacency, my friend. I know exactly where you're coming from. It wasn't the money with Ashton. I won't tell you I minded all the luxuries his big bucks brought, that wouldn't be entirely true. But I let Ashton use me as much as I used him— because he was comfortable, and even though I'd fallen out of love, I grew lazy. I knew the score with Ashton until he found a new scorekeeper."

"And look at us now," Frankie commented wryly.

Jasmine smiled into the cold night, her grin filled with mischief. "Yeah. Ain't it a bitch when you find yourself after your life's already half over?"

"I think I'm still in the finding process."

"Well, hurry up. It's damned cold out here." Jasmine rubbed her hands along her arms to emphasize the raw wind blowing down the cheerfully decorated sidewalk.

Yet, discovering she'd subconsciously avoided Mitch, thus totally blocking out any sign of his extracurricular activities when, had she been more interested, she might have been more aware, brought with it the sting of Nikos's admission. "Nikos should have told me."

"Yeah, but he's a man. He wasn't thinking long-term repercussions. Hence teenage pregnancy and the clap."

Frankie giggled at Jasmine's joke. "He sucks."

"I don't either," Nikos denied, hauling a limp, passed-out Marco out the restaurant door. "I just wasn't thinking ahead."

"Because you didn't think you had to," Jasmine shot back. "You were procrastinating. Very typical. I'm disappointed."

"Grrrrrr," Simon purred, pulling up the rear behind his friends. "I love it when you're saucy."

The roll of Jasmine's eyes was meant to show Simon her irritation, but there was also something in them that said Simon didn't trouble her nearly as much as she'd have everyone believe.

"I promise to bow and scrape accordingly, but first, we have a problem," Nikos stated.

"Oh, you bet you do, Antonakas," Frankie muttered.

Nikos ignored Frankie's comment. "We need a lift, ladies. I walked from the diner. Simon has no wheels, and Marco isn't going anywhere unless it's to detox. Plus, we can't find his car keys, just the keys to his apartment. Can you give your boss a lift? Marco doesn't live far."

"You mean the boss who potentially could have created more drama for me and my fragile instability?" Frankie asked, all sweetness and light.

He rolled his tongue in his cheek in impatience, but his expression turned sheepish. "Yes. That's the one."

Jasmine sought Frankie with her eyes, sending another girlfriend question.

Frankie nodded her head. "Fine. But I want next Tuesday off to Christmas shop, and there better not be a single joke about kelp wraps and seaweed facials or it's on."

Jasmine dug in her purse, pulling out her car keys, and whispered in Simon's ear, "Catch, quarterback." She jingled the keys before lobbing them at Simon, whose hand shot up, following the direction of the jangle of metal. "You drive, superstar," she said on a giggle.

Simon was one step behind her. "I love a woman who isn't afraid to take risks." He cackled, obviously pleased.

Looping her arm through his, Jasmine led him to the edge of the sidewalk. "You break my CRX, and you'll find out just how far I'm willing to go. I saved for a year to buy it."

"You have a C-Rex? Jesus, they're like a thousand years old."

"So am I," Jasmine snickered. "We're a match made in heaven."

Their voices trailed off, leaving Frankie with Nikos and the boozed-out Marco. "Wait here. I'll get the car, and if he unloads his misery in my backseat, then I want Tuesday *and* Wednesday off."

Nikos grinned. "You just want Wednesday off because Nails by Noreen's having a twofer special. She told me when she was in for lunch and dropped off flyers."

Frankie chuckled her way into the parking lot. "Perfect. I can have my upper lip waxed and get my nails done. It'll be like Christmas and my birthday." She beeped her car, jumping in and cranking up the heat with a hard shiver.

Pulling up to the curb, she got out to help Nikos get Marco into the backseat. He slumped against the door with a drunken murmur. Getting into the driver's side, she shook her head at Nikos, wrinkling her nose. "He's snockered. Tomorrow's going to totally suck for him."

"Among other things," Nikos agreed as she pulled out of the parking lot. "Look, Frankie. I'm sorry I didn't tell you about Marco, but it wasn't to protect him as much as it was to keep one more stress off your plate."

She caught a glimpse of his profile in the dashboard lights, angular, sharp, so sexy, and forced her eyes back to the road. "I appreciate your looking out for me, but I don't need to be treated with kid gloves. Was I surprised Bamby wasn't Mitch's first foray out into the land of the infidel?" Frankie shrugged. "I guess not as much as I thought I'd be once I got used to it. But Marco's your best friend. That's way too close for comfort. I can only imagine what you must have thought when Maxine brought me in for that interview."

He pointed a finger toward the windshield. "Turn left here—this is his apartment complex, and truthfully, I forgot all about Marco until after our notorious interview."

"Because I wowed you with my culinary resume? No, wait. It was my serial-killer glam, right? You know, the crazy hair and baggy clothes?" she teased.

His hand brushed hers, making her pulse thump. "It was just you," he said into the quiet hum of her tires.

Frankie's stomach jolted, stupidly wishing he meant her and not just the nuttiness that had been her on that day. "I'm an awesome first-impression maker."

Nikos's laughter made her tingle. "First building straight ahead. And you definitely made a first impression."

Frankie swung her car into a slot and shifted into park. "Do you need help?"

He turned to her, his eyes a deep black. "Nah. I got him. If you don't want to wait, I can always call Cos to come get me."

She gulped at the thought of her and Nikos in the close confines of her car—alone. All alone. "No, don't wake him. Chef Boyardee's cranky enough. When he's tired, he's the pits. I'll wait."

Nikos slid from the car, popping open the rear door and grunting when he dipped his head inside to pull Marco out and launch him over his shoulder, fireman style. "Be right back." He kicked the door shut with his foot and made his way into the complex, walking with an easy gait despite the fully grown man on his back.

She flipped on the radio while she waited, settling on a station exclusively playing Christmas music. Her head fell to the cushioned headrest as she closed her eyes and pondered the loyalty Nikos showed not only his family but his friend, broken by the end of his marriage. Maybe he wasn't as much like Mitch as she'd first thought. Maybe his magnetic charisma sprang from genuine feeling.

Maybe.

The questions she had about the where and when of Mitch's hooking up with Carrie drifted off when she sank farther down in her jacket, comforted by the strains of "Silent Night" and her Nikos musings.

A hand, callused and warm, flitted across her cheek. "Frankie?"

A small sigh escaped her lips when her name was called, breathy and content. "Hmmm?"

"Do you want me to drive?"

Her eyes popped open, her hands gripped the wheel. "No. I'm okay. How's Marco?"

"Trashed. I put him to bed and left him a note. He'll be fine."

Frankie started the engine as Nikos clicked his seatbelt into place. "Sounds like you've done this a time or two," she said, backing out of the parking space, fighting to forget Nikos's fingers on her cheek and the tremble it wrought. *Composure, composure, composure. Find some, girlie.*

"Like I said, he took the breakup pretty hard. He's been boozing it up off and on ever since."

Her nod was of understanding. She knew all too well the acute pain a betrayal of trust created. It hurt your bones to move. For her, it had stripped away every shred of her identity. Took her purpose and smashed it to smithereens. "I get it. Some people drink the depression away. Some people, like *me* people, sleep it away. Whatever it takes to dull the pain."

Nikos's jaw hardened, but she caught a glimpse of his eyes, and they were soft. "That doesn't excuse his behavior, Frankie. He can't keep this up. He'll lose his partnership at the practice. I really thought a few months away from here would help."

"I'm not saying that to excuse how he behaved tonight, Nikos. He behaved badly in a public place, and that's not okay, especially because he's sort of a public servant. Riverbend's a small town. I'm saying it from a place of understanding, from sympathy. I'm also thinking if Maxine can drag me out of bed and make me suck it up, maybe Marco should call her and see if she can help him, too. I know he wasn't a trophy wife, but there must be a male version to the 'suck it up, princess' technique."

His jaw relaxed, and his tone took on a smoky quality. "You're a really good person, Frankie Bennett."

She chuckled with a nervous twitter, pulling into the diner's parking lot to come to a stop. "This from a man who watched my kitchen-gadgetry meltdown. It takes guts to label me anything but certifiable."

Nikos turned in the passenger seat to lean into her, placing one arm on the dashboard. His eyes were no longer playful, but serious. "I mean it, Frankie. Marco made a real scene in there tonight with you right in the middle of it. To find a common thread with him because he's in self-pity mode instead of flattening him with a good right hook makes you a decent woman."

Frankie's throat tightened, but she couldn't tear her gaze from his. "Contrary to the impression I created during my last television appearance, I'd never hit anyone."

His smile lit up the interior of her car, the grooves on either side of his mouth deepening. "You kinda suck at accepting compliments."

"Looking the way I do, they're pretty few and far between these days," she quipped, low and shaky, unable to move away from the draw of his luscious lips, the tangy scent of his cologne. Her hormones awakened with a fierce flame in her lower belly.

"I was complimenting your character."

"Which could be the only thing I have left to compliment."

"That's not true," he responded, his voice suddenly a whisper, a whisper that left her mesmerized, transfixed on their close proximity. The car became nothing more than the two inches of space between them.

Her breathing shuddered, hitched, then almost entirely subsided while she tried to think of something to refute his words. "No. I know what the truth is. The truth is, I'm a hot mess—a shadow of the woman I used to be."

Nikos tilted his head, his jaw covered in dark stubble. "Maybe you're still in the discovery process of finding the woman you'll become."

God, she really hoped there was truth to that statement. After all the shit, she was due some awesome. "May . . . be." Somehow, her eyes had drifted half-closed, Nikos's cologne surrounding her with its heady undertones, making her head swim. The heat of his body, bulky, strong, encompassed her while Johnny Mathis sang "O Holy Night."

"I'd be very interested to see who you turn out to be on the other end of this mess you've been in," he murmured, inching closer until, from hooded eyes, she saw that his eyes were drifting shut, too.

Her heart began to crash when he husked out a breath of air, fanning over her face with the scent of wine and something minty.

Frankie's stomach muscles tightened like a clenched fist.

This was it. All her nighttime fantasies come true. Every hot Greek second of them.

Fear, excitement, and more fear swelled when Nikos moved so close to her his lips all but grazed hers. Wait. Did she really want him to kiss her? Maybe the buildup was going to be far better than the payoff.

But then Nikos took care of any misgivings she had when he let his forehead fall to hers while her heart slammed against her ribs and her hands itched to reach up and drag her fingers through his thick hair and tug him back toward her.

Okay, so yeah. She really did want him to kiss her. And if it dispelled a myth or two—so be it. At least she'd know. Plus—bonus—she'd finally get a restful night's sleep.

Disappointment, heavy and stinging, settled in her belly.

He huffed out a breath she couldn't decipher as regret or irritation. "I won't do this. Not this time." The arms that had bracketed either side of her moved away to the tune of her puzzled frown, leaving her cold even with the heat in the car on.

Nikos sat back, his hand on the door, his face granite hard with a determination Frankie didn't get. "Thanks for your help tonight, Frankie. I'll see you tomorrow."

The passenger door clicked before Frankie had the chance to so much as blink.

But not before some serious regret set in.

What. The. Hell had just happened?

You just experienced your first almost kiss, Frankie. Delicious, no?

Her cheeks were back to flaming again while questions swirled in her head.

What exactly wouldn't Nikos do "this time"?

And why, why, why wouldn't he do it the hell with her?

~ ℓ ~

"Frankie Bennett?"

Her head lifted, wary with caution. Oh, if the universe were feeling charitable, this wouldn't be someone who wanted to experience her crazy firsthand by way of an autograph. "Maybe," she said without turning around, scrunching her eyes shut to ward off the stranger's next words.

"It's Marco Sabatini."

When she turned, she half smiled, her eyes teasing when she took in his sharp suit and tie and his freshly scrubbed, albeit, lined face. "Sorry, I didn't recognize you because you didn't slur your words."

He let his head hang to his chest, the curls on it gleaming and still damp in the stream of sun from the diner's window. "I'm ashamed,

Frankie. I had way too much to drink last night, and I'm always an ass when I do."

Throwing the towel she'd just cleaned the front countertop with over her shoulder, Frankie nodded in total sympathy. "I get it. Not the drinking part, but the 'find a way to dull the pain' part. I didn't drink when Mitch and I split, I slept. For six solid months."

He smiled, though Frankie wondered if it was just out of courtesy. There was nothing in it beyond its dental perfection that said he felt it. He was as numb as he could be without the aid of booze. "Nikos mentioned that on the phone this morning. I bet you were a lot less hazardous that way, though."

"Well, there is that. So how do you feel this afternoon?"

"Like a shithead. That's why I'm here. To apologize."

"Not necessary, and I'm sorry, too. For what Mitch did to your marriage. I really had no idea. I thought Bamby was his first affair. Crazy that, huh?"

Scrubbing a hand over his face, he pulled at the lines beginning to form under his aquamarine blue eyes, as though he could erase the dark shadows forming there. "I don't know who Bamby is, but I'm sorry you had to find out about Carrie by way of my out-of-control behavior. I'd like to make it up to you."

Frankie cocked her head to the left. "You don't have anything to make up, Marco. It's over. Though, would it upset you too much if I asked you a question?"

"Shoot."

"I don't understand the Mitch-Carrie thing at all. When did this all go down?" *And which part of stupid was I lost in when it did?*

Marco shoved his hands in his trousers, his face grim. "Your hus . . . Mitch was checking out diners to do some show or something."

Bells clanged in her head. The road trip to scout potential places to shoot the show. Of course. The original plan for *Mitch in the Kitchen* had been to call the show *Mitch in* Your *Kitchen*. Mitch would show up, take over the restaurant's kitchen, and have a cook-off—or something like that. The idea was canned in favor of the production costs at a time when the Bon Appetit Channel still wasn't sure Mitch could fly solo. She sighed. "I remember—about a year and a half ago, right?"

Marco's nod was somber. "Yeah. Carrie was a real fan of his from his days on some other show—"

"*Road to Randall,*" Frankie interrupted as the memory rushed back. "He and Chef Randall were friends. Well, until Mitch's popularity rose and Randall's didn't. That's when the Bon Appetit Channel offered him a test run for his own gig."

Marco's grim look returned. "Carrie was excited to meet him. So when Nikos accepted the invitation, mostly because Carrie begged and pleaded for him to at least meet with Mitch and the production crew, she was beyond herself. She told Nikos he could always say no and that would be that. No harm, no foul. Nikos only agreed because Carrie was my wife. He never would have let Mitch film here. Trouble is Carrie didn't follow her own advice. No doesn't seem to be in her vocabulary. Not where Mitch was concerned, anyway. They met while I was at, of all things, a dental implant convention. She, according to Nikos's version, got pretty friendly, and well . . . you know the rest."

Embarrassment flooded her. Her fingers gripped the ties on her apron, fiddling with them while she struggled to come to terms with her ex-husband's philandering. Philandering that clearly stretched across at least two states. "I'm so sorry."

Marco placed a consoling hand on her shoulder. "It's hardly your fault, Frankie."

Her eyes held Marco's. "Then why do I feel like it is?"

"Probably because all good mothers, even when murder's involved, always ask themselves how they could've missed the signs," Nikos said, all smiles and lighthearted chuckles this fine afternoon. The afternoon after the night where he had almost kissed her, then run off as if she'd held a gun to his head and forced him to almost mack on her.

Humph.

It was all she could do to get to sleep last night, and he was behaving like he hadn't given her the diss of all disses. Charming and carefree as always.

Though, his analogy about Mitch and her playing the role of his mother wasn't exactly far off the mark. There were many times when she'd felt like Mitch's conduct required motherly attention.

He slapped Marco good-naturedly on the back with a playful grin. "How's the head this morning? Did you take the aspirin I left on your nightstand?"

Nikos's presence brought another thought to mind. One Frankie had yet to allow the freedom to process because their almost kiss had gotten in the way. Oh, but when she had a minute to herself, she was all over it.

"It's got a freight train running through it right now. I can't wait to get to the office and fire up the drill," Marco commented, his face sheepish. "I was just apologizing to Frankie."

"Good thing, too. Mama would have your hide if she knew what you did last night. Come in back and see her, huh? She's missed you."

Marco shook his head, his eyes avoiding Nikos's. "Not yet. Maybe another day. I need to get back in the swing of things again." His eyes sought Frankie's once more, soft and filled with a sorrow she could almost taste. "So how about dinner—to make up for screwing yours up last night?"

Nikos's face did that light to dark thing again before he said, "Frankie's probably busy."

Really? Had Nikos taken to looking at her day planner? Okay, so she didn't have one, but if she did . . . . *Frankie* was most certainly not busy. She might have been busy if Nikos had manned up and kissed her last night. As of now, she was as free as an ex-con out on parole. She gave Nikos a cocky glance before smiling at Marco, bright and shiny. "Nuh-uh, *Frankie's* not busy at all. So I'd love to have dinner with you, Marco. Two victims of Mitch and some spaghetti—it'll be like *Dawn of the Living Dead* meets *GoodFellas*."

Marco chuckled, with a warm, and this time, genuine hint to it. "Great. I'll drop back by soon and we'll make plans."

With a raised eyebrow and a cocky swing of her neck, she popped her lips in Nikos's direction before addressing Marco. "I look forward to it."

Nikos glared down at her. "Don't you have onions to peel?"

The smile never left her face. Whatever was pissing Nikos off, and she had to hope it was because his best friend had just asked her out, made her almost coo with pleasure—loud and proud. "You're a mean one, Mr. Grinch." She wiggled her fingers over her shoulder at Marco. "Byyye," she said flirtatiously, pushing her way through the kitchen doors, pleased she'd left that conversation with the upper hand. Nikos had no right to her personal life. He'd made that clear last night.

Voula gave her a nod and a wink of approval. "I like you today, Frankie."

Frankie put her arm around Voula's abundance of shoulder and grinned. "You know what, Voula? I like me today, too."

"Frannnkieee?"

"Mr. Grinch?"

"What was that about?" Nikos demanded.

Hurling a bag of potatoes up on the large island, Frankie gave him a look of pure innocence. "What was what about?"

His face went all thunderclouds with a chance of rain. "Marco."

"He apologized."

"I know that much. But why would you go out with him?"

"Why would you care?"

Voula snorted along with Cosmos and Hector as they ducked out of the kitchen.

Crossing his arms over his chest, Nikos's lips thinned. "I didn't say I cared, but he is my best friend."

"So he can't have more than one friend? Is that like a man rule? Because if that's the case, your math sucks. Simon makes three of you." She began to peel the potatoes for shredding, with an extra bit of enthusiasm in each swipe of the peeler.

Nikos glowered. "That's not what I meant, Frankie, and you know it."

Pausing, she placed her hand on her hip. "No. I don't know what you mean. Why don't you explain?"

Nikos grappled for a moment before finding what she was sure he considered a suitable cover. "I just mean that Marco's in a bad space right now."

"And spaghetti would trap him in the bad space forever?" she asked, her words dipped in sugary sweetness.

He rolled his tongue in his cheek to emphasize his aggravation. "No. I just mean you saw the way he behaved last night. What if it happens again and you can't handle it?"

Nice. Convenient. Not so well executed. "In case you've forgotten, I'm in a bad space, too. In fact, there's plenty of room on the couch in the bad space. I'm happy to share, and if Marco even considers ordering a thimbleful of booze, I'm out. So don't worry your Neanderthal head about it. We'll be fine."

"Fine," he gritted out.

She gave him a wide grin full of sadistic mockery, taking pleasure in his fight to keep his ire in check. Maybe there was some truth to what Jasmine said last night. Maybe. "Yeah. It is."

Nikos turned to stalk off, his broad back rigid with tense muscle, but Frankie called him back when she remembered something about her conversation with Marco. The something she hadn't quite been able to process but had a total grasp on now. "Hold on one minute, cranky pants. I have a question for you."

"Does it involve what Marco's favorite flower is?" he cooed, dripping sarcasm and discontent.

Frankie had to look down at the potatoes to keep from giggling, pleased he was so clearly jealous. "No, but it does have to do with Marco."

Nikos raised an arrogant eyebrow while he waited.

"How about you tell me a little something about Carrie and Mitch."

His eyes became hooded, cautious. "What's there to tell? Didn't *Marco* tell you everything?" he asked with a flippant tone.

Surely he didn't think she was going to let him get away with the defensive crap, did he? Frankie shook the potato peeler at him. "Oh, he told me plenty. What I want to know is why *you* didn't tell me their affair virtually happened right here in your diner? You've met Mitch! Or was that something else you wanted to protect me from?"

"You know, I sort of feel like all I've done is apologize to you when I did nothing wrong but try to protect you." He gave her his best remorseful face, probably counting on the beauty of it wowing her into submission.

And it might have—if not for last night.

Not. Today.

"Uh, no. That isn't going to work. You knew Mitch had slept with Carrie long before I interviewed for this sweatshop."

"If you're mad because I didn't call you and tell you he'd tapped another chick before Bamby, I don't think I can be held responsible. It's not like your number was listed."

She paused for a moment, gathering her words as another revelation hit her. "That's not what I'm saying at all. You knew as far back as my interview that Mitch had slept with Carrie—worse, Mitch was right here in your diner when they were testing concepts for his new show. You knew all of that and you still made like you had no idea who I was. And even after you admitted you knew who I was, you didn't say a word about Marco. Thoughts on that?"

"It's not like we were BFFs, Frankie. You'd just walked in off the street. I was an employer looking for an employee."

"But Marco is your BFF. Did you think he'd never come back from Botswana, like, ever? Did you really think we'd never run into each other? You lied to me!" she accused.

"Ohhhh, no, lady!" Nikos yelled right back, his eyes squinting at her. "I didn't lie. You just never asked the question."

Frankie snorted loud. "Please. How random is that? 'Hey, potential boss, was my ex-husband ever here at your diner, sticking his man bits in your best friend's wife?'" she yelped. *God, this man!*

There was a moment of silence before Nikos let out a cackling laugh, long and sharp to her ears. He leaned against the island's top with the heel of his hand while he caught his breath. "Man bits?"

Frankie's eyes narrowed. "Oh, no, Antonakas! There'll be none of that changing-the-mood bullshit so you can avoid conflict. Not this time. So tell me—is there anything else I should know? Did Mitch have orgies here, too? Did he try to cop a feel from poor Voula? Because I gotta tell ya, there doesn't seem to be a whole lot Mitch hasn't tapped around these parts! What else don't I know that I should on the off chance I might have another messy, very public incident like last night?"

Nikos instantly sobered, placing a warm hand on hers. "I honestly just wasn't thinking ahead. I only knew you needed a job, and I felt like it was the least I could do after what I saw happen right in my own diner with Mitch and Carrie. You were pretty raw when we met, Frankie. You looked like you'd been through the mill."

She swatted his hand away and made a face at him. "Poor, poor Frankie Bennett, right? Lost, alone, tabloid fodder. But never fear, Nikos Antonakas to the rescue," she said with pointed sarcasm.

Throwing the potato peeler down, Frankie fought a ridiculous rush of hot tears. Her humiliation, finding that Nikos knew things about Mitch even she hadn't known, made her feel like a complete fool. Like every aspect of her life, aside from her television debauchery, was a raw open wound, exposed for anyone to rub salt in.

Worse, it was the dismal caricature she'd become. One everyone wanted to feed or save or protect. Enough. "You felt sorry for me. So you gave me a job. Thanks. No lie when I say I *really* appreciate the paycheck, but do me a favor—stop looking out for me and my fragile state, and stick to running diners!"

As she made her way to the employee bathroom to throw some cool water on her face, Frankie made a decision. No more pathetic, loser divorcee in need of everyone's pity and sympathy.

Even if she eventually found out Mitch had tapped every twenty-five-year-old from here to Sheboygan.

Even if.

～ℓ～

"You've done it now, brother," Cosmos commented with a wry tone.

Nikos let his chin drop to his chest with a tired sigh. "I made her cry."

"You did. You suck."

"Big," he agreed.

"We told you to tell her."

Nikos nodded his head, picking up the peeler. "You did."

"And now look."

"You know, I'm really sick of Mitch inadvertently fucking up my love life."

Cosmos frowned. "Uh, sorry? You have no love life. If what you told me about last night with Frankie is true—you blew it, pal. You skipped out on her, resisted your manly urges, whatever—it's exactly what you should have done because for the hundredth time, no good can come from you hooking up with a woman who's on the rebound. Besides, you left the door wide open for Marco and his well-worn coat of pain and self-pity to cloak the fair Frankie and win her heart. There's nothing a chick digs more than a guy with gen-u-ine feelings. She'll be his problem in no time flat. And then you can forget all about Frankie and her issues that you seem to find so irresistible. Did it ever occur to you to maybe date a woman who isn't on the most-wanted list for rebound relationships?"

Nikos yanked another potato from the bag with a rough hand and said with a sharp, unforgiving tongue, "Cos, shut the hell up. I mean it. Shut up *now*."

"I'm just looking out for you the way you seem to want to look out for every woman who needs a knight in shining armor. Not to mention, stray animals, and even drunk gamblers like Hector," he whispered, looking over his shoulder with a guilty glance toward Hector's corner of the kitchen. "Admit it, you're a sucker for anyone who needs help. You've been that way all your life. Stray animals, lost souls—whatever. You're in for saving them."

"And that's a bad thing? Look at how well Hector's turned out."

"You feed the homeless guy who sleeps on the bench outside, Nikos. The point is, you have a savior complex."

"Benny's a good guy. Just down on his luck," he defended. "Mama feeds him, too."

"Look, all I'm saying is you don't need Frankie's shit rocking your world, and I'll say that as many times as it takes to get it through your thick skull."

Nikos remained silent, refusing to take his brother's bait. The hell he'd let Marco have a crack at the woman he wanted. The. Hell.

He didn't like that he was coming to want Frankie far more than even he was comfortable with. Forcing himself to leave that car last night had been an act of sheer willpower so physically difficult, he had a sore jaw this morning from clenching his teeth.

Frankie was a woman newly free of the marital ties that bind. One who hadn't yet experienced what her life could be when she found out who she was. A woman who could still possibly have feelings for the man she was married to for eighteen years. He'd been burned by that kind of woman—a woman in transition, on the rebound.

But he didn't want a woman in transition.

He wanted one forever.

And Frankie just wasn't a woman he should be considering to play the role of his partner.

Yet, here he was.

Still.

Considering.

CHAPTER NINE

From the journal of Frankie Bennett: Oh, I'm not reluctant at all when I write—game on, sistah! No more dastardly deeds, Chloe Whatserfaceopolus. Got that? You've picked the wrong loon with a wooden spoon. Heh. My crazy—it rhymes. Oh, and in the spirit of the season—Fa-la-la-la-la-la-la-la-la this, you troublemaker, 'cause I'm gonna rain all over your Silent Night with so much shit, you'll pray it's *you* who's run over by a reindeer instead of Grandma!

Jasmine snuggled closer to Simon, shooing a jealous Gary away. Closing her eyes, she inhaled with a deep, cleansing breath in mind. She wasn't the most experienced woman when it came to keeping things uncomplicated, but she was certainly going to try.

Which meant not reveling in the sheer joy of having a strong, sexy-as-hell man holding her against his tight, too-young-for-her body. "You should call Win," she forced herself to say. It was the last thing she wanted, but she was sticking to her guns. A relationship on her terms, and her terms meant no sleepovers for the quarterback.

She wouldn't have any man getting too comfortable in her hard-won space. This was hers. Paid for with money she earned herself every week. That fact used to make her smile with such pride. Pretty Jasmine making an honest living all on her own without the aid of a sugar daddy. All of her so-called ex-friends who fully expected her to hunt down the nearest senior citizen capable of taking care of her could piss off.

Yet lately, since she'd met Simon and they'd culminated this wild, physical thing between them, those very things had taken on a rather narrow, pointless meaning.

Somehow, calling the couch she'd found for such a bargain at the Salvation Army "hers all hers" was no longer as much of a coup as it once was; now, it was—just a couch.

It was her couch. Indeed. She was pathetically proud she'd saved to buy it. Yet who really cared that a couch represented her struggle for independence? Early on in her divorce, the material things she was afforded by her own earnings had left her glowing. Now, other things left her glowing. Other less materialistic more emotionally satisfying things.

And that was becoming damned uncomfortable. She didn't want to feel this way about Simon—or anyone—but most especially the rich, fun-loving Simon. She wanted to live life on her own terms, be free to do as she pleased, when she pleased without having to atone for her every movement. She wanted to lie around in her pajamas and not have to gussy up unless she chose to.

You couldn't do that if you had an anchor around your thigh—even if the anchor was luscious. Even if.

Simon brushed her hair from her shoulder, planting soft kisses on it, working his way down to her nipple. "Why should we wake Win when you have a perfectly nice bed I can sleep in?"

Yeah, Jasmine. Why? "Because you have your own perfectly nice bed, and it's only nine o' clock. I'm sure Win's still up watching *Supernanny*. A good thing, too. He could use all the tips she has to offer on parenting a spoiled, out-of-control man-child," Jasmine said, realizing there was no hard, accusatory edge to her tone this time when she teased Simon about being a boy in a man's body.

Simon laughed against her breast, the warm ripple of air making her squirm with delicious anticipation. "If you'd just let me, I'd spoil you right along with me."

"I've been spoiled, bad boy. I don't need any man's gifts or trinkets or fancy meals to keep me coming back for more. I come back for more because I *choose* to come back for more. Period."

The determination in her voice rang sour, even to her own ears. But she couldn't let go of her need to prove she wasn't in this for anything more than the physical pleasure it wrought. If Simon knew how close he was to touching a place in her heart she didn't want touched, he'd have the upper hand.

No can do.

Simon had gone in for the kill on his hunt to date her in a big way. Initially, he'd come off like every other clown who had some cash to throw around. He'd infuriated her from the start. But that fury had turned into a playful game. When she'd finally given in, she'd made the terms of their relationship clear.

So instead of pushing her with lavish meals and gifts, Simon allowed himself to be pushed, something Jasmine knew he didn't like. Pulling her lips to his, he chuckled again. "I get it. You're sleeping with me on your terms, but do you think maybe you could ask for a raise some time soon?"

She wrapped her hands around his thick wrists when he covered her with his body, spreading her legs apart while fighting a groan of unadulterated pleasure. "Why would I do that?"

"So I can have something better to eat than a number three combo at McDonald's."

Her smile was peevish. "That's all I can afford."

"But it's not all *I* can afford, fruitcup."

"Keep your financials to yourself and learn to love the Quarter Pounder, buddy."

"If I can love a Quarter Pounder, why can't you learn to love my personal chef?"

"Because I can't pay for a personal chef to love."

"You're being ridiculous." He'd given this same argument since they'd begun dating, or whatever they were calling this. Simon just couldn't grasp the concept of a divorced, working woman's freedom and all its blissful budgeting on a shoestring.

"You dare say that now when you're about to tap this?" she said playfully, nuzzling his neck.

"There is that," he murmured with a husky groan before sinking into her, making her forget Quarter Pounders and budgeting and her rebellious need to keep him at a safe distance.

~ total ~

Frankie hit the diner two days after her scuffle with Nikos a new woman. With her sparkling new attitude, she breezed past the narrow-eyed Chloe without so much as a rumble in her not-so-nervous-anymore stomach.

So, neener, neener, neener.

She had to remind herself she was a new woman when she almost ran smack into Nikos, who was taking inventory. "Morning," she said with a cheerful smile, the one she'd rehearsed nine hundred gotrillion times in the mirror on her days off. The happy, secure, well-adjusted, "not in need of help from the psych department" smile.

"I suck," he said, deadpan and somber in all his gorgeousness.

"Did you lose count of the olive jars again? You want help?"

"That's not what I mean, and I think you know it."

"Ohhhhh, you mean the other day, right?" she asked, all breezy and carefree as part of her new-woman package. "Forget it. What's done is done." She looked for the fresh green peppers in the fridge. "Now, I know Cosmos must need peppers chopped. I heard two orders for omelets on my way into the kitchen. What's on tap for today, slave driver?"

"Frankie?" He grabbed her arm, swinging her to face him.

She gave his hand a pointed look, lifting her arm in question, returning to her promise to remember he was just a man. No matter how manly. "What? C'mon, haste makes waste."

"Slow down and listen to me make nice with you for being a jackass. It doesn't happen often."

"That you're a jackass or that you make nice?"

He grinned, warm, sexy. "I'm sorry I didn't tell you about Mitch and Carrie and Marco and whatever else I didn't tell you about. I swear in the future, anything Mitch does, if he so much as thinks about behaving badly, when I psychically tap into his mind, you'll be the first to know."

She couldn't help but laugh. "Well, thanks, but I don't care what Mitch has done anymore. I didn't care as much about what he'd done as about what I didn't know he'd done. I think it was more about how utterly humiliating it is to be the last one to know what was right under your nose. I felt stupid and blind is all. But I'm over it because his past bad behavior is out of my control. So let's get on with the business of this thing called slave labor."

Now he chuckled, too, deep and rich, something she'd missed on her time off. *So pathetic, Frankie.* "So, friends?"

She backed up against the cool exterior of the refrigerator with a grin. "You mean like the kind who call each other on the phone and talk nail polish, *Tiger Beat*, and Scott Baio crushes? Or the kind that have a peaceful, *honest* working relationship with no random surprises that leave one another blindsided?" she teased.

"It's a tough choice. I mean, we are talking Scott Baio here, but I'll take peace, honesty, and goodwill toward men for five hundred, Alex."

Frankie stuck out her hand. "Deal."

Nikos took it, entwining his fingers with hers. "Deal. Now in other important news. Christmas," he said, still holding her hand.

"What about it?" she asked, forcing herself to keep her fingers from trembling.

Nikos wiggled his eyebrows. "The Antonakas Christmas bash, ma'am. It's huge. Like invitation-to-the-White-House huge. Well, maybe not that huge, but there are at least as many people at our annual Christmas party as there are at a White House formal. I know it's late in the game and you might already have plans, but I forgot to tell you before your day off. It's Christmas Eve. I know that's tomorrow, but we have tons of food, family by the busload, more nieces, nephews, and grandkids than ten daycare centers, and more chaos than a three-ring circus. It's loud, bad for calorie counting, and there's usually a drunken brawl with ringside seats, and we try to keep it all-inclusive for every faith. It's also one of the rare few days a year when the diner's closed. And of course, both you and Gail are invited. All the employees and their families usually at least do a drive-by if they have other plans."

Of which she had none, and that hadn't depressed her much at all until Nikos described his family's celebration. Then disappointment crept into her thoughts. *Employees. Know your place, Bennett. Got it.*

Frankie's smile waned, but her tone, she was proud to say, remained steady as a rock. "Sounds like fun. I'm in, but I wouldn't count on Gail. She was hedging about some invitation her gentleman caller extended to her, but she didn't want to leave me alone. She'll be happy to know I have plans. You know, the *employee* kind. So sure, I'd love to come. Need help prepping for it? Bring something? Maybe something with goat cheese and figs?" she joked.

Clearly, he'd missed her emphasis on "employee" because he

skipped right over it and zeroed in on the party planning. "Nope. The rest of the family gives us a day off and they do the cooking. Anyway, good deal. So now that we've made nice, I have some details to work out for tomorrow's party."

"Then I'll get to work," she replied with forced good cheer.

By her late-morning break, Frankie smiled with the satisfaction of a job well done. A mountain of chopped onions and garlic even Barnabas couldn't criticize lay in wait for Cosmos to marinate his next batch of brisket in, and she'd reorganized the fridge so each item he needed was at the ready.

The rumble of her stomach led her to find Voula and her infamous meatloaf. "Look at my Frankie," she said with a gleam in her eye. "Now Mama doesn't have to force her to eat. The horse finds the grass all by herself."

"Water. You're leading a horse to water, and if I eat any more of your water, I'll need a bigger car," Frankie said, smiling back, giving her a squeeze to her shoulders.

Voula pinched her at the waist. "In no time we have to buy you bigger pants. That makes my cockles warm. Now eat and make Mama smile." She winked, piling the meatloaf and fries high on the plate, then dousing it with an overflowing ladle of brown gravy.

Frankie took the plate, and she and Voula headed to Nikos's office, where he'd kindly offered to let her bring Kiki in for the afternoon while Gail was in Atlantic City on a senior overnight trip. As she walked, she scooped up a heaping forkful to stuff it in her mouth with a blissful sigh. "Voula, you should market this. It's the best meatloaf I've ever eaten. It's simple and rustic and there are so many flavors, my mouth does the happy dance. Trust me when I tell you, when I was married to Mitch, I tried a million different ideas, variations on the original theme, trying to make the perfect meatloaf. They all paled in comparison."

Voula's eyebrow rose as she made her way around Nikos's desk to gather up Kiki from a napping Barnabas's lap. "You mean mine is better than the bad Mitch's?"

Frankie giggled, smiling at how comfortable Kiki was with Voula. "Yours is better than some of the best chefs in the world, Voula. It's like uber-meatloaf."

She frowned, her round face wrinkling. "Uber?"

"Like the crème de la crème. The *best*," Frankie assured her around a crispy-tender French fry.

Voula nodded, as if she knew she had the world at her feet with just one bite of her concoction of ground beef and spices. She dug around in her apron pocket, pulling out a treat for Kiki, who took it with her usual somber gratitude. "It is a secret I tell you one day, Frankie." She chuckled, tapping the dog's nose with affection. "But you know, my memory is so bad, I have to look at the recipe every time I make."

Frankie gave Kiki a quick kiss and waved a fork at Voula on her way out of the office, plate in hand. "Whatever's in it, it's hardcore, and you should guard the secret with your life."

Voula's chuckle followed her out into the dining area where she went in search of her bottle of water and her latest magazine endeavor into finding a hobby, poetry writing.

"Frankie?"

A foreboding chill of unease skittered up her spine. No. It couldn't be. How? And more important, why?

"Frankie?" An all-too-familiar hand tapped her shoulder.

Dear Universe, would it be an insult to my mother if I legally changed my name? I don't think she'd be too upset with me, seeing as each time someone says it, the destruction of my fragile psyche and my newfound happy place typically occur.

Damn it all. Just when she was getting her groove back, or if not her groove, then at least a safe distance from the ledge she'd so precariously teetered on—in walks the one person who almost sent her over the edge.

She sucked in a breath, mentally arming for battle.

Okay, Frankie, time to man up. In the spirit of this changed-woman gig you've hired on to—face the ex. Like a big girl. Like you mean it.

Like the prick owes you money.

Her turn was a slow execution while she composed her face, forcing her body language to express an air of casual indifference. "Mitch."

He smiled, that charming "come let me show you my spiderweb" smile. Nothing about him had changed. He was still handsome and camera perfect. His periwinkle blue shirt had not a crease in it, and his steel gray silk trousers were as smooth as glass. "It's so good to see you, Frankie." Mitch opened his arms as though she'd fall right back into them.

At one time, maybe as little as just five months ago, maybe, just maybe, she might well have dived back into the shallow end of the pool. Even with his infidelity, if only to find comfort in the routines of her old life with him and not to have to face life alone.

Yet, seeing him now, she was never so glad she'd slept her postdivorce trauma almost entirely away. The only emotion she could summon for Mitch was distaste and a mild case of anxiety. Anxiety that had nothing to do with his physical presence but rather stemmed from her question as to what exactly he wanted.

Booyah for time and distance and oh, yeah, functioning brain matter.

Frankie took a step back, placing her half-eaten meatloaf on the front counter. "How did you find me?"

His smile upped its wattage. "What difference does it make? I'm here now."

As though that made everything all right as rain. "Phew, thank God, right? I mean, how was I going to go on breathing like I have for the past seven months without you?" She raised a condescending eyebrow to pack her punch.

Mitch chose to ignore her snipe, and instead, sat down on one of the counter stools, laying his forearm beside his identical, as yet untouched plate of meatloaf. "Can we talk?"

Frankie's head cocked in an absurd parody of "what the fuck?" "About?"

He patted the stool next to his in a gesture of friendly warmth. "What's been going on in your life. How you're doing. You know, conversations people have when they haven't seen someone they care about in a long time."

People you care about? Seriously? Oh, tongue don't fail me now. "When you find that someone who cares about me, have your people call my people. Until then, go away."

"Aw, Frankie. We have some hard feelings between us, don't we?"

"Well, they're not soft and squishy."

Mitch gave her his best "I haz a sad" expression. "Can't we let bygones be bygones?"

"Oh, they're bygone. All gone, in fact. Now go back home to Bamby."

"Bamby and I are over."

"Did she find out about Carrie?" Frankie asked like butter wouldn't melt in her mouth.

"Carrie?"

Frankie marveled at how dumbstruck his perfectly aged face appeared. How many women had there really been before Bamby? Something to ponder as she sent him packing. "I know how hard it must be to keep track of all the female pairs of eyes you've wobbled," she sympathized, letting her words drip with false consolation.

"Carrie was a woman you met right here in this diner. A foodie, so to speak. A foodie married to someone else. But that's all water under the proverbial bridge now, Mitch. The past is the past and all that jazz. I don't know why you're here or how you found me, and frankly, I don't give a prostitute's checkup why, because we have nothing to say to each other. Now, you're interrupting my lunch hour. Go. Away."

Mitch's face went hard for a moment, before he recovered and slapped on his smile especially made for his fans. The "I am the great chef and you are the minion" smile. "I can't believe you're working in a diner." He pushed his food around his plate, wincing as though the mere idea that the food didn't cost a hundred bucks physically hurt him.

"I can't believe you have the balls to mock my job or the food here. First of all, that's the best meatloaf you'll ever eat, *Chef Mitch*. So if you plan to be insulting, take it elsewhere or I *will* bring my wooden spoon out of retirement. Second of all, at least here the only monstrous ego I have to contend with is the homeless guy's out front who claims I'm blocking his sun when I park in the space in front of his bench. Believe me when I tell you, being employed here is like rainbows and rocking horses compared to working for you."

But Mitch was ignoring her again. He'd decided to brave a bite of food for heathens and was too busy making groans of chef pleasure. "This is amazing." Mitch held up a forkful of meatloaf. "Just amazing."

Frankie gave him a sour glare. "Sometimes food for heathens can be that way."

"Any chance I could get the recipe?" he asked, licking the fork like a cat licking cream from his whiskers.

Beyond flabbergasted at Mitch's bold request, Frankie held herself away from the counter with stiff arms. "So you can tell the world you created it like you did with all of my recipes for the show? Fat chance, Mitch. Besides, it's a family secret, and even if I did know it, I certainly wouldn't give it to you so you could claim it as your own stroke of genius."

"How's my Kik?"

"*Your* Kik? You mean the dog you cared so much about you had a clause put in our divorce that said you wouldn't be held responsible for any of her veterinary bills? That Kik?"

His face didn't change, but his eyes shifted. "I loved Kiki," he defended so weak and insincere, it was all Frankie could do not to gouge his eyes out with her fork.

She shook her head with an angry swish. "No, you loved the ratings she brought the show. You loved letting everyone believe the PETA-loving Mitch had saved her. But we both know the truth about that, don't we?"

His mouth thinned, but only for a moment before he took his next turn in his attempt to keep things light. "So, created any interesting recipes for your new job?"

Frankie's eyes narrowed. Now she knew what this was about. Oh, yes indeed. Mitch was recipe dry. What he lacked in food creativity, he'd made up for in charm, and that was how he'd nabbed the show at Bon Appetit. Because although she hated to cook, she had once loved to blend spices and create concoctions for Mitch. She'd had a good sense of what worked and what didn't. She was also a master at substitution when they re-created a recipe and couldn't decipher a spice or ingredient. So sayeth the great and powerful Mitch.

Her eyebrow shot up. "What's the matter, Mitch? Running out of new and original recipes for the show?"

"I miss your input." Mitch shot her a remorseful glance.

"No, you miss me doing all the work. Too bad you and Bamby broke up. Maybe she could have helped you with your lack of originality." So shazam.

With a lean into her, Mitch's eyes feigned contrition. "I admit I've had a setback or two. Ratings . . . well, they've been . . . Never mind." He shooed the sentiment away as though he hoped she'd wring it out of him. When she remained silent, he added, "Maybe you'd like to come back and consult? I know Bon Appetit would love to have you."

"I'd rather be hooked for cash," was her dry response. One that surprised even her. "I like my job here, and I like the people I work with. Being left high and dry without a pot to piss in made me realize I'd rather be poor than be your wife."

Oh, revelation. It was true. She was beginning to love more than just Nikos's hot abs and suh-weet ass. She was in love with his family, their love of one another, their laughter, and even their bold, honest opinions. She even loved getting up at four in the morning to be in by five. Okay, maybe she didn't love it, but it had come to represent a labor of her love for these people who gave her a reason to want to get up.

"You don't really mean that . . ."

Mitch had said that often in their marriage, and she'd let herself believe it. But not anymore. "Oh, on the contrary. You can bet your bippy I do. Now for the last time, go away!" She hissed the words as quietly as she could, attempting to slide away from him to the next stool over.

But Mitch grabbed hold of her sweater, tugging her back to him, leaving her pressed against his body. "This is a public place, Frankie. I have every right to be here, honey." The words themselves might be threatening, but they had a seductive hint to them she wasn't liking.

"Yeah, and it's *my* public place, and if I say you go, *you go, honey*," Nikos said from behind them, a clear threat in his words.

Frankie swung her head around to find Nikos, hands on his lean hips, an angry scowl tightening his usually relaxed face. Her first inclination was to stop Nikos from rescuing her one more time, but that notion fled, because seriously, her radiant warmth over having a real live hero was winning the race against her new-woman independence.

Mitch swiveled on his stool, waving his fork around to point it directly at Nikos. "Do you know who I am?"

Oh, the celebrity card. Well played, but clearly not making the intended impact with Knight In Shining Armor Nikos.

"We have a problem here?" Cosmos growled.

"No," Frankie began, holding up a hand. "It's okay—I'll handle—"

"I think we do. I'm being harassed by the pseudo Calvin Klein model," Mitch said caustically. "Maybe his jeans are so tight he's lost his ability to behave properly in a social setting."

Uh, eek.

The situation went from mildly threatening to all-out warfare when Cosmos gathered Mitch up by the collar of his wrinkle-free, periwinkle blue shirt, pushing Frankie away from Mitch and smack into Nikos. "Yeah? Well, I'm Calvin's little brother, and you're not welcome in this diner. If I were you, I'd hit the bricks that led you here."

Mitch blustered, his passive face going from pale to an angry crimson red. "Take your hands off me!"

Out of nowhere, Voula was sprawled across the top of the counter, hip deep, waving her rolling pin as flour spewed in the air, with Barnabas right behind her. "You go away, bad Mitch, or I show you what I do with this rolling pin!" she shouted.

Barnabas tugged at Voula, but not to thwart her efforts to clock Mitch. Nay, he wanted a shot at him, too. He shook the three-pronged fork from the kitchen at Mitch's shoulder. "Go back to your TV kitchen, Mr. Fancy Pants, and you leave our Frankie alone!"

Nikos diffused the situation with two hands by snatching Voula's rolling pin away from her and simultaneously latching onto Cosmos, then blocking Barnabas. "Knock it off. *All of you!*" he roared, making Frankie glad the lunch hour hadn't quite begun. "Mitch, take it on out of here, and don't come back. If you bother Frankie again, it'll be your ass on *my* plate! Now get the hell outta my diner!"

Mitch shoved his way between Cosmos and Nikos, yanking at his shirt with an angry hand to straighten it as though someone lesser than him had touched him. "I'll have you arrested, you animals! This was assault!"

Cosmos opened his mouth, but Nikos clamped it shut with just one glare, pulling Frankie tight against his strong side. "You be sure and get my name right when you file your complaint, Bennett. It's Nikos Antonakas. Write it down now. One O, three A's in my last name. Or do you want Frankie to do it for you? You know, because you're incapable of wiping your own ass without an assist."

Mitch shoved his way toward the doors of the diner, brushing against the small Christmas tree with so much force it fell over in a heap of crashing gold bulbs and sprays of tinsel.

Chloe backed away from the corner she was skulking in, but not before a look passed between her and the retreating Mitch that Frankie didn't have time to question. "You'll hear from my attorneys!" he yelped into the cold rush of air.

Frankie was speechless—mortified at the plate of meatloaf dripping down the front of the counter in globs of ground beef and gravy. Voula huffed her fury as Barnabas slammed the heavy fork down on the counter. Cosmos's nostrils flared, and Nikos's jaw clenched.

Tears for the trouble she'd brought welled in her eyes, flustering her. "I—I'm—I'm sorry. Omigod . . . I'm sorry. I don't know how he found out I was working here. I'll clean it up," she said with haste, dropping to her knees to recover the broken pieces of plate. The moment she knelt, scrambling to clean the mess, a memory of her old life collided with the new.

Her on the floor, clearing away some mess Mitch had made in a fit of temper or just out of carelessness. Would she always be the one who had to clean up the messes Mitch made? Or could she hand the baton over sometime soon?

Voula was the first to come around the counter, pulling Frankie to her feet to envelope her in a hug. "This is no your fault, Frankie. Mitch, he is bad. Dirty, dirty bad. We don't let no one treat family bad," she spat, the stray strands of her hair puffing out from the wind of it.

Barnabas was instantly at his wife's side, reaching for Frankie to engulf her in a hug doused suspiciously in garlic and onions. "I won't have that Mitch here bothering our Frankie. Even if you don't chop like Barnabas does it, you are family."

Frankie leaned out from him and burst out laughing. "Did you rechop what I've already done?"

"Bah," Barnabas scowled, shamefaced, his dark hair falling to his eyes. "It just needs a little more." He held two chubby fingers together to emphasize what a little more was.

Frankie gave his thick neck a tight squeeze, fighting tears of gratitude. "I'm sorry he made such a mess."

Barnabas pinched her cheek. "S'okay. Nikos will help you clean it up, and I'll take over the chopping while you do."

"Papa," Cosmos warned. "You come with me, old man. Sit and I'll make you a patty melt, just the way you like it." Cosmos led his father out of the dining area while Nikos stooped to help her.

Frankie waved him away, unable to look him in the eye. "It's okay. This was my fault. I'll clean it."

Cupping her chin, Nikos forced her to look at him. "No, Frankie. This wasn't your fault at all. You think you might wanna stop taking the blame for Mitch's asinine behavior any time soon? He's a big boy, you know."

Her cheeks warmed to his fingers under her chin. All that resolve, bolstered by all those little talks with herself about how she wasn't going to fall for another man who could rival Mitch's charm, was sliding.

Do you hear that, Frankie Bennett? You're slipping . . .

Shut up, already. Nikos the dreamboat Antonakas just played Robin Hood to my Maid Marion. The least I can do is thank him.

But it doesn't have to be with those big gooey eyes and that hitch in your breathing. A handshake is perfectly acceptable—socially proper even.

Shhhhh. "Thank you for coming to my rescue," Frankie whispered.

"Wow—did that hurt to say or what?" he teased, his eyes liquid pools of black silk.

"Well, sometimes even I can admit, rescuing is okay."

Nikos winked, bushing her hair away from her eyes. "Especially when family does it, eh?"

With a lean back on her haunches, she giggled. "This makes you my brother, Antonakas. I always wanted an older brother."

"Who said I'm older?" Nikos pretended to be affronted.

"I'm betting you're at least forty."

"Was it my sagging ass or the crow's-feet around my eyes?"

"Hah!" Like this man had to worry about sagging anything. "No, silly. It was your mother. She spilled the beans when she was bemoaning her lack of grandchildren."

"Ah. Well, I'm working on it."

"With Chloe?" Omigod. Had that burning question just escaped from her thoughts and out through her lips? The one that had tortured her since Jasmine told her Chloe was supposed to marry Nikos?

Nikos's face took on a serious slant, the sun shining through the window lingering on his chiseled cheekbones. "No. Not with Chloe.

That was never an option. No matter how Mama feels. And I'm forty-two, funny lady."

"So you are my older brother. You know, in the spirit of *family*."

His pause lingered between them, as though he was measuring what he'd say next. "Maybe we should just label me a kissing cousin," he chuckled out.

Well, sure, that'd work if he'd actually kissed her. The thought sobered her. "Maybe. Now go help your brother stop your father from rechopping everything I already chopped."

Nikos rose, taking the broken pieces of plate with him. "Chloe? Would you get the mop and grab this, please? I'll catch you later, cuz," he snickered.

Frankie wiped down the stools' legs before rising only to come face-to-face with Chloe and her mop. She leaned against the handle of it with narrowed eyes, her stance defensive. "How long do you suppose you can keep this up?" she asked.

Frankie sighed. If she could contend with Mitch, Chloe was like a day at Six Flags. "Keep what up, Chloe?"

"The damsel-in-distress gig? It's pathetic to watch you fall all over Nikos."

Armed with Nikos's admission and still fuming from Mitch's intrusion on an otherwise perfectly good day, Frankie couldn't hold her tongue. "You know, Chloe, maybe it's time *you* gave it up."

"What's that, Frankie?"

"The idea that you and Nikos are ever going to be anything more than employer and *waitress*." She crossed her arms over her chest with a return glare of defiance. So, yeah.

Chloe's face went glacial, her eyes like chips of ice. "Why don't you go back to Mitch where you belong?"

An ugly suspicion made Frankie ask, "Why would I do that, Chloe?"

"Because you don't belong in this diner, and you never will."

"How do you suppose Mitch found out where I worked, Chloe, or that I worked at all?"

She had to give Chloe credit for never batting an eyelash. She shrugged her slim shoulders. "How should I know?"

"It was *you*." Frankie stated it plainly, no question in her voice. She knew Chloe had somehow gotten in touch with Mitch and brought him here to stir up trouble so Nikos would be angry with her. The urge to wrap her hands around Chloe's neck made her fingers itch.

"I don't know what you mean, Frankie. The only thing I do know is this: Nikos may not want me, but he doesn't want you either, or if he does, it won't be for long. A woman like you could never hold a man like Nikos's attention for long."

A woman like her. Skinny, painful to look at, jacked-up Frankie. "Ah, well. I guess it's better than never having his attention at all, isn't it, Chloe?"

Chloe's lips formed a sneer.

Score one for the hot mess.

"You watch yourself around me, Frankie. Just watch it," she seethed, shoving the mop to stand upright against the countertop, then stomping off in the direction of the bathrooms.

Frankie's eyes narrowed in thought.

Well, then.

Anger, spiteful and rebellious, reared its ugly head.

Chloe of the long dark tresses and the legs of a runway model was in for a little surprise tomorrow tonight.

Frankie Bennett was out for a taste of some jugular.

Chloe's.

The hell she was going to let that woman have the best of her. She'd had enough taking it up the ass to last her a lifetime. No more quiet, reserved, well-behaved Francis.

She'd show her what jacked up was all about.

There weren't many people, at this stage of her life, who'd guess Frankie had once been considered pretty hot. She'd laughed with Mitch about it when her picture was labeled as such in a gossip rag. Sadly, he'd laughed, too. But Mitch had, at one time, paid a lot of money to have people actually show her how to achieve pretty hot.

So pretty hot it would be.

Well, it would have to be only pretty hot because she really didn't have the money to be ultra hot.

Or the boobs.

So affordable hot would have to do.

But she'd work every last hot nerve she had until they were raw and bleeding.

Nikos Antonakas'd better hope his eyeballs were securely in their sockets. Because she planned to wobble them with her fabulousness until they fell out of his head. (And if his nether regions enjoyed the view, too, well, booyah.)

And with that went the very last shred of her efforts to just say no to the gregariously charming.

CHAPTER TEN

From the journal of a "very sick with nerves, and more reluctant by the second" Frankie Bennett: Note to self: Maybe in the future, you idiot, when you decide to spin a fantasy about rutting with the man who's essentially your boss and the only source of income you may potentially ever have, you might want to have those ugly misgivings whilst you're in the safe zone otherwise known as "fantasy." That word implies it hasn't happened yet, you twit. Once you slap on those false eyelashes—you're committed. So says Jasmine.

"Jesus, Jasmine. How much glue did you use? I won't be able to see my target if my eyes are glued together. Not to mention the fact that these things are like bat wings. I could annihilate an entire small African village with the virtual windstorm I make when I blink," Frankie said, trying to pry her eyes apart after Jasmine applied the ridiculously long false eyelashes they'd giggled over at Walgreens. "It's like the eyelash apacolypse."

"Oh, shush, and stop complaining. You said you wanted a dramatic effect. Drama and all its effects have their sacrifices. Wait until you've worn that cheap push-up bra we bought for longer than an hour. You don't know sacrifice until then." Jasmine gave a fond glance to Kiki, sitting at Frankie's feet. "Tell Mommy, Kiki. Beautiful takes work, right, gorgeous?"

"I said I wanted effect. I definitely didn't mean the kind that inspires the throwing of small change."

Jasmine giggle-snorted. "Stop. I can't line your eyes if you're making me laugh. Would you just be quiet and trust me? I know what I'm doing. You're going to be drop-dead, stone-cold gorgeous, and you'll be so classy Webster's will be beating your door down to put your picture next to the word. Now shut it, and let me finish your lipstick. Do not speak."

Frankie kept silent, yet she couldn't help but wonder, now that her anger had cooled, if this was a stupid thing to do. Whatever issue had held Nikos back the night he'd almost kissed her, it was probably a good enough reason to dissuade her from trying to pull this off.

Seriously, who did she think she was?

Jasmine tugged at her elbow, pulling her to stand in front of the mirror, then scooping up Kiki from the floor. She chucked the dog under her chin. "Doesn't Mommy look hot, Kik?"

Frankie's first glimpse of herself in full makeup since her divorce almost knocked her backward on her three-inch heels.

Jasmine nudged her from behind with a conspiratorial smile. "Would Jasmine steer you wrong?"

Wow, Frankie mouthed, but couldn't quite express in full syllables.

"Uh-huh," Jasmine crowed. "I told you I knew what I was doing. You've got some serious gorgeous going on, lady."

"I'd forgotten . . ."

Jasmine threw up a dismissive hand. "I know. After all the weeping and wailing is over and you get a gander at the woman you used to be, it's jaw-dropping to see the old you again. But look at yourself, Frankie. Really look. You're a beautiful woman."

Her reflection shimmered back at her, forcing her to scrutinize the Frankie Jasmine had created. The eyeshadow they'd chosen, a smoky green with charcoal and dark brown accents, gave her eyes a smoldering, seductive glow.

As it turned out, the eyelashes weren't ridiculously long at all, but framed her eyes, making them mysterious, as though she hid a secret only she knew the answer to. Adding the swipe of eyeliner beneath them gave her eyes an almond shape. Jasmine had managed to create cheekbones for her, too, taking away the gaunt, undernourished look everyone accused her of and replacing it with a high slant she'd only seen on runway models.

Jasmine squeezed her shoulders with affection, grinning from behind her. "I think the lipstick works, huh?"

Oh, indeed. It worked. It wasn't the red Frankie had originally chosen. Instead, it was a matted taupe, glossed over with a touch of peach, making her lips look full and shiny-lush. "I bow to your expertise. You know your stuff," Frankie agreed, giving her hair a fluff, hair that Jasmine had insisted needed the dye job of a lifetime.

In still more of Jasmine's wisdom, she'd picked a red that left Frankie's long, thick strands a muted gold and auburn. The color shone in all the loose curls flowing over her shoulders and three inches past her breasts to cascade over a bronze, sleeveless shirt littered with rows of circular, shimmering dots, hanging by invisible threads.

The neckline was prim, stopping at her collarbone. Yet, once Jasmine had worked her seamstress magic, it hugged her body, emphasizing her pushed-up breasts and tapering at her waist to flare over her slender hips covered in an ivory skirt that fell to just above her knees.

Jasmine waved tape at her. "Okay, kiddo, let me run some of this over that skirt one more time. Gary decided it was his latest conquest in the game of luuuurve." She chuckled, slapping the tape against the black patches of stray cat hair until she was satisfied. "Okay—you're good to go."

Hearing Jasmine's final approval made Frankie's stomach heave so hard, she had to catch the edge of her aunt's vanity to hold herself up.

"Hey, princess," Jasmine taunted. "Stop. Stop now. I will not have you flipping out. After all the work I've done on your overhaul, I deserve a public showing."

"I can't do this, Jasmine. Who am I kidding? I'm no man-eater." Oh God. What had she been thinking when she'd decided to take Chloe out with her va-va-voom? It was all fun and games till people laughed and pointed.

"Nope. You're definitely not a vixen, and if you change your mind once we get to the party, fine. Cold feet happen, but let me remind you of one little thing."

Her freshly waxed eyebrow rose. "That is?"

"You'll probably still want Nikos tomorrow in the cold light of day just like you did yesterday and the day before, and then you and regret can become strange bedfellows. If you're too chicken to go get your man, okay. I'd never want you to do something that makes you uncomfortable. But, remember, it was you who called me from your car, desperation in your voice, begging me to teach you how to nab a hot Greek. Wasn't it?"

Yes. That had been her. There'd been ranting, some whining, and then, after much egging on from Jasmine, a war cry. But earlier she'd been fueled by her anger and an irrational wish to see Chloe squirm in her tight miniskirt until she imploded, scattering little pieces of her lithe body all over the diner.

Now? Not so much. Not after a good night's sleep and some much needed perspective. Yet, there remained that wee niggle that all her Nikos dreams could possibly come true if someone just made a move. The niggle Jasmine had planted when she'd said Nikos was attracted to her. The niggle Chloe found such a threat. That was the one that still sparked her engine.

"Yes. That was me, but then the adrenaline rush of all those stark images you put in my head of Chloe turning on a spit like a leg of lamb . . . uh, passed."

Jasmine's blonde head shook back and forth. "Right. Because of all that time and perspective bullshit. And that's fine. If you don't ever want to explore what *could* happen between you and Nikos because neither of you will get off your ass, more's the pity. But listen, if you do nothing else tonight, you're going to that Christmas party as the beautiful, confident woman I know festers inside of you. And you can bet your ass, I'm not letting six-dollar false eyelashes go to waste."

Frankie threw her head back and laughed. "It would be like breaking a commandment or something."

"Or my heart. Whatever," Jasmine said with playful sarcasm. "Now"—she held her hand out, palm up—"we out?"

A shaky breath later, hoping to absorb some of her friend's confidence, Frankie slapped her hand in Jasmine's. "We're out."

Gail's whistle of approval from the kitchen made Frankie chuckle. She spun around on her heels. "You like?"

Gail matted her lipstick with a tissue. "You look pretty fancy there, sassafras. So, you ready to get your man?"

Frankie bristled, pulling on the long, light beige trench coat Jasmine had loaned her, and putting Kiki in her crate. "Who said anything about getting a man?"

Both Jasmine and Gail rolled their eyes. "You have a push-up bra on, honey. It's a dead giveaway when a girl puts her wares on a push-up platter. Now you go have a yummy Greek for Christmas, and I'll see you in the morning for hot chocolate and blueberry scones, okay?"

Tradition. It had been her mother's and Gail's Christmas morning tradition to make blueberry scones and have hot chocolate while they unwrapped presents. The twinkling of the lights on the small Christmas tree they'd bought together made Frankie's heart clench with yearning for her mother.

Frankie gave her aunt a hug, squeezing her hard while inhaling the scent of everything she considered warm and welcoming. "Definitely. Have fun with Garner and say hello for me."

Gail snickered, throwing her Christmas silk scarf around her freshly washed and roller-dried hair. "Don't you worry about me and Garner. We wrote the book on fun."

Frankie gave her aunt a gentle shove toward the door before she revealed any more intimate senior deets on fun. "Bye, Aunt Gail."

"So, let's get going. Simon and Win are meeting us there. I'll drive," Jasmine offered.

A long, cleansing breath later and she was following Jasmine out to what she'd fondly called her C-Rex. A rusty red bucket from 1984 on four wheels, it was her pride and joy because the purchase had been a step toward the freedom she seemed so hell-bent on making sure everyone knew was hers.

The passenger door opened with a rusty creak, catching the wind and almost dragging Frankie with it. As she climbed in, her palms grew sweaty. To take her mind off what she was planning to do, Frankie asked, "Speaking of Simon, how's that working out?"

Jasmine turned the key in the ignition, her hand shaking from the frigid air that had moved in the night before and headed out of the village. She was silent for a few minutes before replying, "It's working—*for now*."

Frankie burrowed deeper into her loaner jacket, hoping the heat worked in Jasmine's clunker. "Wow, Jasmine. You think you could be any less enthusiastic about a guy like Simon wanting to date you?

I know pretty girls like you are used to rich, fabulous men chasing after them all the time, but Simon's different. I have a gut feeling."

"I don't want to judge, Francis, but your gut is what led you to threaten to kill your ex-husband on national television."

"Hater. It wasn't my gut. It was my crazy," Frankie said with a laugh. What she adored most about Jasmine was her balls-to-the-wall ability to call it as she saw it.

"Which makes you and your gut unreliable sources. Simon isn't any different than any other man."

"Is what you keep telling yourself," Frankie finished for her.

Jasmine sighed, gnawing at her lower lip with a distressed frown. "Sort of."

"So why won't you just let it happen?"

"Because after it happens is usually when the magic mysteriously wears off and they're off to the next younger, bigger-breasted babe."

Frankie clucked her tongue, chiding Jasmine. "You can't hide the look in your eyes when Simon walks into a room."

"Sure I can," she said, turning into the diner's parking lot. "He's blind."

Frankie covered her mouth to keep from snickering. "I meant from everyone else, you insensitive meanie-butt. And you know, I've been too caught up in my own crap to do any research, but if you don't mind me asking, how did Simon lose his sight?"

Jasmine ran her tongue over her lips and grimaced. "A car accident. The windshield smashed and he got glass in his eyes."

"I don't know, but the way he handles it, joking about it all the time and without the kind of bitter sarcasm behind his words you'd expect, makes him that much cuter to me, don't you think?" Frankie prodded.

Jasmine pulled her car into the first available space, stopping it with a groan of her tired brakes. "I think we should focus on our mission, Wonder Girl, and forget about Simon and me. So far, he's been a good boy about keeping this thing we have going, on my terms. We do a little dance, make a little love, and then he goes home. It's all I can handle right now."

Frankie shook her head, the long curls of her hair sticking to her lip gloss. "No. It's all you'll allow. Big difference."

"Listen, Maxine junior, back off with the advice, and let's go get your man. Now hand me my purse, hot stuff. We have a man to snare."

Frankie reached down to grab Jasmine's purse while her stomach swelled with fear. Jasmine took it with a raised eyebrow. "Get out, Frankie."

"You know, I really don't feel up to snaring a man tonight. I mean, it's soooo much work. All the small talk, the ego stroking, the ridiculous twirling of your hair and wetting your lips—and for what? Some sex?" *Ohhhhhh. Some sex. Sex, sex, sex.*

Jasmine popped her lips. "I get the impression sex with Nikos wouldn't just be 'some' sex. Look. It's cold. Simon's waiting. I'm hungry. The food is free. I can't afford to pass that up because it's not often lately I can save five ninety-nine for an extra value meal because I've happened upon free food. So either you take your skinny ass in there, or I drag you in there, keeping in mind I eat at least two and a half meals more than you a day, Big Macs being my energy bar of choice. Do you have any idea the kind of punch I can pack after eating so many Big Macs? You *do not* want to go with me, sister. Now hit it." She pointed a pink, home-manicured nail at the car door. Then, taking the matter into her own hands, Jasmine got out of the car, walked to the passenger side, and yanked the door open. "Out."

Frankie's breathing accelerated when the frigid air hit her lungs. She reached for Jasmine's arm to help her get onto the sidewalk in her spiky heels. "I can't breathe."

"That's because you have on a push-up bra. Breathing is a luxury meant for women with perky breasts. Stop stalling, Frankie. There are people in there who genuinely like you and respect your mad chopping-prep skills. Focus on them. Remember, the only thing you have to do is go inside. What happens after that, it's up to you."

"Yeah, yeah, yeah," she mocked, teetering across a patch of ice on the stairs leading to the door. "I'll be all regret and remorse if I don't go through with it. I'll still want Nikos tomorrow if I chicken out tonight. Don't you dare waste six-dollar false eyelashes, Frankie, blah, blah, blah."

Jasmine threw open the diner door with a sweep of her hand, her teeth chattering. "After you, Ms. Your Cup Runneth Over With Self-Esteem."

Her first step into the diner wobbled, her eyes focusing on her feet and a graceful entry. When a rush of warm air greeted her, she relaxed a little, letting her shoulders ease back. Until she looked up.

At all the eyes zeroed in on her.

There was a momentary hush in the room crowded with so many heads of dark hair, Frankie struggled to tell one from the other.

Was there schmeg on her lipstick? More cat hair on her skirt?

"I think you've officially made an entrance, Ms. Bennett. Don't you ever tell me again that false eyelashes might be just a little too over-the-top," Jasmine whisper-mocked from behind her, giving her ribs a jab with her elbow. "Go on. This is your moment."

"Frankie?" Voula, wide-eyed, arms opened, called. She pushed her way through the crowd, now recovered but still eyeing Frankie with gaping mouths. Voula caught her by the cheeks, cupping her face with warm, kitchen-rough hands. Hands Frankie had come to love for their straightforward, hardworking honesty. "Do you see what Mama's meatloaf does?" She clapped her hands together in delight, her eyes twinkling. "You are so beautiful tonight. Like Snow White at the ball."

"Cinderella, Mama," Cosmos chimed in. He was definitely a treat for the eyes in his dark gray trousers and red, tailored-to-fit shirt. The Santa hat he wore lay on his head in a crooked slant. He gave her a quick kiss on the cheek, then stood back and whistled his approval. "Uh, wow. Somebody got nailed by the smokin' hot fairy," he joked his appreciation, but then his expression sobered. "You look terrific, Frankie. Really."

She couldn't help but grin. Approval in any form from Cosmos was rare. "Well, thank you, sir. I clean up all right, eh?"

Maxine's head popped up in the crowd of people, her handsome husband not far behind. They held hands as they approached her, giving Frankie that familiar stab of envy. "Frankie?"

"If I had a nickel for every time someone's said my name with that 'no way' tone in their voice as of late, I'd have a shot at actually having a bank balance."

She grinned when Maxine reached out a finger to lightly touch one of her long curls, her mouth forming a small O. "You are *stunning*. I can't believe it's you! Campbell," she called over her shoulder to her husband, "would you just look at how beautiful she is?"

Campbell smiled, warm and kind, the hands he placed on Maxine's shoulders a gesture of sweet possessiveness. "You look terrific," he added.

"And I don't want to say I told you so, Frankie Bennett, but—"

"You told me so. Yes, yes, you did, Maxine. I do feel better. A million times better, and I know I was selfish and ill-behaved the last time we saw each other, but I really owe you a big thank-you for dragging me out of bed. So thank you." Frankie pulled her into a hug. "Jasmine's responsible for reminding me what it is to care about what you look like again."

A tear welled in Maxine's eye, one she brushed at with an impatient swipe of her finger. "Did you see the reaction you got when you walked in? Holy jaw-dropping. And Nikos? I thought for sure he'd fall over in the tray of lasagna." Maxine gave her another tight squeeze. "I'm so happy, not just because you're utterly gorgeous and have reinvested in you, but because it seems like you've found a place to fit—even if it's only temporary and you move on to something different, you've adapted. You've grasped the beginnings of a new start. There's nothing that makes me happier. It's the best Christmas gift I could have ever hoped for. You had me really worried, but look at you now."

Yeah, yeah, yeah. New start. Fitting in. Christmas gifts. Could they go back to the Nikos falling in the lasagna part? No. That would be rude and ungrateful, something Frankie definitely was not. She owed Maxine a shining moment because she was the woman responsible for forcing her to recognize the mess she'd allowed her life to become. Frankie gave her an extra hug, her gratitude honest and heartfelt.

"Jasmine!" Maxine squealed, hugging her and forgetting Frankie for the moment.

Frankie mouthed to Jasmine her intent to hit the long buffet spread out on the diner's counter, then made her way through the crowd, stopping when Voula or Cosmos wanted to introduce her to someone in their family.

A tall, regal-looking man waved her down from his spot in the corner of the room where he and Simon mingled by a cluster of fake potted palms that had been lit with multicolored Christmas lights. "Miss Frankie, is it?"

"It is," she said on a smile. "How'd you know? Has Simon been talking out of turn?" she teased, patting Simon on the arm.

Simon reached for her, pulling her to his lips for a peck on her cheek. "Me. I heard all the commotion when you walked in and the muttering of your name in vain from Chloe's lips."

She blushed, giving a covert glance around the room for Chloe, whom she found buried in a sea of dark heads, her eyes avoiding Frankie's. "It's so good to see you." She tucked her hands under the lapels of his suit jacket. "You look pretty hot, Simon."

"I hear you do, too," he chuckled, waving his hand in the direction of his friend. "This is Win, by the way. My babysitter." He winked with a grin.

Win took her hand, lifting it to drop a light kiss on it. His chuckle of amusement was like a mug of hot chocolate, slipping into your belly to warm your insides. "Ah, Simon, I wouldn't hold the title for oldest babysitter if you didn't hold it for oldest man in history in need of a babysitter. It's a pleasure to meet you, miss. You are truly a vision of everything lovely and heart-stopping. Glad tidings to you."

"So where's my woman?" Simon asked, tucking his cane beneath his arm. "I swear if one of these Greek cavemen scoops her up, I'm not afraid to call disabled and at a disadvantage," he cracked.

Frankie laughed, loving that Simon was so well-adjusted to his blindness he was able to joke about it. Frankie squeezed his arm, tugging a piece of his blond hair. "She's not far behind me, and I don't think you have to worry, Simon. She only has eyes for you. But you didn't hear that from me."

"Hah! I told you, Win. She's nuts about me."

"Who's nuts about you?" Jasmine crooned.

Simon reached a hand out toward her voice, pulling her to him to engage her in a swift kiss. "There she is. You look beautiful, baby."

"For all you know I have on sweats and a dirty T-shirt," she said dryly, though when her lips met Simon's, a breathy sigh, almost inaudible, escaped her cherry-colored lips.

Frankie laughed again. "I'm off in search of food. Anybody want anything?"

Jasmine shooed her away. "I've got it from here. You go . . . you know . . ."

Simon's freakish ability to detect even a hint of Jasmine's change in tone asked, "Go what?"

Jasmine purposely steered both Simon and Win away, one on each of her arms. "Nothing. Now c'mon. This is your chance to ply me with booze and take advantage of me while I indulge in food that doesn't have a number attached to it and can't be supersized."

Frankie drifted off, her eyes scanning the diner with a low-key glance for Nikos. She scooted her way to the buffet table, bumping into the elusive Adara, who was manning the food.

"Frankie?"

The surprise in Adara's voice had become familiar. She grinned at the third fabulous Antonakas family member. "In the flesh."

"You are all kinds of awesome. You look unbelievable!" Adara gave her a hard hug, brushing the long strands of Frankie's hair from her shoulders.

"Thank you! You, too, but then you always do. When I see you anyway. Where've you been?"

"Oh, you know. Studying," she said with a conspiratorial chuckle, reaching for an empty bowl from the counter.

"Ahhh. Boyfriend?"

Her finger flew to her lips. "Shhh. Yes. And you're not getting anything else out of me." She winked a long-fringed eyelash.

Frankie winked back. "I know nothing. You need any help?"

"Would you be an angel and go fill this back up with more pickles? These animals wiped me out."

Frankie grabbed the bowl. "You got it." Holding the bowl over her head, she inched her way toward the kitchen, smiling and nodding at the unfamiliar faces with still no Nikos sightings. She pushed her way through the double doors with her shoulder, squinting in the dim lights of the kitchen usually so bright and full of activity.

Someone's feet shuffled as they approached her.

Her stomach jumped in fear at the black silhouette outlined by the fridge. Wouldn't it be just like her luck to get herself whacked on Christmas Eve, of all things, and before she ever had the chance to hunt Nikos down and make him want her?

And when she looked so flippin' good, too.

Oh, irony.

But she reminded herself, she did have a weapon in the bowl she carried. It wasn't like she was afraid to use a kitchen item to take someone out.

A hand, lightning fast, arced upward, plucking the bowl from her hand in one swift motion.

Damn. Where was a wooden spoon when you needed one?

~ ℓ ~

Nikos heard Frankie's gasp of surprise when his arm snaked around her slender waist and hauled her to him. He even heard the grunt she made when the force of their bodies connected.

He chose to ignore her whimper of protest when he finally, Jesus Christ, *finally* planted his lips on hers. Hard and fast, Nikos drew her mouth to his, fighting the swell of the deepest groan he'd ever experienced, driving its way with force to lodge in his throat.

When she'd walked through the diner's doors tonight, like some slinky, auburn Tabby, his head had nearly exploded. The trouble all along with Frankie was how hard it was to stay away from her.

No way could he do it now, when her skirt clung to her hips like a second skin and her shimmering top begged him to tear it over her head and bury his lips against her small, firm breasts. His cock throbbed with white-hot heat at the chance to drag his hands through her silky hair, feel her soft skin against his, touch every square inch of her, make her scream when he devoured the heat between her legs with his hungry mouth.

Desire ratcheted up a notch when she realized it was him, and not only did she succumb to his lips on hers, but she willingly parted them to allow his tongue a taste of her own.

He backed her up against the refrigerator, flattening her to the cold steel, driving her tight skirt upward to find the lacy tops of her thigh-high stockings attached to what he considered the sexiest piece of lingerie a woman could wear. A garter belt.

Jesus, this woman was going to be his undoing.

Fire screamed along every nerve he possessed when Frankie lifted her leg, wrapping her ankle around his waist to drive his body so flush against hers, he had to fight not to come.

His breathing rasped when her fingers dug into his scalp, his heart nearly jolted out of his chest when Frankie didn't stop him from pushing the edge of her shirt up over her breasts to finally, after many a sleepless night, cup them in his hands.

Fuck, Nikos thought with a vague warning to his overheated body. He had to slow down. He wanted to lavish Frankie with the kind of attention she deserved, in the right setting, one befitting her first encounter outside her marriage.

God damn his conscience when she was so willing—so fucking hot.

He dragged his lips from hers with a grunt. "Frankie, honey. We have to stop," he murmured against her luscious lips, totally aware his voice was deep with need.

Her head fell back against the fridge, her eyes, amber and sultry, were glazed. "Stop . . ."

Nikos pressed his lips to the top of her head, inhaling the scent of her shampoo, forcing himself to find calm and the reason that went with it. "Not here, honey. There are too many people who could intrude, and if you knew my family, most of whom are out there now, you wouldn't want that, but if you trust me enough, come with me."

He backed off, using his hands to push off and away from her, searching her eyes to look for a reaction.

This was her chance to bail. If she had any doubts, he had to give her the opportunity to say no.

It would suck beyond measure, wanting her the way he did, but he'd respect any hesitation on her part.

But then Frankie, as beautiful to him when she was chopping parsley as she was dressed to make a man's heart jump from his friggin' chest, smiled. Easy, with a small hint of confidence. "You lead," she said, husky and laced with matching desire.

Nikos dragged her back to him, lifting her up to settle her at eye level.

Frankie responded by wrapping her legs around his waist.

"You're sure?"

Her eyes held his, fiery and alive. "Antonakas?"

"Bennett?"

"Make haste."

CHAPTER ELEVEN

From the journal of the "never less reluctant in her life than I am now" ex-trophy wife Frankie Bennett aka Da Vixen: Okay, so boom! All I have to say at this point is I wish someone had told me sooner. For sure, in the waning years of my marriage when my sugar cookies all but went stale in my goody jar, I'd have left Mitch in a nanosecond for just one night like last night with Nikos. I'd have gotten a divorce all right and proper first, but still—leave I would have. And I swear, by all that's holy, if I ever see Mitch again, I'm going to give him a nuggie for telling me one orgasm was all any decent woman could hope for.

Nikos carried Frankie out the back door of the diner and about two hundred feet away to a small cottagelike barn house lit with white twinkling Christmas lights around the windows. A fir wreath hung on the door; red ribbons and silver and gold ornaments swayed against it when he popped the door open with one hand while still holding her against him with the other.

The icy air and reality had begun to sink their sharp talons of anxiety into her gut. When Nikos closed the door behind them, her shock at her surroundings was matched only by her "sex with someone other than Mitch" fear. "This is yours? How did I not know you lived behind the diner?"

Had she ever given thought to Nikos as anything other than a secret fantasy and a real life playa? Had she ever once considered he ate, slept, showered like everyone else?

His hand was tender when he trailed the back of it along her cheek, letting her slide down his body to rest her heeled feet on the floor. The dark green cable-knit sweater he wore made his black eyes darker, if that was possible. "Believe it or not, this was the house my parents lived in when they first came to America, long before Riverbend was more than a blip on the map. I renovated it to suit my needs when I moved out of the city. They actually had the diner built in front of it. They've long since moved to the house right back there."

He pointed out the front window and to the left to the top of a steep hill where an enormous white house with tall white columns spanning the length of it was nestled against the deep purple of the sky.

Turning away from the window, Frankie scanned the rustic interior of the cottage, where braided carpets were scattered across an old barn wood floor and red and taupe plump-cushioned furniture braced by finished logs surrounded a stone fireplace.

The warmth of the fire crackling in it took the chill off, heating her back. "It's incredible," she breathed, taking in the pictures hanging on the wall in chunky wooden frames. A collection of single and group photos, solely in black and white, of Cosmos, Adara, Voula, and Barnabas, all smiling, were artfully arranged in clusters.

"Not nearly as incredible as you, Frankie," Nikos said, tugging her to him once more, the rustle of his black trousers making what she was embarking on a reality.

Her sigh was of completion, and she had no way to hide that, despite the jitters her nerves were expressing. Nikos holding her, fitting her body to his, was like some kind of revelation. A realization that life had color, texture, and dimension.

It frightened and excited her in one simultaneous act like nothing else.

Without letting her go, he walked her backward to an end table also made of finished logs, reaching down to grab hold of a remote. With the press of a button, he clicked on the stereo. Christmas music filtered to her ears in muted surround sound, Bing Crosby's crooning, mellow and sweet.

Nikos settled her against him, swaying their molded hips while resting his chin on the top of her head. "You're afraid."

"Afraid might be a little exaggeration."

"Okay, you have hesitations."

Yeah. Of all the retarded things to have after all her mental buildup. "At this moment, yes. Back at the diner? Not so much."

"That's because I didn't give you a chance to have anything. So you wanna talk about them?"

No. She just wanted to leave her head smothered in his hard chest and never talk again. Frankie inhaled, allowing his musky male scent to infiltrate her nostrils. "You're my boss." There. She'd said it. It was the one word that always popped up to rudely intrude upon all her midnight musings over Nikos. Things could get sticky if they did this and it didn't work out—or as unbelievable as the thought was, if it wasn't all she'd cracked it up to be.

Oh, Christ and a sidecar. What if it sucked? What if he was just hot to look at but not so hot in bed? What if she thought it sucked and he didn't? What if he thought it sucked and *she* didn't? What if they wonked each other's eyeballs crossed and it went terribly wrong and she had to look at him over a ten-pound bag of onions indefinitely until she could find another job?

"Say again?" Nikos prompted.

"I said, you're my boss . . ."

"Correction. Your slave driver."

She giggled softly at the laughter in his voice. "Yeah. If this—I mean—if we're . . . I've never done this before. I kind of don't know the rules for . . . for . . ."

"Engaging in carnal hijinks with your employer," he finished for her. "So are you asking me if this is a one-night stand?"

No. She wasn't asking that at all. She didn't know what she was asking, but now that the subject was all out there . . . "I don't know what I'm asking. I'm . . . I don't know."

"I'm glad you brought it up."

She pressed a knuckle to his pec and grinned when it flexed against her cheek. "I didn't bring it up. You did."

"Right. Well, now that it's been said, let me be clear."

Frankie's eyes scrunched shut, bracing herself for the inevitable "this has to be our little secret" speech. Or maybe it would be the "I'm only in this to get laid" line. She watched MTV. She got it, and she was still willing. In fact, she'd never thought past the point of Nikos's lips all over her girly parts.

None of this had come into her fantasies. There was never any talk of happily ever afters or commitments or even anything more than drive-by casual sex. There'd only been . . . well, the rutting. The fornication. Jesus, the shallow, emptiness of that thought made her just as bad as Mitch. "Okay, I'm all ears."

Nikos forced her chin upward with a gentle hand. "I'm not about casual sex. I've thought about this for the past month, Frankie. In fact, I'm not at all embarrassed to tell you, I've thought about it probably every twenty minutes or so since I first laid eyes on you."

"Are you sure Simon's the blind one here?" she teased, hoping to look away from his intense black gaze.

"Don't do that anymore, Frankie. Stop beating yourself down. It insults my taste in women. So to be clear, I am not, nor will I ever be, the kind of man who only wants to score and move on to the next game. Hear this and hear it loud and clear. It's long, so settle in." Nikos tucked her to him, spreading his thick thighs to encompass hers then pulling her arms around his waist.

"I want you. You and all your postdivorce trauma. You and your mussed-up hair in a ponytail with the yellow and blue scrunchie. You and your baggy clothes—which I might add, hid a body I wanted before, but now want all up in mine. I want you and the tossed-aside mess you think you are. I want to get to know you beyond the external things everyone else sees. I really want to know what you find so great about the Go-Go's, because you put Gail's iPod on every day at your lunch break and listen to 'We Got the Beat.' I find myself astounded at your poor taste in music when there's so much good Slayer out there to be had. I want to know if you like mustard or ketchup on your hot dog. I want to know if you even like hot dogs. I want to know what brand of toothpaste you use, what kind of soap. I want to know if you're ever going to decide on a hobby because it seems so important to you. And I won't deny, I really want to know what else you have on underneath that skirt that's so tight, you brought me to my knees in it."

Whoa. Her silence was outweighed only by his while he appeared to wait for her answer. The sharp planes of his face, tight and expectant, made Frankie bite her lip.

The words, when she found them, were slow, though offered in complete honesty with no hidden agendas attached. "Okay, first. Mustard and sometimes relish. Second, whatever's on sale at CVS that whitens and moisturizes. Third, I can't choose between raising ant farms as a second income or making furniture out of Hefty bags and beer cans. Lastly, and I'm going to be really truthful when I tell you, I never thought past the actual . . . well, you know. It never occurred to me there'd be anything to talk about but the—"

"So you saw me as just a plaything?"

Well, "plaything" was kinda harsh. Maybe partner in all things sweaty and grunting was more appropriate. "No . . . but . . . it never occurred to me you'd be down with anything else because you can have your pick of women with far less issues than I have. So I never let my imagination go any further . . ." Oh, sweet mother. She could really use a roll of duct tape and an extra pair of hands to wrap around her mouth.

Nikos didn't stop swaying, his hands never stopped swirling in enticing circles over her back muscles. "Whatever you thought, if it wasn't along the lines of what I was thinking, like exclusivity and getting to know one another, then all you have to do is say it."

And so then what? It was over. No gettin' jiggy wid' it? Jesus. How had she managed, after the train wreck that was Mitch, to find herself a man, the first one out of the gate after her divorce, who actually had boundaries and morals when all she thought she'd been looking for was a little some-some?

What did this say about her as a human being? What did it say that a man as divine as this one wanted to pursue a potential relationship with someone as mediocre as her, and she'd never once considered he was capable of it?

Wait, strike that. She'd never even given him enough credit to consider he'd know how to do anything other than run a diner and boink. She'd never allowed the love he clearly shared with his family, the hard work he put into running his father's business, to connect with the sex god she'd turned him into in her mind.

She'd never considered it because her way of thinking was what she knew. Mitch's way. Superficial, shallow Mitch, whom she'd let lead her to believe she could never be enough. Because he had chosen the young, nubile, undoubtedly prettier-than-Frankie-would-ever-be

Bamby, she figured, by default, all men made their choices in the same way her ex-husband did.

Oh, low didn't get any lower than what she was feeling right now.

"Frankie? Did I freak you out? It's not my intention, but I'm determined to begin as honestly as I can. Or not begin at all. All or nothing. That's up to you."

From the look on Nikos's face, she definitely saw some sort of resolution she didn't understand, but it was there.

Huh. Right here, right now, she had the most delicious man she'd ever laid eyes on in the palm of her hand, and she didn't know what to do with him unless it involved ravishing his luscious body, and even then, she was riding the fence about her ability to please all this hunk. "I think . . ."

What did she think? "I think I wasn't at all prepared for you to say something as sweet and profound as you just did, and I'm a little shocked, but if you give me a good, solid twenty minutes, and maybe some shots of tequila, I might be able to wrap my brain around it," she joked.

"You thought I'd just want to screw, didn't you? What is it about women and that line of thinking with me?" He gave her a mocking, tragically crushed look, but his question was genuine.

Oh. Priceless. He was just golden. He was gorgeous and he didn't have a clue. "Oh, I dunno, Nikos. I'm going to take a stab here and guess it might have to do with the fact that finding women who'll drape themselves at your feet while the masses line up to hand feed you Twinkies would be the least of your problems. Maybe that has a little something to do with it. In the interest of honesty, and along with the humiliation of showing my cards, you're in a different league than the average man."

"Translation?"

Her smile was watery. "Oh, now you're just fishing, Antonakas."

"I'm wounded."

Frankie rolled her eyes. "Fine. If you need to hear it out loud. You're pretty hot. No, you're unbelievably hot, and for someone like me to hear you talk about anything other than tossing my ovaries around, casually, and without a single shred of misgiving, is like having Scott Baio show up at your door and propose to you."

His chuckle was low, husky, and sweet to her ears. "I am not a casual tosser. When I toss, I do the whole enchilada."

"So I've come to discover," she whispered with a shaky timbre to her voice.

"Is that more than you can handle at this point?"

"If I say yes, does that mean there'll be no tossing?"

His smile was tender but firm. "I'm afraid it does. But I'd totally understand if that's how you feel. I'm not suggesting we buy wedding rings and book a flight to Vegas, but I am suggesting you consider having all of me."

Or none of him. Disappointment for that notion seeped into her brain. Yet, what he offered was such a big leap after having been dumped so callously by Mitch. Her heart clamored with fear, but it was her gut that reacted with a toe in the shallow end of the pool. "I come with more baggage than an overbooked flight to Boise."

"Yeah, but I'd be so disappointed if you flew luggage-free. You'd never value arriving on time because you would have never experienced the hell that's losing your bags in Tijuana when your destination's Hoboken."

Frankie didn't want to lose again. Not ever again. And she was never going to allow a man to own so much of her that she retreated back to the dark confines of her cave to mourn him. But she was afraid to fall for more sweet talk. She'd done it once. Twice was unacceptable—especially at her age, when she was supposed to be more mature and semi-capable of differentiating between sincerity and bullshit.

She'd only just begun to gather not only her wits but also a paycheck free and clear of Mitch's influence. She was so afraid to screw that up by getting involved with someone and ending up hurt. "Losing your bags sucks."

"But it can make you appreciate having to buy those Louis Vuittons to replace your old Walmart brand."

"You do not know who Louis V. is."

"Not only do I know of him, I did some account management for someone on his staff. That's not the point. The point is, if you're not ready for the physical part of this relationship, or the beginnings of something more substantial than a sheet wrinkler, then we'll wait until you are. And if you never are, I'd appreciate your honesty. And you don't have to make any rash decisions tonight. We can go as slow as you'd like."

Tell that to her hormones, who, as obnoxious, uncontrolled crowds go, were voicing their desires in the way of raw, exposed nerves and a desperate need for the show to go on. There was nothing in this choice Nikos posed that held anything unappealing. It was only her fear that she'd end up humiliated by picking the same man in a different body that kept her from jumping at the chance to get to know Nikos better.

However, there was beauty in the thought that nothing could ever be worse than flipping your lid on national television. "I think I'm in."

Tilting her head back, he gazed down at her. "I think I like the sound of that. You do realize what that means, don't you?" Nikos arched her back as he hauled her hard against him.

It meant her nether regions better sing their chorus of hallelujahs in their indoor voices so she wouldn't embarrass herself. Relief, excitement, along with a hot dose of anxiety over unfamiliar territory made her voice hoarse. "What does that mean?" Frankie asked with a coy smile, suddenly unsure.

"First, it means you can't go on a date with Marco. Then it means we get to see each other naked," he said against her mouth, whispering over her lips with a lick of his silken tongue.

Frankie had to fight another swell of panic mingling with the heat Nikos was stirring deep in her belly. Naked. Sex meant she had to be naked. Oh. Dear. Lord. "That means I have to take my clothes off?"

"Nope," he muttered against her neck, making her tremble. "It means I get to take them off for you."

Wait, where in her fantasy had she been naked? She'd always had something flowy and shimmery on, and her hair was fabulous and lush. But no naked. Her heart began a race against her lungs to screech out of her chest in a game of who was more panicked.

But then, her head fell back on her shoulders as Nikos trailed a hot path along her sensitive flesh, nipping and kissing his way back to her mouth, making her forget her fear. When her head lifted, she remembered. Panic about the naked reared its ugly head thanks to the Christmas tree and its soft lights twinkling in the corner of the room. "It's bright in here, don't you think?"

He chuckled, deep and vibrating against her neck. "It's the getting naked thing, right?"

Oh, Death. Where are you when I need you? "No . . . yes. Well, I guess I just didn't think . . . my entire fantasy out."

Nikos's head bobbed upward, leaving the flesh of her neck mournful. "Fantasy?" His question was deep and hoarse.

Okay, Death, if you're off for the night, could I get a little help from Mr. Destruction? Maybe an earthquake that shifts the floor and swallows me whole? "I—it's—I don't know what you're talking about, Antonakas. I said nothing about fantasies." She gave him an indignant glance before looking over his shoulder at the brightly colored wall.

Taking her by the hand, Nikos smiled over his shoulder. "I know what I heard, Bennett, but I'll let you slide until a later date. We have a room with no windows or lights to find."

They ended up in his bedroom. "You do, too, have windows in here," she accused.

"Hang on to your skirt there." Tugging her fully into the room, her feet sinking into the plush carpet with each step, he stopped at the bedside table and picked up a remote. With a click, shades slid from the tops of the windows to the sill, blanketing the room in total darkness.

In fact, it was so dark Frankie could no longer see two feet in front of her. As Nikos pulled her near, she stumbled, falling into his hard chest with a grunt.

Her body tensed, but Nikos molded her to him, soothing her with the strength of his arms, letting the warmth of his length seep into hers. Frankie relaxed in increments, sighing while shivers of anxious anticipation slithered along her spine. Her arms wound around Nikos's neck like they were meant to rest there.

He nuzzled the top of her head, inhaling, his wide chest expanding against hers, making her nipples rub with delicious friction against her bra.

"So, about the naked thing," he muttered, kissing her earlobe.

"What about it?" she mumbled back, lost in the sway of their bodies.

His fingers ran the length of the edge of her shirt, toying with her, teasing her hot flesh. "You ready for it?"

Her breathing hitched. *Yes. No. Yes, yes, no.* "Is this a sticking point, or is there room for negotiation?"

Nikos's chuckle was thick and sinful. "I hear it's part of the deal, but I'm pretty creative. I'm sure I could find a way to work around it. Though, I'll just say here and now, I think you're worried over nothing."

"That's because you haven't seen me and my ribs sticking out or the cellulite on my thighs." Her stomach jolted at the idea of his perfection meeting her imperfection in a blend of perfect imperfection.

"And I won't because I can't see two inches in front of me. So we're good to go?"

Point. "Wait. One more little niggle. What *if* I'm really crappy in bed? What *if*, because I am a total novice, and I don't know much more than a recently deflowered eighteen-year-old about, you know, stuff, I end up being the pits in the sack? Will you laugh at me behind my back with Simon and Marco while you slug back brewskis and eat chicken wings?"

"Simon doesn't like beer. He's a booze snob, and we all know what happens to Marco when he slugs back anything alcoholic. But I'm sure he'd be the voice of admonishing reason in our quest to mock your skillz," he teased against her ear, entwining his fingers with her shaking ones.

"So you will laugh at me. I should have known you were too good to be true," she joked back, knowing full well Nikos was trying to ease her fears.

"It'll only be just a snicker, but then I'll move on to the next post-divorce ex-trophy wife and forget all about you and your not-so-wicked bedsport ways. Promise."

Frankie smiled. "I'd feel so much better knowing you'd move forward with such eloquence and tact."

"I'm nothing if not eloquent, and on a serious note, Frankie, here's the deal. Let's just say, for all intents and purposes and to ease your apprehension, we don't see fireworks and rainbows. I guarantee you it'll be a helluva lot of fun working that out until we get it right. I do have faith we'll get it right, if not tonight, eventually."

Oh, this man. Either he was the smoothest operator this side of the Mason-Dixon, or he was a really genuine find. In a diner. In Jersey. Of all the places. *God, please—don't let him be like Mitch. Please, please, please, don't let me get this wrong again. I just can't be a loser in such a big way more than once in a lifetime.* "You're a very patient, decent man, Antonakas. Or you're full of shit."

Another chuckle rippled from his throat. "Well, you won't know that until the day after, and I'll have achieved my dastardly goal by then. So I have time on my side."

"You're very charming . . ." Jesus. That word.

"And that reminds you of Mitch."

"How did you know?"

"I met him. My kind of charming is a whole different breed, Frankie."

The sincerity in Nikos's voice was definitely different than Mitch's brand of genuine. It was a subtle difference, but it was there.

Her sigh was shaking, rattling on its way out. "Then, okay . . . I think I'm ready. 'Think' being the operative word here. As long as you think you have enough constitution to possibly see me naked in the light. There's still that. And it troubles me. Big. I mean, moonlight can be a mighty powerful thing. What *if* some of it escapes through your fancy blinds and you happen to see what you're contemplating, you know . . . uh, tapping. What *if* that very light does happen to escape through the blinds and you do see me naked and it totally squicks you out? That would be embarrassing for both parties concerned, don't you think? Then things would be even more awkward than when we originally set out to, you know . . . If we planned to do it, then didn't do it because you freaked out, think about how uncomfortable we'd be when we have to look at each other over a tray of marinating brisket. Oh, the horror—"

Nikos's silken lips quieted her, soothing her fears with their deliciousness.

Clothes shifted, lifted, then fell to the floor in whispers of linen and popping buttons. Shoes were kicked off and landed with a heavy thud to an unknown destination. Now she wished she hadn't wanted total darkness if only to see all of Nikos, naked, sculpted, hard. Her hands clung to his neck, longing to boldly run them over every plane of his body. Yet uncertainty warred with desire.

Though, there was no wasting time for Nikos when he opened the clasp on the front of her bra, brushing the straps from her shoulders with skilled hands. Hands that were warm, firm, lightly callused from the physical labor he put in at the diner.

Frankie shivered with anticipation when he ran his fingers between her breasts, skirting the globes of flesh, pressing his mouth to hers and sliding his tongue inside.

Her legs trembled, turning to room-temperature butter from the heat of Nikos's tongue, swirling to meet hers. The white-hot pleasure of his mouth encompassing hers was like nothing she'd ever experienced.

Stabs of desire rose and fell in her belly, pricking nerves, making them aware of sensations she didn't know existed until the touch of Nikos's mouth on hers as his fingers traced the outline of her breast.

His groan was deep, rumbling with approval, bringing a jolt of unexpected pleasure to her. When his thumb grazed her nipple, Frankie bucked beneath his hand, moving closer, seeking more of the crazy need he so easily evoked in her.

Disappointment followed by sheer anticipation shivered over her exposed flesh when Nikos left her breasts to run his hands over her ass, plucking at the garters she wore. "I like," he said with a husky silken tone, drawing her thigh up over his lean hip still clad in boxer briefs she now regretted not seeing.

Frankie's heart crashed against her chest in an almost painful agony of rhythm when Nikos artfully released the garters one at a time, letting them drop to her thighs and pull at her nylons.

He cupped her ass, drawing her hard against him and releasing a hiss of approval when their flesh made full contact. Skin to skin, Frankie was almost dizzy from the combination of warm flesh and the rigid press of Nikos's cock against her.

She fought a sharp groan when he slid his fingers under the edge of her panty line, caressing the skin where her thigh met her most intimate place. Frankie's head fell back on her shoulders as Nikos tugged her underwear off, following with his until they were both the naked she so feared.

There was nothing between them but her thigh-high stockings with the sexy line up the back.

More fear swept over her in waves of dizzy reminder.

Nikos's mouth sought hers again but not before he whispered, "Do you hear that?"

Frustration made her question almost desperate. "What?"

"Nothing. Absolutely not a sound, and you're very definitely naked," he pointed out, nipping at her bottom lip. "No gasps of horror. Definitely no screams of terror from any of my southern locales. In fact, you're getting a resounding cheer of 'more, more, more.' You know what this means, don't you, Bennett?"

His voice slithered along every inch of her flesh in a blanket of smoky decadence. "What does this mean?"

"It means you're a total hottie," he said before thwarting any more conversation by pulling her to his cushy bed with him.

She lay on top of his solid weight, soaking in the sweetly sharp contact of their flesh in unison, reveling in doing nothing more than discovering one another.

Fingers skimmed, soft moans filled the room, heated flesh shivered, giving way to the flex of muscles straining against one another.

Nikos drew her hard against his cock, allowing her clit to experience the hot length of him. Crisp pubic hair scraped her swollen flesh, leaving her needy and with an ache she didn't care to find an explanation for.

With two hands, Nikos lifted her to the top of the bed, setting her on plump pillows she sank into with a trembling sigh. Parting her thighs, he centered himself between them, running his hands along her hips, past her ribs, along her collarbone until he came to her hair, dragging his fingers through long strands of it. His wide chest whispered against her cheek, smooth and leaving her with a feeling of security.

Lips pressed to hers in brief kisses, skirting along her jawline before stopping at her breasts.

The sensation was so exquisite; Frankie bit her lip to quell her gasp of pleasure when he cupped them, kneading the globes of flesh. His mouth lowered until she felt his hot breath, hovering over her nipple. It was all she could do not to beg him to envelope it.

When Nikos did, the world tilted upside down, only righting itself when she curled her fingers into his thick head of hair and arched her back to encourage the hot swirl of his tongue. His mouth moved over each nipple with sweetly flaming strokes as he reached between her thighs and dipped his fingers into her wet flesh.

Frankie bucked beneath him, rising up to meet the exploration of his hand with a cry she couldn't stop. Nikos's thumb on her clit, swollen with need, rolled in lazy circles, waiting to discover which motion made her moan with the most pleasure, which turn of his finger made her tighten her grip on his hair.

Dizzy, Frankie struggled to hold back the thrust of orgasm, but the need for sweet relief crashed hard against her will for restraint. The writhing of her hips refused to be thwarted as she pressed hard against his fingers, riding the crest of release.

Her shoulders slumped as the breath in her lungs left in a whoosh of pleasures now met.

Leaving her breasts, Nikos clearly wasn't done. He ran his tongue in electrifying strokes over her ribs, along her belly until he came to the space between her thighs.

The cool air of the room hit her exposed flesh with a scintillating tingle, leaving Frankie gasping for breath, still recovering from her orgasm.

Hot and confident, Nikos took his first taste of her clit, teasing the bud with short, measured strokes, then laving her in long swipes of raspy tongue. His finger found its way to her slick passage, slipping inside her with ease, increasing the once more mounting need for release.

Her groan of pleasure elicited a groan of approval from Nikos, heavy and thick with his ministrations. Frankie cried out when he hit her sweet spot, hooking his finger against it and bringing her to a height she'd never attained before.

Her hands had a will of their own when they reached down, clutching his wrist with frantic fingers, fighting the swell of another climax in the hope of making it last.

Yet, she couldn't thwart the kind of intense pleasure he created with his tongue and finger. It rose and peaked, hot and so stingingly sharp, she came with a crash of her hips against the bed and spikes of decadently sinful liberation.

There wasn't enough air to satisfy her lungs when she attempted to force some into them. Her huffs resounded in the bedroom, clinging to her ears.

Nikos crawled back along her body, moving upward to settle above her. He stroked her hair, trailing his fingers through it, soothing her until her raspy breaths became easy puffs. Cupping her chin, he brought her mouth to his, and Frankie, for the first time in her life, tasted herself on Nikos's lips.

Forbidden and intoxicating, she didn't stop him when his tongue delved back into her mouth, licking, stroking, while his hands ran in tender impatience over her thighs and hips.

Her heart stopped when she finally made contact with his cock. Her hands had a will of their own as curiosity got the better of her and she reached between them to take a tentative stroke of his rock-hard length. His hips shifted, straining against her hands, the cords of muscle in his back bunching with tension.

Frankie wanted to touch every inch of his flesh, but his groans of pleasure, muted against her lips, were too inviting as she enveloped him between her hands. Thick and just long enough to make her sigh, his erection responded instantly to her touch, and she luxuriated in the pleasure Nikos appeared to derive.

"Frankie, honey," he husked against her lips.

"Hm?" Her response was thick and sluggish.

"Condom. *Now*," he gritted out with a clenched jaw, fumbling in the dark for what she assumed was a nightstand.

The sound of a drawer opening and closing broke her haze of desire for a moment until Nikos rose above her, the warmth of his body hovering over hers sending a shiver of longing from head to toe.

In that fragile moment, while his arms bracketed her, while he was poised above her in the velvet cloak of darkness, Frankie understood what it was to feel cherished, treasured. It burrowed into her gut, threading its way to her heart. A heart she thought would always be at odds with even the idea of another man in her life.

The simple purity of that thought made her burrow beneath

Nikos, pulling him to her to mold their flesh together. His groan, muffled against her lips, spurred her on, making her wrap her thighs around his lean hips and encourage him to enter her.

The thrust of Nikos's cock was swift, a silken glide of white-hot heat, driving into her and stealing her breath. Her chest expanded, crashing against his with the sweet sting of impact. Her nipples tightened to hard points, rubbing against his hairless chest as he took stroke after masterful stroke.

Frankie's arms tightened over the solid planes of his back, her fingers kneading his well-muscled flesh while she clenched her teeth at the delicious stretch and tightening of her aching body.

Nikos ground against her, pushing forward, then holding back, thrusting, retreating until the need for another round of completion tore at her. Frankie tightened her legs, hooking her ankles against his lower back until the slap of their flesh became hypnotic.

The noticeable tension in his strained muscles, the hiss of his breath brought with it her own mounting climax, so intense, it bordered sweet agony.

With her head buried in his tightly corded neck, the scent of his mouthwatering cologne in her nose, Frankie came again, with a flaming streak of electricity She reared upward, clinging to Nikos, the sweat of their bodies gluing them together.

He threw his head back with a growl, rocking into her, driving against her with a force that left them both haphazardly strewn across the bed until they both became boneless heaps.

Nikos was the first to raise his head, his pants for breath easing. He cupped the side of her face, running his thumb over her lips. "So, have we dispelled all the fears about the naked and the sex not being all we cracked it up to be?"

Her smile was genuine, topped with the bliss of completion she still couldn't wrap her head around. Sex with Mitch had been good, even satisfying, but it wasn't electric blue with streaks of purple. And it never entailed more than one orgasm. "You're not considering turning on those lights, are you? I won't have it, pal. My hair's an entity all unto itself after all that sheet wrecking."

Gathering her in his arms with a chuckle, he slipped from inside her but held her close. "Your hair's pretty sexy. I'd really like to see it in all its afterglow glory."

"You're a masochist."

The shrill ring of the phone stilled any reply Nikos might have readied. Frankie stiffened. "Oh, boy. I'd bet we've been gone a long time. Jasmine's probably looking for me because she's my ride, and your family's bound to be wondering where you are. We're in deep doo-doo if they come looking."

Nikos laughed, dragging a blanket over her. "Cover up so I won't burn my retinas when I turn on the lights. I can't find a phone I can't see."

She giggled, hearing the teasing quality to his tone, burying herself under the warm comforter, grateful now that her body had returned to room temperature.

Much stumbling and a choice word or two was had while Nikos found the bedside lamp and lunged for the phone. "Hello?"

From beneath the cover of blankets that smelled like Nikos, Frankie peered at him in all his buff gorgeousness. Oh. God. For as long as this lasted, he was never allowed to see her naked. There was no measuring up to such incredible, well-preserved perfection. Every lean, olive-skinned, sharply planed inch of his, right down to the smooth skin between his pecs, was glorious. His hair was mussed, his cheeks flushed but not in an unattractive way. Instead, their lovemaking had left him more fabulous than he was before.

The frown marring his forehead sounded out an internal alarm. "Yep. I'll tell her." Nikos hung up the phone after his curt parting words.

Her concern mounted. "What happened? Is Jasmine looking for me? Oh no. Did something happen to Aunt Gail?"

Nikos sat at the edge of the bed, so evidently unashamed of his nudity, his face unreadable, but his eyes scanned hers with a hawk-like gaze. "You got an urgent phone call."

"From?" she prompted, sitting up.

His eyes sharpened to two onyx points of discontent. "Your ex-husband."

CHAPTER TWELVE

From the journal of ex-trophy wife Frankie Bennett, aka Wannabe Vixen: I swear on my life I will, as long as I live, never, ever let Jasmine Archway talk me into wearing false eyelashes again. Oh, and I'm actually going to follow more of Maxine's advice about your first postdivorce relationship. Lay out the rules for your relationship requirements from the beginning and make them crystal clear. Do not be charmed into bending them even a little by the wiles of a man who's to-die-for delish. Because I don't give a hot Greek and some meatloaf with gravy how winningly Nikos Antonakas smiles at me—I'm not budging. Go. Me.

"Hah! Everything with Mitch is urgent. He probably just lost his garlic press." Frankie's eyes narrowed. What was up with Mitch these days? He hadn't spent this much time with her in all of their marriage. Suddenly she was on his most-wanted list? Twice in the matter of a few days after seven solid months of total silence while he cranked out his angst, looking for the Fountain of Youth in Bamby's girlie bits, just wasn't acceptable.

She was not the weak, helpless, afraid-of-her-own-shadow woman who'd left him. And he certainly wasn't going to take advantage of her now. Mitch owed her some afterglow. Damn him for ruining her afterglow. He was allowed to do it when they were married—it came with the marital ups and downs, but not now when the afterglow wasn't his to take.

But Nikos was grabbing at his pants and tugging his sweater over his head, his face unreadable. "Cosmos sounded like it was serious, Frankie. I think you should get dressed."

Hookay. So was this the perfect excuse to get rid of her after all that talk of exclusivity? Maybe she hadn't left him wanting more like he'd left her, and he wanted out? Maybe he had some kind of code with Cosmos that would allow him the op to bail because she sucked. Misery began to form a knot in her stomach. The empty one that was apparently ravenous now that all the bedsport had given her an appetite.

"Stop thinking what you're thinking, Frankie."

Frankie looked away, her eyes scanning the room for her clothes, taking in the heavy log armoire in the corner and the puffy red and taupe striped chair in the corner.

Nikos sat on the bed, clasping her wrists in his hands, his thumb caressing her skin. "There really was a call from Mitch, Frankie. Cosmos isn't my alibi to escape from your less than experienced clutches."

The sting of stupid tears filled with doubt wet her eyelids. "Okay."

"No. It's not okay, and you're not okay. Your reservations are written all over your face. It makes sense that that would be your first thought because of how Mitch treated you. He created suspicion and the fear of being lied to for any man you happened across after him, but I'm telling you the truth. Now let's get dressed and see what Mitch said."

Someone pounding on the door made Frankie spring into action without allowing her to dissect Nikos's insightful, sensitive words. Tearing the comforter from the bed to keep her covered while she hunted for her clothes, she searched the floor for her ridiculously high heels.

Nikos left her with quick strides, heading for the front door. She hurried to throw on her push-up bra and top, dragging her panties and her skirt over her hips with hands that shook.

The rumble of voices beyond the bedroom door made her run her hand over her hair, which was now scrunched into balls from the hairspray Jasmine had sprayed at her like an exterminator killing an infestation of roaches. Shit. Her purse with the brush in it was at the diner.

She popped open the bedroom door to find Cosmos standing on Nikos's front step, a frown on his face, muttering something to Nikos.

"Cosmos?"

His face went from impatient to grim. "Frankie, Mitch's assistant called. He's in the hospital."

Frankie smoothed a hand over her skirt, pausing to gather her wits. Did it make her a horrible person to wonder why she was supposed to care so much it warranted a phone call to her? They were divorced. Had she been in the hospital during their seven months apart, would Mitch have cared? Would anyone have called to tell him? Didn't divorced mean those kinds of emergencies no longer applied to each other? "Juliana called?"

He nodded, shoving his hands in his pockets. "Yeah, that's her name. She said Mitch is in the hospital and he needs you."

Needed her. To what? Find his pulse? Straighten his IV pole? Give him a sit-bath? Though, eighteen years of obligation tore her in two different frames of mind. They had been married. She had once, admittedly, loved Mitch, and now he needed her.

Yet, the rebellious side of her wanted to scream that had she needed him—*when* she'd needed him during the course of their marriage, he'd never been there for her. Not to mention the way he'd left her with next to nothing without even so much as a call to check on her well-being. So why did she have to be there for him if their marriage was over? Did Mitch's medical emergency beat her pain and suffering because it was only a little divorce? "Did she say what was going on and if it was serious?"

Cosmos shook his dark head in the negative. "She was pretty

vague, but she gave me the address at the hospital and said that Mitch asked you to come right away. Then she hung up before I could ask her any questions. Sounded like some kind of commotion in the background. I think it might be serious, Frankie."

Frankie wasn't thinking about Mitch, she was seeking Nikos's eyes—eyes that filtered his thoughts with such obvious caution it hurt her to look into them. Maybe this made her selfish, but the odd vibe between her and Nikos worried her more than Mitch and his emergency did.

Maybe she could just call the hospital . . . She sure couldn't call Mitch or even Juliana. They'd changed their numbers shortly after her television debut, claiming, via Mitch's attorney, that she was insane and unstable—maybe even prone to homicidal threats. She'd found out purely by accident when all she'd wanted to do was get inside the brownstone to find her second set of car keys.

Nikos was the first to speak, clearing his throat. "Maybe you should go to him, Frankie."

Why did that statement feel like a test?

Nikos solved her quandary by saying, "I'll drive you. It's late, and I don't want you out on the roads on Christmas Eve alone."

Jasmine was suddenly there, her car keys dangling between her fingers, with Simon and Win in tow. "We can always take the C-Rex," she cooed.

Frankie frowned, running her hands over her now frigid arms. "You don't want to go to some hospital on Christmas Eve. You go home and enjoy the rest of the evening."

Nikos grabbed his jacket from a wrought iron hook by the door. "Thanks, Jasmine, but I've got it. You two go do Christmas Eve things."

Jasmine pushed past Nikos, drawing Frankie's jacket around her shoulders and handing her her purse. "You sure? I don't mind coming for the ride. Not to mention, I'd love to know what the hell that snake wants with you on Christmas Eve."

Frankie gave her a quick hug. "I'm fine. Go and stand under some mistletoe with your man." Pulling her close, Frankie whispered in her ear, "And thanks for everything."

Jasmine's smile was Cheshire when she whispered back, "Never doubt Jasmine's ability to rope in a man, or read one, for that matter. I hope it was everything you wanted it to be. Don't forget, I want to hear all about it tomorrow. So call me. Now be safe, and I really hope it's nothing serious with Mitch. Just FYI, I have my doubts it is. He's a prick, but still, I don't wish anything more horrible on him than a limp dick. Anyway, Merry Christmas, honey."

Simon gave her a quick kiss before taking Jasmine's hand in his. "You call if you need anything, Frankie. Don't let that jackass sack you, okay?" He wiggled his eyebrows. "I'll be at Jasmine's if you need us."

Jasmine rolled her eyes, pulling him out the door and directing him over a patch of ice as Win took her hand and brought it to his chest, leaning in toward her with a hushed voice. "Truly, miss, you are lovely tonight, but might I suggest you allow me to straighten your hair for you? It would seem a stray eyelash has met its fate in your hair." His hand discreetly reached to the top of her head where he plucked the eyelash out and stuck it in his pocket. "All's well," he said on a wink. "A Merry Christmas to you and yours. It was a pleasure meeting you. Safe journey now."

Frankie smiled up at him in gratitude as her hand flew to her eyes. Shit, both of her eyelashes were missing. No one could ever mistake her for anything remotely like a vixen.

She watched Win's back as he made his way out, fully expecting Cosmos to follow. Yet, he lingered, waiting in skulking silence.

Nikos turned to her. "You ready?"

Frankie shook her head, catching the hard gaze Cosmos shot her. "I can't let you take me, Nikos. You go spend Christmas Eve with Voula and everyone. I'll be fine. If you could just give me a lift to the village to get my car, I'd appreciate it." No way was she letting Nikos and Mitch in a room together—especially if Mitch really was having some sort of medical emergency. He was nothing short of an asshole when he had a mere hangnail.

"Not gonna happen," he said with a definitive tone and a shake of his head. Yet still, there was a new tension between them Frankie didn't understand but really wished they could take a moment alone together so she could try and navigate it.

Cosmos shook some keys. "I'll drive. You two can argue about it on the way. Let's go." He stomped off through the cold night air toward a detached two-car garage and a large, white Suburban.

Frankie followed behind him with Nikos at her elbow to keep her from falling. "Cosmos! Voula will never forgive me if I take not one but both of you away on Christmas Eve. I'm a big girl. I can drive myself."

Cosmos scoffed, popping open the driver's-side door. "Voula would never forgive us if we let the 'bad Mitch' have at her Frankie without us there to protect her. She was the one who said we should go. Now get in," he ordered with a snap to his words while Nikos remained stoically silent.

Oh, tonight was just turning out to be the bestest evah. She'd boffed herself dizzy with an amazing man who appeared genuine and deep when all she'd ever known was shallow and immoral, and instead of basking in that revelation, she was on her way to the hospital to see to Mitch's needs.

Yet the tug of years of obligation made her feet move and get in the backseat.

Nikos slid in beside her, but his hand didn't reach for hers, leaving her even more miserable than the news that Mitch was in the hospital.

Thankfully, the traffic was light due to everyone being where they should be on Christmas Eve. At home. With their families. Warm. Safe. Nikos looked out the window as they passed a blur of decorative lights, but his glance didn't stray to her. Cosmos's silence was palpable, leaving Frankie feeling awkward and an imposition.

No one spoke while Christmas music played, soft and bittersweet to her ears.

Cosmos pulled into the emergency room entrance with a jolt. Frankie yanked the door handle and hopped out as fast as her heels would allow, the sharp wind whipping at her jacket, relieved to get away from a tension she couldn't figure out. "I'll go find Mitch and Juliana and meet you back here in the waiting room."

Frankie took off in the direction of the reception desk to find Mitch already there, sitting in a wheelchair, moaning and holding his chest with one hand, clinging to a blanket with the other. Juliana was at the desk, scrolling through papers.

Her approach to Mitch was hesitant, her steps sluggish. "Mitch?"

"Frankie!" Juliana called to her, her full cheeks red, her misshapen clothes askew. Frankie felt a pang of remorse for her. She looked run-down. No doubt, now that Mitch didn't have her to run ragged, Juliana was likely taking the brunt of his workload.

Frankie smiled in her direction, drawing her coat tighter around her neck. "It's good to see you, Juliana. How've you been?"

Her cheeks puffed outward. "Tired, but okay. Listen—"

But Mitch cut her off, managing to roll his wheelchair between the two women. His hands shooed at Juliana in impatience. "You go fill out the forms, Juliana, and go home. It is Christmas Eve. I'll speak to Frankie." He coughed, his eyes searching hers.

For what, she didn't know.

Frankie's lips pursed as Juliana cocked an eyebrow in Mitch's direction before making a reluctant retreat and turning her attention back to his release forms.

Frankie crossed her arms over her chest. "So what's going on, Mitch? You look fine to me. I'm not sure why you called me to begin with, but seeing you, it doesn't look like it was anything dire." And definitely nothing that should have dragged her from the warmth of Nikos's bed.

His lined face went slack with a defeated, hurt expression. "I disturbed your Christmas Eve, didn't I?" His hand reached for hers, cold and smooth, so different than Nikos's. "Accept my apology?"

Frankie's sigh was a mixture of impatience and frustration. The hell he was going to pull the martyr act with her. It drove her absolutely insane. Whenever Mitch wanted something, he put on his sacrificial victim pants and had at her, twisting the situation to his advantage by creating guilt because she was aggravated. Nope. He didn't get to do that anymore. "Why did you need me here, Mitch? What was so urgent you asked for, of all people, me? Because this doesn't look urgent, Mitch. You're being released, for crap's sake. It's not like you're dying."

He let his wide shoulders crumble inward. His gray-blue eyes grew watery. "But that's just it, Frankie."

Her teeth clenched, her hand remaining slack in his clingy grasp. "*What's* just it, Mitch?"

"I *am* dying, Frankie."

She blinked.

Shock washed over her in a wave of disbelief.

Dying?

Mitch was dying? Of all the horrible things she'd wished on his person after he'd trashed her life, never once had she wished death as his fate.

Wait—honesty check. She'd never wished it and truly meant it.

Frankie's shock was followed by the sharpest stab of guilt she'd ever experienced in her life, bar none. She'd been so aggravated with him for dragging her away from her antics with Nikos and now look.

She'd even gone so far as to accuse him of martyrdom.

Dying trumped martyr-ish activities—big.

Frankie's hand went to Mitch's cheek just as Nikos and Cosmos whisked into the emergency room on a cold blast of air.

But the air wasn't nearly as cold as the glare Nikos gave her.

Whoever said timing was everything could stuff it up their ass for being so spot on.

⌒

"Did we really just give that asshole a ride home?" Cosmos sneered at Nikos, who stood in the middle of plastic Mitch's living room, wondering how Frankie had ever fit into this lacquered, glass, and white-marbled sterile world. Not a single square inch of this brownstone felt like Frankie.

Nikos clenched his jaw, narrowly avoiding a gold and glass sculpture shaped to resemble something he totally didn't understand. He pulled his brother to a corner away from Mitch's bedroom. Their old bedroom, he assumed. The bedroom with the bed Frankie was busy settling Mitch into with comforting hands that should be only on him. Not fucking Mitch. God, that was a shitty thought to lob at a dying man. "Cos, shut it. Yes. We gave him a ride home. Did you hear what Frankie told us? He's *dying*," he hissed low and infuriated. "So quit being a shit and knock it off."

Cosmos jammed his hands into the pockets of his jacket with an angry grunt. "She's divorced. Why does Mitch's dying involve Frankie?"

Nikos positioned himself in front of Cosmos, letting his lips thin.

"Because she's a decent human being, Cos. That's why. What was she supposed to say? 'Sucks to be you. Merry Christmas, gotta run'? Don't be a moron today, okay? Just for once, take the day off and stop running at the mouth with the first thought that comes to mind, and keep your opinionated yap still."

Cosmos pointed an angry finger at Nikos's chest, his white teeth clamped together, but his face screamed disbelief. "Do you really believe all that crap about all these tests he's supposedly had since the last time he came into the diner? Seems to me finding out he had cancer happened pretty quick."

Nikos's eyebrow rose. "How long does it really take to find out you have cancer? It just takes one test."

"So why do you think he chose *tonight* to tell Frankie? Tonight of all nights?"

"You heard what he said, Cos. He wasn't feeling well, and he panicked. I suppose if I had cancer, I might freak over every little ache and pain, too. When you have a terminal diagnosis, I'd imagine you're always on red alert. Reaching out to Frankie was just a gut reaction born out of the fear this might be it. Maybe he wanted to apologize for being such a shit to her? You know, like making things right before you buy the farm? They *were* married for a long time." Even he couldn't believe he was defending Mitch. But there it was.

"Okay, fine. Then tell me this. Does he look like he's dying, Nik?"

There was that. "Just because he's not on life support doesn't mean he's not seriously ill, Cos. Plenty of people look fine and don't stop living until they're forced to. You heard what he said."

"You mean while he was slapped up against Frankie in the backseat, clinging to her like she was a starving man's last jelly donut?"

Nikos ignored the jab and the subsequent anger he'd felt since he'd had to bear witness to that. "The doctor told him to keep living his life while he gets treatment. You heard the doctor say that himself. Wouldn't you want to do the same?"

Cosmos blinked. "You're kidding, right? I don't know about you, but that doctor looked like he'd just graduated kindergarten. Mitch's playing her just like she's playing you. Jesus Christ, Nik, I can't believe you did her!"

Anger, spiky and jagged, gripped him, making him gather Cosmos up by the collar of his jacket with rough hands. "Never, ever, as long as you live, refer to her that way, Cosmos, or I'll *kill you*." He shook him off with a hard shove, leaving his brother to fall back against the pristine white wall.

Cosmos threw his hands up in a gesture of acquiescence. "Fine. I'm sorry. I like Frankie, too. But I'm just calling it like I see it, brother. It's Anita all over again. Plain and simple. All you have to do is look in that bedroom and see it with your own eyes."

Nikos ground his teeth to keep from bashing in Cosmos's. No. This was nothing like Anita. He'd never felt this way about Anita. "When I need your opinion, I'll let you know. Otherwise, I'm a big boy, and I can take care of myself."

A snort escaped his brother's lips. "Right. I remember how well you took care of yourself the last time shit like this went down—"

"Shit like what, Cosmos?" Frankie asked from behind the two men, making them cringe in unison. "And shhhhh. He's finally asleep."

"Color me all kinds of happy the Sandman's taken Mitch to peaceful pastures," Cosmos retorted.

Frankie stepped between Nikos and his brother, putting her painted nail at Cosmos's chest. "Look, I don't know what I did to tweak you, but *you* offered to bring me to the hospital. Yet the entire way, you were a total cranky ass. If you've got some kind of problem with me, spit it out, Cosmos, and do it while you can still claim to have a set of balls."

Nikos's mouth fell open before he had to clamp it shut so his laughter wouldn't wake Mitch. He made a face at Cosmos over Frankie's shoulder.

She whipped around, facing Nikos, her eyes luminous with a harsh glare up at him. "That goes for you, too, Antonakas. You have some nerve offering to bring me here, then grudging about it the whole way. Very passive-aggressive, if you ask me, and totally not okay by this girl. So those sticks you two have up your asses? Be good boys and help each other by pulling them out!"

Frankie pushed past Nikos with a hand to his shoulder to gather her jacket and purse. "Now be quiet and let's go. Juliana's on her way over, and I need to get back to Gail before she finds out what I'm doing. And you two beasts need to get home to Voula before she has my head for killing you both. Which I will do if you don't spit out your beef with me by the time we get in that car!"

With that, she stomped past both of them toward the elaborate front door—its etched-in-gold glass pristinely smudge-free—while two sullen, checked men followed her on heavy feet.

Nikos couldn't stop himself from noticing how hot she was when she was riled up. She was damned sexy all seething and spouting orders.

Nikos leaned over her and said, "You're a little hot when you're angry."

With a sigh of disgust, Frankie folded her hands together under her purse. "I'm glad you feel that way because that means by the time it takes to get back to Jersey, I'll be smokin'. Now get in the car and spill the problem."

Shit. Now he'd have to explain his irrational, knee-jerk reaction to her running to Mitch's aid. That meant they'd have to talk feelings, and he'd have to have an explanation for his feelings, which had to have some basis. Otherwise they'd appear knuckle dragger-ish and petty.

That basis was Anita.

Scrubbing a hand over his face, Nikos groaned.

He hated to talk feelings when they were his. He was a much better listener.

Though, if Frankie's stiff spine and dour expression were any indication of what was to come, he'd probably be better off deaf.

Cosmos pressed a button on his key fob, starting the engine via remote.

Nikos held the back door for Frankie to slide in, then followed suit by climbing in beside her.

Cosmos snorted. "You're being taken for a ride, Frankie."

She bristled in her heated seat. "Meaning?"

"Cos thinks Mitch is lying to you because he wants something," Nikos offered, averting his gaze once more, tight of jaw, eyes gleaming.

Now Frankie snorted. "Weren't you there when Doogie Howser gave us the skinny?" She still couldn't believe Mitch was actually dying.

She couldn't *believe.*

Oh God. Had she just thought that? Was she doubting Mitch? Yet, she'd heard the news herself. With her own ears, she'd heard a doctor who was all of twelve if he was a day tell her Mitch had cancer and his chances of survival weren't good—complete with stats and percentages she couldn't remember for the attempt to process it all. He'd said it while he'd looked at the wall behind her instead of directly in the eye.

He'd said it with a tone that had been as impersonal as if he'd been ticking off grocery items on a list.

"Yeah," Cosmos snorted, interrupting her thoughts of doubt. "I was there, and I still don't believe it. Mitch wants something."

Frankie snorted back. "Right, because I have so much to offer. Really, Cosmos, what is it that you think I have that Mitch wants enough to tell me he's dying of cancer for?"

"Maybe he wants you back? He wouldn't be the first guy to pull a desperate, stupid stunt like that."

"And when he doesn't die? Then what?" Frankie reached over the seat and patted Cosmos on the shoulder, ignoring that niggling fear Mitch was lying. "Good try, but I doubt Mitch wants me back, and for the record, even if he did, I don't want him back."

Ah, revelation. Saying those words out loud felt good, but better, they felt right. If she'd had even a small misgiving about any residual feelings for Mitch, they'd been quashed tonight. Even in light of a possible terminal illness, it didn't change how she felt. Though, she'd be there for him when she could. What decent human being wouldn't offer at least some solace? Yet, it didn't change the fact that she was so over Mitch and ready to continue her life, move forward, and maybe toward Nikos, she'd barely paused.

Her words clearly changed Nikos's attitude by the way he walked his fingers across the leather seat and reached for hers.

Frankie's eyes warned him he'd better back off. "Oh, no," she whispered with a fierce glance at him, flicking the back of his hand and snatching hers away. "There will be no making up until we talk about what led us to have a reason to make up. *Again.* So back on over there, pal. Now, your crazy theory, Cosmos? Any other nefarious conspiracies you'd like to share?"

Cosmos gave a light tap to the steering wheel with the heel of his hand. "I don't know. I just know he's up to something and it smells. I just haven't figured it out yet, but I will."

Sitting back in the seat, Frankie turned to Nikos with flashing eyes. "Pearls of wisdom you'd care to share?"

Nikos's jaw cracked before he spoke. "Look, I'm not saying the guy's a liar, but you won't catch me discounting the idea that he's capable of it. He did cheat on you. That requires lying. Pearled enough for you?" He followed up his sarcasm with a grin. The one he seemed to innately know made her melt.

But all melting was on hold until she found out what bug he'd had up his ass. "That's true. Point taken, but cheating and dying are huge leaps apart. So here's what I think. I think I'm a big girl and I can take care of myself. There aren't many who know Mitch the way I do. He's been known to stretch the truth to suit his needs, definitely. But this . . . Telling me he's dying for some unknown purpose is disgusting and cruel. If he's not telling the truth, I guess I'll know when he doesn't turn up dead, but he'll wish he was. Until I hear otherwise, as far as I'm concerned, the least I can give him is my compassion, and that's just how it's going to be."

Cosmos shook his head. "So why does he need you to help him finish out the season's shows, Frankie?"

"Because he's sick? All he asked me to do was help him with a recipe or two so he can finish up the season before he begins treatment. It's not a big deal. I did it all the time for him when we were married. Do you blame him for not wanting anyone to know, Cosmos? Especially his audience? Look, I don't think I have to explain to you both that Mitch might have been a shitty husband, but don't you think he at least deserves some kindness because he's a sick man, not to mention a human being?"

Her gut tightened. She was torn in half by the part of her that wanted to spit in Mitch's face for not just hurting her, but not even caring enough to see if she was all right after her media blitz. The half that wanted to tell him to go to hell—he didn't deserve her sympathy when he'd given her not an ounce.

While the other half of her reasoned that Mitch was a man she'd once loved and he could die if the chemo he'd talked about didn't work. There was just no way she couldn't at least try and do something.

"Consider it fulfilling a man's dying wish . . . or whatever. Either way, I make my own choices and if I choose to help Mitch at his request, that's what I'm going to do. What kind of person would I be if I didn't? So deal."

Boom.

First single, postdivorce, "live your life the way you want to" serious decision made. Though, the doubt Cosmos's words created niggled at her, made her sympathetic heart twist in indecision. Would Mitch do something so awful? And why? He wasn't exactly above some pretty low-down stunts, but that sort of lie would make him a much shittier person than she could've ever imagined.

"It's a bad idea, Frankie. That's all I'm saying." Cosmos's tone was lighter, but his statement held the intent of his supposition.

She pursed her lips in the dark warmth of the car. "Noted. Now let it go, and take me home. I'm tired. I'm cranky, and I haven't eaten in twelve hours."

"You missed that entire spread at the party? How could you possibly miss all that food?"

"Ask your brother," Frankie offered.

Cosmos paused, then cleared his throat. "Sorry. Never mind."

Nikos inched his fingers over her knee. "If you make up with me, I'll cook you something back at the diner. But only if you stop giving me the evil eye."

"You're due evil eye, mister. You evil-eyed me the whole way here. And I'm not sure you have enough food in two diners to make that up to me." She gave him a condescending glare, turning to look out the window.

His grin was sheepish in the passing headlights of other cars. "I can try."

Frankie made a face at him, tightening her jacket around her.

Nikos slid over closer to her, walking his fingers up her arm until they tangled in her hair. He twirled a long piece of it. "But it's Christmas."

"And that means you can be an eternal shit with me? No. I don't think so," she whispered, turning to look at him, fighting the warm swell of emotions gathering in her belly when he grinned. "If you want to make it up to me, you'd better tell me what's stuck up your ass, and then—and only then—can you cook for me." She gave him a flirty smile filled with this new brand of sass she'd acquired. "You have your relationship requirements, and I have mine. Mine include no covert attacks I can't defend myself from because I don't know what the attack is for. I had enough of that in my last relationship."

"That means you have to talk about your *feelings*, Nik," Cosmos crowed, clearly enjoying antagonizing his brother.

Nikos flicked the back of his brother's head. "Can it. And don't you have headphones for your iPod, or those ear things? Put them on and mind your p's and q's." He pulled her closer to him, and while she wasn't reluctant, she wasn't losing her footing either. "Now, where were we?"

"The part where you tell me why you acted like I'd taken away your World of Warcraft privileges."

"Yeah . . . the feelings part."

His tone had a distinct ring of disgust to it. A moment of concern struck her. "Is that a problem for you? Talking about your feelings?"

"What do you consider a problem?"

"A problem is when you don't open that mouth of yours—and we both know you're not afraid to do that—and tell me what the problem is. Instead, you clam up and become sullen and moody. You have all these requirements from me, and you definitely didn't have any trouble spitting those out, but I can't have any? Not happening. So I have some, and if you don't like it, then it's like you said—all or nothing. One of those requirements is to tell me when you're pissed."

Yes. That was definitely a standard she wouldn't compromise on. No more sneaky, behind-her-back blindsiding. Bamby was enough clunked-in-the-head for one lifetime. Maybe if Mitch had shared his apparent lack of interest in her and their faltering marriage, she could have saved herself the pain of a televised near homicide.

"Okay. I don't love sharing my feelings."

His admission was hard-won. Frankie read that in his tone, but it wasn't enough. Suddenly, absolute honesty was the only thing she'd settle for. Maxine was right about one thing—you definitely learned as you went.

Frankie met his eyes dead-on when she said, "Well, I don't always love it, but I'm not too much of a chicken to do it when it has to be done. Not anymore. So enough of changing the subject, using your good looks and devilish smile to charm me into ignoring the fact that there *is* a problem, and hit me. Be a brave little warrior now, or I'm going home and there'll be no more communication until you fess up. Not. A. Word."

"You think I have a devilish smile?" He winked, tracing the line of her nose with his index finger, making her insides turn to goo.

Now there was a feeling she was all too familiar with. When Mitch had decided she was his next kill, he'd wooed her with his savvy "man on the hunt for a mate" skills. Oh. No. Her head was on straight this time. No amount of charm and good looks was winning this battle.

She leaned forward, out of Nikos's embrace, tapping Cosmos on the shoulder. He popped the earbuds out of his ears with a question on his face as he pulled off the turnpike.

"There's a McDonald's open—even on Christmas Eve, right? The one just a couple of blocks up the road from the diner? Would you be an angel and stop there for me?" She gave Nikos a pointed look while she pulled a ten-dollar bill from her purse. "I have a sudden hankering for a Big Mac meal. *Supersized.* Oh, with a milk shake. Chocolate. Wait, no! Strawberry. Ohhhh, and maybe an apple pie, seeing as I missed the one your Aunt Dora makes. You know, the one Voula raves about all the time."

"Sure—"

"Okay, okay. Fine. We'll talk," Nikos spat, his mouth a thin line of reluctance.

Her lips pursed with sour disapproval. "Without the 'tude, thank you. Funny how you can turn that smile on and off at will to schmooze me, isn't it? But I ask one little thing and you're a cranky pants again."

"Look, lovebirds, it's after midnight. Man up, Nik, or shut up. I'm tired, and you know Mama'll have me out in the backyard on that spit, roasting the leg of lamb at the crack of dawn for Christmas dinner. So make a choice or I'm dropping you both here and going home to get into my warm bed where I'll laugh about ditching the two of you in this frozen tundra. Oh, yes, I will. Laugh and laugh."

Nikos grunted. "Go to the diner, knucklehead," then to Frankie, "I said we'd talk."

As Cosmos pulled into the diner's parking lot, Frankie sat back, pleased with herself for not allowing him to steamroll her.

She popped open the door, wincing at the rush of frigid air when she slid to the ground. "Thanks, Cosmos, and have a Merry Christmas. I'll see you at work in a couple of days. Oh, and apologize to Voula for me, would you, please? I'm sorry I took you and Nikos from the party to tend to Mitch."

"Night, Frankie," he called. "Oh, and, Nik?"

Nikos stopped before sliding out the back door. "Yeah?"

With two fingers, Cosmos plucked something spidery and black out of his thick hair. "Tell Frankie she needs more glue."

Her hand flew to her eye. Well, if Cosmos and Co. didn't know for sure she and Nikos had slam-bammed each other, they did now. Her face turned red at Cosmos's chuckle, making her pivot on her heels and run to reach the safety of the warm diner.

Nikos was right behind her, jamming the key into the door, then taking her hand and pulling her inside to push her up against the counter, placing his lips on hers.

The warmth of his mouth gave her legs a reason to wobble, but not her resolve. She placed her palms on his chest in objection. "Food and icky feelings. In that order before I die of starvation or lack of emotional fulfillment." Frankie gave him a shove toward the kitchen, pulling her jacket off and draping it on the back of a stool.

Nikos shoved his way into the kitchen, going to the fridge to dig out some of the party leftovers. Yet he remained silent.

Frankie crossed her arms over her chest, determined to clear the air. "So, how is it that we only decided like three hours ago to become involved, and already your nose is out of joint? As records go, I think we're, hands down, the winners."

Nikos pulled the sauté pan from the shelf below the stove and threw a square of butter in it. "I don't know about you, but I don't mind being labeled a winner."

The hearty scent of leftover stuffing wafted to her nose, making Frankie rethink her demand that he take her home if he wouldn't cough it up. So she'd give this one last try. Because she really was starving. "Okay, so here goes—because you're rusty at this. I ask you a question and you answer."

He didn't look up from the pan, but he nodded his dark head, his fluid hands stirring the contents of the pan. "Done."

It's now or never, Frankie. "Who's Anita and what does she have to do with me?"

CHAPTER THIRTEEN

From the journal of ex-trophy wife Frankie Bennett: Dear Santa, you're all kinds of awesome drenched in awesome sauce. This year's Christmas present beats an impersonal gift certificate to the spa at the Four Seasons from Mitch, hands down. I think you even managed to beat the year I got the Barbie Dream House and not one, but two Barbies. No easy feat there, sir. Love and a lifetime supply of whateverthehell kind of cookies you like.

His shoulders stiffened, instead of turning around to face the music. Nikos opted to keep his face buried in the sauté pan. "You heard."

"Well, I didn't just pick her name out randomly from the universe. So yes, I heard."

"Why do you want to know?" A stupid question meant stupidly to fend off the inevitable stupid explanation he'd have to give. Thus, making him look stupid. Something he didn't have much love for.

"You know why I want to know, because Cosmos mentioned her name in the same breath as mine and that breath wasn't exactly favorable. So who's Anita and why's she such a big deal?"

"She was my fiancée." He heard Frankie's breathing halt, but it didn't thwart her quest.

"So what does she have to do with me?"

Here we go. "Her circumstances weren't unlike yours."

"She was an ex-trophy wife who worked for you for little more than sweatshop wages?"

Nikos picked up on her tone, teasing and light, but the subject of Anita was anything but light in his mind. "No. She was on the rebound."

Frankie clucked her tongue, coming up behind him to peer around his shoulder. "And that's what makes Cosmos say her name like it's some Satanic curse?"

Nikos's chest loosened a little when he barked a laugh. "No."

"Oh, one-word answers. So insightful. Look, Nikos, if anyone has a right to have some serious issues with spilling their guts, it's me. But here I am, willing to spill my guts if it means we won't have residual leftover bad-relationship crap between us before we ever even start. If it's going to affect your mood like it did tonight, then I deserve to know. So I think it's only fair you tell me the crime Anita committed so I can prep for my sentencing. One I don't deserve the rap for, but one that's apparently scarred you enough to make you angry that I even entertained the idea of going to see Mitch. Who's *dying*."

Fair. That was more than fair. He switched the burner to low, turning around to face the woman he wanted to bring into his life. "I met Anita when I worked in Manhattan. She was a client, just recently divorced from a wealthy, high-profile defense attorney. I was helping her invest her divorce coup long-term. I should have known better. Not only was she a client, but she was also freshly divorced. I should have realized she wasn't even close to working through her issues, but that didn't stop me from getting involved with her. I fell in love, and she claimed she had, too. Until her ex-husband came calling, that is. She went back to him. That's it."

"And it hurt you," Frankie prompted, her amber eyes flooded with understanding.

"It made me do stupid things I don't want to do again." He had a jealous bone. 'Nuff said.

"So because Mitch called, and I went to see him, you were angry because it was too reminiscent of what Anita did."

Her words weren't a question, but they were right on target. Christ, he hated this—this weakness of his for women who'd been crushed. "That thought came to mind."

"I'm on the rebound. So you assume I'm going to do the same thing and end up wooed by Mitch and his sweet words of love? Are there really any words to make up for him banging Carrie and Bamby, Nikos?"

"For some women? Definitely."

Frankie pursed her lips at him, placing her hands on her hips. "Well, maybe I'm not some women. Look, no matter what happens with me, you, us dating or not dating at all, Mitch and I are done, and I don't care what he says. I'm sorry that he's so sick, but I don't love him anymore. I don't wish him ill, even after what happened between us, but we're never getting back together. If that's not enough for you, then I don't have whatever it is you seem to need."

He grabbed her hand, caressing the soft skin he'd luxuriated in just a few of hours ago. "Look, here's the thing. Anita wasn't completely over her ex-husband. She said she was, but if she'd been over him, she wouldn't have run like a marathoner doing the 5K every time he called. It was always little things like he needed help with something at his hip new bachelor pad or he couldn't remember the phone number of a friend they'd had as a couple. Fredrick, her ex, cheated on her, too, but sometimes that's not enough hurt to stop someone from going back for more."

Frankie cocked her head, the fall of her silky auburn hair catching the light in the kitchen, making her more irresistible than ever. "You can't always help who you love. It's sad but true."

"Yeah, well, you'd think the ultimate betrayal in a marriage would cinch the deal, but Anita didn't seem to feel the same way."

"Did she cheat on you with her ex?"

Another question he'd battled with and had to eventually let go of without a clear answer. Nikos shrugged his shoulders. "I don't know. She said she didn't, but doesn't everyone who gets caught deny it at first? When I say I understand what you've been through, I do to a degree. The thing with Anita left me pretty raw and definitely overly suspicious. I'm admitting this up front—I can't promise I won't have irrational moments of manly stupidity. Either way, it doesn't matter. Anita's back with Fredrick and it's over."

No one understood irrational better than she did. "How long has it been over?"

"Two years."

Frankie's head fell back when she laughed, the column of her throat enticing and creamy. She cracked her knuckles.

"What's so funny?"

"I'm sorry. I don't mean to make light, but wow. You're way worse off than I am, Antonakas. I've only been divorced seven months now, and I'm not nearly as trashed as you are, and we know for sure Mitch cheated on me. Not to mention, I was married for *eighteen* years."

"I have a hot temper sometimes. I react before I think. I'll work on it."

"Like I'm one to talk. I've been known to *react*," she said on a grin.

Nikos pulled her against him, inhaling the scent of her perfume and the remainder of their lovemaking still clinging to her skin. "Is this a competition? Who can take the most pain?"

Her arms slid around his neck, a gesture of such ease and innocence, it made his gut clench. "Oh, I know I can take more. I'm a woman. It goes without saying we're made of tougher stuff. We bear children. You lot just put them in us." She smiled, infectiously, flirtatiously, surprising him.

"Speaking of children. Why didn't you and Mitch have any?"

"Mitch wouldn't have made a great father. I realized that early on, and I'm pretty glad I did after hearing Maxine's story, but I'm also infertile."

He gazed into her face, waiting to see a flash of pain over revealing something so personal, but he didn't find any. "And you're okay with that?"

Frankie paused for a moment, making Nikos wonder if she was as okay as she'd first appeared to be. "I really wanted children. I had a great mother. She raised me alone after my father left us, and with the occasional support of my Aunt Gail. We were really close, but she died just after I met Mitch. I wanted to be a great mother, too. It just didn't work out. Something about my fallopian tubes and sperm and all sorts of complicated mumbo-jumbo we didn't look into further because Mitch didn't really want children—he just couldn't say it. Some days, like the day I found out he was doing Bamby, I'm glad. Mitch was a lot of work—adding a child to that would have tipped me right over the edge."

Nikos felt a shift in his chest, a hard jolt of remorse. "But you wanted them?"

She looked over his shoulder. "Yep. At one time, I did. What about you? Did you want children?"

He smiled. "Yeah. I did."

"And no one ponied up to ride the Antonakas train of love? No one? What has this world come to? Madness surely," she teased with a grin. One that had different components to it he hadn't seen till just now.

"Let's just say, I spent the early part of my adult life going nowhere, thought I'd found out where I was going, then changed directions. I didn't date anyone seriously again until Anita."

Her eyebrow rose. "Again?"

Nikos winced. Yes. Again. He'd done the rebound thing not once, but twice. Which made Frankie number three. Christ, it had to be a charm. "Yep."

"Are there more love misdemeanors I'm blissfully ignorant of, but am sure to be blamed in the name of?" she asked sweetly.

"There was one in college. But in my defense, she'd broken up with her boyfriend back home in wherever she was from. Nebraska, I think. Anyway, they'd broken up until he showed up in his beat-up old Ford pickup with a bouquet of handpicked daisies and a guitar. The very guitar he used to sing a love song he'd written just for her— below *my* dorm room window."

She laughed again, the sound rich and inviting to his ears. "Oh, that's priceless. Crappy, but priceless. How long did you date her?"

"The last year of college. I was going to ask her to marry me."

"Ah, but you didn't have a guitar and daisies, now did you?" she joked.

He took a nip of her lips, now bare of the shiny gloss she'd had on earlier. "Uh, no. Just some meatloaf and gravy."

She tilted her head back. "You know what this sounds like? It sounds like you're a 'damsel in distress' kind of guy. Always rescuing someone. But I don't need to be rescued, Nikos. Just some honesty and some respect will do."

He *was* a "damsel in distress" guy. Simon said it was because he was a bleeding heart. Stray animals, kids, women—God save him from the women. "I'm definitely much better at respect and honesty than I am at squishy, girlie feelings."

"Hey," she chided, "if feelings were squishy and girlie, you wouldn't be saving women from their nefarious exes."

"You have a point." She had too many, but still, she was right.

"And for what it's worth, I love meatloaf and gravy, especially Voula's, but I'd kill for peanut butter and jelly at this point. So feed me, Antonakas. Before I keel over. It's been a busy day that began at eight this morning for me. That's how long it takes to put on false eyelashes."

He winked down at her, marveling at this carefree side to her. "Ohhhh, right. Food. So are we done with the caring is sharing? Or do you want to wring more embarrassing relationship disasters out of me?"

She chuckled, tugging at the collar of his sweater. "You can't ever top mine, buddy. I own humiliation and made embarrassing my bitch. But yeah, for now I guess we are. Just do me a favor from here on out?"

Reaching around her, he gave the stuffing one last toss and turned off the stove, still meshing their bodies together, reluctant to let her go. "Name it."

Those amber eyes, once so dull, gleamed with determination. "Don't skirt things that are important to you and get angry with me for something I have no idea about. You're not allowed to be sullen and pouty and not tell me why. If we're going to give this a test run, it's a real sticking point for me. After Mitch, I think you should be able to see why honesty and telling me what's going on is something I'd want. No amount of charm's going to keep it from eventually coming between us. If Mitch had told me he was unhappy, or for that matter, if I'd told him I was unhappy, he still would have been a lying shithead, but maybe I could've saved myself a run in the tabloids. See where I'm going?"

His spine stiffened. "I'm nothing like Mitch."

Yet hers relaxed against his hands. "And I'm nothing like Anita and Miss Nebraska."

"Deanne and touché."

"I'm over Mitch."

"I'm over Anita."

"Then we're all about the over, aren't we? So we understand each other?"

"We do. Want me to show you I understand?" he teased, skim-
ming his tongue over her lips, hoping to drag her back to his place for
just a little while longer.

She groaned, low and sexy, making his body respond with a fierce
spike of electricity flooding his veins. "Not before you feed me like
you promised. I'd never make another round if I don't eat. Now give
me the food or suffer the wrath of my discontent."

Keeping one arm around her, Nikos reached up and grabbed a
plate and some silverware from the overhead shelf, then scooped
some stuffing up and dumped it onto the white surface.

Frankie looked at the plate. "That's it? After all that, this is all I
get?"

Nikos chuckled, leaving her to move toward the fridge. He
propped it open with his foot. "How about some cold ham and maybe
some cold cuts and cheese?"

Frankie dropped the plate to the counter, digging in with zeal.
"Bring it all."

"Wow. What a change from a month ago when getting you to eat
was like asking for an exorcism from the Catholic Church." He
dragged out several plastic-wrapped platters, depositing them in
front of her with a pleased smile.

She shoveled a heaping forkful of stuffing in her mouth while
grabbing for a roll of salami and provolone. "It was all that baggage
unloading. Makes a girl ravenous."

Nikos pulled up a stool next to Frankie, content.

Really content.

For the first time in a long time.

A sense of peace stole over Nikos as they talked while Frankie ate
and Christmas lights twinkled outside the diner. The kind of peace
he wasn't quite sure he'd ever experienced in exactly this way before.
Not with Deanne and not with Anita.

Not ever.

Whoa and shit.

In that order.

~ ℓ ~

"All I wanna hear you say, sassafras, is Nikos is a good boy and he wrapped his willy. Then I can go back to bed."

Frankie's cheeks flamed, her hand self-consciously reaching for her crazy, messed-up hair as she made her way into the living room to find Gail and Kiki curled up on her aunt's favorite chair. So much for the hope of not having to explain. "Aunt Gail! Shame on you. How do you know anything other than decking the halls went down?"

Gail set Kiki on the floor and shoved her hands into her quilted green bathrobe pockets. "Nothing to be ashamed of. I make Garner wrap his, and you decked something, but it wasn't a hall, that's for sure. Good on you for gettin' your spunk back, toots. Your uncle and I might not have had any children, but I know the look of a night in the sack. Your old Aunt Gail's no dummy."

Frankie winced, dropping her coat to the couch and leaning down to rub Kiki's head. "Well, here's what one of those kids would have said to you if you'd had one. TMI. As in—"

"Too much information. I know what it means, girlie. I watch that *Bad Girls Club*. I know all you kids think we seniors don't have it in us, but I'm here to tell you, hoo boy, can we—"

"Nooooooo!" Frankie held up a hand, covering her eyes with the other, giggling. "I don't doubt you have it in you. Not for a second. I just don't want to know about it—hear about it. Visualize it," she said on a rough chuckle. "So how about we just conclude, I was as safe as any good adult should be and call it a night?"

Gail laughed witfh a throaty chuckle. "Aha, somebody had a Merry Christmas. Can't say's I'm surprised or unhappy about it. Nikos

deserves a nice girl like you after that last round he had with Whatserface."

Frankie frowned, still troubled by Nikos's admission. "Are we talking about Anita?"

"Not sure of her name. I don't think Voula ever mentioned it. I
just know she was upset about his troubles at our bridge games about
two summers ago."

Nikos was turning out to be one revelation after the next. He'd
been hurt just like her. Yet, she'd learned from Maxine's nutty theo-
ries, the key to finding happiness was in dealing with what went
wrong and letting it go in favor of getting a grip and not repeating
past mistakes. How odd that she wasn't the only one who needed to
do that.

That she was taking the sensible approach to a new relationship
venture left her feeling very proud of herself. Nikos had a way about
him, one that could distract her from almost anything with his delicious kisses and disarming grin. Yet, she couldn't afford to budge. No,
she wouldn't budge. The instant she'd made her demands clear to
Nikos was the instant she knew trust and honesty were two things
she wouldn't go without again.

Frankie rubbed her aunt's shoulder with an affectionate hand, in
need of some time to herself to think. "You go to bed, Aunt Gail, and
get some sleep. I'm cooking tomorrow. Oh, and you'll be tickled all
shades of the rainbow to know, I invited Nikos over for dessert. How's
that pin-curl your hair?"

Gail chuckled, cupping Frankie's jaw, sweeping a kiss over her
cheek. "You're a good girl, Frankie. A good girl who's moving on.
Your mother'd be so proud."

The long events of the night, the turmoil over Mitch, making
spectacular love with Nikos, topped with Christmas, made her long
to talk with her mother. "I hope so, Aunt Gail. I hope that's true."

"You can bet your bippy on it. I'm off to bed now. Night, honey, and Merry Christmas." She gave Frankie a squeeze before treading off to her room.

Frankie flopped back on the edge of the couch in front of the small Christmas tree, staring at the lights draped over gold and silver ornaments, and kicked off her shoes.

Tired. Euphoric. Afraid. Excited.

Afraid.

She was back in the dating pool—a pool she'd spent not nearly enough time swimming in to begin with before she'd committed her life to a man she outgrew.

Yet, here she was, hot-man nabber of the year, all getting involved and setting records straight like she knew what she was doing.

Frankie smiled secretively.

Yeah. She didn't just have a fantasy man, she'd scored one.

And she was terrified.

~ℓ~

"Merry Christmas, crabby," Simon crowed. Pleased with himself and the gift he'd bought Jasmine.

He heard the crinkle of the envelope as Jasmine took his gift. He also knew the look that flashed across her face was akin to what one might expect had he given her something he'd dug out of a Jersey land-fill. The breeze of her waving it under his nose sent her perfume to settle in his nostrils. He grinned. She was pissed. He loved when she was pissed because it gave him the opportunity to prove her wrong.

He loved proving Jasmine wrong because it only strengthened his case that they should be a couple. Permanently. "So go on, open it."

"I thought we weren't exchanging Christmas gifts. In fact, I remember expressly telling you no gifts. I can't afford gifts. I can barely afford to pay my rent and keep you in Cheetos."

He rubbed his chest with the palm of his hand, preparing for battle. "I offered to buy my own game-time snacks. You refused, Independent Woman of the World. Just open the damned thing and quit complaining, honey." He'd never tell her, but he loved to hear her complain. He loved to hear her, period. Simonides Rhadamanthus Jones was in love. Whether Jasmine liked it or not.

She shifted in the bed, moving away from him. "Didn't your mother teach you any manners at all? Giving someone a gift who can't afford to give you one back makes that someone uncomfortable."

"My mother is too busy enjoying marriage number two in Saint Moritz to teach me anything. Didn't your mother teach you to be gracious?"

"My mother was a tough broad who didn't take any crap from anyone right up until the day she died. You leave my mother out of this."

Simon let his hand stray along the sheets until he located her knee, giving it an affectionate squeeze. "Well, at least now I know where you got your balls. Now open the present, honey."

Jasmine flicked his hand away with one of her pretend irritated gestures, but he knew her vibe, and while she was playing like he'd given her the gift of chlamydia, she was actually pleased. He sensed it in the unbidden sigh escaping her full, soft lips. He sensed it in the way she leaned toward him and in her overall body language.

"Fine. I'm opening, but if you think you can buy me with jewelry and trips to exotic locales, you're wrong. I've been everywhere, and I've had all the trinkets I can pawn. So don't go thinking . . ."

The way she drifted off in the midst of her hundredth saucy rant told him she'd sliced open the envelope.

"Oh, Simon."

Yeah.

Simon folded his arms behind his head, pleased when he heard Jasmine sniffle.

"You bought me a six-month supply of cat food and a year's worth of veterinary care for Gary . . ."

"Yeah, because I'm like that. I know how much you love Gary and worry you won't be able to afford his shots. A healthy Gary's a happy Jasmine. But there's more," he prompted.

She giggled, the sound warm and slipping into his ears like soothing oil being poured over him. The rustle of the envelope indicated she was still digging into it. "Gift certificates to McDonald's. You're determined to find a way to make me let you pay for dinner, aren't you?"

"I wouldn't want you to have to cook." Actually, after the can of SpaghettiOs she'd burned, he'd prefer she never touch another utensil again. "So how can you be mad at that? Because if there's a way, you'll find it," he teased.

She was silent for a moment, and he knew when he slid a hand to her cheek, it would be moist from the tears she was trying not to shed. "No one's . . . no man's . . . ever given me a gift so . . . so thoughtful."

No man better ever give her a gift, thoughtful or otherwise, Simon thought.

Climbing over him, Jasmine straddled him, leaning down, her long hair brushing against his cheek. "Thank you," she whispered, pressing her lips to his.

His chuckle was deep, and for the first time since his accident, he wished he could see, so his eyes could meet hers. So she'd know what he was sure she wasn't ready to hear. "What, no beat down? No protests? No refusals? Who are you?" he joked softly against her mouth.

Her response was almost inaudible. "I don't know, but thank you." She settled on top of him then, curling her hand under her chin, nestling her head against his shoulder.

That tight feeling that never failed to constrict his gut sat deep in his belly. The feeling that told him all he needed to do was wait this out. It was happening whether Jasmine wanted it to or not, Simon thought with satisfaction. She would fall in love with him if it killed him. He wouldn't accept less.

Yet, Win was in his head in an instant, admonishing him for not telling Jasmine everything.

Everything.

Resting his head against the top of hers, Simon shoved away the eventual mess he was bound to make in favor of the woman he held in his arms. The woman who, after spending so much time with him, had managed to turn his childish grudge into something he'd never expected.

The woman he'd originally set out to hurt because her ex-husband was a pig, and now only wanted to love.

CHAPTER FOURTEEN

From the journal of ex-trophy wife Frankie Bennett: Sorry it's been a while, but props to Maxine. I gotta give it up to her. She was right about more than just the thrill of being self-sufficient and the boost to your self-esteem when you learn to stand on your own two feet. Sex, when your ass is less than perfect, and your thighs cramp at the mere mention of the position doggy style, can still be awesome. In fact, now that I've sort of adjusted to dim lighting—very dim—okay, really dim, it's begun to rock my socks off. It almost beats getting my own place to live. Wait. No it doesn't. Making love on Nikos's bed, couch, sunken tub, shower, wherever, beats sex at my new place on a cold tiled floor where if we move an inch in the wrong direction, we'll end up having to call the paramedics. But it's a real close second.

Nikos dumped a small box on Frankie's kitchen counter, Kiki under his arm, gazing lovingly at him, while Gail arranged her cutlery drawer. A drawer that held nothing more than three forks and one large serving spoon, but they were hers and they were in *her* drawer, in her studio apartment. "You have no knives, sassafras. How will you cut those big pieces of steak you're going to cook for you and the hunk here?" Gail asked, thumbing over her shoulder in Nikos's direction.

Frankie laughed, draping an arm around Gail's shoulder. "I hate to cook, and you know it. And it'll probably be a while before I can afford much, but at least I'm out of your hair, and you and Garner can ... you know ... in peace." She winked with a conspiratorial smile.

Gail gave her hand a squeeze. "You know I loved having you, and I'm sure gonna miss that coffee you make, but I'm real proud of ya for getting your own apartment."

Frankie smiled at the blank walls and empty space. Yeah. She was proud, too.

"There goes the neighborhood," Jasmine teased, dropping a large gift bag on the kitchen counter.

Frankie laughed, giving her a quick hug. "You have no one to blame but yourself for the state of your neighborhood. If it wasn't for you, I wouldn't have gotten away with not having to give that shark of a landlord of ours a deposit." Jasmine had charmed the pants right off of Rocco, their landlord and an all-around ladies' man. By the time she was done, Frankie had the corner apartment, lower level, two parking spaces, and was located right across the way from Jasmine.

"Did my woman use those pesky feminine wiles she's always complaining are the death of her to get you your own crib, Frankie?" Simon teased, close behind Jasmine, his hand on her waist.

"She did," Gail confirmed with a shake of her silvery head. "Hoo boy. I ain't never seen anything like it 'cept in the movies either. She's one smooth talker, this sexy cookie is. I think he'd have agreed to let Frankie have an elephant for a pet by the time Jasmine was done with him."

Jasmine threw up her hands with a grin. "I figure I may as well use all of this for something—even if it's for evil." She poked at the bag on the counter, shoving it in Frankie's direction. "Open it."

Her cell phone rang, interrupting her excitement over Jasmine's gift. She held up one finger in a gesture for Jasmine to wait and whispered into the phone, "I told you I'd have it for you, didn't I, Mitch? I'm in the middle of something, but I'll call you back later." She flipped the phone shut and returned her attention to Jasmine, briefly wondering why Simon had such an odd expression.

"Well, hurry up and open it!" Jasmine encouraged.

Frankie stuck her hand inside the big lavender foil bag and pulled out several items wrapped in blue tissue paper. "It's a shower curtain and towels. Oh my God, I forgot about towels! Ohhh, and a toothbrush and soap holder, and wait—Scrubbing Bubbles and a sponge."

"That's because you're now officially the maid, but don't worry. I'll teach you how to scrub the toilets so there's no nasty ring," Jasmine taunted good-naturedly.

Nikos laughed, unfolding the lone plastic chair she'd gotten free from the bank when she'd opened up a savings account, and setting it in the middle of her small living room-slash-bedroom. He set Kiki on it, scratching her ears. "Look at you. The only thing you need to make the old homestead complete is a velvet Elvis portrait for the wall."

Frankie giggled, her heart skipping a beat when she caught Nikos's gaze from across the room. "Hey, I had to start somewhere, right? And once I get my tax return, I'll pick up some more essentials, funny man." Thankfully, she'd remembered she was owed one of those due to her job at Bon Appetit last year, and she'd filed an early return. A definite bright spot when she and Nikos discovered her quest to get out of Gail's hair wouldn't have to be thwarted quite as long as Frankie had originally thought.

And here she was. The walls were cracked, the crazy blue and green bathroom was uglier than a boil on your ass, the kitchen was the size of a shoebox, and the front door sagged, but it said "Frankie Bennett" on the rental agreement.

There was no two ways about it, she'd have to stick to a strict budget, one she'd learned how to create with Jasmine and Maxine and the girls at Trophy, but if she was careful, and barring any unforeseen tragedies, she was going to do this.

Her way.

"Knock-knock!" Maxine called, milling her way through everyone to find Frankie. "I come bearing housewarming gifts for a woman of independent means," she said on a wide smile. Pretty and always tastefully put together, Maxine gave her a hug.

"I come, too," Campbell called from behind her. "Because the gifts for the independent woman were too heavy for the other independent woman to carry alone."

Frankie's eyes widened as she counted three boxes and two more gift bags. "Oh, no, Maxine. I can't. It's too much."

Maxine's smile grew wider when Campbell placed his hand on her shoulder. "Well, you might want to wait on that until after you open them. There's booty to be had, oh, and this." She handed Frankie a small black tote. "It's a survival guide for women striking out on their own. You know, coupons for local stores, emergency numbers, suggestions for energy saving, tips on how to get a stain out of your carpet because your maid's gone the way of the dinosaur. All important stuff."

Frankie laughed again, giving Maxine a hug. "Thank you. I wish you hadn't spent so much."

Maxine tweaked her cheek. "You won't feel that way when you have coffee already made in the morning. It's crucial to a single girl's survival. Besides, you'll need it for those early morning demonstrations at the mall with the Slap Chop."

Nikos had given her later hours at the diner in order for her to take on a part-time position at the mall, ratcheting up his supportive factor to the nth degree. He'd offered to give her a raise, but they both knew he was overpaying her as it was, and as it stood, the diner needed another cashier to replace Adara when she'd gone back to college.

Her refusal hadn't made him angry at all. In fact, instead of trying to save her, Nikos was the one who found the ad for the demonstration hostess and showed it to her.

Which made him crazy irresistible, which was always followed by more of the afraid thing.

Nikos came up behind Frankie, throwing his arm around her shoulder. After almost a month and a half of dating, she was still getting used to her insides always feeling like a bowl of Jell-O whenever he was near. He leaned in, placing his lips against her ear to whisper, "How long before we can get everyone out of here and christen the new homestead in the style to which it's due?"

A chill of delicious anticipation swirled low in her belly. Nikos created a special kind of fire in her she'd never expected, and it involved more than just the fire he created in her loins. He made her want to succeed at getting on her feet. He made her want. End of.

More importantly, and more and more frequently, he made her smile secretively, when she was alone and it was just she and Kiki.

"Frankie! I brought you some stuff from Voula, who insisted every good girl should have a set of knives and a meatloaf pan." Cosmos held up a box and several bags. "There's more in the car, and Mama's on her way with Papa."

She took them from him, plopping them in the middle of her living room with a beaming smile. Voula held a warm spot in her heart. She'd coddled and nurtured and encouraged Frankie day by day at the diner until she'd made her feel like she belonged—like she was an integral part of this crazy bunch of unruly clan members and the running of their diner. Even Barnabas had begun to come around with the occasional grunt of approval for her chopping methods.

Each day that passed, each moment she spent with the Antonakases, each lunch shift when she worked side by side with Nikos, had become a soothing balm—a place of respite where she didn't have to be anyone but Frankie.

In increments, she was becoming more successful at tamping down the idea that something or someone was going to take what she'd found away from her. The notion never failed to make her heart skitter sideways.

Which scared the living shit out of her.

These days, she wasn't sure what was scarier—how easy it was to be nuts over Nikos, or how easily everything could fall apart. Yet, deeper and deeper she fell . . .

"Oh, look at our Frankie," Voula cooed, patting Gail's arm as she arrived a few moments behind Cosmos. "She is leaving the tree, eh?"

"Nest, Mama. She's leaving the nest," Nikos corrected, winking at Frankie and leaning in to give his mother a peck on her forehead, his strong, tanned hand cupping her chin.

Voula pinched Frankie's cheeks with a fond smile. "Yes. She leaves the nest like a big girl. I am so proud of our Frankie."

Barnabas followed Voula in, then knelt beside Kiki, scratching her under her chin with an indulgent smile and that little noise of pleasure he made whenever Frankie brought her to the diner to sit in the back office and watch TV with him. He'd even picked up a bed for her to sleep on the desk in. A princess bed with fluffy pink and white marabou fur. "How's my Kooky today? She is a good girl for Uncle Barnabas? Look what I bring for my good girl." He dug in his pocket with a grin, pulling out one of Kiki's favorite new treats.

Kiki preened, her typically solemn approach to almost any situation all but lost when Barnabas paid her even a little attention. Her tail wagged as she burrowed on the chair, giving Barnabas a coy, playful peek from beneath her tiny paws.

His laughter, hearty and rich, made Kiki rise on her haunches to stretch against him and beg to be picked up.

Frankie shook her head at how indulgent he was. "She'll get fat, Barnabas," she chided with a chuckle.

He waved a chubby, wrinkled hand at her in dismissal, tucking Kiki into the top of his gray sweater vest. "Ack. My Kooky is a good girl. Good girls get treats."

Jasmine tapped her on the shoulder. "Okay, sweetie. Gotta run or I'm going to be late to work."

"Heaven forbid you should be late to Fifi's," Simon said with a roll of his eyes.

"Fluffy's, and that job pays for my playpen. So lay off, poor little rich boy, and let's go."

Simon pecked Frankie on the cheek with a grin reserved especially for the kind of crazy Jasmine drove him. "This woman."

"Cosmos, we go," Voula directed. "We don't want to leave Hector alone for too long. Last time he almost burned the whole batch of lamb stew because he flirt with the girls. Frankie? Tomorrow we talk curtains. I make, okay?"

She gave Voula a hard hug and chuckled. There was never any telling Voula no. Whether it was food or curtains. Everyone said yes to Voula. "Curtains. I'm in. I'll see you tomorrow. And thank you, for everything. You're too good to me."

Voula pinched her cheek again with nimble fingers. "You are family. Family needs curtains. Barnabas, come. Put Kooky back and we go see what Hector's doing."

Barnabas gave Kiki one last kiss and an ear scratch, handing her to Nikos, then kissing both of Frankie's cheeks with a wide smile. "*Kalh Tuch*, Frankie. You are a good girl. Not as good at the chopping as me, but a good girl."

Nikos clapped his father on the back and translated. "That's 'good luck' in Greek."

"Okay, pussycat. I'm out, too," said Aunt Gail, leaning in for a hug. "I have a hot date with Mona, Mary, and some bingo. You call me if you need anything. I'll miss you, sassafras."

Frankie hugged her hard, forcing back the sting of tears. "What will you miss more, me wandering around in my pajamas with greasy hair, or the big lump in the bed of your guest room?"

Gail gave her a pat on the cheek, buttoning her coat. "But look at you now, huh? That dirty bird didn't get the best of you. I'm proud of you, kiddo."

Frankie smiled in grateful satisfaction as Maxine and her husband Campbell left behind Gail. She was proud of her, too.

Now that they were alone, Nikos began to organize boxes and gift bags against the wall. He whistled, putting his hands on his lean hips, clad in stonewashed jeans. "You know, Bennett, I'm thinking this divorced, poor gig is a real racket."

Her eyebrow rose. "Why's that?"

"Did you see some of this stuff everybody brought? When I got my first apartment, I had one pot and like a box of dry spaghetti. My own mother didn't bring me even one set of sheets, but you get two. From Macy's—and Egyptian cotton, no less. I don't want to sound petty here, but I'm beginning to feel like my people love you more than they love me." He pouted his bottom lip.

She giggled. "I am pretty loveable."

Nikos gave her the look when he scooped her up, fitting her against him. The one that was a mixture of smoldering black eyes and playful sinfulness. The one that made her toes tingle and her heart thrash around in her chest with giggly, bubbly joy. "Oh, that you are, but loveable enough to buy you an entire kitchen aisle from Macy's? I dunno . . ."

Her glance at him was coy, but her body sought his in the arch of her back. "I am. I can prove it."

Nikos wiggled his eyebrows at her in a lewd response. "Do I have to take you to task, Bennett?"

"Will it involve a cold, hard floor and the potential need for some Tiger Balm?"

His hand slid under her sweater to cup her breast, caressing the underside of it, dragging his fingers along the sensitive tip of her nipple. "If I promise to rub it on all your sore spots, are we a go?"

Like she had the kind of will of iron it took to deny him. The playful, flirtatious side of her, one she didn't know existed until Nikos, twirled a strand of her hair as she leaned back in his arms. "Oh, I don't know. You could just be trying to score, and when all's said and done, I'll be left to try and figure out how to reach the middle of my back while you brag about your coup over a football game and sliders."

He ran his tongue along her lower lip, eliciting a shiver of anticipation from her. "I would never brag. Not over sliders, anyway. Maybe peach pie. That always makes me give it up. "

Frankie let her arms slip under his, wrapping them around his waist with more giggling. "Fine, then. Do what you will with me," she said on a mock sigh, fighting to hide the shudder of need rippling through her.

Nikos's laughter was gruff when he pushed her back against the wall and popped open the button on her jeans. Jeans that now fit the way they used to thanks to some Antonakas love. He slid them over her hips with slow hands, caressing her skin as he went.

Frankie's head fell back against the wall when he kissed his way along the side of her hip and down along the inside of her thigh. Her heart almost stopped, much like it always did, when he reached the most intimate place on her body.

Nikos relieved her of her panties and jeans, lifting her feet to pull her ballet slippers off. His hands were hot, untamed, running over her thighs, down along her ankles, and back up again to rest at her waist. His groan was unbidden, muted against the tender skin of her belly. He used a single digit to take a long draw of her swollen flesh, dragging a whimper of a plea from her lips.

The world tilted when his tongue sunk deep into her, swirling the aching bud of her clit with the tip. Her hips bucked against his mouth, hot and all encompassing. The silken glide brought her fingers to knead at his shoulders as his hands pulled her flush to him, kneading her ass in a circular motion.

Her nipples beaded, painfully tight and hard against her sweater, the delicious friction of Nikos's mouth bringing the white-hot flood of heat she'd begun to allow herself to crave.

When he slid a finger inside her, thrusting it into her with a force that left her gasping, she cried out, her chest heaving forward, her shoulders pushing against the wall as she rose on her toes to consume every last lick of his raspy tongue.

Frankie drove down hard against Nikos's lips, writhing with blissful pleasure when climax, sharp and sweet, began its upward climb. Her hand gripped his shoulder, the other wound into his hair, gripping the back of his head to keep his mouth as close as she could.

Her orgasm was a flash of brilliant white light behind her eyelids and the molten grip of sweet relief. She gave a final violent shudder before collapsing against him, boneless and replete.

Nikos shimmied up along her frame while clothes were discarded and breaths of need rang in her ears.

Their bodies met, naked, hot, heaving against each other, their skin sticking and pulling apart as they ground together. Like so many times in the past month, Frankie instinctively raised a thigh, curling it around Nikos's waist. She reached between them, grasping his cock, silken and straining against her hand.

His groan, throaty and low, made her smile, much the way it did when she recalled it when she was alone. The sinful pleasure that single sound brought her left her feeling feminine and empowered as she dragged her body along his to kneel in front of him.

His hiss of pleasure when she cupped his tight sac and enveloped him in her mouth made her sigh around him. She'd just begun to learn what brought Nikos the most pleasure, what brought him as close to the edge as possible. Drawing the tip of his cock against her tongue, Frankie began the slow downward spiral, letting her lips drag over his hot shaft.

Nikos's hands found her hair, clenching fistfuls of it, thrusting into her mouth until his hiss of need and the tug on her shoulders had her once again, back against the wall.

A condom came from somewhere, sliding onto his cock with skill, and then he was above her, taking her lips, devouring her with the thrust of his tongue.

Her hands were frantic, pulling him close, hiking her leg around his waist until she felt the hard tip of his cock against her slick entrance. A single drive upward, and Nikos was filling her, groaning against her mouth until he took all focus away but the need to find fulfillment.

Each second, each grind against one another, each crash of their hips sounded out in the small space. Their breathing became rapid, heaving in and out until Frankie's teeth clenched together from the building pressure.

Nikos cupped her face with one hand, using the other to keep them fused. His mouth pulled from hers to settle on her cheek, his warm breath fanning it as he drove upward.

Frankie could no longer bear the electric current sizzling along her veins, the slap of their flesh, the aching-sweet pleasure he wrought from her. With her breasts scraping against his chest, her nipples hard and aching, she came in a rush of colors and sounds.

Nikos bucked, too, groaning long and low, stroking her hair, kissing her lips.

Frankie shivered against the shelter of his chest, fighting that swell of completion she harbored each time he smiled, when they made love, when he rested his chin on the top of her head.

Her internal battle for complete emotional independence from anyone or anything warred with the onslaught of this deep-seated need she had for Nikos. The safety his embrace brought her was one she'd never fully experienced with Mitch.

Yet, nothing frightened her more than losing all the ground she'd gained. She never wanted to allow the expectation that someone else would always take care of her to overrule her common sense.

But Nikos drew those very feelings from her, from deep inside her where they were no longer cast aside in favor of sensibility.

"So where's the Tiger Balm?" he teased, withdrawing from her and pressing a kiss to her forehead.

Frankie snuggled deeper against him, rubbing her arms. "Forget the Tiger Balm. I'm starving. Feed me, Seymour."

Nikos stopped to gather some of their clothes, wrapping his sweater around her shoulders. She burrowed into it, catching the scent of his cologne and doing that secret-smile thing. "You want me to cook or you want to go out, mistress?" he teased, grinning at her when he handed her her jeans.

Frankie loved to watch him cook for her. It wasn't like watching Mitch cook. Nikos didn't care if crumbs fell on the floor or if egg yolk spattered his ceramic stovetop. It was, instead, a completely relaxing experience, one enjoyed over a bottle of red wine, with her sitting at his small breakfast bar watching while they talked and she skimmed the paper for a part-time job. She cleaned up, sometimes with Nikos's arms wrapped around her from behind as she rinsed dishes. "I'd love for you to cook, but we lack the basic essentials. You know, food. I haven't shopped. Not to mention, I don't have any pots or pans to cook anything in."

Nikos shook one of the wrapped packages on her floor that Maxine had brought over. "I think you probably have a whole kitchen here."

Slipping on her jeans, Frankie smiled. She was so grateful to have found these people who'd dragged her out of her sinkhole of depression and made her choose to not just survive, but to live—really live.

And eat awesome meatloaf.

Her brand-new cell phone, the one she and Voula had shopped for, rang to the tune of "Vacation" by the Go-Go's. Nikos glanced at it, then frowned. "It's Mitch. *Again.*"

Frankie's sigh was exasperated when she took the phone. Mitch had approached her about possibly helping him create some recipes for *Mitch in the Kitchen*'s last three or four shows of the season.

Since he'd asked her, she'd avoided his phone calls when she was with Nikos due to what was occurring right now: the old jaw clench Nikos had perfected to beat back his jealousy whenever the subject of Mitch came up, and unfortunately for her, he came up often—mostly on TV, and ironically, almost always when she and Nikos were together. Though Nikos said nothing, Frankie knew Mitch's constant contact was a bone of contention between them.

Her glance at Nikos was an apologetic wince. "I've been avoiding him for about a week. I really think I should take this, and then we'll hit the Stop & Shop and utilize my mad coupon-clipping skillz. Whaddya say?" Frankie tacked on a sweet smile, flirtatious and cute for good measure.

Nikos's eyebrow rose with a cynical slant to it. Yet he voiced not a single jealous word. "I'll go look for coupons."

With a deep breath, she flipped open her phone. "Hi, Mitch. What's up?"

He coughed into the phone. "I really need you, honey."

Bristling at the word "honey," Frankie narrowed her eyes. "What's wrong?"

His moan echoed in her ear. "I feel simply awful, and I really need to give the producers something that resembles a recipe to keep them off my back. Please, sweetness?"

"Have you told the execs what's going on with you? I'm sure they wouldn't be angry with you, Mitch. You have cancer, for God's sake."

Nikos coughed his displeasure from his place on her lone folding chair, rooting in the big yellow coupon holder Gail had given her.

"No!" was his quick reply, followed by another cough. "I don't want anyone to know anything. You know what the press is like, Frankie."

Oh, the irony. "Uh, yeah. I kinda do. Remember the headlines, 'Celebrity Chef's Wife Wreaks Wreckage With Wire Whisk'?"

Mitch paused, sending a grating sigh through the phone. "I really could use your help, Frankie. That's all I'm asking. Is it too much?"

Fuck. The pity card. Well played, Sensei. Since her chat with his doctor in the emergency room, and despite the urging of Gail to check the validity of Mitch's pending doom, Frankie had decided she had no right to dig around in her ex-husband's affairs. Legally, she was no longer entitled to that information anyway.

Yet each time someone brought up the possibility that Mitch was lying, her doubts gave her gut a good, hard twist. Frankie shoved that notion aside in favor of a "better safe than sorry" attitude. She'd never be able to live with herself if she was wrong. "When do you need the recipes, Mitch?"

"Tonight."

"Are you serious?"

"I *have* been trying to tell you that for a week, Frankie," he scolded with the tone one used for a ten-year-old who'd left the light on in the hall yet again.

"Mitch, some of those recipes took me weeks to figure out! How am I supposed to come up with three in one night?"

"If you'd just called me back . . ."

She ran her fingers over her temple and gave Nikos a sheepish look. "Okay. I'll be there in an hour, providing traffic doesn't prevent it. I'll call you on the way with a list of things we'll need for test runs. Can Juliana pick up the items for me?"

His voice instantly lightened. "I'll make certain of it."

With a click, she turned off the phone, wincing when she caught sight of Nikos's dark gaze. "He is dying, Nikos." It really was the best defense around. How could anyone ever say no to someone when they were dying? What request was too much?

He shook his head, rising from the chair, his handsome face resigned. "I know, I know. I get it. This is me trusting you. You go tend to Mitch and his kitchen, and me and Kik will make up a list of things you need from the grocery store." Kiki hopped out of her princess bed and stood on her hind legs to lean on Nikos's calf, stretching against him. He scooped her up and planted a kiss on her nose.

God, he really did have some gush-worthy moments. "You don't have to shop for me. I can do it . . ."

"When, tomorrow? Your shift starts at seven, Frankie. It's already three. By the time you get there and *create* and get back here, you're going to be dead on your feet. You go. I'll take Kik for the night if you don't make it home by eleven, okay?" He gave her a quick peck on her lips. "Go. It's okay," he emphasized with a reassuring pat on her backside.

Taking Kiki from Nikos, Frankie gave her a quick snuggle before handing her back. She squeezed Nikos's arm and shot him a smile before grabbing her coat and purse and running out the door.

As she headed out of her apartment complex, she smiled again when she remembered his body pressed to hers.

And then she blushed because she was having carnal flashbacks she neither regretted nor didn't want to repeat. A. Lot.

Add in the fact that while she knew Nikos wanted to throttle Mitch, sick or not, he didn't object to her going. The clench of his jaw and the flash of irritation in his eyes had told her he wasn't happy about it.

But that he had, in fact, not made a big stink of it, and even offered to take Kiki for the night, meant he was beginning to trust her.

Like a flash of lightning, it hit her: Nikos's trust in her had become very important.

She smiled.

To herself.

Like time number two million and two.

CHAPTER FIFTEEN

From the "red-eyed, snot-dripping-from-her-nose" journal of ex-trophy wife Frankie Bennett: Recipe for Disaster equals one part dying ex-husband, two parts enraged new boyfriend, and a pinch of paparazzi with telephoto lens. Oh, and *Hollywood Scoop* is the debil, and all the people who work for that fucking show are ass-licking, debil worshippers. I have to go now, because I need another tissue and some ointment for my raw nose. And the want ads. In that order.

Frankie glanced at the clock and yawned wide. Wiping her hands on the apron Mitch had provided, she untied the strings and laid it on the countertop, looking in Mitch's direction. "So I think you're good to go. This should get you through to the next-to-last taping and keep the execs happy. I'll email you one more recipe before the end of the week to finish it up."

Mitch's eyes, still so youthful despite his fifty-eight years, crinkled at the corners. "Do you think it could be that meatloaf recipe from the diner?"

Her head cocked. "I told you, that's an Antonakas family secret. End of discussion."

His charm turned up a notch. "You know, you're a lifesaver, Frankie. The powers that be would have known something was up if I didn't produce. I just couldn't come up with anything. I can't seem to focus with . . ."

Right. Who could focus with their head in a guillotine? She brushed her hair from her face, ignoring the mess they'd made in favor of digging out her purse from the pile of computer paper on the marble countertop. "I'm an exhausted lifesaver. As it is, I won't get back until almost six, and then I have to go to work. And you should be in bed." Mitch didn't look sick. In fact, he looked better than he ever had. Maybe all that colonic garbage he'd given a thumbs-up to really was the answer: youth in an enema.

As they'd worked, she'd been hesitant to ask too many questions about the doctor he was seeing or his course of treatment for fear he'd consider her interest more than just humane. Too much of the evening, and the intimacy Mitch injected into every other word, had left her feeling uncomfortable.

Though, tonight had been a milestone. No matter how many times Mitch brushed her arm with his, no matter how many warm smiles he shot her way, no matter how many frickin' times he'd cornered her against a counter—he just wasn't Nikos.

Wee and doggie to growth.

Wiping his hands on a linen towel, he cornered her again. "Why don't you just stay here, honey?"

Frankie backed away. "Because I have an apartment I'd like to spend my first night in, not to mention, work in two hours."

"Right. The diner." Oh, the sarcasm those words dripped.

"Yes, Mitch. The diner. I know it's beneath you because the label isn't five-star, but I love it there. I love working there. I love the people there."

"And that Nikos. Do you love Nikos, too?"

"Did you love Bamby?" she countered.

"Not like I loved you."

Hookay. They were traveling into the muddy waters of lying and so much bullshit. She was out. What was the point of arguing when he had much bigger issues to consider at this point in his life? "None of that matters anymore. I have to go."

But he took her by the arm, pulling her to him, his body still quite obviously in peak condition due to his personal trainer Gustav. "Don't you miss me, Frankie? Don't you miss us? Like we were tonight? Cooking together, laughing?"

Laughing? Had there been laughter? She'd made it a point to keep this get-together strictly business minus laughter. Frankie pulled back, letting her arms hang loose. "Us? Us? Do you even know what that word means?" She shook her head, trying to remember that the man with the grip of steel was sick. "Look, let's not do this. You're not well."

"Of course I know what it means, honey, and I'm well enough to know I miss you. We had some good times. Great times."

"Before or after I became your bitch?" The words slipped out before she was able to stop them. That Mitch was diagnosed with a terminal illness didn't change the facts. The facts were these: he'd done something awful to her. Then he'd left her broke and a YouTube sensation. But she was letting her old anger surface when it was of the utmost importance she keep it in check.

So checked.

He trailed a finger down her nose. "That's unfair, Frankie. You asked for something to do."

Frankie sucked in a deep, calming breath. "I don't want to have this conversation, Mitch. I want to go home. Let go of me, and we'll forget this ever happened."

"No. I deserve to hear this. Let's clear the air before I leave this earth."

She softened a bit, cringing at the bold acceptance of his fate. "We don't know that you're leaving anything."

"But if I do, I want to know you had your fair shot. Now, go on.

Give it to me. We're adults. You asked me for something to do. I gave you something to do on the show, didn't I?"

"Right. Something to do—I didn't ask you to do *someone*. I didn't ask to become someone you battered with constant demands and endless complaints until exhaustion set in all while your minions fanned you with palm fronds and hand-fed you grapes. I was your wife, Mitch. Not your slave." Wow. Talk about unload.

Mitch heaved an exasperated sigh, as though he'd said this a thousand times before and she was boring him by making him repeat himself time one thousand and one. "We've been through this, Frankie. You know how passionate I am about my work in educating people about quality food. That takes hard work and dedication, honey."

Those very words, words she'd heard time and again while Mitch had walked all over anyone he had to in order to get where he wanted to be, were hot buttons of long-suppressed anger. "Your work . . . You really are an egomaniac, aren't you? It's *food*, not the cure for erectile dysfunction. And you're right, we've been through this—you know, when I found out you were banging Bamby. What you claim to be passionate about, Mitch, is meaningless in the overall scheme of things. We definitely need food to survive. We don't need pears soaked in one-hundred-year-old brandy to do it. We also need an answer to world hunger. Do you think because you grace people's TV sets every day you're doing them all some sort of favor? Like your humanitarian efforts will make the world a better place? Please. Let's be real. You're a guilty pleasure to your viewers. So stop making it sound like you're the Gandhi of food, saving the hungry one black truffle at a time. I know this will totally blow your mind because it was a real cluster fuck for me when I found out, too, but there are people in the world who'd eat a Whopper every day if it meant they wouldn't be homeless or they'd have a steady paycheck. But none of that matters. What does matter is you didn't have to treat me like I was the maid instead of your *wife* all for the sake of your *work*."

The look he gave her was pained, threading through the light wrinkles at his mouth, and she might have fallen for it if the man standing in front of her wasn't Mitch. "I honestly didn't know you felt that way, Frankie."

This was pointless. "I didn't have the time to know I felt that way until you took every single thing I owned right down to my cashmere socks and skipped off into the sunset with Bamby." She fought not to yell, tamping down her rising anger. "I don't think I ever saw who you truly were until the night of the live broadcast. You did it right under my nose and then you left me with next to nothing, Mitch, and it didn't trouble you even a little. I didn't even get severance pay for time served. I worked just as hard, if not harder, than you to get you where you are at this very second of this career you're so passionate about, and oh, look, I got a Nissan Versa and *my* dog. The dog you never liked to begin with. You didn't know whether I was dead or alive until you needed me to help you."

She'd have given him credit for showing shreds of remorse if he hadn't said what he said next. "I told you, Bamby and I are over."

Her eyes rolled in disgust as she squirmed her way out of his arms and headed toward the door, swinging it open and rushing out, making a beeline for her car. "Yeah, you sure did. Was it her sagging ratings or her sagging implants that did you in? Look, Bamby isn't the point anymore. I don't want to go over this with you. You need to rest. What's in the past is in the past. Let it go."

"I got caught up in the fame, Frankie. It just happened," Mitch called from behind her as his quick steps thunked on the pavement.

Frankie beeped her car door before whirling around. Damn him. Why couldn't he just let this be? Her words began somber and as calm as she could muster, but they ended up loud and screeching in the chilled night air. "You were always caught up, Mitch. In you. You were self-absorbed long before you hit national television. And nothing just happens when it's about shedding your drawers and sticking your man bits into another woman's special lady. That's premeditated boinking. So spare me the age-old excuse!"

Mitch caught her up against him again. He sure was quick for a dying man. "I'm sorry, Frankie. I've made some mistakes, but so have you."

Whoa. Why was it that when something most excellent happened, it was all due to Mitch, but if something craptacular occurred, she'd had a hand in it?

"Oh, you bet your ass I did! I made plenty of mistakes. I let you turn me into your whipping boy. But my mistakes didn't leave you in poverty, living in your aunt's retirement village. They didn't leave you humiliated and some sideshow freak on national TV either. You, as always, came out of this smelling like a rose. I was the one who was painted unstable and a raving lunatic. I'd bet my ovaries people give you their sympathetic face when I come up in conversation, don't they, Mitch? Poor, poor celebrity chef with the crazy wife. But it isn't you who has to deal with the constant scrutiny when someone recognizes you, is it? They want your autograph. Me? They want to know if my straightjacket's on tight enough to keep me restrained."

Mitch's control was slipping, his patience waning—which meant it was time for him to sound like the reasonable half of this conversation. Like she was the loon in all of this. "Let's be honest here, Frankie. You did that to yourself."

Shoving against his shoulder, she tried to loosen his grip. "I damned well did. I flipped. But let's also be honest about something else. You did me wrong, pal. Not the other way around. There wouldn't have been a scandal if you hadn't created one to begin with.

Yet I'm the one paying for it. Well, not a flippin' second longer! I will not be embarrassed for calling you out because you're a lying, cheating bottom-feeder, and I won't be your victim! I like my life now, Mitch. It's a whole lot less complicated when I don't have to chase after you with a roll of toilet paper in hand so I can wipe your ass. I like that I'm in control of what happens to my life. Nay, I love it, and you can't ever have that back. No one will ever control me the way you did again. For any cause, five-star food or otherwise."

His lips thinned—a sure sign he was fighting to keep his notorious temper in check. Yet his next words were a shadow of sincere. "I don't want to control you, Frankie. That's never what I wanted. I just got a little carried away. All I really want is you to consider us getting back together."

"Because you need me to help create recipes for the show."

"No—"

"Oh, yes!" Frankie all but shouted, forcing herself to keep her voice down. "My recipes won't help that. Keeping your dick in your pants might. Now go inside before this gets any worse. Go back to your precious multimillion-dollar brownstone with its ridiculously overpriced paintings and marble floors and let this go. Please. Getting you all riled up can't be good for you. You're ill. I'm here for you in the most vague sense. I'll help you in any way I can, but we're never getting back together."

Mitch scooped her up in his arms, then cupped her ass as though he had a right to it, and dying or not, that just wasn't gonna happen. "Are you sure you won't reconsider getting me that meatloaf recipe? It could be a big hit. Think about the business it would bring the diner."

Anger not only at his presumptuous behavior but also at the size of his balls slithered in an ugly climb from her toes to the tip of her head. With a pinch to his ear, Frankie drew him down to her lips.

"Oh, I'll give you a meatloaf recipe—meatloaf this, Mitch Bennett, and take your hands off my ass or I can promise you, you'll need a proctologist as well as an oncologist. Let. Go. Now."

Mitch did as she requested, letting her go so that she almost fell into her car. Frankie cracked the door open and gave him one last glance. "I'll email you. Good-bye, Mitch." It was all she could do not to snarl the words at him before she started the engine, slammed the door, and left.

Terminal or not, there wasn't a shred of guilt left on her plate for finally letting Mitch have it.

Consider the air all clear.

~ℓ~

"So you and Chloe are never going to make Mama grandbabies."

Nikos cocked his head and gave his mother a sympathetic smile. Running a hand along her cheek, he leaned in to kiss her. "No, Mama. I've told you over and over. I'm not interested in Chloe. I know she's Greek, and in your mind the perfect fit to the family, but you don't want me to be unhappy for the rest of my life, do you?"

She spread her hands across her ample hips. "But you like our Frankie. You can't hide this thing from Mama."

Shit. "I wasn't trying to hide it from you per se, Mama. We were still testing the waters, so to speak. Feeling each other out, seeing where everything would lead before we made any official announce-ments about anything. And I know she's not Greek, Mama, but you and Papa will just have to live—"

"Bah," Voula said with affection, cupping his cheek with her weathered hand. "I know Papa and me always say we want you to marry a nice Greek girl, but really, we just want you to marry some-one. Anyone. I don't even think she needs to be nice now you're so old," she teased. "We teach Frankie how to be a good Greek. If she can be married to that bad Mitch for all that time, teaching her to make good baklava should be a cupcake."

Nikos barked a laugh. "Piece of cake," he corrected, love in his tone.

Voula shrugged. "Same thing. I just want you and your fresh brother to be happy. If Frankie makes you happy, I'm happy."

"And Papa?"

Voula grunted, making a fist she shook playfully at her son. "He is what your Frankie calls a cranky pants, but he is not mad about you and Frankie. He's mad he does not feel useful anymore. It's time we talk about that Florida you say would be so nice for your Mama's creaking bones. I want to play shuffleboard and sit by the big pool with a tall, pink glass of silly juice. I know if we leave the diner with you, you will take good care of it."

"You have enough in your retirement fund to last you two lifetimes, Mama. But I don't think Papa will go for it. He's nothing if he can't micromanage the diner."

She shook her chubby finger at him. "You don't worry about Papa. He'll come with me if I tell him Seamus Mavros is there . . ."

Nikos gathered her in a hug. "You are one crafty lady, Mama."

She patted him on the back. "Speaking of my Frankie, where is she today?"

Nikos gave a worried glance at the clock. Frankie, since the first and only time she'd been late, was nothing if she wasn't punctual to the point of early. On most days, she was a half an hour early, but it was already ten till seven.

He'd spent a restless night with Kiki curled up next to him, refusing to give in to his bullshit insecurities. It wasn't even Frankie he didn't trust; something just didn't smell right with Mitch. Still, lying about kicking the bucket was a drastic extreme to go to in order to woo a woman.

"Morning, Voula," Frankie called from just inside the kitchen, dark shadows under her eyes.

Voula clapped her hands in delight. "Ah, there she is." Then she frowned, cupping Frankie's chin. "You look so tired, my baby. You don't sleep?"

Nikos watched as Frankie waved his mother off, giving her a quick hug before going to get her apron. "I just had a long night . . . er, unpacking. I'm good to go."

Voula reached for her again, pressing the back of her hand to Frankie's forehead. "You don't feel sick, but you come to Voula at lunchtime break. I make you soup. It feeds the heart."

"Soul," Frankie corrected on a tired giggle, grabbing her favorite knife. "I'll see you at lunch."

More and more, when he observed Frankie with his mother or even his father, Nikos also observed tightness in his gut, an electric tingle in his chest he'd been unsuccessful at pinpointing. His eyes strayed to the woman he'd come to look forward to seeing across from him every day. Her auburn hair was in that messy ponytail, and her amber eyes were indeed rimmed with dark shadows.

Nikos nudged her slender shoulder with his, keeping his ludicrous suspicions and potential outbursts to himself. "How'd last night go?"

Frankie's eyes didn't seek his. Instead, she looked down at the chopping block. "Okay. No big deal."

"Did you come up with anything solid—or are you going to have to go back?"

She frowned down at the carrots she was slicing for the stew. "No, no. I don't have to go back. I think we sewed it all up. Was Kik okay? Is she in the back with Barnabas?"

He nuzzled her neck, ignoring the weird vibe she was giving off. "Yep, she's with Papa, and she spent the night plastered up against me like we'd been surgically attached together." Leaning in closer, he let the tip of his tongue skim the outer shell of her ear. "We missed you."

Frankie waved him away with a gloved hand and a terse giggle. "Stop. Your mother."

He took the knife from her, forcing her to look at him by hauling her close, bringing to mind the lascivious notion of taking her right here and now. "She knows."

When her eyes finally found his, they were weary and hesitant. "Am I in the shit because my last name doesn't have an 'opolous' on the end of it?"

Nikos laughed. He loved her sharp wit. "Nope. Mama loves you. She's fine with it. Happy it's you, in fact."

"Really?" Her genuine surprise was evident.

"Really, sweetheart. Why are you so surprised?"

"Because while I'm clearly diner material, I didn't think I was 'big, hunky Greek son' material."

Nikos found her lips with his for a quick kiss. "Well, I say you're Greek material. Now get to work, and if you need a break before lunch, take one. You look like you've been up all night."

Automatically, her eyes strayed elsewhere before she rested her head on his shoulder and sighed. "Don't be silly, Antonakas. I need at least eight to deal with a slave driver like you. Ten if I hope to be quick of wit."

Another quick nip of her luscious lips and Nikos said, "I gotta go do payroll. Meet me for lunch in the back?"

She grinned, making his stomach do something he was sure only girls' stomachs did. "It's a date."

Nikos left her chopping carrots and green peppers with a satisfied smile. Today, life was good. Not that she would have prevented him from pursuing Frankie, but his mother wasn't going to harp on him about Frankie's less than Greek-ness. Topping that off, Voula was going to talk Barnabas into retiring—something long overdue but much needed.

And Frankie was here.

Opa.

～ℓ～

"My Nikos, he likes you."

Frankie gave Voula a look of caution she was unable to hide while she nibbled a cracker and stirred her chicken soup in the back office.

Voula gave her a shoulder-to-shoulder nudge. "You like him, too, eh, Frankie?"

"He's . . . he's . . . uh, very nice."

"S'okay. You don't have to hide the feelings with Mama. Then we all walk on eggs. Eggs are no good on your feet."

"Eggshells." Frankie gulped. Despite the fact that Nikos had given her the green light, she'd seen Voula in action when one of her cubs had a mere scratch.

"Yes. The eggshells," she said on a wide smile. "I know Nikos, and I see how he looks at you when he don't think I'm looking. It makes my heart glad. But he has bad thing happen. I don't want that to happen again, Frankie."

You've been warned, Bennett.

Wiping her hands on her apron, Frankie approached the topic with caution. "I can only promise to do my best not to leave any carnage."

Voula frowned. "What is this carnage?"

"Wreckage. I mean, I promise to try not to hurt Nikos."

Voula rubbed a flour-covered thumb over Frankie's cheek. "It's not you I worry about. You know about the bad because you were married to the bad. But you're a smart girl. You learn from your mistakes. It's Nikos. He has the stupid disease. He doesn't always pay attention before he say something stupid. He is the most like my Barnabas. Green with the monster."

Frankie laughed, sliding back in her chair to scratch Kiki's head. "You mean the green-eyed monster? Like jealousy?"

"That's it. He is jealous and he does the stupid."

"Because of Anita . . ."

Voula winked, slipping Kiki one of the treats she carried around in her apron pocket at all times. "She had no business with my son when she really loved somebody else. She don't look at my Nikos the way you do. Eh, but what can I do when I see disaster? Nikos is a man. He does not listen to his mama anymore, even when I try and warn him. But he did not listen, and look what happened. Mama is always right. So you be patient, okay? If he opens his big mouth?"

"I promise to try."

"You're a good girl. Does not matter that you are not Greek. You're still a nice girl."

"Well, this very nice, not-Greek girl thanks you for the kind words." The warmth of acceptance made her cheeks glow and her heart shift.

Voula laughed, winking conspiratorially at Frankie when Nikos and Barnabas entered the office.

Nikos pulled up a chair next to Frankie, pulling Kiki into his lap and settling her under his chin while Barnabas flipped on the wide-screen television Nikos had installed just for him.

Barnabas settled into the chair, patting Voula's hand when she let it rest on his shoulder.

Frankie smiled at the people she'd come to treasure, sipping at her soup and fighting back a bad case of the sleepies. She felt only a little guilty about not telling Nikos she'd been at Mitch's all night. Later. She'd tell him later when she was better equipped to have a possible argument she hoped to avoid.

The voice of the newscaster on the TV droned on, familiar to Frankie's ears, but vague and buzzing due to sleep deprivation. "In our 'Actual or Nonfactual' spotlight—celebrity chef, Mitch Bennett."

Frankie instantly cringed, shrinking down into her seat. God. Mitch was like a bad case of herpes—always with her.

"As seen here on *Live! with Regis and Kelly*, the wandering-of-eye and playboy food fanatic of the once popular *Mitch in the Kitchen* was all smiles when he revealed a hint to the morning cohosts that he has some rather exciting plans for the future, involving, of all things, meatloaf. But that's not the real question you should be asking yourselves, fine fans of the preserved like well-aged wine prince of palette pleasure—the real question is, will Mitch Bennett and his one-time wife and candidate for best impression of a psych-ward escapee revisit their recipe for love? Check out this footage, taken just last night, from *Hollywood Scoop*'s intrepid reporter Dan Winter, and judge for yourself if it's actual or nonfactual."

Frankie's eyes were wide open now, her hands clenching the bowl of soup.

As scenes from last night flitted across the screen, all forty-two inches of screen, Frankie didn't have enough breath left in her lungs to even gasp.

And there they were. Displayed in plasma, Mitch's hands on her ass, her lips near his ear.

The video of her supposed tryst with Mitch undoubtedly had been edited to make it look as though she and Mitch were in some kind of passionate lover's embrace, and they'd conveniently left the words "meatloaf" and "recipes" in while cutting out her protests.

Yes. Today was all kinds of awesome.

Barnabas clicked the television off, letting the remote slide to the pocket on the side of his chair, wordless. Voula's horrified face, the shape of her mouth in that O of disbelief, was matched only by her muffled sob and escape out through the doors of the office.

Frankie cleared her throat, praying the raw, cracked feel of it wouldn't lend to a squeaky, disjointed explanation. She laid a hand on Nikos's arm, but he yanked it away, making her jump. She fought for calm. "Listen to me—"

Nikos's lips thinned, his jaw tight and unforgiving. The muscles of his free forearm clenched, flexing with tension. "You were with Mitch all night last night, weren't you?"

Frankie scooted forward in her chair, imploring him to look at her. Her pulse crashed in her ears and her stomach heaved. "Yes, but it's not what you think. They're making it look like something it wasn't, Nikos!" If Mitch wasn't dying, he would be when she got her hands on him. He'd never looked more youthful and glowing than he had in that clip from *Regis and Kelly*.

The idea that she'd been had made her want to yark.

"Don't insult me by lying, for Christ's sake!" he roared, making even a deaf Kiki jump. "You did just see what we all saw, didn't you, Frankie! God damn it, they have video of you and Mitch at his house with the clothes you had on last night. You sure as hell didn't look like you were reluctant to have his hands all over you."

No, no, no. She would not let this slip away. Not when she was so close. Her eyes remained pleading, but her resolve was unshakable. "Whoa, hold on there, knuckle-dragger! Do you have any idea the way the tabloids twist things to make it look like something it isn't? That video's been edited to hell and back!"

Nikos scraped his chair back, his body rigid with his palpable anger. His black eyes grew hard like two onyx stones, but his voice, Jesus, his voice was eerily together and ominous. "I might not be Cordon Bleu–educated like Mitch, but I'm not an idiot, Frankie. It doesn't change the fact that his hands were all over you. I saw it with my own eyes, and you didn't look unhappy about it."

"Right, but the part of our conversation you didn't see was the part where I told him if he didn't take his hands off my ass, I'd remind him how stealthy I am with a wooden spoon! You're jumping to conclusions again, Nikos—you're sentencing me without giving me a fair trial!" she shouted, jumping up and sloshing her soup to the floor with trembling hands.

But he was in a zone Frankie knew all too well. It was painfully obvious in his stance and by the tightening of his jaw he couldn't hear her anymore. "I knew it," Nikos said with so much disgust in his voice, it left the marrow in her bones aching. He dragged a hand through his hair. "I knew something was going on, but I swore to myself I'd trust you. You can't deny what I just saw, Frankie, so don't you throw Anita at me. Don't. I ignored that little voice in my head that said you wouldn't ever go back to a piece of shit like him—"

"Nikos Antonakas!" Barnabas shouted, popping up from his chair to stand in front of his son. "You do not use this language with our Frankie no matter what. You will be a gentleman!" he commanded in a tone of force Frankie would never have guessed he possessed.

Frankie's heart raced when Nikos's eyes scanned her in distaste. "Don't worry, Papa. It won't ever happen again. Get the hell out, Frankie."

Voula's cry from outside the door preempted any further explanation, leaving everyone assholes and elbows to see what was going on.

Nikos was first to her side, Kiki still tucked under his arm, blissfully unaware of the newest commotion. "Mama? What's wrong?"

Her round face held disbelief. "My recipe for the meatloaf. It's—it's—gone!"

Cosmos bolted through the doors of the kitchen and took hold of Voula's shoulders. "Did I just hear you right?"

Tears streamed from Voula's always cheerful face. "It's gone, Cosmos! I know where I put. Every night I put it away because I need the next day. My memory is so bad. I must look always to be sure I make it right. It's not there," she sobbed.

The few remaining lunch customers in the diner sat in stunned silence just as Simon burst through the diner doors with Jasmine literally flying behind him. The clickety-clack of his cane led him to where they all stood. From where Frankie was positioned, she noted Simon looked deeply troubled. "Nikos? We need to talk, champ. *Now.*"

"Not now, Simon," Nikos said with clipped words.

Voula leaned against Cosmos, her eyes reddening by the second. "We must find the recipe! I cannot make meatloaf for the customers."

"I'll help," Frankie finally chimed in, her chest tight. "C'mon, Voula. Let's double-check."

Simon blocked her from moving toward Voula. "I wouldn't do that, Frankie."

Her heart began a hard rhythm in her chest. "What?"

"I said, don't bother. I know who took Voula's recipe."

Oh, thank Jesus and all twelve, Frankie thought. She sighed her relief, ignoring Jasmine and the wave of her hands from behind Simon. She was doing the girlfriend thing again, but Frankie was too tired to figure out what she could possibly be warning her about.

"I think it was Frankie."

Note to self: When your girlfriend sends you the girlfriend signal, no joke—at all costs, heed.

CHAPTER SIXTEEN

From the journal of the "right back where she started from" still ex-trophy wife Frankie Bennett: All I want to know is this—why is it that when Mitch dumped me, I slept like a newborn in my cocoon-like cave of despair, but when Nikos Antonakas did it, I couldn't catch some shut eye if the Sandman and every last one of his merry band of Sandettes combined hurled all the sand from the Jersey Shore at me? Thoughts? Bueller?

"What the hell do you think you're doing, Simon? Who the fuck do you think you are?" Jasmine demanded as they pushed their way out of the diner and headed for the parking lot. During her lunch break at Fluffy's, she and Simon had both been witness to the TV footage of Mitch and Frankie. Jasmine had seen and Simon had heard that stuffy, snarky bitch of a reporter take pleasure in exploiting Frankie.

Instantly, Simon had put his idea of two and two irrational thoughts together, formulated Frankie's alleged deceit, and sentenced her.

It had taken Simon all of two seconds to demand Win drive him to the diner to share his thoughts with Nikos. Jasmine had followed behind in her car, alternating between worried for her friend, sick that she'd momentarily considered Frankie would have anything to do with Mitch's stealing the meatloaf recipe, and furious that Simon wouldn't listen to a single word she spoke in defense of Frankie.

The hell she'd let Simon accuse her friend before she had the chance to defend herself.

Simon's face was pained in the harsh light of the midafternoon sun. "You didn't really think I wasn't going to tell Nikos what I heard, did you? Not on my watch. I know she's your *friend*, if that's how friends roll these days, but Nikos is mine, and I'll look out for him whether you like it or not."

She rounded on him, almost wishing he could actually see the fire she knew flamed in her eyes. "That son of a fucking bitch stole the recipe for Mama Voula's meatloaf, Simon. I don't know how, but he did it. You heard what that gossip show said just like I did. Mitch suddenly has some secret that involves meatloaf? Meatloaf? What kind of goddamned *chef* brags about meatloaf? I know it was him. I know it in my bones. I don't know what he's planning to do with it, but it can't be good."

"How do you suppose Mitch got ahold of it to begin with, Jas? Who else would give it to him? Who else works that closely with both Mitch and Mama V? Look, I just laid it out there. They can do with it what they will." He cracked his jaw, wincing against the harsh wind that stung them both with icy whips of air.

Shit. There was that. Shit, shit, shit. Yet, Jasmine refused to believe otherwise. Refused. Oh, Christ on a cracker. She couldn't be wrong. "Chloe—maybe it was Chloe!"

Simon's shoulders lifted. "Maybe, but I didn't hear Chloe on the phone with Mitch. I heard Frankie. Whether it has something to do with what just went down or not, I don't know."

"I just can't believe Frankie would ever do something so awful, Simon. She adores the diner. She adores Mama Voula. She's nuts about Nikos. Why would she ever do something like that?"

Simon cocked his head in the direction of Jasmine's voice, his words tight between his clenched teeth. "Why does anyone do anything? Maybe she was just pretending to adore them until she could get her hands on that recipe and skip off to Mitch for some cash. She's not the first person to want that recipe."

"What proof do you have she's responsible for this?"

Simon gripped his cane, his gloved hand tense and tight on it. "I just told you. I heard her talking to Mitch on the phone. The day she moved into her place."

Jasmine slowed, but only a little. "And what did the great Simon hear with his finely honed hearing skills?"

"When we went to her apartment the other day for her house-warming, I heard her tell Mitch she'd *have it for him*. It's not hard to add the two together, Jasmine."

Jasmine poked his chest with an accusatory finger. "Yeah, well dumb jock that you are, I'd bet you sucked in math. She could have meant a million different things, Simon. So your theory's officially just been shot to hell. Now shut up, and let's go back in and help Frankie sort it out."

He remained in the middle of the parking lot, unmoving. "The hell I will. I'm just looking out for Nikos and the people who love me like I'm their own, and after her phone call with Mitch, that *Hollywood Scoop* bullshit, and some pretty incriminating video of her and her ex-husband, I laid it out there."

Jasmine's eyes narrowed. "How do you feel about blind, deaf, *and* mute, quarterback? Mitch did something shitty to Frankie, no way would she help him do something shittier, and she wouldn't go back to Mitch for all the Betsey Johnson in the free world."

"You've only been friends for a few months. Can you seriously claim to know her? Think of all the money she'd regain if she got her hooks back into Mitch . . ."

Fury sizzled along her spine, racing toward her mouth. One she wasn't afraid to lambaste him with. "I don't think I need to know

Frankie longer to know she'd never do something like that to another human being after the way she was hurt, and she doesn't want to get back together with Mitch. I just want you to look at this with the possibility she's innocent."

"I'm just bouncing the idea that Frankie's seen some hard times lately. Some cash wouldn't make her cry."

"Way to bounce," Jasmine torpedoed the words at him. Suddenly, she was doubt-free, and angry about Frankie's juryless trial. The trouble was, her anger wasn't just about her friend's dilemma.

"You're angry." Simon said it as though he was surprised she'd be angry he was accusing her one and only friend of not just stealing, but sleeping with a bottom-of-the-barrel licker.

Jasmine scraped her heel on the pavement in disgust, but it wasn't just on Frankie's behalf. Part of her disgust stemmed from the notion that her fears about Simon were justified. "You're a real Mensa candidate. I *am* angry. I really was beginning to think you were different. I don't know why all men with two dimes to rub together and a couple of annuities are assholes, but I was this close to believing you were different. You see all women as opportunistic gold diggers, don't you, Simon? There's no way you'll even allow that maybe some distortion of the truth is happening here. Maybe what you heard and what *Hollywood Scoop* reports is just a little skewed toward the nasty gossip end of the spectrum. You know what those story-loving whores are like firsthand. Jesus, I thought I was jaded. I think we're done, Simon."

When Simon approached her, his nostrils flared. He knew exactly how to locate her because she was wearing the perfume he claimed to love. Standing before her, his face held myriad emotions she didn't bother to decipher, even if she had the luxury of doing so without ever having to meet his condescending eyes. "Any excuse'll do, right, Jasmine?"

"Excuse? You're accusing my friend of being a backstabbing, money-grubbing bitch without giving her a chance to explain."

"But Frankie's the perfect excuse to get rid of me so you don't have to face the fact that you're falling just a little in love with me."

"Simon!" a female voice called from over his shoulder, thwarting Jasmine's response. A slender, sharply dressed woman approached them, microphone in hand and a cameraman just an inch shy of her ass, scrambling to keep up with the heavy equipment.

The trouble with that attractive woman was this: she was only the leader of a pack of attractive women, and men, hell-bent on getting to Simon.

"Shit. The press," Jasmine muttered to him, setting aside her fury in favor of protecting an unarmed man. She shoved Simon behind her, steadying herself against his chest.

The woman Jasmine had initially caught sight of jammed a microphone in her face. "Aren't you Jasmine Archway?"

From the corner of her eye, she saw Win fight his way through the crowd with limited success. Who cared who she was? Ashton was a tire mogul—more boring than watching your nails dry. He was rarely, if ever, in the tabloids unless he was banging a rich socialite, and even then, the razzi lost interest pretty fast if the socialite wasn't Paris Hilton.

Jasmine fought to keep her answer from coming off as hostile, yet the vibe she was picking up was anything but friendly. The woman's face, lovely and unlined, even in the harsh midday sun, swam in her line of vision. "Yes. I'm Jasmine Archway." She was . . .

"What's your take on the intimate relationship you're having with your ex-husband's biological son?"

Simon's groan swished through her eardrums.

The world tilted, the parking lot's pavement rushed upward in a wave of crushed black stone to stare her in the face, then sink back to the ground again, the pack of faces before her blurred into millions of prying eyes.

Summoning all of her former life's limited paparazzi etiquette, she responded, "I have no comment."

Oh, but that wasn't entirely true.

Jasmine did have one last comment before she planned to shove her way through the throng of gossip-mongering whores, get in her car, and go back to her small apartment where it was safe. Uncomplicated. So she could nurse her repeat performance of naïve idiot in private.

Jasmine yanked Win forward through the crowd, pulling him as close to Simon as possible. He'd need help getting through this mob of foaming-at-the-mouth reporters.

Just before she pivoted on her heel, she turned around to take one last look at the man she'd been this close to falling in love with. Her face was impassive, her tone dead. "I guess you're right, Simon. *Any* excuse'll do."

Before the bitter tears of her foolishness could fall, she ran toward her battered car and away from Simonides Rhadamanthus Jones.

Her ex-husband's son.

God bless us, everyone.

～～

"I'm going to go to that diner and drag Nikos out by his ear. Then I'm going to show him my senior citizen's right hook," Gail snarled, pacing across the small space of threadbare carpet in Frankie's living room. Maxine snorted at her words.

Frankie's eyes followed Gail back and forth. She sighed from her place on the lone folding chair, almost but not quite amazed at how worked up everyone was. To be properly amazed, she'd have to be involved. To be involved, she'd have to actually care about taking any further action.

"And I'll help ya. Then you know what I say, Gail Lumley?" her Aunt Gail's best friend and Maxine's mother, Mona, asked.

"What do you say, Mona Marie Henderson?"

She raised a fist, wrinkled but agile, toward the ceiling. "I say we go dig that talleywhacker Mitch out of his plastic kitchen and show him what senior Tae Bo is all about!"

Frankie slumped in her chair, running a hand over her greasy hair. "I say we just let me go back to my air mattress. It's actually rather nice. Kik loves it."

Maxine whirled around to face her from her stance in the kitchen doorway. "Oh, no, Frankie Bennett. You've been moping for too long now. You are absolutely not going to crawl back into your cave. You'll get up off your ass and do something about this!"

Disinterest returned full force. Each time Frankie thought she might be able to conjure up the will to fight the unfair situation she'd been presented with, her AeroBed called like a siren's song. In her defense, it was a really good song. Irresistible, in fact. There was nothing like just lying around feeling sorry for yourself.

Tugging the blanket she'd dragged around with her since she'd been unfairly accused of cheating up under her chin, she pondered with slow words. "I'm not sure what you want me to do. Beg Nikos to listen to me? Beg him to believe I'm not some lying, whoring thief?"

"Yes!" Jasmine shouted, the jingle of her bangle bracelets jarring Frankie's peace in the quiet place. "Yes, that's exactly what we want you to do, Frankie."

Frankie shot Jasmine a bored look. "Look who's giving out advice."

Jasmine wagged her finger in warning. "Don't you dare, Francis. Nikos is not your ex-husband's son. You were not some pawn in a sick game of payback."

She shrugged her shoulders, unaffected. "According to Simon, neither were you."

"And he's sooooooo honest and forthright. Please, Frankie. He'd say whatever he had to to the press so he ends up looking like the upstanding, cancer-society-donating hero everyone thinks he is. I'm not buying. Regardless, this isn't about me. I'm not stinking up the joint with my pity."

No. That was true. Jasmine was as beautiful as always. Perfectly coiffed, perfectly made up. Perfectly together. Frankie would cringe in embarrassment at her own greasy, rumpled appearance—if she cared, that is. Alas, for the moment anyway, she didn't. She'd forgotten how grand the quiet place was, and she just wanted to pay it a little visit. Just for another hour or so. Then she'd see about clearing her name.

Besides, no one in the quiet place called her a purveyor of falsehoods.

Mona was quick to stick a finger under Frankie's chin, giving it a nudge. "You will not lie down and die, missy. I won't have it. You will get up off your skinny keister and go prove that penis pimp was the one who stole that recipe and leaked that video of you two to the press because he wants you to come back and be his slave again. He knew if Nikos saw that video, it would finish you two off!"

Frankie sighed with an apathetic yawn attached. "Mitch is a sick man, Mona. What would you have me do, beat up a man with cancer?"

Mona stomped her foot. "Yes! He's about as sick as I am a twenty-five-year-old blonde with perky taters and a size-two dress! Now let's prove he's not above that kind of trickery!"

"So I can what, Mona? Make Nikos believe me? Nikos didn't trust me enough to even consider I was telling the truth to begin with. He didn't even bother to hear me out. That's all there is to it."

Jasmine swiped at a strand of Frankie's hair covering her eyes. "I hate to defend the hothead, but he's had a bad experience in the past—not to mention, that footage on *Hollywood Scoop* was pretty misleading."

"Yet here you all are, trusting that I'd never do something like that to anyone, but the man I . . ." Her voice cracked. Oh, no. There'd be no more sobbing. She caught herself, gripping the arms of the chair.

"I'm going to make a horrible admission here, Frankie," Jasmine said with a wince. "I doubted for a minute, too. It was only a minute. Okay, maybe three, but I did doubt. Then I forgot about my doubt because I was so furious with Simon."

"The point is you gave me a chance to explain. Nikos didn't. To think I was was so close to falling in love with him, I was almost ready to let him see me naked in broad daylight."

Both Gail and Mona, heads cocked in thoughtful pause, hummed in sympathetic understanding, acknowledging the serious commitment she'd considered making. Maxine nodded her recognition of Frankie's sentiment.

But Jasmine came to Nikos's defense. "Our emotional investment in you is very different, honey. I don't know about the rest of you ladies, but I've never had one of my friends, you know, of the girl variety, cheat on me in the physical sense. You can't hurt us in quite the same way. Nikos is another story. He was dumped by a woman he thought was truthfully over her ex-husband," she pointed out.

Gail, Mona, and Maxine hummed more unified agreement.

Which served only to make Frankie angry. "You know, I was cheated on, too. Hello. Or have we forgotten how my marriage ended? Nikos admitted there was no proof Anita cheated on him. If anyone should have been suspicious and jealous, it should have been me. In fact, I should have been a raving lunatic every time Chloe stuck her big, perfect hooters in his face or whenever any number of women who ate at the diner flirted with him. But I wasn't, because I don't want to be that person. I listened to Maxine's advice about letting go of past hurt, for all the good it did me. I *want* to trust a man again. I wanted to have faith that all men weren't barely evolved apes. That's where Nikos and I are very different. I went into this thing with Nikos with my eyes wide open, and with the idea I'd at least get the benefit of the doubt if a problem arose."

She had said that the first time he'd become sullen and moody over Mitch, hadn't she?

Yes. Yes she had.

Frankie settled back in her chair. Phew—that diatribe had been exhausting. If she raised her hand to her brow, odds were, there'd be beads of sweat on it.

How was it, when you did everything in your power to change all of your bad relationship habits, when you tried to be as open and honest as a person could be, you still ended up back in the same stupid spot you began in?

Mona was the first to respond. Her sharp eyes took in Frankie with a mixture of sympathy and purpose. "And do you remember how your marriage ended, Francis? With you screaming like you were on fire on live television. You *reacted*. Maybe not the way you would have if it wasn't such a sock in the kisser, or the way you would have preferred to, but you went berserkers, kiddo. I think I know what Jasmine means. Nikos reacted. Badly, yes, but it's because he's been knocked around a time or two. He saw what we saw, and it looked pretty damn bad for you. I'm not saying what he did was all right by me. I wish he had listened to you. All I'm saying is he lost his marbles. You know what that's like. I'd also like to think if the situation was reversed, and you were the one who behaved like a big, fat baby, Nikos wouldn't give up so easily."

Jasmine saluted Mona with her coffee cup and a grin. "I couldn't have said it better myself."

"I reacted because Mitch really *did* cheat on me with Bamby. I didn't cheat on Nikos, and I didn't steal . . ." She fought back that lump in her throat—the one filled with her grief over losing the Antonakas family as a whole. "I didn't . . . I would never . . ." She choked on her words. "I would never steal that recipe."

"Different circumstance, same reasoning, sassafras," Gail offered, running her fingers over the small pearl buttons on her sky blue sweater.

Her resolve was beginning to soften. Her longing for Nikos was penetrating her safe cocoon of anger. She missed him so much; her heart was like a heavy lump of rocks in her chest. "I understand what you're saying. I hear your reasoning, but here's the problem. I did try to call Nikos on several occasions before I finally decided I was going to be dubbed not just mentally unstable but stalker worthy if I didn't give up. He refuses to talk to me. I'm not going back to that diner until we at least talk. Not after the way he looked at me like . . ." She fought the hitch in her voice. "Should I keep begging and pleading? Shouldn't I have some kind of self-worth?"

"You mean the kind that involves baths and a hair brush?" Maxine chirped with a cocked eyebrow and a teasing smile.

It was all Frankie could do not to flip her the bird. Even if she was right. "I mean the kind that allows me to see this for what it is and to let it go in favor of moving forward." Again.

Fuckall. She didn't want to have to start over again.

But a thought occurred to her—she'd have to simply because she was right back where Mitch had put her when she'd left him anyway. Wallowing. Swimming in the deep, soothing waters of self-pity.

A small ember from her recently stamped-out fire ignited.

She'd let another man, despite how lick-o-licious, drag her down.

No. Nikos hadn't done this to her. He'd crushed her with his mistrust and doubt, but she'd let herself go right back to square one. She'd let his reaction defeat her when she knew she was right. Okay, so maybe Nikos would never believe her. Maybe she'd never convince him she wasn't a cheat.

All that mattered in the end was that *she* knew she wasn't a cheat.

All that mattered was she was right with Frankie when she went to sleep at night.

How stupid of her not to hang on to that at all costs.

Maybe Mensa wasn't going to reserve a spot for her just yet.

"I let this happen," she muttered, reaching down to scoop up Kiki, considering.

Jasmine smiled, bright and beautiful. "In part, yes. You're doing what you did when you left Mitch. Instead of getting back up on your feet, you're sitting on your ass in your own cloud of dust. No man, even one as fantastic, albeit stupid, and as ridiculously jealous as Nikos, is allowed to reduce you to this, Frankie. You can hurt. You can cry. You can feast on a high-caloric diet in your mourning, but you can't stop functioning. It would mean you've learned absolutely nothing since your divorce. So get the hell up."

Maxine grinned at Jasmine. "Grasshopper, I bow to your sage wisdom." She held out her hand to Frankie. "I'll help."

"And I'll make us some sandwiches," Mona added, rubbing her hands together with glee. "While we figure out what our next plan of attack is, girls."

Frankie took Maxine's hand, wobbling when she rose, clinging to poor Kiki, who missed their daily routine—and seeing Nikos. Each day since this had gone down, Kiki had waited patiently by the door at six sharp, eyes wide and expectant. She was waiting for Frankie to scoop her up, put her in the car, and take her to the diner so she could be with the people she'd come to love.

If Kik only knew her beloved Nikos was the person keeping her from doing just that. No fair. Even if Nikos refused to believe anything she said for the rest of his miserable, jumping-to-conclusions life, he had no right to take away everyone she'd come to love just because he was a bonehead.

Whether she loved his bonehead or not.

Then she had a lightbulb moment.

Wow, did it suck when all you did was alternately cry and drink copious amounts of caffeine in various forms.

And as it turned out, Oreo-cookies-and-cream pie was not part of the four essential food groups some would claim was so critical for energy and a well-balanced diet. Her innards said so when she attempted to move out of her own way.

Frankie's stomach rolled, but Jasmine pressed an arm around her waist to right her. "You know what pisses me off about you, Francis?"

"What's that, Jasmine?"

"You did nothing but eat pie and guzzle coffee, and I think you're skinnier than when this whole thing began. Screw you, Bennett."

Frankie giggled, righting herself. "So what can we possibly do to fix this mess I'm in?"

Jasmine's eyebrow arched. "We need to get to Mitch. He's got that recipe. I feel it in my gut, and he played you like a Stradivarius. He's no more dying than I am a size four."

"But you said you were a size four . . ."

"And I lied, all right? All of those McDonald's french fries with that asshole Simon and the pressure of your skinny ass made me do it, okay? That's neither here nor there. Mitch isn't dying, and he got his hands on Voula's recipe while using you to help him."

Frankie nodded her agreement, almost sure what Jasmine said was true. It added up, and it pissed her the hell off. "But how did he get it? I mean, it wasn't like Voula kept it under lock and key, but who'd help him do something like that?"

"I'm thinking Chloe. She's the obvious suspect. She was pathetically jealous of you and Nikos together. Why wouldn't she do something that crappy to get rid of you?"

For the first time in a week, Frankie felt the blood in her veins begin a slow simmer. "I know it should have, but the thought never crossed my mind."

"That's because you're not a devious bitch. Chloe is."

"And what do I do about that, Jasmine? Take her out in the diner parking lot?"

"Chloe's the least of my concerns right now. Right now, we need to figure out how to get the recipe back from Mitch. Dealing with Chloe can come later." Jasmine's cell phone chirped. "Shit. I have to get that. If it's one more reporter, I'm going to have to change my number."

Frankie sympathized. Reporters had been calling Gail all week long. You'd think Mitch was Jim Morrison reincarnated. He made cookies and frou-frou delicacies. Yet he was all the rage as of late, and she was a part of that shit storm.

Though, it was so much worse for Jasmine. They'd been hounding her since last week about Simon and his long-lost father. When Frankie's heart wasn't aching for Nikos, it was aching for Jasmine. Simon had proven her right. Give a man some bags full of money, and they discovered everything had a price tag. They became invincible and above common decency. Yet, in the process of walking all over you, they ended up breaking your heart.

While Jasmine gave good face, Frankie knew during the brief clearing of her caterwauling and whining that her friend had come to care for Simon. She'd never admit it now, but the hurt that flashed across her face at the mention of Simon was a very real pain.

Jasmine's lips thinned to an ugly line as she listened, with the phone pressed to her ear, to whoever was on the other end of the call. She shook her head in a distinct "no" motion. Then she bit the tip of her fingernail in thought, her features softening. With a confused, furrowed brow, Jasmine said good-bye and hung up her cell with a grimace.

"Is everything okay?" She put a hand on Jasmine's arm.

Jasmine's eyes narrowed, gleaming like she'd just eaten her prey alive. "It just might be, Francis. It just might be."

Frankie frowned, hiking up her sagging drawstring flannel pajama bottoms. "Who was that?"

"Simon."

Frankie's stomach lurched, making those pastrami and Swiss sandwiches Gail and Mona were making much less appealing. "And you haven't twitched once. Or spoken in tongues. I'm impressed, kemo sabe. What gives?"

"We, my friend, have a whole new ball game with Mitch and his kitchen. Get your mitt, Frankie. We have a recipe to catch."

CHAPTER SEVENTEEN

From the journal of Frankie Bennett: I have decided a career as a superspy is off the table for me. That I allowed myself to hatch a plan of diabolical thievery with a blind man, his babysitter, two crazy senior citizens, and the hottest blonde, genius mathematician ever is just shy of bungee jumping off the White Cliffs of Dover. So a potential reprisal of Jennifer Garner's role in *Alias* is quite safe from me. Jesus. The things we do for love.

"You did the stupid thing, didn't you?"

Nikos ran a hand over his hair. "What's the stupid thing?"

Voula clucked her tongue and perched herself on the arm of his couch, letting her pudgy, sneakered foot swing. "Do you remember little Angie Staniskoppas?"

"Vaguely."

"She lived down the road and you had big crush on her, Nikos. You used to play together all the time. Do you remember why you stopped playing together?"

He ran an impatient hand over his chin, sipping at his beer. "No, Mama. Look, what's the point here?"

"You watch the tongue with Mama. I get to the point when I get there. Answer the question. Do you remember why you stopped playing together?"

"No." Okay, so that wasn't totally true. He did remember Angie and how she'd ditched him for Jason Antonetti.

"Because you did the stupid thing. You see her talking to another boy, and you don't ask her what they are talking about, forgetting you don't own her. Instead, you think she likes the other boy better. So you tell her she's not your friend anymore and you make her cry."

"Point. Please, Mama," he said, softening his tone a bit.

"This is the point, Nikos. Angie was borrowing a pencil from the other little boy. Her mother tells me this when she calls to say Angie is crying and she doesn't know why you are mad. I know why you are mad. Because you do the stupid thing. You do this all the time. You don't listen. You don't think before you open the mouth. You just see colors."

"Red. I see red." Damn right he'd seen red. Lots and lots of red.

"Red, blue, purple. I don't care. You said mean things to Frankie, and I don't care what the television says, my Frankie would never do what they say. What you say. I know there is a—a . . ." His mother frowned, unable to find the word she was looking for.

But he doubted the word she was looking for was what was needed where Frankie was concerned. "An explanation."

Voula waved a finger in the air. "Yes. One of those. But did you listen to Frankie? Did you ask her? No. You yell at her, and you send her away. Now she is too afraid to come back, and you won't return her calls. You did the stupid thing. But I want you to hear me, Nikos Antonakas. You will be sorry. I love you no matter what silly things you do because you are my son, but I am not afraid to tell you when you have done wrong. This time, I think you are wrong. I don't believe Frankie played cootchie-cootchie-coo with Mitch. I don't care if he makes piles of money with my recipe for meatloaf either. Not if it mean we lose our Frankie."

His frustration grew, threatening to bubble over and splatter his mother. Couldn't anyone see she was the root of this problem? How was it even Cosmos had his doubts? Cosmos, who'd all but labeled

Frankie from the get-go. Since Frankie had been gone, the diner's atmosphere had changed.

Barnabas mourned the loss of his Kooky by way of longing stares at her vacant princess bed. Voula virtually sat shiva during the hour she'd once spent each day making her meatloaf, giving him the evil eye every time he was left to do Frankie's prep work. Adara had called him from school just to let him have it for buying into the accusations against Frankie, and then she'd hung up on him—with zeal.

Each day was heavier than the last, and no one was laughing the way they once had. They weren't even laughing the way they'd done *before* Frankie Bennett came on to the scene. But facts were facts. "She stole from us, Mama. Am I the only person of sound mind to know that?"

Voula's head shook in typical dramatic Voula fashion. "No. You are wrong to believe the newspapers and television. Do you believe that Jennifer Aniston has baby by aliens? No, but you believe Frankie was making kissy-face with that bad Mitch. The television is lying! But when you find this out for sure, it might be too late. If I have no grandbabies, I will blame you." Voula kissed the top of his head, gathering her scarf and purse and heading for his front door. "You remember what Mama says. She will be right, and you will be sad again, Nikos."

The click of the door left Nikos alone with nothing but his hot anger and the residual need for one Frankie Bennett.

"How does it feel, sir, to eat crow? Is it as unpleasant as everyone claims—or does it taste just like chicken?"

Simon pressed his forefinger and thumb to the bridge of his nose. "So *Hollywood Scoop* had a heavy hand in the editing process of Mitch and Frankie's allegedly rekindled romance. Doesn't mean she didn't steal the recipe, Win." Though, that nagging feeling he'd had since this had all begun nagged harder.

Win placed his arm around Simon's shoulder, holding the disc one of Simon's contacts at *Hollywood Scoop* had managed to get his hands on. The one with the real scoop, sans some artful editing. "Sir? Do you really believe that—or is that what's helped you sleep at night? You *heard* just as I did. Frankie most certainly did not betray Nikos with Mitch. You added uneccessary fuel to Nikos's fire with a stupid assumption. You were wrong, Simonides. I do believe the expression 'own it' applies directly to you."

"I did own it," he offered, hearing his defensive tone ring throughout his ridiculously large kitchen and cringing. "I called Jasmine. I told her I jumped to conclusions. I offered to help. I'll show Nikos the disc."

Win snorted his disapproval. Simon knew the one. It meant he had to atone bigger—harder—and faster. "And the lovely Jasmine? How do you plan to make up for forgetting to mention her ex-husband is your father? Would you just chalk it up to 'oops, my bad'? Or are you willing to go the extra mile?"

Simon let his head sink into his hands. "First, he's not my father. He donated some sperm. Edward Jones was my father right up until the day he died ten years ago. And I did apologize. Well, at least as often as she'd pick up the damn phone. If I hadn't yelled Frankie's name right out of the gate, she'd have hung up again."

"It's nothing less than you deserve. I told you from the start, honesty would be the only route to take with Jasmine."

He sighed, turning his head away from Win's open admonishment. "I was going to tell her. It just kept getting harder and harder."

Win tapped his finger on the table Simon sat at. "Which part was the hardest, young man? The part where you planned to steal what you thought was Ashton Archway's finest possession—his wife—like you were snatching up a Ming vase, and rub it in his face—or the part where you thought you could get away with it? Clearly, sir, you underestimated your opponent. Ashton Archway quite obviously didn't find Jasmine as valuable as he should have—or you've come to. It would have been no skin off his nose, as you say. He would have just replaced her with another Ming vase. A warm, beautiful, smart woman like Jasmine is nothing but a replaceable toy to a man like your *father*."

Simon slammed his fist down on the table. "I get it, Win!" he roared. "I get it—lay the hell off."

"*Do not* raise your voice with me, Simonides. I'm most certainly not afraid to take you over my knee. Now, no more mewling like a newborn kitten. You did this. You shall find a way to fix it. I shall help. Pick that phone back up this instant and tell Jasmine and Frankie we'll be right over, not only with the proof of her innocence, but with a plan."

Win's hand clamped down on Simon's shoulder in that warning from days of old. "*Now, Simon*."

Nothing had changed since Win had come into his life when he was eight years old, and Edward Jones had insisted Simon have consistency in his, up until then, reckless, resentful early youth. He'd hired Win to take care of Simon while his mother traveled with him. When his mother met and married Edward, a wealthy lawyer and part owner of a minor league baseball team, he'd changed everything in little Simon's world.

Edward treated Simon like his own son in every sense of the word—even when Simon didn't welcome it. Instead, he continued to love Simon without his consent and much to his aggravation. And while this new man in his life had more money to spare than God, he made Simon tow the line.

When Simon was sixteen, Edward insisted he get a job, and then smiled proudly when Simon told him it was at the local convenience store as a cashier. He patted his son on the back and took him to open his own savings account.

There were no fancy sports cars, no private schools, no expense accounts, no overindulgences on behalf of Edward. Outwardly, most wouldn't have known Simon's father was a multimillionaire, and that was because Edward wanted Simon to learn the value of hard work, honesty, and the ability to spot sincerity from a mile away.

What there was in return was an abundance of Edward's love and constant support. His advice, his warm bear hugs, his infectious chuckle, his evident pride in his son Simon, and his legacy as one of the kindest, most genuine men Simon had ever known.

His father made him work through college, and he suffered the wrath if his grades didn't meet Edward's approval. He wouldn't have a boy who could only catch a piece of cowhide—he saw to it Simon got his degree in finance. His father also was responsible for keeping his head on straight when he'd made it to the NFL. Edward kept his ego from exploding. He'd taught Simon to give back instead of recklessly indulging.

Edward was the man Ashton could never be—the father he could never be.

Winchester was whom Edward had entrusted Simon to all those years ago, and when Simon's accident took his sight, Win picked up where Edward left off. Win never failed to remind him exactly who was in charge, and he wasn't afraid to tell him he was wrong. He kept him in line.

Win had frowned upon Simon's old childhood resentments when his mother had no choice but to tell him who his biological father was after he'd found a picture of them together.

And then Simon began to nurse his anger about Ashton's rejection like a bottle of booze. He nursed the resentment that while he lived in a rundown trailer with his mother, Ashton Archway lived in a mansion. He nursed the tears his mother had cried when jobs were scarce, and she'd almost lost their home, forgetting that shortly after that, life had become pretty damn good with the entrance of Edward.

It burned his gut that Ashton was once a huge fan of the team Simon had played for. The man who'd spawned him, in what could only be called irony, loved the star quarterback.

Meeting Ashton wasn't a problem. He was, after all, Simon's biggest fan. Yet it was after that very meeting, at which Ashton let Simon know under no circumstances did he want anything to do with him and his "married into money" mother, that Simon began to cultivate a plan. His plan didn't change when he lost his sight—it was what got him through the grueling heartbreak, the endless hours of relearning how to walk across a room without taking out a lamp. In fact, it strengthened his hell-bent plan for revenge.

To take what Ashton Archway called his most prized possession. Jasmine.

It mattered little that Ashton divorced Jasmine to buy up, as she'd put it. What mattered was showing him he could have *whatever* he wanted now, because Simon Jones had turned out just fine—and he had more money than he knew what to do with.

The goddamned trouble with all of this was, his revenge might as well have been plotted by an eight-year-old. He should have told Jasmine about Ashton from the start. From the moment he'd decided he was no longer interested in hurting the tire mogul who'd left his mother like so much trash.

Each moment spent with Jasmine made it harder and harder. Each moment spent with her, he fell more deeply in love.

He toyed with the cell phone Win left at his fingertips.

Christ. He'd fucked up. Every lesson Edward had ever taught him, he'd defiled. Disgust for his behavior welled up in him, threatening to incapacitate him.

And Win was right—it was time to atone.

~ ⚬ ~

Simon arrived at Frankie's apartment three hours later, hangdog, and with the biggest bouquet of flowers she'd ever seen in hand.

Win gave him a hard nudge inside. "Miss, it's always a pleasure to see you." His warm eyes smiled, his big hand reached for Frankie's.

Taking a deep breath, Frankie addressed her accuser, fighting to keep her anger with him from her voice. "Simon, how's life treating you?"

He winced. "Better than you?" He held out the flowers to her, his face hesitant. "I don't know what they look like, but Win assured me the cost of them was on par with a space shuttle ticket."

She sniffed them, savoring the lilies of the valley interspersed with so many roses, she lost count. "He's right."

Simon almost grinned. "Good. So what's next? A kidney? My pituitary gland? I'm down with whatever you need."

"If that's not the truth," Jasmine drawled from the doorway, though she couldn't hide the look of longing flitting through her eyes when they landed on Simon's big frame. Frankie noted her friend erased her yearning just as quickly as she allowed it.

An uncomfortable pause turned into at least a full minute of awkward before Win finally said, "We are here to profoundly apologize for the devastation Simon's brought you, Frankie, and you as well, Jasmine. He shall bow and scrape appropriately at your command. I'll see to it."

Frankie couldn't help but laugh. Simon was like a chastised child, still smarting over his wrongdoing. "How about I make us all some coffee, and we sit down and talk?"

"I'll help," Jasmine added. "To be sure we put the proper amount of arsenic in Simon's cup. We want a clean kill."

Win's head reared back and he laughed when Frankie nudged Jasmine and scowled. "I'd hold the measuring cup. However, I fear we need Simon as our pawn in our dirty game of pool. Thus, for now, I declare he lives. After we've had our way with him, he's all yours, Miss Jasmine."

Satisfied, Jasmine and Win went into her small kitchen to hatch Simon's diabolical end over a pot of freshly brewed coffee.

"Frankie, I was wrong," Simon said, using his cane and his nose to move closer to her.

Her chin lifted, and her voice was strong and clear when she replied, "Yeah. You were. You totally tightened my noose. But I'm not sure if that bothers me nearly as much as what you did to Jasmine. It was cruel. So I'll just say this and then I'll let it go. Win told us about you and Ashton, and the way he treated you . . . why you wanted to hurt him like he hurt you and your mother. I know what that kind of anger can do to you. But you really blew it. I know I'm like the pot calling the kettle black when it comes to anger management here, but *wow*. That said, for some ridiculous reason, I don't think you're a horrible person. I can't say the same for Jas, but I believe you truly feel something for her you didn't expect."

Simon blew out a breath he'd been holding, his wide chest deflating. "I did something I'll have to live with for the rest of my life. But I swear to you, Frankie, the second I sat next to Jasmine in that bar, everything changed for me. All I can do now is apologize to her, and to you. I'll make sure Nikos has a copy of that disc if it's the last thing I do, and I'll help you do whatever you need me to do with Mitch."

Frankie paused, unable to see anything but genuine concern on Simon's face, genuine remorse. She put her arm around him and gave him a hug. "So let's go get us a piece of Mitch."

Simon held out his arm to her, and Frankie took it, and together, they walked to the kitchen.

———✺———

Win attached the Bluetooth securely to Simon's ear. "How does that feel, sir?"

"Good, Win. Thanks."

Jasmine's heels clicked against the floor almost twenty-four hours after they'd sat huddled in Frankie's tiny kitchen hatching the best plan of attack. "Gentlemen, Frankie, are we ready to go slam some hokey chef ass?"

Simon smiled in Jasmine's direction, so sweet and loving, Frankie hurt for him. "Ready as I'll ever be, cupcake."

Jasmine placed a finger on his chest to stop him. "I'm not your cupcake. We're doing this for Frankie, who deserves to be exonerated after you all but pounded more nails of suspicion in her coffin."

"Let it be, Jasmine," Frankie chided. Simon had only been looking out for Nikos. She'd had all night to do some thinking—what else was there to do when she couldn't sleep?—and while she didn't like it, Frankie understood the bigger picture. Simon had reacted the way any good friend would. She only wished it hadn't been in front of everyone at the diner.

Jasmine straightened her sweater, smoothing it over her svelte hips. "The hell I will. Now let's go get that damned recipe from that douche bag, and then I can be rid of the whiny ex-football player." She stalked from the room, the crunch of her heels an indication of her fury with Simon.

"Hey! I'm not whiny, just blind, and I said I was sorry," Simon reiterated.

"That's so not working in your favor anymore! Not the blind and definitely not the sorry, pal!" Jasmine called on her way out of Frankie's back door.

Frankie shared a glance with Win. "You're worried, miss?"

She ran a hand over her forehead, shoving the stray strands escaping her mussed ponytail away from her face. "Are you kidding? How can we ever hope to get the recipe back if we have to mediate the Hatfields and the McCoys? We need clear heads and distractions while Simon looks for it. Maybe we should just revert to plan B and beat the recipe out of Mitch—or at least demand he just give it back to us." They'd nixed that idea in favor of having no solid proof Mitch actually had the recipe.

Win placed a reassuring hand on her shoulder. "Please don't fret, Frankie. I know my Simonides, and his remorse for putting that thought in Nikos's head knows no bounds."

Her sigh was shaky. "I know he was just standing up for his friend. If I'm honest, it did look pretty bad."

"All evidence did point to you, miss."

Anger tingled in her gut. Redemption, vindication motivated her. "Just like Mitch wanted it to." She knew that now without a shadow of a doubt. Mitch had used her as his patsy. Dying or not, he epitomized shithead right to the bitter end. He'd known exactly what he was doing. Though, in all of her hours spent thinking, she couldn't figure out what he planned to do with the recipe. Revealing its ingredients on the show was totally crappy, but what would Mitch gain from it other than happy fans?

Win held out his arm in his usual gallant fashion. "Shall we go catch a snake, Frankie Bennett?"

"All or nothing," she muttered, allowing him to escort her to Simon's car, waiting by the crumbling curb in the back alley so if any lingering paparazzi were about, they could escape. Frankie took a deep breath, relieved to find no one.

As they drove the last leg of the trip to Mitch's, Jasmine went over the plan one more time. "Okay, so here's the deal. Simon, open your ears because if you screw this up, you won't just be missing your sight."

"Sooooooo sexy," he crooned from the backseat with a seductively playful tone.

Frankie squeezed his hand to quiet him when Jasmine flashed an irritated frown in his direction.

"Frankie, you called Mitch and told him Simon wants to meet him and that you have the finished recipe for his last show, right?"

"Check," Frankie confirmed, the memory of that phone call making her stomach gurgle uncontrollably. "He was all over the fact that a famous ex-pro football player wanted to meet him. Mitch is nothing if he's not being properly adored."

"And he has no clue you know anything about *Hollywood Scoop*?"

She shook her head with a devious grin. "Nope. When I asked him how the show was going with the new recipes, he asked why I didn't watch to find out for myself. I told him how sorry I was I hadn't answered his phone calls, but I'd been really busy getting settled in my new apartment, and I couldn't afford a television. Oh, and I told him Gail's been out of town as casually as I could so he wouldn't know reporters have been calling her." Which wasn't a total untruth. She really didn't have a television. But Jasmine did . . .

Jasmine snickered. "He really is a complete ass. I guess we can be thankful those reporters haven't found out where you live or we'd be sunk. Now, Simon—"

"Yes, lover?"

Jasmine reached over the seat and flicked his arm. "Knock it off.

I'm not your anything." She cleared her throat. "So your job is to appropriately gush and talk about kitchen whatever."

"Gadgets," he provided. "I've done my homework. He has all sorts of overpriced doodads, but I'm particularly fond of the magnetic measuring cups."

Frankie watched Jasmine fight a sneer. "Yeah, yeah. A-plus. You did your homework. Whatever. So after you're inside for a couple of minutes, you get a phone call and that phone call will be me—out on the back verandah, looking into the prick's study. Frankie, are you sure I can see into the windows?"

She nodded, clenching her fists, her heart starting to pound faster. "Absolutely. Mitch had them replaced with floor-to-ceiling windows because he worked best in the mornings when the sun was brightest on that side of the brownstone."

Jasmine frowned. "Wasn't it you who did all the office work?"

God, hindsight was a beautiful thing, wasn't it? "For all the good that does me now."

"Don't give up the ship, kiddo. The fat lady hasn't even warmed up. Now, Simon, you make like the phone call's important and ask if there's somewhere you can go for a bit of privacy. That's where I come in, and Frankie, you keep Mitch busy. Do whatever you have to do until Simon finds his way out of that study." She bit the tip of her nail with a worried frown. "Jesus, are we sure Voula's recipe's in the study? Really sure?"

Frankie chewed her lip, fighting back the worry that had plagued her for the past week. "It's where Mitch keeps everything important. At least it was when I was married to him. It'll probably be in the third drawer down on the left side of his desk just like we discussed. He kept all of his financials there, everything that had to do with anything of importance. If it isn't there, then I'm essentially screwed, but no harm, no foul. We just leave like we never planned to steal anything."

Jasmine sneered. "No. Then we beat it out of him. He's got it. I know he does. I don't understand for what purpose, but he does. Don't worry, honey. Please. The only thing you have to worry about is that the whiny ex-ball fumbler will screw this up."

"I am blind, Jasmine. It will be *you* who's directing me from the verandah."

"Always with the blind card. It didn't stop you from being a liar."

With a snarl, Frankie snapped, "People! Please, please knock it the hell off! I'm already eggshell fragile here. I haven't slept in a week worrying about what Voula and Barnabas think of me. I'm tired, and I'm afraid to screw up my one shot at making this right. So stop fighting and let's focus on getting Voula's recipe back before Mitch turns it into a three-ring meatloaf circus, okay? Please?"

Jasmine reached back and squeezed her friend's arm, narrowly missing Simon's also consoling touch. "I'm sorry. You're right. So I'll be hiding in some bush on the verandah, directing you, Simon. That's it. That's the plan."

Now that Jasmine had laid it all on the table, out loud, Frankie had to fight back the million and one misgivings she had and take a deep breath.

Jasmine looked at them all. "We good?"

They pulled up to Mitch's brownstone with a hushed glide of Cadillac, parking in Frankie's old spot. Her stomach jolted again, her hands shook. "We're good."

Jasmine grabbed her cell phone with a grimace. "Ring-ring, Mitch's minion calling. It's that Juliana again."

Frankie chewed her lip again. In order for this to work, Mitch had to be alone. If Juliana was with him, they were screwed. She'd specifically told Mitch that Simon didn't want anyone else present because he was a private man.

Jasmine pushed the phone at her. "I think you should take it. If she's with Mitch, if she starts asking questions, hang up and pretend you lost the signal, and we table this for another day."

"Jesus, Jasmine. You're the most devious person I know."

"How do you think I caught Ashton tapping his latest victim?"

Frankie took the phone, praying she could pull this off. "Juliana? Hey! How's it going?" Jasmine smiled and gave her a thumbs-up of approval.

There was the smallest of sobs before she said, "Frankie, I'm sick over this, but if I don't tell you, I'll never sleep another wink."

Frankie imagined poor Juliana, tired, rumpled, beaten by Mitch and his demands. Instantly, she pitied the woman who'd had to step into her shoes. "O . . . okay. What's on your mind?"

"Mitch is a liar. A low-down, dirty, rotten douche bag."

Frankie almost barked a laugh. Ah, enlightenment.

"He's lying to you, Frankie! He isn't dying of anything. He's healthier than a twenty-year-old. He's not dying of cancer. He wasn't even a little sick on Christmas Eve. It was all part of a plan to get you to come back to the show. Mitch paid some out-of-work actor to come to the hospital and feed you that story. He knew damn well it would take something drastic to get you to come back. He knew it!"

Frankie's mouth fell open. That fucking bastard. She gripped the phone tighter to her ear, fighting for composure. "Are you joking?" She knew Juliana wasn't. Knew. Yet those were the only words of disbelief she could find.

Juliana sniffled and blew her nose into the phone. "I swear it, Frankie. I have the proof. I'll give it all to you, but not before I go to Bon Appetit and expose him for the pig he is! You *have* to believe me. I was suspicious about you coming back so easily. Mitch said it was because you wanted him to consider reconciling, but I didn't believe it, so I started to dig. It took a little while, but it wasn't hard to figure

out. Mitch is such an idiot he left a paper trail. He was so smug and
sure you'd never find out."

Frankie's stomach heaved. "Mitch lied to you," she murmured,
holding up a hand to thwart Jasmine's concerned gaze.

Juliana snorted her displeasure. "He lies to everyone. I begged
him to tell you the truth after I found out what he'd been up to. I
knew he needed your help with those recipes because his ratings
have tanked, and the execs were considering cancellation. I knew he
was cheating on you with Bamby, I just didn't have the guts to tell
you, but I never thought he'd stoop so low and tell you he was dying.
I never thought he'd be so afraid to lose his limelight that he'd steal
some poor woman's recipe and try to sell it to someone to mass produce for the frozen food section of grocery stores."

Frankie gasped. The depth of Mitch's fucked-up-edness was endless. She put a hand to her mouth to bite her finger to keep from
screaming. She'd fallen for it. Nikos and everyone else had been
right. Mitch was that much of a scumbag. How she could have ever
believed otherwise bordered unreal. Stupid, stupid Frankie.

Juliana didn't appear to hear Frankie's gasp; clearly, unloading
her burden was the only goal. "I don't know where that recipe is, but
I *know* Mitch has it. He caught me eavesdropping on him when he
was talking about the terms of this contract he's trying to finagle with
that frozen foods corporation and fired me, but it was only seconds
before I was going to quit! And now I'm going to hang up because I'm
so disgusted with myself for hiding Mitch's affair with Bamby and
everything else that I can't stand being in my own skin. I'm disgusted
that I was afraid to lose my job. But no more. I won't be a part of
something like this. Not anymore! I'm sorry, Frankie. I'm so sorry!"

The phone went dead.

Well, now. That bit of information made everything so much
easier.

Mitch wasn't dying right now, but, oh, when she was done, he'd be on his knees, praying he was.

"Frankie? What's wrong? Are you okay?" Jasmine prodded.

She smiled then.

Wide.

Sly.

"You bet I'm okay, and if I were you, Simon, when we get inside that brownstone, I'd listen for the scrape of a kitchen knife against Mitch's neck. Does anyone know if they have the death penalty in New York?"

~ ℓ ~

After retelling Juliana's story as quickly as she could, Frankie fought the urge to forget their best-laid plans and storm Mitch's castle instead.

"You have it together, Francis?" Jasmine asked.

Frankie's nod was curt. Sure, she had it. It was all together.

"Okay then, Mouseketeers. This is it," Jasmine announced, sliding down in her seat so Mitch wouldn't catch sight of her. "Good luck, sweetie, and go get 'em!"

"Aw, thanks, cookie—"

"Not you, dumb ass," she retorted from her hunched position in the front seat.

Simon turned his head in Frankie's direction. "Ah, love. Ain't it grand?"

Frankie fought a snort, escorting Simon up along the walkway lined with decorative stone she'd specially ordered herself from Italy. "She'll forgive you, Simon. Maybe not exactly in the way you want, but she will. Just give her time."

He paused in his step for a moment, pulling her hand under his arm. "You do know I feel like grade-A shit for buying into this, don't you? I was just looking out for Nikos. After Anita . . . I just didn't want to see him hurt like that again."

Frankie gulped crisp air into her lungs. "I almost understand. I think I was forever going to pay for Anita's sins, so it's probably better it's over between Nikos and me." Christ, that hurt to admit. But Nikos had allowed his mistrust to overrule even the slight possibility that she was telling the truth. Mitch's betraying her with another woman didn't match this kind of hurt.

"I should have given you the benefit of the doubt, but it looked so bad, Frankie."

"You know a thing or two about the tabloids, Simon. You're an ex-pro football player. If it isn't bad, or if it doesn't look bad, how would they ever sell papers or get ratings? Forget that. This isn't just about Nikos. It's about Voula and Barnabas and how they welcomed me when I was as low as I've ever been. I care about them, Simon. If anyone can buy Voula's meatloaf in the frozen food section, which is what Juliana claims Mitch plans to do with that recipe, then why would they travel from all over just to have some at the diner? That recipe's been in her family for generations, and if it wasn't for me, Mitch never would have known about it. I feel partially responsible for this."

"I don't think Nikos will want things to be over when he knows the truth, Frankie. He's a little head over heels for you."

Her heart throbbed in anguish for Nikos, but facts were facts. "For me? The real me who's fighting for what she wants in life, or the Frankie who needs a knight in shining armor? I can't live without trust, Simon. I wouldn't do it with Mitch and I won't do it with Nikos."

"How about this—we go and get this damned recipe from that slug, and we don't make any final decisions until we return it to Voula?"

Her mind was made up. No amount of crying at night before she finally fell asleep, no amount of missing Nikos would make her budge. But for the sake of this working, she nodded her head. "No final decisions."

They took the five steps leading to the door and stopped. "So here we go, sunshine. You got your game face on?"

Frankie forced a smile as she rang the doorbell. "Ready, set, hut."

Mitch opened the door, his face a wreath of smiles and goodwill. His greeting was warm, despite the dismissive glance he gave Frankie.

"Simon, it's wonderful to meet you." He extended his hand, touching Simon's.

And Simon responded by grabbing it and pulling it to his chest as though he held the very hand of God—like a teenage female who'd just stumbled across Robert Pattinson. "Omigahhhhhd!" he squealed, rivaling any third-grade girl. "You're Mitch in the Kitchen! Oh, man, I love you. Just big love from old Simon to you. You are hands down, the best chef ever. I mean, I know a lot of folks think that Tyler Florence is the shit, but he's no you!"

On that note, the one that left Mitch's ego appropriately fed, she and Simon entered the lion's den.

CHAPTER EIGHTEEN

From the journal of ex-trophy wife Frankie Bennett: As I reflect, again, I reiterate—spies we ain't.

"Do you know your left from your right?" Jasmine hissed in Simon's ear?

"I do." He at least kept his answer vague so if Mitch heard him, he wouldn't suspect foul play.

"Then take approximately three steps forward, make a hard right, and turn around, numbskull."

"Hey, quit with the name-calling. You'll mess up my step count."

"Would you shut up? You're not supposed to say anything suspicious, superspy! If Mitch hears you, he'll catch us." Christ, if Simon didn't get this right, she'd beat him with his walking cane personally. A deep breath later and she was watching him fumble in his pocket for the bobby pin to pick the desk's lock. "Be careful, Simon!"

Well, it was too late for that. Jasmine gasped. The bobby pin fell and skidded under the desk. "Oh, for the love of!"

"Blind here," he whisper-yelled back. "If you'd just stop barking orders at me, I wouldn't have dropped it. Jesus, Jasmine."

She crouched lower in the rhododendron bush to get a better view with the binoculars Simon had purchased for just this reason, fighting the sting when a branch cut through her nylons. "Oh, stop, please. You weren't so blind you couldn't lie to me. Wait! I see it. Get on your knees, bad boy, and slide your hand forward to about one o' clock." Simon did as he was told, clasping the bobby pin to stand up, thwacking his head on the edge of the large antique desk.

"Ow! Damn it, Jas, you're supposed to be my eyes."

"Oh, suck it up, girlie, and pipe down. Weren't you the one who played football? Did you cry like a girl when someone tackled you?"

Simon cleared his throat. "I did not, but I had a helluva lot better guards watching my back than you, gorgeous. Now stop barking at me, and let's do this before we get caught."

A shaky breath later and she was back to directing him. "Reach forward, Simon, and hang on to that bobby pin like it'll win you the Super Bowl." On closer inspection, Jasmine saw his hand hovered right in front of the keyhole. "Good, now make sure that thing's right side up, and jam it in there."

He tried not once but four separate times before she lost her cool with a slap to her forehead. "No, fool. Stop. Catch your breath. *Listen* to me. Lean forward."

Simon did as he was told.

"Niiiice. Now keep your hand straight and feel for the keyhole."

His chuckle slipped into her ear, making her shudder uncomfortably. "You're hot when you play spy."

Her sigh was ragged. "Simon—this is for Frankie! You know, the woman you helped trash because you wouldn't listen and who now no longer has a paycheck?"

Instantly, Simon was all business, successfully jamming the bobby pin into the keyhole. "Yes!" she cheered, then slipped on the rocks in the garden. She grabbed on to a branch of the bush to right herself, glancing around to see if anyone had caught her yet. "Okay, you're in. Pull out every paper in that damned drawer."

Simon began digging, setting everything on the desk in front of him.

"Hold each one up so I can see it clearly," she ordered, her heart racing. "Ohhhh," she cooed, "their divorce papers. Put that one down and say something random, like you're talking to a business associate. Say it loud, so that dipshit hears you, and Frankie knows we're in the thick of this."

Simon obeyed by barking into the phone, "How many times do I have to tell you, Don, no more endorsements for Nike! Jesus Christ, I'm blind, and even though blind men 'just do it,' too, we don't do it while we're running alongside a horse!"

Jasmine straightened. "Your agent did not suggest you do a commercial running alongside a horse."

"Yeah, yeah, he did." He held up another paper over his shoulder.

"No! Damn. That's not it. But wait, it's his checking account statement. Stop right there. I'm not ashamed to say, I wanna know how much he's bilked Frankie out of."

Simon slapped the paper on the desk. "That's not nice."

Her next words were petulant. "What would you know about nice?"

"I know what I was going to do to you *wasn't* nice." He sifted through more papers, holding them up.

"Using people never is, and no, no, and no. It's not in that batch. Damn!"

"That was only how it started, Jasmine. The moment I sat with you at Foofy's, I knew revenge wasn't what I wanted anymore."

"Fluffy's, idiot. Will you ever get that right? And it doesn't matter. That you even considered doing something like that to me—to anyone—makes my skin crawl."

Jasmine refused to continue her internal battle about Simon. That she could remotely consider still caring for him after he'd set out to do something so immoral made her wonder who she hated more—herself for still wanting him or Simon for having the kind of gall it took to do something so malicious.

"Hatred, resentment, years of it, does ugly things to a man. Win told you what I said only minutes after we met, didn't he?" He flashed another piece of paper.

"No, that's not it, and yes, Win told me, but why would I believe him any more than I believe you. He has *your* best interests at heart, dirtbag, not mine."

"Win only does what's right. I think it's obvious because I'm here with you right now. He wouldn't have let me get away with not making this thing right."

"And would you have been making this right if Win hadn't forced you?" She plucked a leaf from Mitch's rhododendron and shredded it with a maniacal smile.

"Yes, Jasmine. *Yes.*"

That one word shouldn't have held much water. It was only a word. Yet it chiseled at her heart like an ice pick, forcing her to see the power of such a long-festered resentment. "Oh, wait! Omigod, Simon, I think you found it!" Jasmine peered closer, adjusting the binoculars to focus on the well-worn piece of notepaper he held. "Ohhh, that's it! Put all those other papers back in the drawer, and let's get the hell out. I can't believe you did it! You did it!"

Simon palmed the recipe, scrambling to drag the pile of papers back to the drawer and shutting it with agile hands.

Jasmine sucked in a deep breath. *Thank you, God.* "Okay, now get the hell out of there before Frankie has to do something drastic."

Simon turned to the windows, his winning smile, arrogant and pleased with himself, wide on his face. He held up the recipe in two fists and gave her the sign of victory.

So caught up in his coup, he completely ignored her gasp.

She ducked behind the bush, fighting a yelp of pain when a branch caught her cheek. "Simon!"

Nothing. No response in her ear. *Oh. Dear. God. In. Heaven.*
"Simon!" she whisper-yelled. "Turn around, you gloating fool . . ."

~~

Frankie was hot on Mitch's heels, fear of being caught at a premium.
"See? I told you Simon was just fine, Mitch. He's really good at being
blind. Gets around just fine, don't you, Simon?"

Simon turned around just as Frankie saw him letting what she
prayed was the recipe slip to the floor. She faked a loud cough so
Mitch wouldn't hear the notepaper rustle as Simon followed suit and
yelled into the phone, "I told you, no, Don! What about me and maxi
pads says ex-pro football player?" He covered the earpiece and whispered into the room, "Agents. You know how it is, right, Mitch?
Always looking for the next buck."

Mitch gave Simon a skeptical glance, then appeared to remember
Simon couldn't see it. He moved toward Simon, and square into the
path of the recipe, all alone and needing someone to pick it up by
Simon's feet. "Here, let me help you, Simon. You'd probably be more
comfortable in the great room anyway. My office gets so cold."

"No!" Frankie jumped in Mitch's path, clutching his arm and
hoping her eyes were doing that smoldering thing Jasmine could
market and sell on a street corner. "I mean . . . er . . . why don't we
pick up where we left off the other night, uh, *honey*?" Eek. As tempt-
resses went, she sucked big ass.

Mitch stared down at her, his eyes narrowed, suspicion gleaming
in them. "I don't think it's appropriate in front of Simon, Frankie, do
you? It's rather a personal matter."

She caught a flash of Jasmine's blonde head over Mitch's shoulder.
Oh, crap! Moving in closer, she slanted her body at an awkward angle,
planting it sort of on Mitch's, slinging her arm over his shoulder to

point a finger at the spot on the floor so Jasmine could see where the recipe had fallen. "Simon knows how I feel, don't you, Simon?" she cooed, breathy and sweet. Well, okay, not quite as breathy as she'd hoped. She sounded more out of breath . . . "He knows how much I've missed you, Mitch. I talked about it the entire way here, right, Simon?"

Simon nodded slowly with a perplexed look on his face, then bobbed his head up and down with vigorous consent. "That's so true, Mitch. So true. Talk and talk. That's all she did. She's just bananas in love with you. In love, love, love. And I ask you, who am I to get in the way of soul mates? You two lovebirds go work things out while I finish up my phone call, mmkay? Go on, you silly gooses. Make nice."

Frankie winked up at Mitch in her best imitation of the seductive winks she'd seen Bamby give him. But her eyelid twitched rather than cooperated due to the fact that it was all she could do not to yak up all that pie she'd eaten. "So whaddya say, Mitch? Is what you said the other night still the truth?"

Mitch sucked in his cheeks, a sure sign he'd never meant a single word. Just as he was about to bullshit his way out of yet another lie, Simon's shoe scraped over the recipe, creating a rustling noise on par with an atom blast.

Hoo boy.

Mitch whipped around, planting his hands on his hips. His eyebrow rose in question when he rounded the corner of his desk. "What do you have there, Simon?"

Frankie flew to his side, shooting a quick glance to find Simon's foot covered almost the entire sheet of paper. "Simon's so clumsy sometimes. I bet it's your list of things to do, isn't it? Simon's always making lists." She bent to retrieve it, but Mitch put a warning hand on her shoulder.

"Don't move," he warned. "I'll get that for you, Simon."

Mitch began to stoop beside her, pushing Frankie out of the way with a rough hand to her shoulder.

"It's now or never!" Jasmine screeched into Simon's ear so loud, even Frankie heard it. "Tell Frankie to hit the floor and then take this bitch out! Go long, Jones!"

"Frankie! Hit the floor!"

But she was already there, sliding under the desk and grunting from the force of her landing.

The crash of Mitch's desk toppling over and the sound of bone crunching as Simon took Mitch to the ground in a crushing tackle screamed in her ears. Frankie eyed the recipe and dove for it while Simon wrangled Mitch to the floor, laying him out in a full-body press.

"Got it!" Frankie yelped in victory. Oh, never was there ever a more fabulous piece of paper than the one she held in her hands right now.

Jasmine skidded into the office, her heels clacking hard against the wood flooring while Win stomped in behind her. She helped Frankie up, brushing dust off her shirt.

Simon looked down at Mitch with sightless eyes. "Dude, you are so screwed. Just thought I'd give you the heads-up. Oh, and ease up on the garlic." Win yanked Simon upward with a grunt, while Mitch moaned from the floor, rising to put the back of his hand to his bloody mouth.

Frankie handed off the recipe to Jasmine, stalking Mitch back to his kitchen, where he screamed, "All of you get out or I'm calling the police!"

Her lips thinned. "You, slimy bastard! How could you stoop so low, Mitch?"

Unfazed, he went to the sink and wet one of his fine linen towels. "I have no idea what you mean."

Jasmine held up the recipe, shaking it at him, her cheeks bright red. "This is what she means. It's called stealing!"

Mitch placed the cloth to his split lip and stared them down with an arrogant defiance even Frankie would have never believed he possessed. "It was Frankie's idea."

So the anger management thing would have to wait, Frankie decided. And she'd go willingly if sentenced.

Just not before she ripped Mitch's dick through his belly button.

There was no thought involved in what Frankie did next. No pausing to gather her senses or to curb her blown fuse.

Frankie reacted, reaching for the first thing she could touch, launching herself at Mitch and pinning him to the wall with the kind of force she'd never have expected from someone who'd eaten nothing but Oreo-cookies-and-cream pie for a week.

Hah, you, Surgeon General.

Though, in her white-hot fury, she did revel in a moment of reflection. Everyone who'd seen her flip on national television would probably have to agree, threatening someone's life with a meat mallet, pointy side up, probably was a whole lot more scary than some silly old wooden spoon.

~ total ~

"Well, Antonakas, you've fucked this up but good. However, pal that I am, I decided to let you in on a little something."

Nikos made a sour face. "What's that, Simon?"

"Seeing as I screwed everything up about as good as screwing up gets, I thought you at least deserved the chance I'll never have with Jasmine."

"Simon, what the hell are you talking about? I'm shit up to here with pretty much everything. Say it and then have Win take you home. I'm in a piss-poor mood."

Simon waved his cane over top of the coffee table, sending empty beer cans flying. "Self-pity by way of Heineken is weak, buddy."

Even in his haze of anger and turmoil, Simon could still amaze him. "How the hell do you always know?"

"I've only told you a thousand times. My other four senses are finely honed weapons the likes of which the government has never seen. I could smell you from outside your door. But that's not why I'm here. I'm here because you owe Frankie big, and when you beg and scrape, if I can't see it, I'd at least like to hear it. Because I promise you, I'm going to giggle my ass off."

Nikos sat forward on the couch, driving his throbbing forehead into his shoulder. "You're not making sense."

Simon rooted in his pants pocket, pulling out an envelope. "One guess what this is."

"A letter from some stray groupie you just couldn't spend the night without, telling you she's having your baby?"

Simon poked him in the chest with his cane and smirked. "Funny. Nope. It's Voula's recipe, shithead, and the footage, with *full* audio of what really happened when Frankie supposedly hooked up with Mitch."

Nikos lunged off the couch, tearing open the envelope to scan the paper. He went slack-jawed.

"I see you're appropriately shocked. Good."

"You don't see anything," Nikos muttered, still too astounded to add much more. His gut shifted, hard and uncomfortable.

"You blew it, buddy. But maybe, just maybe, you can make it up to Frankie if you do that scraping thing I mentioned. She didn't steal the recipe, Nikos. Hector did, the little weasel. Mitch gave him all of five grand for it, and the dipshit took it. Mitch stood to make a whole lot more, and the idiot took but five bills."

Nikos sank to the couch along with his stomach. "Oh, Jesus."

"Yeahhhhh," Simon drawled. "I admit I had a hand in leading you astray. Now I'm admitting I was a jackass."

"How do you know for sure it was Hector?"

"Oh, you silly. Mitch sang like a fat, yellow canary when Frankie threatened him. He was such a little Mary about it, too. All this squeaky whining and begging her not to ruin him after he left her with a car and a dog, and he threatened to take the dog."

"Frankie threatened Mitch?" His Frankie? *Correction, ass. Not so much your Frankie anymore.*

"Oh, you should have seen it. I should have seen it. I'd have given my left nut to see it. She threatened to go to the press and that big food company about Voula's recipe and tell them how he stole it. That's what he planned to do with it. Sell it and turn it into a frozen entrée. Frankie told him even if no one believed her, it'd still make his life a little more miserable than it already was."

Simon made his way over to the couch to plop down next to Nikos. "Bon Appetit was thinking of canning Mitch's show anyway, his ratings were on the downward spiral. Mitch was going to lose his time slot because he couldn't keep his dick in his Dockers. He didn't need any more trouble than he's already had since Frankie flipped on him the first time. Seems women all over the country were sending him hate mail about what a scumbag he was. That's why he was going to tell his viewers it was Frankie who'd helped him create those last shows. It made him look like a hero for taking her back and her look like she was trying to make up for her freak-out. It also made him look like all the bullshit he spewed to the press about how Frankie needed mental help was true."

Nikos groaned. "God, he's a fuck." And he'd fallen for it. Hook, line, and sinker.

Simon nodded. "Either way, he confessed. While Frankie had him flattened against a wall, and I think Jasmine said she had one of those meat mallets at his throat. Pointy side up. Either way, he gave up Hector. So while I almost wish it had been the president of the Annihilate the Competition Club, because I totally liked Hector better than Chloe, it wasn't Chloe—our first suspect. I'd lay bets Hector's drinking and gambling again. Hector's an addict. Five grand equals a lot of booze and slot machines."

"How did all this go down? How did you get your hands back on Mama's recipe?"

"Dude, superlong story—one I'll tell you when we have more time."

The haze Nikos had been in began to clear, and with that clearing came sharp stabs of guilt for not seeing what was right in front of him. "So why didn't Frankie come tell me this herself?"

Simon slapped him on the back, the sound making him cringe after all that beer. "That, friend, is part of the pickle you're in right now. She doesn't want to see you, though she did ask me to tell Voula she'd meet her for lunch next week."

"Mama made plans with Frankie to have lunch?" He didn't know whether to be angry that his mother had clearly chosen a side or glad she'd been hell-bent on sticking to her original theory. That Frankie was no liar.

"She did. We're the only two cavemen who believed Frankie would steal. The only thing you were right about is Mitch isn't really dying. Another long story I'm all shiny about sharing once we get you cleaned up."

Nikos sat stunned into complete silence.

And then the impact of Simon's words, his behavior toward Frankie, and his mother's warning sunk in.

Fully.

He ran his hands over his tired eyes. "I so suck, eh, friend?"

Simon's sigh was exaggerated. "Oh my God. Like you wouldn't believe."

"All the evidence pointed toward her," was his pathetic, sissy defense.

"Uh-huh. And I helped point," Simon admitted, his eyes going remorseful.

"You suck, too." Like that should make him feel any better.

"Not quite like you."

No. Not like him. "I have to explain."

"You didn't trust her when she told you she'd never steal from you or Voula and that she didn't sleep with Mitch, and I have the doctored footage to prove she didn't. I'll force you to watch it later. Anyway, isn't trust the thing a chick wants most? Don't they want you to take their word above everyone else's? That's what Jasmine said when she found out that douche of an ex-husband of hers was my biological father. She said betraying a trust is the slimiest thing a man can do in a relationship."

Nikos's disbelief grew. "You finally told her?"

Simon snorted, letting his head fall to his chest. "Noooo, that's the problem, amigo. She found out that day at the diner from the press. Nice, right? I wasn't up front with her. I was going to be. I just didn't do it in time. I put it off. Which makes me not so smart in hindsight. And now look. Like a lovesick teenager. So, in the interest of not letting you end up in this boat with me, as much as I'd appreciate someone who could see in order to steer it, I have a plan. All you have to do is shave."

"How the hell do you know I haven't shaved?"

Simon grinned. "I can hear your stubble scrape the collar of your shirt. Now quit with the questions and get to crack-a-lackin'. And grab a shower, for the sake of all of us who have to endure your stank. Brush your teeth, too, so you don't pollute a small Indonesian village, and then I'll tell you my idea for winning back your dream girl, lover boy."

Nikos rose on unsteady feet.

His longtime friend held out his hand to grab at him, pulling him into a quick shoulder bump.

Simon wrinkled his nose. "Jesus, Nik. You stink."

No truer words.

~

"Why are we here again, Aunt Gail?" Frankie surveyed the nonexistent audience in the studio of their local cable channel.

Gail looked away, making a big deal out of digging in her purse. "I told you, Myrna Tuttle's doing book reviews for WBDH. You know, for the live local show *Gil and Lil in the Morning*? What kind of friends would Mona and me be if we didn't show up to support Myrna?"

Mona popped her lips, looking around the darkened studio. "The good Lord knows she's gonna need it if she's reviewing that crap we read last book group. I can tell you this for sure: there'll be no more dagnabbit astral projection for this girl. Not when I can read one of those spicy romance novels. You hear me, Gail Lumley?"

"So where's the rest of the book group?" Frankie asked, sliding her coat off and helping Gail with hers.

"We *are* the book group," Mona said.

"Ladies," Maxine intervened with an odd nervous twitter to her words Frankie didn't miss. She clasped her hands together, then rubbed her knuckles. "We'd better grab a seat."

Because they were filling up so fast. Frankie plunked down next to Gail, patting the seat beside her for Jasmine. She leaned in to her friend and whispered, "I'm sorry I talked you into this."

Jasmine pulled her nail file from her purse, passing Frankie a purposefully bored look. "I'm all about the seniors and being supportive. Won't be too far down the road when old Jasmine's going to be glad she got a head start and made friends with them early in the game. They know AARP like RuPaul knows a wig and a girdle."

Frankie chuckled at the visual of Jasmine wearing polyester pants or a housecoat. "You'll be the hottest broad attending Sing Along with Engelbert Humperdinck night."

"Oh, shh! Here come Gil and Lil!" her aunt said, excitement in her voice when she patted Frankie's arm.

Frankie rubbed her eyes, exhausted from the past two days of job hunting and forcing herself to try and set Nikos's obvious rejection behind her.

Simon had called her to let her know not only that he'd given the recipe back to Nikos with the proof she wasn't a backstabbing whore, but also that Hector had been officially fired and, apparently, Mitch had lost his time slot. As for Chloe, she'd quit after openly declaring her happiness that Frankie was gone, resulting in Voula chasing her with a rolling pin.

And still her cell phone remained silent, crushing what little hope Frankie had left that Nikos would at the very least apologize. Two additional long nights of missing his arms around her, missing the craziness of the diner.

Missing.

Those tears she'd fought since everything had gone down threatened to return full force. Oh, no. She would not go back to a self-pitying, pathetic wreck.

But she really, really wanted to.

Really.

Commotion from the stage in front of them forced Frankie to refocus, using the techniques she'd read in Maxine's ex-trophy wife guide. Onward ho—at all costs.

The lights went up and Gil and Lil began their dialogue. "Welcome back to *Gil and Lil*! Today we have a very special guest, a local celebrity of sorts who's here to share a very special recipe. Put your hands together for Riverbend's own Nikos Antonakas, owner of the Greek Meets Eat Diner!"

Frankie's eyes widened while everyone around her clapped.

A lot. Wildly, even.

And then she glared at them—every last one of them.

CHAPTER NINETEEN

From the journal of ex-trophy wife Frankie Bennett: Television, live or otherwise, is the root of all evil. Excuse me, but I have to go now. I'm going to blow up Best Buy's electronics department.

Jasmine shot her a catty smile.

Maxine's grin was Cheshire.

Gail and Mona just ducked.

"How could you all do this to me?" Frankie hissed at them. "You lied to me!"

"Suck it up, princess, and shut your trap," Jasmine whispered with a giggle.

Oh, the hell. How could they even entertain the idea of supporting Nikos's television debut when he'd treated her the way he had? Fury and Frankie became one. She clunked Jasmine in the leg with her shoe so she'd move out of the way when she made her escape.

"If you don't sit your ass down and behave like the lady I know you are, I'll clock you in the head with my new heels from Payless. Don't make me do that, Frankie. I had to save a long time to buy these." Jasmine clutched the sleeve of her shirt and pushed her back into her seat.

Gil stuck his hand out, giving Nikos's a warm shake. God, it shouldn't hurt so much to see him. Having someone *force* her to see him just plain tore at her heart. Yet her eyes couldn't look away.

Nikos's large frame loomed over Gil's; his raven black hair glistened under the set's lights. He was wearing her favorite color, a royal blue tie. "Welcome, Nikos." Gil smiled, camera perfect. "First up, tell us about Greek Meets Eat. Lil and I had lunch there just the other day, and the meatloaf is out of this world!"

And out of Mitch's hands without so much as a "thank you," Frankie thought with derision. She blocked out most of the conversation between Gil and Nikos, opting to fight tears with her head down.

"So show us what you've got for us today, Nikos," Lil directed in super-shiny tones.

Frankie's head popped up to catch sight of Nikos, staring with this awkward hesitance at the demo table where some bowls, a mixer, and some measuring cups sat. He pulled out a piece of paper from the pocket of his suit and had to catch it to keep it from falling to the ground. With a clearly uncomfortable glance, he squinted out into the audience. "Uh. I have a recipe."

Uh, you sure do.

Lil's lilting giggle swirled in Frankie's ear. "And what's the recipe for?"

"Um, it's called a Recipe for Forgiveness."

Gail and Mona shuffled in their chairs while Maxine encouraged Nikos to smile by pulling at the corners of her mouth in an overblown motion like some teen beauty queen's stage mother.

Jasmine rolled her fingers at him in a gesture to continue.

Clearly, with the lights from the set, he couldn't see his audience. Nikos paused, shoving a hand in the pocket of his trousers.

Gil stepped in to help. "What's the Recipe for Forgiveness's ingredients, Nikos?" he prompted with a theatrical flare.

Nikos instantly looked down at the paper he held. "Oh, right. Um—one cup of shamefaced . . . Shamefaced? What kind of word is that?"

Gil redirected Nikos to the paper with a flick of his finger and whispered something Frankie couldn't make out.

Nikos nodded to Gil. "You're right. Okay. One cup of shamefaced, uh . . . two cups of behaving like a total dumb ass, and a pound of . . ." Nikos squinted, then let out an impatient sigh. "Jesus, Simon—is this your chicken scrawl? How the hell am I supposed to beg the woman I love for forgiveness if I can't read the damn ingredients to beg with?" Nikos balled up the sheet of paper and threw it to the table in front of him.

Frankie couldn't move.

Nikos's eyes looked for the camera Gil pointed to, so deep and dark, she couldn't tear herself away. "Forget all of that. Wait, don't forget *all* of that. I *am* all of those things—ingredients, whatever. I, Nikos Antonakas, did a stupid, unfair, crappy thing to Frankie Bennett, and I was wrong. Really, really wrong. This is me, so pathetically sorry, I've resorted to apologizing on cable TV. Do you have any idea how much airtime costs even on local cable? But I want it on record, I'm owning my mistake, and it was the biggest one I've made in my life up to this point. Almost as big as letting Simon write up that stupid Recipe for Forgiveness." Nikos's eyes strayed away from the camera to narrow in someone's direction off set.

She'd bet it was Simon. Frankie stuffed a fist in her mouth to keep from laughing out loud or bursting into tears. She couldn't decide which emotion would win.

Nikos held up a hand, his beautiful face hard with determination. "So here's where I stand. I don't know if you're watching, but I hope Gail and gang made you tune in. Or at the very least, someone TiVo'd this so you can watch it later."

He had no idea she was in the audience . . . Frankie held her breath while Nikos clenched his jaw and continued like his teeth were being pulled from his head with no anesthesia.

"I love *you*, Frankie Bennett. I don't want to save you. I don't want to own you. I don't want to keep you from doing anything you want to do, whenever you want to do it. Most importantly, I *trust* you. I was an irrational, jealous idiot, and if you'll forgive me, I promise to spend the rest of my life making it up to you. Oh, and to sweeten the deal, I'm including my crazy, loud, unruly family, and all the Tiger Balm and meatloaf you want—available in a lifetime supply."

Frankie's heart screamed in her chest, her pulse skipped beats in erratic thumps.

And then it happened. A rush of complete certainty flooded her veins. The kind where you know, beyond a shadow of a doubt, there's just no fighting what's meant to be. What you've waited your entire life to get a taste of, and now you've been offered the whole damn pie.

Frankie rose as an expectant pause filled the air with such pungency; she could taste it on the tip of her tongue.

Her purse fell on top of Jasmine, her jacket to the floor.

She pushed her way past the folding metal chairs to stand a few feet away from Nikos. Her voice was shaking with emotion, but her words were sure. "So, Antonakas, how much did this little stunt cost?"

Nikos's head popped up. The dull lifeless hint to his eyes was gone and replaced with a glimmer of amusement. "Oh, it was big, Bennett." He spread his broad hands wide. "Big money."

She clasped her hands together behind her back. "Was it at least as much as you'd have had to dish out if you hadn't *fired* me?"

Nikos snorted and grinned, taking two steps closer to her. "I didn't fire you per se . . ."

"Technicalities. So? Answer the question."

"At least a hundred times that."

Frankie upped the ante and took three steps toward him, inhaling a whiff of his cologne, one that left her smiling with the comfort it brought. "I guess that means a raise is out in my near future."

"Oh, yeah. Probably the next ten futures." His smile was cocky when he stretched his leg out and took another exaggerated step, bringing him almost directly in front of her.

Frankie rolled her tongue in her cheek and sidled closer until she could see every delicious groove on either side of his mouth. "Damn. That's too bad, Antonakas. I really, really need a couch and some curtains. Wow, do I need curtains."

His hand reached for hers, clasping her fingers in a loose embrace that made her heart skip with joy. "You could always use my couch."

She let her fingers curl into his. And it was as right as she'd suspected. Right and so sweetly good. "You're too generous. So when can I expect you to drop it off?"

He took a long breath. "I was kinda hoping we could *share* mine."

Frankie wiggled her eyebrows. "You mean like partial custody?"

Nikos wiggled his back. "I mean like partial visitation."

Frankie pretended to give that proposition serious thought. "It is a *nice* couch."

He finally closed the space between them until their noses almost touched. "It just hasn't been the same without you."

Frankie's hand reached up to cup his cheek, running her thumb with a contented sigh over the planes of his jaw. "Do you think your couch and my folding chair will hit it off?"

Nikos wrapped an arm around her waist, dragging her to him so that her back arched and her upper body was squarely pressed to his chest. "I think it could happen. I mean, as long as my couch doesn't do anything stupid."

She chuckled, wrapping her arms around his neck. "Don't you worry. My folding chair has legendary skills with a wire whisk."

Nikos's laughter showered over her like a balm, but his face grew serious once more. "I can't offer you what Mitch did, Frankie. I'm not poor, but I'm no multimillionaire either. I run a diner in New Jersey, and soon, it'll be mine entirely. But I love my diner and I love working with my family. I don't want to be famous, and I don't ever want to go back to my old job. My hours suck, my employees are unruly, loud, opinionated, and unmanageable, but we make the best meatloaf anywhere in the world, and not to be taken for granted, you'll never want for a single thing if you take a chance on me. I love deaf dogs, cats, too, deaf or otherwise, and women who can't find a decent hobby, hate to cook, and listen to the Go-Go's. Also, if pressed, I'll watch reruns of Flavor Flav's *Flavor of Love*. I know you thought I was asleep, but I caught you riveted to it at two in the morning. Though, I can't promise I won't nap during it. And finally . . . I love *you*, Frankie Bennett."

Frankie closed the distance between their lips, but not before adding, "Phew, color me relieved, because I love you, too. It would have sucked if I was all alone in this, huh?"

Cheers from the once silent and darkened backstage rose up to meet her ears as Nikos planted his lips on hers and soundly kissed her.

From the left side of the set, Voula, Barnabas, Cosmos, and Simon burst onto the stage, clapping Nikos on the back and hugging Frankie.

Gail and Mona sniffed into their tissues while Maxine and Jasmine checked their compacts to be sure their mascara hadn't run.

"Oh, my Frankie!" Voula tweaked her cheeks. "I have missed you. I told my big, stupid son you would never steal from me." She tucked Frankie's hand under her arm. "You come now and we go back to the diner for some meatloaf to celebrate."

Nikos put a hand on his mother's shoulder. "I was kinda hoping for some alone time with my main squeeze, Mama."

"Bah!" Barnabas barked. "You have plenty of alone time when Frankie comes back to chop. Now we celebrate!"

Nikos wrapped his arms around her waist from behind. "You game?"

She giggled, snuggling closer to his chest. "Are you kidding? I hate to tell you this, but I don't know what I was jonesin' more from lack of—you or Mama V's meatloaf."

He chuckled, tucking her head under his chin. "Then meatloaf it is, but later, you'd better make sure you've taken out every lightbulb from every room in your apartment. We have some making up to do."

Her stomach bubbled in decadent anticipation. "Well, then, *opa*."

"Oh, definitely there's some serious opas in your future," he whispered in her ear, sending delicious tingles along her spine.

Hand in hand they made their way out of the studio in one large, loud group. Frankie caught sight of Simon, stopping to call him out. "You." She pointed a finger at him with a grin. "You had something to do with this, didn't you?"

"He arranged the whole thing, honey," Nikos said, kissing the top of her head.

"You arranged all of that? The apology, the show, the whole thing?" Jasmine asked, pushing past Nikos and Frankie.

"Yep. Simon's not just a national celebrity. He's a local one. Gil and Lil almost fell over themselves when he called and asked them to set this up for me," Nikos added. "It's good to have friends with connections for bennies."

"*You?*" Jasmine said again, her beautiful face surprised.

Simon shrugged. "I owed Frankie. I was wrong. I had to do my part to help Nikos make up for listening to a dumb ass like me. I steered him wrong. It's only money. Of which I have plenty. Not a big deal."

Frankie watched while the frigid outer layer of Jasmine's heart began to thaw. It was in the hint of her gaze. Her eyes strayed to Frankie's, hesitant and full of her fear for the next step. A step she knew Jasmine was petrified was a trap.

Frankie came to stand beside Jasmine. "Forgiveness feeds the soul, my friend. I just fed mine."

Jasmine eyed Simon in obvious hesitation. "He did such a bad, bad thing, Francis," she whispered with shaky words. "Yet, even after doing such a bad, bad thing, I still want him so, so much."

"I get it. Believe me, I get it," Frankie whispered back.

With a roll of her eyes and a sigh, Jasmine put a tentative hand on Simon's arm. "Okay, so here's where you're at. *You* are on probation, quarterback. One wrong play and it's over. During your sentence, you will come clean about anything and everything that could affect me even a little, especially the paparazzi. You will never, so long as I allow you to play in my sandbox, ever, lie to me or accuse someone of something without a thorough investigation headed by me. And if you ever make me cry as hard as I did when I found out about you and Ashton, you're paying for my eyelid lift. Understood?"

"You, the great and powerful Jasmine, cried over me, the dumb jock? Like real, live tears?" Simon taunted.

Frankie intervened. "Were I you, I'd reconsider going there." She gave him a kiss on his cheek with a giggle. "Now go make up, and thank you."

Simon held out his arm to Jasmine, and she hooked hers through his. "So we shouldn't talk about the tears? Did you eat Häagen Dazs, too? I thought your ass *sounded* fuller, but I have to feel to be sure."

Instead of decking him, Jasmine's head fell back and she laughed as she guided him out of the studio. "I'll eat what I want, when I want, big ass be damned—whether you can see it or not. Oh, and by the way—way to cream a guy. You took out Mitch like he was a pin and you were the bowling ball. Sooooo hot," she squealed, their voices drifting out of the studio, leaving Nikos and Frankie both laughing.

"Meatloaf calls!" Cosmos yelled from the exit of the studio.

Frankie smiled up at Nikos, her eyes a window to this crazy, exciting, all-consuming love for him. "Ready for some make-up meatloaf?"

He pressed a kiss to her lips that left her sighing with anticipation. "I think that's an order I can fill."

EPILOGUE

From the journal of Frankie Bennett-Antonakas: I think the last name Antonakas on the end of mine says it all, don't you, dear journal? This concludes my postdivorce discovery entries. I've discovered—hoo boy, I've discovered. Probably more than the Discovery Channel. I've discovered happiness, true fulfillment, and most of all, I've discovered my life is now so full, I don't have time for journal entries either. So it is with great fondness that I bid you a big ole later gator.

Eight months later

"Mrs. Antonakas?"

Frankie groaned from beneath her new husband's talented lips as he spread her sex and nipped the swollen flesh. "Why are we talking *now*, Mr. Antonakas?" she complained in a teasing tone, then shuddered a sigh when he stroked her with his tongue, drawing another orgasm from deep within her. She groaned her pleasured approval, clinging to his shoulders and dragging him to her lips.

Nikos rolled her to her side, his chest pressed to her back, taking her mouth against his, and cupping her breast, stroking her nipple to a tight peak. "Are you sure we won't hurt the baby?"

Frankie clasped his wrist, her head falling back to the pillow when she lifted her hips to encourage Nikos to enter her. She smiled at how utterly freaked he was, before reaching down between them to run her hands along his rigid cock. "I'm definitely sure, Nikos. It's really okay. You heard the doctor. I am, however, not so sure I won't hurt you if we don't get it on—soon. So do me," she said on a chuckle.

Nikos lifted her thigh, pulling it back over his hip, entering her with such care Frankie's chest grew tight with love. Her arm wound up around his neck, her back arched at the never-ending pleasure he created when he was deep inside her.

His breaths grew harsh, mingling with hers as he drove his cock into her with easy glides, running his hands over her now much fuller hips, caressing her skin until it was on fire.

When he cupped her breasts, the force of white-hot heat erupted within her, making her drive downward against his lower torso. Nikos's familiar shift in position, the tightening of his muscles as he pulled her closer to him, was a sign his release wasn't far off.

Frankie clutched wildly at his wrists, gritting her teeth when her climax took away all reason, leaving her mind numbed but her senses screaming.

Nikos huffed from behind her, a long, harsh rasp of a breath, his chest expanding and deflating against her back. As the air returned to her lungs, she smiled, burrowing against her husband's hard body with a wiggle of her hips.

He nuzzled her ear. "Hmmmm. I like you today, Antonakas. A lot."

Frankie giggled with utter contentment. Life was so good—with Nikos—at the diner she now managed alongside him—with the frequent visits they made to Voula and Barnabas in Boca and the Tuesday night dates they shared with Jasmine and Simon, now engaged, for dinner at Little Anthony's and even the occasional drink at Fluffy's. Good, good, good. Better still, she'd been entrusted with the meatloaf recipe. It was now her job to prepare it. "You'd better.

You knocked me up." Boy, had he ever. In record time since she'd had a procedure to clear the block in her fallopian tubes.

"Who knew Antonakas sperm was so potent, huh?" he asked, nipping at her shoulder.

"Especially since it's so old," she teased. Their ages had concerned Frankie for about three minutes after they'd gotten the news of her pregnancy. She was almost thirty-nine. Nikos was almost forty-three, but then Jasmine reminded them, she, at nearly forty-seven, was like the new thirty nowadays, and suddenly, the prospect of watching their child graduate college when they'd be nearing or almost in their sixties didn't seem like such a big deal.

Nikos ran his hard hands along her ribs, ribs that would shortly disappear beneath weight gain. "Hey! Lay off the old there, woman. I still have all my teeth and my colonoscopy's all clear. Besides, how many old men can do what I just did? I'm in tip-top shape."

Frankie stretched luxuriously against his solid warmth, arching into the trail of kisses he left along the column of her neck. "I say you prove your youth and do it again," she teased.

Nikos's cock grew rigid against her once more, pressing with sinfully delicious pressure against her ass. "Are you sure you're up to it again, honey? I mean, you're no spring chicken either, and you are with child. *My child*," he reminded her, his tone of possession sending that wild thrill of bliss through her.

Frankie rolled to face him, sliding her body seductively against his with a hiss of pleasure when their bodies made contact. "I think I can manage one more round without breaking a hip. I took my osteoporosis prevention pills today."

"That's so hot."

She nodded her agreement, shivering when his tongue glided over her lower lip. "I know, but it's only going to get hotter from here.

While this little one is off finger painting in preschool, we're going to be scoping out AARP for deals."

Nikos tightened his hold on her, massaging the curve of her hip. "As long as we do it together, I'm totally in."

"Then together it is, Antonakas. Opa," Frankie said, breathless with her love for him.

Together.

What a crazy awesome word.

Opa, indeed.